## THE SOLDIERS' HOMECOMING

Brett, Logan and Sam were best friends and three of the finest soldiers in the Australian SAS K9 division. But one day Sam was killed, tearing their friendship group apart and leaving Brett and Logan with memories that would haunt them for ever.

Now, back in Australia, Brett and Logan are adjusting to life outside the army. But they haven't counted on two gorgeous, intriguing, captivating women who swan into their lives and present them with challenges they've never faced before!

Look out for
**HER SOLDIER PROTECTOR**
Coming in April 2014

# THE RETURNING HERO

## BY
## SORAYA LANE

MILLS & BOON

Published in Great Britain 2014
by Mills & Boon, an imprint of Harlequin (UK) Limited,
Eton House, 18-24 Paradise Road, Richmond, Surrey, TW9 1SR

© 2014 Soraya Lane

ISBN: 978 0 263 91265 4

23-0314

Writing for Mills & Boon® Cherish™ is truly a dream come true for **Soraya Lane**. An avid reader and writer since her childhood, Soraya describes becoming a published author as 'the best job in the world' and hopes to be writing heart-warming, emotional romances for many years to come.

Soraya lives with her own real-life hero on a small farm in New Zealand, surrounded by animals and with an office overlooking a field where their horses graze.

For more information about Soraya and her upcoming releases visit her at her website, www.sorayalane.com, her blog, www.sorayalane.blogspot.com, or follow her at www.facebook.com/SorayaLaneAuthor.

For Hamish and Mackenzie.
I'm so fortunate that you both share my love of dogs!

*In Dogs We Trust*

The unofficial motto of the soldiers
within the Explosive Detection Dog Service

# CHAPTER ONE

BRETT PALMER LEANED against the door of his vehicle. Visiting had seemed like a great idea before he'd left home, but now he was here…turning up unannounced wasn't so easy. Perhaps if he'd planned what he was going to say, had a good reason for not touching base with her before now, but he'd just jumped in the car and decided to chance it.

He sucked back a big breath and forced himself to walk forward. He'd known Jamie Mattheson for years, so it wasn't like she'd get a shock to see him, but still. It wasn't as if he'd ever spent time with her on her own, either.

Brett swallowed the memories, refusing to go back in time, and jogged the last few steps to the front door. He knocked. No one answered. There wasn't even so much as a shuffle from inside. Brett knocked again.

He could either get in his car and leave, or head around back to see if she was there. The sun was already out in full force, typical of Sydney at this time of year, and he had more than a hunch that she could be out in the garden.

Brett stepped back down and walked around the side of the house. It was looking nice, but then he knew Sam had painted the weatherboards before he'd left for their last tour, had made sure he'd done all the maintenance so Jamie had nothing to worry about while he was gone. He'd put money on it that she'd prefer the house to be falling down around her if it meant she could go back in time and have her husband back.

Brett pushed the side gate open and looked around the corner. *There she was.* Standing with her hands on her hips, like something was really frustrating her. Then he saw the something, sitting in front of her, alert, nose pointed in the air.

Bear. She had Sam's dog. How the hell had she ended up with Bear so soon?

"Jamie," he called out, not wanting to startle her but not wanting to be caught staring at her, either.

The dog had given up sitting patiently and was now barking and thundering toward him. He'd been his best mate's dog, but right now he was protecting his new owner, and Brett wasn't exactly game to take the massive canine on.

"Bear, it's me," he called out, as the black dog hurtled toward him. "Bear! It's okay, boy."

The dog slowed, still looking protective, but Brett was comfortable that he was no longer about to be attacked.

"Brett? What are you doing here?"

Jamie was suddenly rushing across the lawn to him, arms outstretched.

"Hey, sweetheart." He held his own arms out, one eye on the dog, until she threw herself against him.

Brett held her tight, holding on to her like his life depended upon it. He'd been best man at their wedding, vacationed with them, had dinner at their house…and now he was comforting a widow.

"It's so good to see you." Jamie stepped back, but she held on to his hands, firmly, like she'd never let go.

Brett looked into her eyes, saw tears there that she was bravely holding in check. This woman had been his best friend's wife, and he'd never, ever wanted to be in this position. He was just grateful that he hadn't been the one to tell her the news when it had happened.

"You've got Bear." He knew he was stating the obvious but he still couldn't believe it.

He turned half his attention back to the dog, who was keeping a close eye on them.

"And I have no idea what to do with him," she admitted, stepping back and letting go of Brett. Jamie had her hands back on her hips as she stared at the dog. "I'm doing my best, but he's, I don't know, smarter than me, I guess. We're not communicating that well."

Brett dropped to his haunches, eye level with the canine. "Hey, Bear. Remember me, bud?" The dog let out a low whine, looking up at Jamie then back to him again. "I know you do. Come here."

Bear slowly walked over to him and sat down on Brett's feet. He gave him a scratch, liking that the dog had accepted him. God only knew they'd spent enough time together when he was serving.

"I'll teach you everything I can, Jamie. He's a pretty

special dog, but he's used to certain commands and lots of them."

She laughed. "Yeah, sometimes I wondered if Sam thought he was more special than me. Probably showed off photos of him to everyone and forgot all about his wife."

Brett reached for her, took her hand again as he stood to full height. "You know that's not true. You meant everything to Sam." He chuckled. "To be honest, we all had to tell him to knock it off most of the time. He talked about you *way* too often."

She laughed, gripping his hand tight. "You always were the charmer."

He put his arm around her, needing to hold her, to show her how much he cared. "I miss him, Jamie. I miss him so bad that I can't…" Brett blew out a breath, dropping his chin to the top of her head. "I just needed you to know that I'm here for you. It's taken me a while, but I'm back now."

Jamie looped her arm around his waist and steered them toward the house. "How about we have brunch?"

"Here?"

"Yeah, why not," she said. "Besides, I haven't had anyone to make pancakes for in a while."

Brett signaled to the dog to follow them, and walked behind Jamie as she went into the house. She was dressed in a tiny pair of cut-off denim shorts and a loose-fitting T-shirt, and he wished she were covered up. She was his friend's widow. She was beautiful. Her legs were so long and tanned…. He forced his eyes to the sky. *Jamie was Sam's wife.* Just because he'd loved her from the moment he'd met her, thought she was the most caring, gorgeous woman he'd ever spent time with, didn't mean it was okay to start giving in to his feelings now.

Sam had been gone only a little over six months. He'd been his best friend. And Jamie was his widow, he reminded himself again.

But deep down, Brett knew exactly why he'd put off coming for so long.

Jamie hadn't stopped moving since they'd walked inside. She couldn't. Because if she stopped even for a second, she'd either start crying or throw her arms around Brett and never let him go.

Having him here was unexpected, unusual, and yet exactly what she needed all at the same time. Since Sam had been gone, she'd had an emptiness inside of her that had ached every single day, but seeing Brett…? It was like the pain was finally easing. Because she could talk to Brett about her husband, really talk about him, and he made her feel like Sam could still walk through the front door, hassling Brett for chatting her up like he usually did. Jamie took a deep breath.

"Maple syrup?" she asked.

He laughed. "Yes, ma'am."

Jamie flipped a pancake and turned around to look at the man seated at her counter. He looked like he always did—handsome and tanned—but there was something different about him now. Something she couldn't pinpoint, except for maybe a hint of unhappiness that kept crossing his face, that made his smile never quite reach his eyes like it once had. There was so much she wanted to ask him, but she wanted to wait until the time was right.

"So tell me how you ended up with Bear?" Brett asked.

She smiled at the dog lying near her feet. He might be hard to communicate with, but he sure was loyal and she loved him for that.

"The detection dog unit contacted me, told me that he had to be retired after the accident, and they wanted to offer him to me first." She shook her head, turning her attention back to her pancakes. "Sam loved him so much, so I couldn't say no. And it is kind of nice having the company, even if we haven't quite figured each other out yet. He's only been here a few weeks because he had to be in quarantine for a while."

She knew Brett had lost his dog in the same explosion that had killed her husband, that he probably wasn't ready to go there yet, but...

"I know I should have come by sooner, Jamie, it's just..." Brett's voice trailed off.

Jamie held up her hand. It seemed like they were both struggling to find the right words. "No apology necessary. We just do what we have to do to cope, right?"

He nodded, looked grateful that he didn't have to explain himself. Instead of asking him anything further, she flipped the last pancake and placed it in front of him, adding it to the stack.

"Looks good enough to eat," he said, grinning as he poured syrup over them.

Jamie sat down beside him, reaching for the coffee-pot she'd left just out of reach. It seemed right having Brett here, even if it was just the two of them, because being alone these last six months, she'd started to forget the person she was, the happy, easygoing person she'd always been. Brett was making her remember how nice it had always been to open their home to friends.

She chanced a quick glance at him, wishing she could resist but unable to. When they'd first met, Brett was dating another woman, and then when he was single she'd already been seeing Sam. *His best friend.* Just because they'd been attracted to one another before didn't mean anything, she knew that, but she had a notion that she should be feeling guilty, shouldn't feel so comfortable in his presence.

"Do you still have your house here?"

Jamie watched as he finished his mouthful before setting his fork back down on the plate. "I decided to put it on the market a while back, and it sold while I was deployed."

"Oh." She hadn't known. "So where are you staying?" She'd been wanting to get in touch with him for months, had presumed he was away again, because he hadn't even been able to make it back for Sam's service.

"I've been at a recuperation clinic. My leg was burned pretty bad when the…" His sentence trailed off. "It's kept me away for a while, then I traveled around for a bit to come to grips with everything, and I only just arrived in yesterday."

She swallowed, taking a deep breath before she asked a question that needed to be voiced. "You're staying in a hotel, aren't you? You only came back here to see me."

Brett looked guilty. "You were Sam's wife. I could only stay away for so long. He'd want me to look out for you, Jamie. You know that. He even asked me as much."

Unspoken words hung between them, words that would never be braved by either of them. Because before it had just been flirting. Now that Sam was gone… It was too soon for either of them, wasn't something that could ever happen. But it didn't mean she wanted Brett to leave, and it didn't mean that he was here for any other reason than because he loved her for being Sam's wife.

"I want you to know that I'm here, no matter what you need, okay?"

Jamie stared at him, raised one eyebrow as she looked into his eyes. "You really want to be here for me? To help me?"

He nodded. "Of course."

"Then help me with Bear," she said. "Turn me into a worthy owner of the dog who meant the world to my husband."

Brett was playing with his fork, looking at the half-eaten breakfast on his plate.

"You're sure you want me hanging around?" he asked. "I mean, you don't have to say that just because…"

Jamie reached for his hand, squeezed it and stared straight into Brett's eyes. "You weren't just his friend, you were mine, too," she confessed. "I've missed you guys—you, Sam and Logan. I miss you all. I didn't just lose my husband, I lost having you two here all the time, too."

Brett grunted. "Bet Logan's been better at staying in touch."

She shook her head. "He's phoned me a couple of times, but I haven't seen him, either. It's been—" Jamie shrugged "—weird. But he did say he was back in town soon, so maybe he's back now?"

Brett looked surprised, but she didn't say anything. He went back to eating his pancakes and so did she.

"Well, if you need help with Bear, I'm here," he said. "How about we start with a few basics today, and I'll come past tomorrow and we can take him out to a park or something."

Jamie stood up to clear their plates. "That sounds like a good plan," she told him.

A niggle in her mind was telling her she should have asked Brett to stay, that her husband would have been horrified that his best buddy was paying to stay at a hotel, but she wasn't ready for that. Wasn't ready for a man to be sleeping in her home, under her roof—a man who wasn't her husband, even if she did hate being on her own at night. Being alone…it took her back to her childhood, brought the ice-cold fear back, and she hated that as much as the reality of waking up without Sam beside her.

And if she were honest with herself, she was feeling nervous about being with Brett too much, just the two of them. They'd always flirted, it was just how he'd always been with her, but back then she'd also been in love with her husband, which meant their joking had always been nothing more than fun. Now?

She just had to take one day at a time. Having Brett

here was better than being on her own, and she knew it was what Sam would have wanted. Even if she was having feelings about Brett that he wouldn't approve of.

# CHAPTER TWO

BRETT DIDN'T KNOW what he'd expected, but being with Jamie was…different. He always knew it wasn't going to be the same without Sam, and he was pleased he was here, but it didn't make it easy.

Thank God they had Bear to deal with. He would have felt weird coming over again without a good reason, without a purpose to help her.

"So did Sam ever teach you any of his commands?"

Jamie shook her head. He could tell she loved the dog, and it looked as if the canine reciprocated—the trouble was plain simple communication. Bear was sitting faithfully beside Jamie, and her hand had fallen to the top of his head, which told him that there was no reason they weren't going to form a good team. They just weren't in sync yet, and that's what he was going to help her with.

"The thing with this dog is that he's extremely easy to teach, so long as you make your commands and actions clear and consistent," Brett told her. "You don't have to be Sam, but you do have to understand how he learns."

"Do you mean like how they need to be rewarded by play?"

Brett grinned. "Exactly. This dog was chosen for the dog detection unit because when we tested him as a youngster, his commitment to a game of ball was un-wavering."

"So I need to play with him?" she asked, staring down at the dog.

"Yeah, you need to play with him, and you need to let him be with you all the time, because that's how Sam treated him whenever they were together."

Jamie was laughing and he loved seeing her happy, as if for a moment they were both here for any reason other than because of what had happened—that they were just two friends catching up under the sun, like old times.

"You guys always act so tough, but when it comes to your dogs, you're like marshmallows."

"It's part of the bonding process, you know that," he told her, pretending to be offended. "And we *are* tough, I'll have you know."

"Yeah, that's what you all tell each other, but really? You're just lonely when you're away and want a warm body in your bed to snuggle up to."

Brett laughed, unable to help himself. "How did you figure us all out so fast, huh?"

Jamie held up her hand to shield her face from the sun. "So are we just going to start with the basics?"

He nodded. "Why don't we run through sit, stay and heel, then I'll teach you how to play with a ninety-pound canine. Sound good?"

The smile she gave him made him drop his gaze, focus on the dog instead, because he was walking a dangerous line between helping out a friend's widow and wanting to be here because he'd always liked Jamie and still did.

And if he were honest with himself, it's why he'd taken so long to come back. It hadn't just been about his injury, it hadn't just been because he was struggling to come to terms with losing his best human friend *and* his canine best friend, it was because when it came to Jamie, he didn't trust himself. He could have all the best intentions in the world, but without Sam here, he was screwed.

Jamie watched as Brett moved across the grass, Bear running along beside him and then bounding ahead to catch the ball.

"You just need to have fun with him," Brett called out. "Let him know you love playing just as much as he does."

She couldn't help but laugh at them as they charged around her small lawn.

"It's not about the space, it's the quality of time you spend with him. He wants you to guide him, to be his leader and his equal, too. He will always look to you for direction, because that's what he's been trained to do."

"So in other words he wants me to be his wife?"

They both laughed and she watched as Brett nodded to the dog to follow him.

"You must miss your dog," she said, wishing she could take the words back the moment they left her lips.

Brett's mouth fixed in a hard line, his jaw clamped before he took a visibly deep breath. "Every goddamn day," he told her, running a hand through his short brown hair. "Teddy hardly left my side in four years. It was like he always knew what I was thinking before I'd even thought it myself. And then…"

Jamie felt like her breath had died in her throat, her lungs refusing to cooperate. The day Teddy had died had been the day Sam had died, too.

They stared at one another. She watched as Brett swallowed. Neither of them wanted to talk about that day, because somehow Brett had made it home and her husband and Brett's dog had been killed. She wished the comment had never come out of her mouth, but it wasn't like she could take it back.

"Have you had any ongoing veterinary care for Bear? I'm hoping after all he did for the army that he's on a full pension."

He'd changed the subject but only just, although she wasn't complaining.

"When I collected him he was pretty much healed, on the outside at least," Jamie told him. "He had a bandaged paw still and lots of missing or singed fur, but they made sure he was almost back to health before letting me take him. And they seemed to look after him pretty well when he was quarantined."

"I was the one who carried him back to the truck," Brett told her, his voice low. "He managed to come toward me, but the ringing in his ears must have been as bad as it was in mine because he couldn't even walk in a straight line, and his paws and legs were badly burned.

There was no part of me that could have tried to get away without helping him, and it was like he wanted to do the same for me."

Jamie refused to look away, no matter how uncomfortable the conversation was making her, because she knew how hard it must have been for Brett to talk about what had happened, even just a little.

"I can't believe you even managed to lift him, after what had happened to you," she said softly.

Brett dropped to his haunches and slung his arm around the dog. "If it hadn't been for this boy," he said, stroking the dog's fur as he spoke, "everyone in that truck would have died that day. It wasn't until I collapsed that I realized why my body was burning so bad, what a mess my leg was, and then I passed out from the pain and shock. Bear was braver than any of us."

Brett was staring past her now, and Jamie didn't want to make him uncomfortable. It was so nice having him here, having a familiar face to chat to, that she wanted to make sure he stayed for the afternoon.

"What do you say we take him for a walk?" she suggested.

Brett smiled, clearly relieved she'd changed the subject completely.

"Do you usually take him out?" he asked.

She grimaced. "It's not that I don't want to, but he's kind of massive and I'm worried I won't be able to control him if we come across another dog or something."

Brett shook his head. "Did that husband of yours teach you *nothing* about this dog?"

She laughed. "No, because it was like they shared the

same brain! Bear just did what Sam wanted him to do, like they had some silent communication thing going on, and he went everywhere with him so it wasn't like I was ever in sole charge."

Brett sighed. "Fair call." He followed her inside and stood back as she locked the doors. "How about you tell me what you'd like to do with him?"

She checked the side door was locked before gathering Bear's lead from a drawer and facing Brett.

"I guess I want to be able to walk down for a coffee and sit without worrying how to handle him if there's another big dog coming toward us. And walk through the park, throw a ball for him and know he'll come back when he's off the leash, that sort of thing."

Brett opened the front door and held it open for her, waiting as she clipped the leash to Bear's collar.

"He's too well-trained to have a fight with another dog, and he will never, *ever* chase a ball and not bring it back to you. It's why he made the squad in the first place."

"Were you with Sam the day he chose him?"

Brett shook his head. "No, but I remember him being so excited that he'd finally found the perfect partner. Bear was with a family who loved him, but they were moving overseas and had put him up for adoption. When Sam went to see him, he tested him out with a ball and he knew straight away that the black giant was going to be his sidekick."

They fell into a comfortable rhythm, walking side by side.

"Is it okay to talk about him?" Brett asked, his voice an octave lower.

The question took her by surprise. "Yes." They walked for a bit more before she continued. "I mean, it's hard, it's always hard, but it's nice talking about him with you."

"I half expect him to be at the house when we get back," Brett said with a smile. "Waiting to give me a telling off about hanging out with his wife."

"Yeah." Jamie was smiling, too, but it was bittersweet. "I guess I'd become so used to him going away on tours, so for me it just seems like this has just been an especially long one. Like I'm just waiting for him to fly home and pick up where we left off." It had been the same when her dad had never come home from deployment—like one day he'd just walk through the door again and everything would go back to normal.

"If it's too hard having me here…"

"No," she blurted. "Having you here is the only good thing that's happened to me in a long while, so please don't think you're making me uncomfortable. It's the complete opposite."

Brett was pleased she wanted him here, but every time they talked about Sam made him feel plain weird for being with Jamie, just the two of them. Lucky they had the dog as a distraction, because it meant they had something to focus on other than the fact that nothing was like it had been the last time they'd seen one another.

"So you just give him a gentle reminder if he walks ahead of you by pulling the lead back," he told her, closing his hand over it and showing her, "and telling him to heel, but you're probably not going to need to do that very often."

Brett didn't move his hand when Jamie's brushed past it, fingers almost closing over his before she realized. It was stupid—they'd touched plenty in the past—but having her warm skin against his reminded him of all the reasons why he shouldn't have been here. Because there had been a time when he'd wished he'd asked Jamie out, before she'd met Sam, and they were dangerous thoughts to be remembering now that she was his friend's widow.

"Brett, I don't want to bring up what happened again, but I need to ask you one question."

He cleared his throat and turned to face her. "Shoot." So long as he didn't have to relive what had happened again, he'd tell her what she needed to know. Those memories caught up on him enough without voluntarily calling on them.

"I keep thinking about the army sending Bear back, once they'd made the decision to retire him. Is it normal for them to care for a dog like that, even though their career is over, and then pay to send them home?"

Brett couldn't help smiling at her. Trust Jamie to have figured out that it wasn't exactly protocol, especially when the handler was no longer alive and able to fight for his dog.

"Let's just say that me and the other boys put a fair amount of pressure on our superiors to make sure Bear had a good retirement. I didn't know he'd be given back to you, but there aren't that many dogs in the world capable of what he did on a daily basis, and it wasn't exactly a tough call to send him home a hero."

Jamie reached out to him, took him completely by surprise as her hand stayed in place on his shoulder.

"Well then I guess I owe you a pretty big thanks," she said, throwing him a smile that made him want to look away, because that smile had always teased him and he didn't want to think about her like that, not now. "It means a lot to have him here, even if I'm kind of hopeless at the whole business of looking after a dog."

Brett fought not to shrug her hand off, and was pleased when it just dropped away.

"So which café are we going to?"

"Skinny latte?"

Jamie looked up. "How did you guess?"

He chuckled and ordered, before peering into the cabinet with her. "And I'm also guessing that you want something sweet. Maybe the chocolate peppermint slice?"

Jamie kept staring at the rows of food, trying to ignore the slice so she wasn't completely predictable. In the end she gave in to her sweet tooth. "Okay, how about we share a piece?"

She walked back outside to where they'd left Bear, not liking the idea of just tying him up and leaving him beside a table.

"He's fine," Brett said, pulling her chair out for her and then taking the seat opposite.

"I can see that. It just seems foreign to me," she told him.

"This dog won't let you down. Trust me. His manners will be better than most of the people in here."

Jamie rolled her eyes, but she knew he was probably right. And she also knew that Brett pulling her chair out for her was the kind of gentlemanly thing that not many guys did anymore. Her husband had, so she was used to it, and she liked being treated like a woman.

Brett's mobile rang and he punched a button to silence it before answering and mouthing *sorry* to her. Jamie touched Bear's head, stroking his fur, not looking at Brett. But she couldn't help but take notice of what he was saying. The fact that it was Logan, her husband's other best buddy, made her want to frown and smile simultaneously.

Part of her was liking being with Brett, but another part of her, like a pang of hunger gnawing at her stomach, wanted Sam back here, too. So she could sit and listen to them talk and laugh and be boys, like she always had. Her husband, Brett and Logan.

Brett cleared his throat and Jamie's eyes snapped up to meet his. She had no idea whether he was waiting for her to say something, or whether he was just watching her.

"Jamie, what do you say?" he asked.

She raised her eyebrows, wishing she hadn't been daydreaming. "To what?"

"Logan's in town for the next week and he wanted to know if you're free tonight. We thought we'd go grab a few drinks, catch up."

Jamie liked that they were trying to include her, but

she didn't want to be a third wheel. "You guys just hang out. You don't need to ask me along."

Brett put his hand over the phone and leaned toward her, eyes never leaving hers. "Please come," he said, reaching for her with his other hand, fingers closing over hers. "I'll pick you up on my way and drop you at your door at the end of the night. Come out and have fun, we both want to take you out."

She looked from his eyes to his fingers over hers, wished that it was just a platonic gesture, that his skin against hers wasn't sending a shiver up and down her spine.

"Okay," she said, not needing any more convincing.

Brett grinned and pulled away, leaning back in his chair again and discussing details with Logan. She was pleased their coffees arrived at the same time as he hung up, needing something to distract her. Somehow she'd gone from hanging out with her husband's friend, to being on edge about agreeing to a night out. It was only supposed to be an evening with friends, so why was her stomach twisting like she was going on a first date?

"Sugar?"

Jamie nodded and reached for it, careful not to touch Brett's hand again.

"So Logan's back for a while, too?" she asked.

"He's still working, but he's based in Australia indefinitely."

"And you're sure he was okay about me tagging along on a boys' night?"

Brett cut the chocolate peppermint slice into two pieces and nudged one in her direction. "Since when are you not allowed to tag along on a boys' night? I don't recall Sam ever leaving you at home when we used to catch up."

"True." Brett was right, she *had* always hung out with them. But now that it was just her, she didn't want them feeling sorry for her and feeling like they had to include her.

"When was the last time you went out?" he asked.

"Can I pass on that question?" Jamie laughed and took a bite of the slice. "It's been a while."

"If another guy so much as looks at you he'll have me to deal with, so you're in safe hands."

Jamie picked at some chocolate and then took a sip of coffee, because she didn't want to make eye contact with Brett. There was only one guy she was worried about, and he was sitting directly across from her. He might trust himself, but she wasn't entirely sure that her thoughts were as pure.

# CHAPTER THREE

JAMIE PADDED BAREFOOT into the kitchen and fed Bear. She poured herself a glass of water and leaned on the counter, slowly drinking it, concentrating on the cool liquid and how it felt as she swallowed. It was the only thing she could think of to calm her nerves, other than going for a run, and after the time she'd spent in the shower and doing her hair, she had no intention of getting sweaty.

What was she doing?

It wasn't the fact that she was going out that was making her feel guilty, because she was in desperate need of doing something fun that got her out of the house. Her problem was that she couldn't stop thinking about Brett, and it was making her feel things that she had no right to feel.

She'd dolled herself up, made more of an effort than she had in months to look good, and it was Brett she was trying to impress. It was as if all the years of flirting had finally caught up with them, and with Sam not here, things were starting to feel awkward, fast. Or maybe not so much awkward as *exciting*.

"Brett is forbidden. Brett is my friend," she muttered, realizing that she was looking at her dog as if he were part of the conversation. "Tell me I'm crazy, Bear. I'm crazy, aren't I?"

He just stared up at her, pausing, before going back to eating his dinner.

Jamie sighed and dumped her water glass in the sink before walking back to her bedroom and looking at the clothes she'd thrown on the bed. She had her little black dress, a pair of satin pants and a sexy top, and her favorite skinny jeans. She reached for the dress and held it up, looking at her reflection in the floor-length mirror behind the door.

She wanted to wear the dress. She wanted to make Brett notice her. *She wanted to feel sexy.*

Jamie stripped down to her underwear and slipped on the dress. She was about to reach for a pair of five-inch black heels that she'd never worn before, that were just stuck in her closet, when her hand stopped moving. Everything stopped. Because just above her shoe rack, hanging on a little hook, was her husband's dog tag on its silver chain.

Jamie slowly reached for it, fingers clasping the cool metal, tracing over the tag that she'd spent so many hours staring at since he'd gone. The same tag that she'd often touched when they'd been lying together, in bed on a lazy morning....

*"If anything ever happened to you, would they give me this?"*

*Sam frowned. "Nothing's going to happen to me, baby, but yeah. They would."*

*She reached for it again, turning it over and reading the inscription out aloud. "Samuel Harvey Mattheson. O positive."*

*"Are you going to recite all my vitals, too?"*

*Jamie lay her head on Sam's bare chest, still holding his tag as she shut her eyes.*

*"Don't ever leave me, Sam. You have to promise to come home."*

*He kissed the top of her head. "Baby, I'm coming home. Haven't I always told you that nothing could keep me away from you?"*

*"How can you be so sure?" She kissed his chest, lips against his warm skin, before moving up and kissing his mouth, trying to stop tears from falling down her cheeks and onto his face.*

*"If I don't, then promise me you'll wear this. I don't ever want you to forget me, Jamie...."*

Jamie had sunk to the floor, tears pricking her eyes then falling in a slow, steady trickle down her cheeks and into her mouth. What was she doing? How could she even be *thinking* about Brett like she had been? What was wrong with her?

But she knew. Deep down, she knew.

There had been a spark between her and Brett for years, a spark that could have easily turned into something more if they'd met at the right time, and now he was here and she was a widow. Her feelings were only natural. But they were also wrong. Being lonely wasn't an excuse to give in to any of those feelings, not now, not ever.

Jamie reached back up for the tag and took it down,

slipping it around her neck. She needed Sam close to her, wanted him close to her, and she was upset that she'd forgotten the promise she'd made to him that she'd wear it.

She also slipped back out of the dress, suddenly not wanting to make Brett notice her like that. She reached for her skinny jeans instead, paired them with heels and pulled a scoop-neck tank over her head. Jamie finished the look with a biker-style leather jacket and hoop earrings, before going back into the bathroom to fix her makeup. She smoothed foundation over her tearstains, put on some more mascara and touched up her lip gloss, before running a hand through her smooth hair—courtesy of her straightening iron.

When the doorbell rang and Bear started barking, she took one final look in the mirror and kissed Sam's dog tag.

Tonight, he was with her, looking out for her, just like his friends were. She couldn't stop her feelings for Brett, but she *could* stop herself from acting on them.

"Bear, it's just Brett again."

He stopped barking as soon as she spoke, but he stayed by her side as she opened the door, like he had no intention of not protecting her, even if he wasn't allowed to bark.

"Hey," she said, opening the door to find him standing a few steps back from the door, hands jammed in his jean pockets.

"Hey," Brett replied, moving forward. "You look, well, *wow*."

Jamie smiled, knowing she shouldn't be so pleased

that he liked the way she looked but unable to pretend otherwise. She reached for the dog tag, fingers closing around it as she looked at Brett, needing the reminder.

"You don't look so bad yourself," she heard herself say.

"Yeah? Well you look like you're going to need a bodyguard to stay safe tonight."

Jamie laughed. "Well, lucky I have two of them, huh?"

It was true—she could have worn the dress if she hadn't been feeling so guilty, because Brett and Logan would act like her overprotective big brothers if a guy so much as looked at her too long, let alone if anyone tried anything on her.

"So shall we go?" Brett asked.

"Just let me check I've locked everything, and I need to grab my purse."

She disappeared back into the kitchen and then the living room, double-checking all the locks.

"You know Bear would maul any strangers who even tried to come in here, right?"

Jamie glanced across at Brett, knew he was watching her. He quickly looked up and met her gaze when she caught him out, but it sent a ripple of delight through her body that he *was* staring at her, no matter what she'd been telling herself as she stood in the closet.

"So not only do I have personal bodyguards escorting me tonight, you're telling me that I have one living in my house now? A big, furry, ninety-pound one?"

Brett held up her purse for her and waited for her to

walk ahead of him down the hall. Her face flushed as she realized he could be checking out her butt.

"I'm saying that you're safe with Bear here, and you're definitely safe with me," he told her, his voice a note lower than it had been earlier.

Jamie glanced over her shoulder and waited for Brett to follow her out the door. Then she locked it and looped her hand through his arm. She could have so easily dropped her head to his shoulder, given him a hug, but she didn't want to blur the lines of their friendship. Once she wouldn't have thought twice about touching him like that, because before it had never meant anything, but she knew he was feeling the change between them and the spark that seemed to have ignited since he'd walked back into her life.

"Thanks for taking me out tonight," she told him, ignoring everything else and saying the one thing she needed him to hear. "I feel like I've been alone for a really long time, and it's nice to just get out of the house and have fun."

The taxi was waiting for them, and he opened the door for her to slide in before sitting beside her.

"Here's to a good night," he said, covering her knee with his hand.

But as soon as he did it, he backed off. Fast. Because the way he looked at her, the way she couldn't help but look back at him when he touched her, must have scared him as much as it damn well terrified her.

# CHAPTER FOUR

"THIS FEELS WEIRD," Jamie said as they walked through the door of the bar.

Brett couldn't have agreed more. He felt like they were on a date, the two of them heading out for the evening, and it didn't help that he was thinking things he wished he wasn't about Jamie. The music was loud but not overpowering, and because it was still early it wasn't completely packed with people yet.

He looked around for Logan, desperate to see him. Once they found him, he could go get some drinks, leave the pair of them to catch up and deal with getting his head in the right space. It was bad enough that he'd spent the day before with Jamie, but seeing her again tonight was too much, too soon.

"There he is."

Jamie was leaning into him, talking into his ear over the noise and the music. He looked where she was pointing, groaning as she took hold of his hand. He got it; she was probably nervous about being out on the town without her husband, was reaching to him for support. But the way he was feeling right now, he didn't need her hand thrust into his, fingers interlaced as she walked slightly ahead of him toward Logan.

When they reached him Brett pulled his hand away and ran it through his hair instead. He needed to get it together, and fast. Logan would notice straight away if anything was going on, and he didn't want to be interrogated by anyone—especially not his best mate. Logan would be the first person to call him to task if he knew even the half of what he'd been thinking.

"Hey, Jamie." Logan jumped off the bar stool and wrapped his arms around her, giving her a big hug.

When he let go, Brett stepped forward and greeted him, grabbing hold of one of his hands and slapping him on the back at the same time. They hadn't seen each other in months.

"How are you, stranger?"

Brett shrugged. "Better now I've seen you."

They stared at one another, so much unsaid, but it only lasted a moment. Logan knew what had happened, would be the only person in Brett's life who would ever come close to understanding what he'd experienced, although even he couldn't imagine how disturbing it had been, how violent. They hadn't seen each other in a long while, had a lot of catching up to do.

Brett shook off his thoughts. "What are we drinking? My shout."

"Start with a beer or straight to bourbon?" Logan asked.

Jamie laughed, and Brett angled his body to better include her. He'd been so wound up in seeing Logan again that he'd almost forgotten about her. Brett touched his palm to her back, moving her forward between them and taking a step back to make room for her.

"I think we'll start with beer. How about you?"

Jamie smiled. "Um, maybe a cocktail for me."

Logan raised his eyebrows and Brett laughed. "So maybe we'll start with bourbon then, if you're hitting the strong stuff straight away."

Jamie leaned over the counter to reach for a menu. "It's been a *looong* time since I've been out. Can't you tell? The only cocktail I can think of is a Cosmopolitan from *Sex and the City*, but there must be something else...."

"Long Island iced teas," Logan announced. "Three of them."

Jamie pushed her shoulders up, shrugging, an innocent expression on her face. Brett needed to warn her.

"They're kind of potent," he said.

Her smile was sweet enough to make him feel dirty for admiring her cleavage when she leaned forward.

"Lucky I have you two to look after me then, huh?" She put an arm around each of them, her smile infectious. "I need a night of just having fun, so order away, boys. I'm in."

Brett did as he was told and watched her walk off with Logan, looking for a quieter, more comfortable place to sit. They all had a lot to talk about, or maybe they didn't. Maybe tonight was about letting Jamie have fun without feeling guilty, just being there for her and making sure she had a good time and got home safely at the end of the evening.

He just had to remind himself that he would have

plenty to be guilty about if he ever let himself give in to the way he was feeling about her. Brett paid for the drinks and stuffed his wallet back in his pocket, before carrying their drinks to the table. He could see Jamie leaning toward Logan, talking, touching his shoulder as they discussed something that had her smiling. Logan was rock-solid, the perfect guy to be spending time with Jamie, because he would honor his word and never do anything that would jeopardize their friendship or the one he'd had with Sam. Trouble was, it wasn't Logan who was spending time with Jamie, because he was still working.

"Drink up," he announced, placing the tall glasses on the table and sitting down beside Jamie.

The way she looked at him took him by surprise, made him hope that Logan hadn't noticed it, but maybe he was just being oversensitive.

"To Sam," Logan said, holding up his drink. "A good soldier, a damn good friend and husband to the sweetest woman I've ever met."

Brett glanced at Jamie, saw her eyes were damp. He held up his own glass. "Cheers to that."

They all took a sip, but Jamie was spluttering as soon as she'd swallowed her first mouthful.

"Are you guys trying to kill me? This stuff is like poison."

Brett laughed. "It gets better. Just keep drinking."

"Has Brett shown you his new tattoo?" Logan asked.

Jamie shook her head, looking at him. "Nope." She took another sip and grimaced again.

"Brett had his done as soon as he was out of recovery, and I got mine when I touched down in Australia."

"You have new matching ones?" she asked. "Can I see?"

Logan pushed his T-shirt up, rolling his arm around to show the words marked in black ink, curling letters over four short rows.

"'Fight a battle for a cause that's worth the victory. Fight a war that's worth dying for. Remain brave in death. Honor those you love.'" Jamie stared at Logan's arm as she finished reading the words.

Brett knew she was fighting emotion, because her voice had become low and husky, a deeper tone than he'd ever heard from her. He responded by rolling up his shirt until he could show her his matching ink, only just able to push the fabric high enough for her to see it.

Jamie turned to inspect his properly, trailing her fingers across each word as if she were writing them, committing them to memory. Her touch was light, and when her hand dropped to land on his thigh, it almost made him lose the drink he'd just reached for.

"You did these for Sam, didn't you?" she asked.

Brett nodded when she looked at him, and Logan did the same.

"Well, they're beautiful," she said, dabbing her eyes with the back of her fingers. "Maybe I should get one, too?"

"No," Brett said, faster than he'd meant to.

"I don't think so," Logan chimed in, almost as quickly.

Jamie raised an eyebrow, looking puzzled. "Because I'm a girl? They're not exactly military tattoos, are they?"

Brett looked to Logan for help but didn't receive any. He cleared his throat, not wanting to dig himself a hole that he couldn't claw his way out of, but not having any intention of letting her ink herself.

"Your skin is beautiful and you don't need any ink, Jamie. Don't go rushing into anything."

"Just keep wearing that tag," Logan added. "It's what he would have wanted."

She laughed and took a hearty sip of her drink, before slowly downing the rest of it.

"Bottoms up, boys," she announced, grinning at them over the top of her glass.

Brett and Logan exchanged looks before shrugging and following her lead.

"My round this time. Another?" Jamie asked.

They both said yes and watched her walk away, like two bodyguards ready to pounce on anyone who so much as bumped into her.

"'Your skin is so beautiful'?" Logan mimicked, punching him in the arm. "Seriously, couldn't you have come up with anything better than that?"

Brett glared at him. "It wasn't like you were stepping in to help me out."

"Yeah, I was too busy watching you swooning over her. You know she's out of bounds, right? Because I'll…"

Brett gave him a playful shove, trying to laugh the comment off. "You don't have to tell me, I know."

"I miss him, Brett. I seriously miss him."

Brett leaned back in his seat, watching Jamie at the bar as she leaned toward the bartender to place her order. He couldn't believe he hadn't noticed the dog tag she was wearing around her neck, but then he'd been trying his hardest not to look at her chest, and the way the tag was being swallowed by her breasts... Brett cleared his throat. That wasn't something he needed to think about right now. Sam had been like his surrogate brother, and he would never disrespect anyone he considered family.

"I can't stop thinking about that day. It's screwed up, Logan. The things I saw, what happened, I just wish I could forget it all, for good."

Brett shut his eyes, blocked the memories out, doing what he always did. Because forcing them away was a damn sight easier than dealing with them, and he didn't want to go there, not now.

"I'm going to go help her carry the drinks back," he announced, needing to move.

Before Logan guessed that he also couldn't stop thinking about Jamie, in all the wrong ways.

Jamie leaned back into Brett, eyes shut, the room starting to spin. She'd had three cocktails, but she wasn't exactly used to drinking and it felt like three too many.

"I don't feel so good."

Brett's arm was suddenly looped around her shoulders, holding her closer to his body. She opened her eyes to look at Logan, but he was starting to blur.

"I think someone needs something to eat," Logan said.

"And water," she mumbled.

Logan jumped up and gave her what she guessed was a salute. "Glass of water and greasy fries coming up."

She tucked back tighter into Brett, starting to feel sleepy.

"Thanks for looking after me."

His chuckle made his chest vibrate beneath her ear.

"They were pretty potent," he told her, his hold on her shoulders loosening as he bent forward to retrieve his drink. "We shouldn't have let you have more than two."

Jamie groaned. "You're going to take me home, right?" She didn't want to have to flag a taxi on her own in the dark, not to mention go home to an empty house. Most nights, she tried to remind herself why she was okay alone, but tonight her brain just wasn't cooperating.

"We weren't exactly going to get you drunk then let you find your own way home."

Jamie shut her eyes again, wishing she had only had two drinks. They'd been having so much fun, and she hadn't been out in so long.

"Brett, can you stay with me tonight?" she asked.

Jamie thought she felt his body stiffen, but maybe she was imagining it.

"Ah, I'm not sure," he said. "I'll see you home, though."

Jamie shook her head and turned, hand on Brett's shoulder as she stared up at him. "Please? I just don't want to be alone tonight."

He looked down at her and she couldn't read his face. Having her eyes shut and sitting still for a few minutes had made the spinning stop, but she was still feeling less than average.

"If you still want me to stay when we get to your place, then I will," he finally said. "Just don't go saying anything to Logan because he'll go off and get the wrong idea and I don't need him getting all crazy protective over you."

She smiled up at him, leaning in to kiss his cheek. It was warm and slightly stubbled, but where she kissed him was soft enough to make her want to keep her lips there. Jamie had only meant it as an innocent thank-you, but she could have easily moved slightly to the left, kissed his lips instead. She was staring at them, eyes unable to leave his mouth, even as his hand came up between them and gently pushed her back into her seat.

"Let's not do anything we'd regret sober, okay?"

Brett's voice was soft, but the hungry eyes staring back at her were telling a different story entirely.

"Who's hungry?"

Logan had returned with the bar food, which looked perfect and greasy.

"Me, please," she responded, her thigh pressed to Brett's as she leaned forward. She was telling herself she needed it there to anchor her in place, keep her steady, but she knew better.

She was drunk and coming on to her husband's friend. It was a hundred shades of wrong, but it felt every shade of right. Jamie reached for a fry and dunked it in ketchup, closing her eyes with delight at the salty, greasy taste.

"These are *sooo* good," she murmured.

Logan laughed. "Drunk as a skunk."

She didn't care what they said. Tonight had been better than good, it had been amazing. For the first time in forever, she felt like herself again, and it had been a long time coming.

Because for a while there, she'd wondered if she'd lost that Jamie forever.

Jamie held on to Brett's arm as she stepped out of the taxi, and she didn't let it go as they walked to her front door. He hadn't said anything about staying or not staying, and even though she'd sobered up a heap, she still didn't want to be alone. Nights like tonight brought everything crashing back to her, even though it had been over a decade ago.

*It had been pitch-black outside, and she'd been tucked under a blanket, alone, waiting for her mom to come home. She knew she'd be drunk, but she wanted to wait for her to come back. When the door had opened, she'd stayed still, not made a sound, knowing her mom would just make her way upstairs and collapse on her bed.*

*Only it hadn't been her mom. She'd hidden, terrified, as two men in balaclavas had burgled their house, never making a noise so they wouldn't know anyone was home. Tears had choked in her throat, but she'd stayed silent, wishing that her dad had made it back. Knowing that if he'd been alive, her mom would still be holding it together, that she would have been safe.*

"So here we are," Brett said when they reached the door, jolting her from her thoughts.

She fumbled in her bag for her keys and called out to Bear as his loud bark boomed through the door. Letting her memories take hold was not something she usually let happen, not that easily.

"Just me," she told her dog, "it's only me."

His barking stopped and she turned the key. Brett leaned past her and pushed the door, standing his ground as she dropped to give the dog a cuddle and then usher him back inside.

"Are you going to be okay on your own?" he asked, looking uncomfortable, hands jammed in his pockets.

Jamie wasn't going to lie to him, especially not now. "I've never been okay on my own," she admitted. "Every time Sam went away, I'd pretend to be all brave because I didn't want him worrying about me, but when he was on tour I hardly ever went out unless I could be back before dark. I was just too nervous coming home to an empty house."

His expression changed, his face sad. "Is it better with Bear here?"

She nodded. "Yeah, a little."

"You still want me to stay tonight, don't you?"

Jamie nodded again. Relief took away the tightness in her shoulders as she realized she was actually going to have someone in the house. That Brett, one of the people she trusted most in the world, was going to be sleeping under her roof, protecting her, letting her have a good night's sleep without her worrying about every creak or rustle outside the window. Without her thinking someone might find their way into her home.

Brett smiled when she stepped back, and he walked into the house and locked the door behind him.

"I'll just bunk on the sofa," he said, following her into the kitchen.

"I can make up the spare bed," she told him, flicking on a light and fumbling in the pantry for coffee. "I don't want you being uncomfortable."

"Hey," Brett said, coming up behind her and taking the coffee. "You go sit down, I'll make us both a cup. I'm sure your head could do without all the movement, might help the pounding stop."

His hand over hers made her freeze, and she resisted the urge to push back into him, to rock her body back into his like she was so desperate to do. She craved his touch like a desperate woman who'd never had the pleasure of a man before.

"Go sit on the sofa," he ordered, voice low.

Jamie reluctantly did as she was told, listening to Brett as he moved around the kitchen. She flopped onto the big sofa, tucked up against a cushion, eyes back on him as he stirred two cups and then carried them over. He placed them down and went to sit on the armchair.

"It's way more comfy over here," she told him.

He hesitated before coming over to sit beside her. Jamie tucked her feet up and changed position, her body against Brett's instead of the oversized cushion. Now she had an oversized, warm, muscled man to lean into.

"Thanks for tonight," she told him.

"My pleasure," he responded, staying still but looking down at her.

Jamie knew she was still a little drunk, that she

needed to just sleep it off and not do anything stupid, but ever since she'd kissed Brett at the bar, on the cheek, she'd thought of nothing other than his lips; his full, kissable lips.

Before she knew what she was doing, she reached up to touch his face, tracing her fingers over his mouth before leaning on him and putting her lips there. It was a sweet kiss, a warm kiss, a kiss that made her skin tingle. And it wasn't easy to pull back from. Brett didn't resist, didn't push her away, but he didn't move closer, either. He just moved his lips enough for her to know that he was kissing her back, that he wanted it, too. Or at least that's what she wanted to think.

He didn't say anything when she pulled away, and neither did she. Brett reached for a cushion, put it at the end of the sofa and leaned back into it, letting her fall down against him. She put her head against his chest, tucked up beside him, like a cat purring into his hold as he put his arm around her.

She should have gone and found a blanket to keep them warm, but she didn't want to move and Brett was warm and snuggly even without anything covering them. Instead she shut her eyes and let sleep catch her and wrap her in its equally warm embrace. She couldn't have fought it if she tried, and Jamie had a feeling that for once she might actually sleep through the entire night without waking, terrified, like she usually did.

Brett stared down at Jamie. She was asleep, he could hear the change in her breathing, but it didn't make him even close to being sleepy himself.

Jamie, Sam's wife, had just kissed him. And he'd done nothing to stop it and everything to encourage it.

Granted, he'd had a lot to drink, but not enough to make him drunk or to make him forget that she was forbidden. Even Logan had reminded him, just in case he'd managed to forget himself, that she was the one woman he wasn't supposed to think about, *like that*. And yet she'd come on to him and he'd willingly accepted her advances.

But then he'd known he was a goner tonight from the moment she'd traced her fingers down his inner arm, along the words of his tattoo, and he'd known he was incapable of doing the right thing when she'd kissed his cheek in the bar. The heat of her breath against his skin, her warm lips, the look in her eyes…like she wanted him, trusted him and needed him, all rolled into one stare. Into one gentle touch that he found one hundred percent irresistible.

Brett groaned, but there was no getting away from her, not now that she was clutching his shirt between her fingers and her head was tucked against his chest like it was her own personal pillow to snuggle up into.

The light in the kitchen was still on, but unless he could teach the dog how to turn it off, he was just going to have to shut his eyes and do his best to ignore it.

He caught sight of Bear watching him, head between his paws, eyebrows raised.

"Don't look at me like that," Brett told him, scowling.

He didn't need a damn dog to make him feel even more guilty than he already felt.

"And don't you be forgetting that I saved your life," he muttered, before shutting his eyes.

The truth was that Bear had saved all of them that day. He'd stopped after Sam had sent him out, body dead-still, tail quivering, head cocked to the side. It had been Bear who'd alerted them to the bomb—only trouble was that it wasn't a standard improvised explosive device. This IED had been remote-detonated, most likely from a local hiding where they hadn't been able to find him. Someone watching, in wait, to explode an entire 4x4 full of SAS soldiers, wanting to blow them all into pieces.

Sam and Brett's dog had been the casualties that day, so maybe he should be showing Bear some respect and thanking *him* for saving his life.

He shut his eyes, knowing sleep wouldn't come easily, because it never did these days. If he managed to fall asleep, he'd wake up in a sweat and twisted in his sheets, mind full of the darkness of that day he was trying so hard to forget. And then he'd lie awake, scared of shutting his eyes again because of the memories that flashed like scenes from a movie beneath his eyelids.

# CHAPTER FIVE

WHEN BRETT WOKE up, the pain in his leg and back hit him straight away. He was all crooked from lying flat, and when he tried to move, he realized he couldn't. Because the woman he'd just been having an erotic dream about was still attached to his chest, her long hair splayed out across him, arm slung down low, cheek to his heart.

He shut his eyes again, remembering how uncomfortable it had been carrying a hundred-and-fifty-pound pack when he was on patrol with the SAS. At least Jamie was warm and… He swallowed away that particular thought. Now he just had to hope that she didn't wake up for a little bit longer, so she didn't have to wonder if it was a gun or if he was just pleased to see her when she realized where her hand was resting.

But…he'd slept. He'd dreamed about Jamie. And he wasn't wet with sweat. Which meant that last night was the first night he'd actually slept through, without nightmares, since *that day*.

When Brett opened his eyes again, Bear was staring

back at him, his nose right beside his face, as if he'd just been waiting for them to wake up.

"Hey, buddy," he whispered, receiving a giant lick in reply.

Jamie groaned then and wriggled closer against him, her arm flinging across his chest. He kept one hand on her to keep her in place, not wanting her to fall off the sofa if she stretched the other way. Another low groan told him she perhaps wasn't a morning person, or that her head was starting to thump.

"Want some pain meds?" he asked, keeping his voice low.

She went still, then put her palm flat on his chest and pushed up. Her hair was all messy, curlier than he'd ever seen it, and her eyes were smudged. She looked lazy and sexy all rolled into one.

"I slept on you."

He chuckled. "We still have our clothes on, so don't worry."

She didn't smile, so he was guessing his joke wasn't in the best taste, but she did flop back down on top of him, face buried in his chest again.

"My head kind of hurts," she muttered. "And don't even try to tell me I don't look like crap, because I know I do."

He laughed. "You actually look pretty good."

Funny how he could go from freaking out to joking with her in two seconds flat, and he wasn't lying, either.

"Warmed-up crap," she muttered. "That's even worse than straight crap, right?"

Brett pushed her gently off him and stretched, being

careful to flex his leg before standing up. He'd missed
a few physical therapy sessions since he'd been back,
and the last thing he needed was to do damage to his
just-recovered leg because he was too lazy to stretch.

"I'm going to get you a glass of water and something
for your head. Where do you keep the meds?"

"In the bathroom," she mumbled.

Brett stood and crossed the room. If he were going to
pretend like he was here just to protect her, to look after
her, he may as well do something to actually be helpful.

Jamie excused herself, went up to her bathroom and
took a long shower. She just stood there under the burning hot water, letting it pour down her face and hair.
Her head had stopped pounding, thanks to the tablets
she'd just swallowed, but she was still feeling a lot less
perky than she usually did.

She forced herself to step out of the shower and
wrapped a massive towel around her small frame, using
a different one to dry her long hair. After what had happened last night she was in no hurry to rush back down-
stairs to Brett, not after she'd gone ahead and kissed
him. Her only hope was that maybe he thought she'd
been too drunk to remember it. *She wished.*

Jamie rubbed moisturizer onto her body, then ap-
plied some makeup, smoothing on some foundation,
then mascara, blush and lip gloss. She didn't want to
look like she'd gone to too much effort, but then she
didn't want him to see her looking hungover with no
makeup on, either.

She heard a noise behind her and jumped, but it was

only Bear. The last thing she needed was Brett walking in on her naked, wearing only a dog tag around her neck. The dog tag that was supposed to remind her, no matter what, that a certain friend of her husband's was out of bounds.

"Hey, buddy." Bear was staring at her with his head cocked to the side, and she was pleased to think about something other than her behavior the night previous. "You hungry?"

Her stomach growled in response to her own question, so she left her hair pinned up wet and signaled for her dog to follow her. She wasn't used to drinking, and she sure as hell wasn't used to dealing with a hangover.

Jamie removed the dog tag and slung it back on the hook by her shoes, feeling like a traitor for wearing it after the way she'd behaved with Brett the night before, and pulled on jeans and a T-shirt. Then she walked down the hall to find Brett with the morning paper, sprawled out over the kitchen counter as he ate a piece of toast.

"Hey," she said as she went straight for the coffee.

He looked up and held his toast in his mouth as he shuffled the paper so it took up less space.

"How you feeling now?" he asked with a grin.

Jamie groaned. "Please don't remind me about last night." She poured herself a large cup of coffee, stirred in two sugars and took a gulp. It was piping hot and burned her tongue but she didn't care.

She scooped a cup of Bear's special dog biscuits into his bowl, aware that he'd been patiently waiting at her feet since they'd arrived in the kitchen, then went back to nursing her coffee.

"I'm feeling a bit responsible for plying you with those drinks," he said, finishing his toast. "Maybe we should have gone with beer, or just let you a have a few girly cocktails instead of the most potent blend on the menu."

Jamie held up her hand. "I'll take full responsibility for drinking them, so long as you don't ever mention the words *Long Island iced tea* to me *ever* again."

Brett laughed and held up his coffee cup. "Deal," he agreed. "You want me to make you anything for brekkie while you nurse your head?"

She groaned again, sipping more coffee. "I'll just have toast, thanks. Cold toast with jam, something easy on my poor stomach."

The way Brett was watching her told her he was thinking about something, waiting to ask her something. Please don't bring up the kiss. The last thing she needed right now was to deal with that particular conversation, especially before she'd eaten anything and had time to process it.

"Jamie, I don't know if you remember, but when we were at the bar, and then when we came back here last night…"

She gulped when he paused, and then he said, "You mentioned that you never told Sam how scared you were coming home to an empty house in the dark."

Phew. She could deal with this conversation if she had to. It might have been difficult to talk about, admitting to that, but given what the alternative topic could have been, she was relieved.

"My dad was a soldier, and he died on deployment, too." Jamie kept her gaze trained on her coffee, not wanting to look at Brett. "When he died, my mom went on a bender that lasted a few years, and I was home alone when we were burgled. I hid until they left, but I guess I've never really gotten over that fear of it happening again. Which is why I'm obsessed with locking doors and being inside before sundown, and my security alarm was always on before Bear came back to live here."

Brett was still staring at her, concern written all over his face. "So I'm guessing you told Sam about what happened, but you never told him how much it still scared you. Because you always knew that he'd be going away and leaving you alone. That there was nothing he could do to change that."

Jamie nodded.

"I can't believe he was away for months at a time, and you had to be a prisoner inside your own house every night. You should have told us."

She sighed and moved closer to him, staying on the other side of the kitchen counter and leaning forward. "I just always had that fear of going to sleep and not knowing if someone could have gotten into the house while I was out. There's nothing Sam could have done for me, except worry like crazy from the other side of the world, and that wouldn't have been good for either of us."

"But you're sleeping okay now?"

She shook her head, not wanting to tell the truth but wanting to lie to Brett even less. "Last night was the first time since before Sam deployed that I've slept through without waking. I've been better with Bear here this last month, so I'm not complaining, but being alone isn't something I've ever been good at. I freak out at every sound and then can't fall asleep again."

Brett stared into his coffee cup, which she was sure must have been empty by now. "Did you sleep better because I was here with you, or because of the alcohol?"

Jamie grinned at him. "Last night might well have been a combination of both, but I have no intentions of turning into an alcoholic just to sleep through the night. Plus I have no plans of turning into my mom."

He smiled, but he wasn't laughing at her joke. "Let me stay for a few days, let you catch up on some sleep while I'm here."

His voice was lower than usual, an octave deeper. She shook her head. "You don't have to do that. I'll be fine."

She might have been telling him no, but inside she was screaming out for him to stay. Having Brett here would make her feel safe, let her relax and just sleep solidly for a few nights at least, but she didn't expect him to do that.

And her intentions weren't pure, either. Because ever since she'd starting thinking about Brett in a certain way last night, remembering how soft his lips had been, how sensual it had been pressed against his body, she'd thought of nothing other than having him here. Keeping him close. Wondering if something could happen between them, and whether he wanted it as much as she did, even if she did know it was wrong.

She took a deep breath. "I don't want you feeling sorry for me."

That made him smile. "I most definitely don't feel sorry for you," he said. "And it's no big deal. If you want me to stay, just say so. Besides, sleeping isn't exactly easy for me these days, and I slept through the night last night, too."

"If I'm honest, Brett, having you here for a few days sounds idyllic." She wanted to stay strong, but she also wanted a man in her house again. Wanted the company of someone she could actually talk to, who wasn't afraid of the truth. Of what had happened to her husband. Because she had no one else to talk to, and no one else to turn to. She'd lost her dad and then her husband to war, and she was tired of being alone. "But only if you're sure."

She listened to Brett's big intake of breath, watched the way his body stiffened then softened back to normal again. When they weren't serving, Sam's two best friends had been as much a part of her life as her husband had, and she missed having them all around. It was like she'd lost all three of them at once.

"Then I'll stay. As long as you need me here, I'll stay."

She dropped her head to his shoulder. "He would have liked you being here, you know that, right?"

Brett shrugged, but she could tell he was finding this as awkward as she was. "You know, he made me promise to look out for you if anything ever happened to him. I just never figured that we'd actually be in that position."

Jamie smiled. "I'll never forget what you've done for me, Brett."

Brett was her friend. Nothing more. She just had to keep reminding herself of that, because falling in love with her husband's best buddy? Not something that could happen. Not now, not ever.

Brett could have been the man of her dreams—*once*. But now wasn't the time to look back. Now was about the future. The one she had to build without her husband by her side. No matter how much she was thinking about *that* kiss.

"Well, if you're staying you're definitely not sleeping on the sofa."

He shrugged. "Whatever's easy for you. I don't want to be any trouble."

Jamie poured herself another cup of coffee and gestured for him to pass his cup over for more. "You never did say how long you were back for? What your plans were?"

Brett took the now full cup from her and looked at her over the counter. "I'm kind of done with the army."

She felt her eyebrows shoot up. "What do you mean by *kind of*?"

"I mean that I've served my time and now I'm retired. Honorable discharge."

"Wow." Jamie hadn't even considered that he might have left the army, that he was done with a role he'd been in for so many years. "Did it have something to do with what happened?" She didn't want to bring it up again, but she also wanted to know.

The relief that hit her body, knowing that there was no chance she could lose Brett, too, was like a physical weight lifting from her shoulders. The last thing she'd need was to worry herself silly the next time both Brett and Logan were deployed. She'd lost too many men in her life to deal with the possibility of losing another.

"I was burned pretty bad on my leg and back, so my injuries were enough to put me out of action for a while, but to be honest I think I've given enough to the cause. I don't think I could have gone back on deployment again after what happened, after what I went through. It's changed how I'd react to a situation."

"So you'll be staying with the army, though?" she asked. "Doing something with dogs still?"

Brett shrugged. "I need to spend some time figuring my life out, what I want to do, where I want to be." He took a sip of coffee, a thoughtful look on his face as he stared out the window. "Right now I can't imagine a life that doesn't involve working with a dog all day, being deployed or training for the next task force operation. So I just need some time to process everything."

"Can you take your time deciding?"

He nodded. "Yeah, I can. I need to focus on recovering fully, then I can figure out what I'm going to do long-term. Start over, I guess."

And he was going to be doing a lot of that figuring out here, if she had anything to do with where he would be spending his time while he was in Sydney.

"So when you say you hurt your leg and back badly…"

she began, not wanting to push him but desperate to know.

"It means I should be doing physio stretches and exercises every day," Brett confessed, "starting this morning."

"Well, it just so happens that I have a heap of work to do, so how about you do what you need to do and I'll sit in my office and try to get this book finished."

Brett grinned. "Deal."

Brett smiled at the physical therapist through the computer screen. It wasn't ideal, but he'd been through rehabilitation and all the hard grunt as far as his leg was concerned, and now it was just a matter of gaining the muscle strength that he'd lost and getting his body back to full capacity.

"So you're not pushing yourself too hard yet?"

He laughed. "Not doing enough is more the problem."

"Well, best I can advise you is to do your stretches daily, and start doing some light jogging if you're up to it. Then you can slowly get back to the point where any type of exercise will be okay."

He gave her a salute. "Yes, ma'am."

She grinned. "Pleased to see you have your spark back. Obviously someone's been looking after you now that you're back home."

Brett glanced up, looked at Jamie working through the open window of her office. "I'm just pleased to be back," he told her.

"Okay, show me your leg stretches, both sides, and

then you can get back to doing whatever it is that's making you smile."

He was pleased he'd decided to use video messaging to contact her, because otherwise another day would have passed without him doing the exercises. Before he'd come to see Jamie, he hadn't missed a day, but she'd been more than a little distracting. The fact that she was working and could look out at him wasn't exactly helping his powers of concentration, but he needed to block her out.

How many times had he had to just focus and get on with a task for work? Ignoring one woman shouldn't have been a struggle, but it was.

Brett ran through the exercises, lifting both legs separately, tightening and releasing and then jumping up and down as he'd been shown to do.

"What do you think?" he asked, slightly out of breath once he'd finished the series of reps.

The physical therapist nodded. "Good work. Just keep it up and extend yourself a little bit more every day. You'll get a feel for how hard you can push your body."

They said goodbye and he stood up, slowly stretching before doing some fast sprints back and forth across the lawn. His leg twinged when he stopped too quickly, but he kept it up, taking care not to strain anything. Bear was watching him from the edge of the grass like he was crazy to be using so much energy in the heat, and he had a feeling Jamie might be watching him, too. He didn't indulge himself in looking in her direction, not yet. Because staying focused was already proving to be a task he wasn't excelling at.

When he finished he dropped to the ground to do two sets of crunches, then press-ups, before shutting his eyes and just lying in the sun. Maybe he was getting old, or maybe his body had just been through a more serious trauma than he was letting himself admit. But he was definitely ready for a shower, or a swim in a cool pool would have been even better.

"You look exhausted."

Brett opened his eyes and stared up at Jamie. He rolled to his side and pulled up to a sitting position.

"I thought you were chained to your desk for the rest of the day?" he asked.

She sighed. "Watching you out here wasn't helping to keep me stuck in there."

"If you'd rather I went…"

"No," she replied, holding out a towel and a bottle of water before he could continue. "What I want is to forget about work and just enjoy the day."

He wiped his face and neck with the towel, before twisting the top off the water and guzzling it down.

"When's your deadline?" he asked as she flopped down to sit on the grass with him.

"End of the week," she said, as Bear came over and leaned against her, looking for attention. "I'll make it, I just can't concentrate today. Or at all, lately, if I'm completely honest. My brain just doesn't want to switch into the right gear."

Brett watched as she tried to push the dog away, laughing as he leaned on her and wouldn't give up. In the end she gave up and Bear laid upside down beside her for a belly scratch.

"For someone who keeps saying she doesn't know a lot about dogs, you're sure developing a good friendship with this one." Bear had his eyes closed now, in heaven at all the attention he was receiving.

"It's not that I don't love him, because I do," Jamie said, smiling with her eyes as she stared at him. "I just haven't ever had a dog before, and I wasn't confident with telling him what to do. Or what to expect from him."

"Love is a pretty good start," Brett said, wishing he'd chosen his words better as soon as they came out of his mouth.

"Yeah? Well I've never found it hard to love, so maybe we'll be okay after all."

Brett stayed silent, wasn't sure what to say. Just because he was thinking about last night, wishing that he hadn't been so damn honorable and pushed her away when she'd kissed him, didn't mean he needed to bring it up. The only consolation was that she didn't have anything to regret now that she was sober, because if he'd let things go too far she might not have the same smile on her face that she did right now.

"As much as I'd like to enjoy the day with you, I think you need to get some more work done."

She groaned. "Have you been secretly talking to my editor?"

Brett grinned. "No, but you don't need this deadline hanging over your head, and you'll feel so much better for doing at least some of it today."

"You're right, I'm just procrastinating."

Brett sat up properly and stretched his legs out in front of him. "I'll make you a deal."

She raised her eyebrows. "Let me hear it."

"I'm going to head out, run a few errands and pick up some groceries. We can cook something nice for dinner, and you can forget all about your deadline, once you've worked for a few hours."

"Promise me we can have chocolate for dessert, and you have yourself a deal."

Brett held out his hand, smiling when her palm slipped into his. He was on dangerous territory, and he was starting to enjoy it.

# CHAPTER SIX

IT HAD BEEN a long time since Brett had shopped for groceries and arrived home to cook dinner. He kicked the door shut with the heel of his boot and carried the bags through the house, before putting them on the ground and calling out to Jamie.

"I'm back," he called, wandering down the hall toward her office.

"Oh, hey," she said back.

He walked a couple of steps backward, looking into the bedroom he'd just passed. Jamie was tucking sheets into the bed, hair pulled up into a ponytail, wearing cutoff denim shorts and a tight tank top.

He could have done without seeing Jamie looking like that, making a bed that was presumably for him. Thank God it was down the hall from her room.

"I just wanted to let you know I was back."

She smiled and threw the duvet on the bed, followed by a couple of pillows that had been sitting on the ground.

"You were secretly checking up on me, weren't you?"

Her smile was infectious, no matter how much he

wished he could distance himself from her. In the car, he'd reminded himself how he needed to behave, how he needed to think about her, but no amount of good intentions could help him when he was faced with Jamie in the flesh.

She didn't seem to notice that he hadn't replied and breezed past him, her shoulder skimming his bicep as she headed down the hall.

"Before you ask, I worked solidly almost the entire time you were gone, so I don't have anything to feel guilty about."

Brett froze before he could follow her, had only managed to turn before his feet refused to move. Because staring at him, eyes on his, was Sam. Sam's smiling photo was hanging in the hall, straight outside the bedroom, and he hadn't even noticed it when he'd walked past looking for Jamie. *For Sam's wife.*

"Brett?"

He shook his head, mouthed *sorry* to his friend, the friend he was so close to betraying, and followed Jamie to the kitchen.

"Are you okay?"

Brett forced himself to snap out of whatever the hell it was he'd sunk into. She'd been Sam's wife for years, he had known that this morning and he'd known it the night before, and yet he was the one who'd suggested he stay, who'd decided to go grocery shopping for dinner. It wasn't Jamie's fault that he was flipping out over something that was every bit his fault, so he needed to pull himself together.

"Sorry, yeah, I wasn't sure what you'd like."

"Mmmm, what are we making?"

He watched as she started to pull things out of the bags. "It's the only thing I can make that doesn't involve packets of sauce or frozen food."

Brett never took his eyes off her as she laughed and pulled out a bag of tomatoes.

"Pasta?"

He nodded. "My mom was a great cook, and it's the only thing I ever learned from her."

Jamie's face lost the rosy glow he'd been enjoying watching, her eyebrows dragging together as she frowned.

"You were only young when you lost your parents, weren't you?"

Her voice was tender and it made him want to walk straight around the kitchen and hold her, to engulf her slender body in his arms and just feel what it was like to have her pressed to him. This woman who was driving him crazy—who'd *driven* him crazy for years—was driving him wild now.

Brett cleared his throat, well past the pain of what he'd endured as a teenager, but still not a fan of dredging up the past.

"I was eighteen, and they both died in a head-on collision," he said, wishing he'd just shut his mouth and not said anything. Talking about what had happened back then was almost as bad about talking about what had happened to Sam. "I was at a party, drunk, and I phoned them to come and pick me up. Turns out they both got in the car that night, and if it hadn't been for me, they would have still been at home."

Jamie was staring at him, palms on the counter. "I can't imagine what that was like for you, Brett, but you can't honestly blame yourself."

"Actually, you're the one person who probably can understand," he said. So many people had acted like they knew what he was going through, but Jamie had only just emerged from that place of loss herself. "It's no different to you losing Sam, it's just at a different stage in your life. The only thing that isn't the same is that you had nothing to do with him dying. Me? I'll never forgive myself for making the call that took them away from me and changed my life forever."

"Brett, you were eighteen years old. Teenagers are supposed to call their parents in the middle of the night when they need them."

Brett shrugged. "Nothing anyone says to me will ever make me believe that I wasn't responsible." He stared at her, watching her mouth as it turned down into a frown. "The only thing that saved me back then was the army. I was surrounded by guys like Sam every day, and they become my surrogate family. They still are, I guess."

"So in other words you found a way to forget about what had happened."

"I'm the first to admit that I ran away from that life, but at the age I was, I didn't really have any other choice. Well, not any choice that would have been good for me."

And this was why he needed to respect Sam, even in death. He'd been family to Brett, just like the rest of his unit had been, and the last thing he needed was more guilt to carry around.

He listened to Jamie sigh before she returned to taking the groceries from the bags. "I'd run away in a heartbeat, Brett, so don't think I'd ever judge you for turning your back on the life you had taken away from you. You were brave to start over, especially in the army."

Brett should have stood his ground, just stayed still on the other side of the kitchen, but he ignored his better judgment and joined her.

"What do you want to run away from?" he asked, voice low.

"From everything about this life, from the memories, just to start over and pretend like this was all a bad dream. That I didn't choose to marry a soldier, knowing that there was a chance he'd die like my father did. I still can't believe that I lost both of them like that."

He wished he could offer it to her, wished he was brave enough to just tell her that he'd run away with her if it meant they could both forget and start over.

"I can't help you run away, Jamie, but I can help you heal."

She smiled across at him, nudged him with her shoulder. He should have resisted, but instead he slung his arm around her and pulled her in for a hug, closing his eyes when she dropped her head to his shoulder and wrapped her arm around his waist.

"I think you've already helped me," she told him, her voice laced with a softness that made him wish he wasn't thinking what he was thinking. That he was just a friend wanting to help another friend with no hidden agenda.

"What do you say I teach you how to cook Mama's tomato pasta sauce?"

She loosened her hold on him until her arm fell away, and he made himself let go of her, too.

"Was your mom Italian?"

He grinned, glanced at her before taking the tomatoes from the packet. "Sure was. And she'd kill me for buying nonorganic produce."

"Ah, well that explains the dark good looks, huh?"

Jamie was laughing and he raised an eyebrow back at her, which only made her laugh more.

"You would have liked her," he said. "And I know she'd have been impressed that I at least remembered one of her dishes."

"I have no doubt that I'd have loved the woman who raised you," she said. "Even if you did lose her young, she sure did a good job."

He looked away when Jamie leaned down to pull out the chopping board, not needing to see the way her shorts showed way too much skin when she bent forward.

"What else do you need?"

Brett reached past her for a knife from the wooden block on the counter, pleased that they were finished with their awkward conversation. He didn't mind opening up to Jamie, but going back into the past was never easy. Not for him. "You can either chop tomatoes or onions?"

"I'll do the onions," she said.

Brett went to question her, to be the gentleman and offer to do the crap job, until she reached for her sunglasses and put them on.

"Ah, smart girl."

She laughed. "Years of experience chopping these suckers. I always keep an old pair handy."

"You know this isn't going to be a quick meal, right?" he said, chopping the tomatoes into even pieces. "It needs to cook for an hour, maybe longer."

"Did you buy wine?" she asked.

"Yes, ma'am."

Jamie dropped her knife and pulled her sunglasses off. "Red?"

He nodded. "Paper bag on the floor."

She crossed the room, pulled out two big wineglasses and pulled the cork from the bottle, before pouring a little into each glass. "We may as well have fun, right? I don't mind waiting if we have something to do to pass the time."

Brett took the glass from her, wishing he didn't have to look at her, that her eyes hadn't locked on his.

"To new beginnings," she announced, holding her glass up to touch his.

"Cheers to that," he said, wishing he'd been man enough to tell her how important the past was.

Brett took a sip as she did the same, swallowing the wine slowly before putting down his glass.

"So what do we do once we're done with chopping?"

They were standing side by side, Jamie with her glasses back on.

"If I was being a purist then I should have skinned

the tomatoes first, but it'll still be great like this and otherwise we'll run out of time," he told her, pleased to take his mind off her by talking food. "We need to sauté the onions first with some fresh garlic, then add the tomatoes, some chopped red capsicum and a few handfuls of fresh basil."

"Sounds heavenly."

"Wait until you taste it with freshly shaved parmesan sprinkled on top with a grind of black pepper."

Jamie's tongue flicked out to moisten her lips and he wished it hadn't. She was clearly thinking about the food, but it made his mind skip off in an entirely different direction.

"Sounds delicious."

"I also cheated with the pasta," Brett told her. "I should be making it myself, but I found a homemade spaghetti at the store."

"I can't believe *you're* teaching *me* a recipe."

He put down his knife and reached for the wine again. "You say that like I'm some uncouth caveman."

Jamie chuckled as she finished the onions and washed her hands. "I guess I just never took a special forces soldier for a cook. I mean, when have you even had time to learn culinary skills?"

"You did hear me say that I can only cook one dish from scratch, didn't you?"

"Yeah, but it's a damn good one from the sound of it," she said, pulling out a stockpot and turning on the gas. "Want me to start on browning the onions? I can be your sous chef if you like?"

He nodded and reached for the cloves of garlic he

hàd sitting on the counter, then started peeling and slicing them. There was nothing he didn't like about cooking with Jamie, about being with her, about having her by his side.

Maybe it would have felt the same with any woman, because it wasn't like he'd ever cooked side by side with anyone else before, but deep down he knew he was kidding himself.

The way he felt for Jamie wasn't normal, which made it all the harder for him to fight. When he'd been out shopping, he'd wondered if he should just call her and say he'd gone back to his motel, that he'd see her again in a couple of days, but that thought had left his mind as fast as it had entered. Because Jamie was addictive, and right now, he was the addict.

"If we don't eat it soon my stomach is going to start roaring."

Jamie leaned back in her seat and gave Brett what she hoped was her most pathetic face. It seemed to work, because he laughed and walked himself and his glass of wine across the room and to the bubbling pot. The aroma of the sauce cooking had filled the room, and her stomach *was* starting to rumble.

"Mama will be shaking her fist up there in the clouds," he joked, turning around with the wooden spoon in his hand. "She'd be telling me that it needs two hours to reduce properly."

Jamie groaned. "I don't care." She took a final sip of wine and joined him in the kitchen. "Is this for me to taste?"

He nodded and held it out, his other hand poised beneath it to catch any drips.

"Tell me what you think," he said.

Jamie leaned closer and opened her mouth, letting him tip the spoon. The taste explosion made her shut her eyes for a second, instantly fuelling her angry appetite.

"Oh, my God," she managed to say after swallowing, her words all sounding like they'd merged into one. "That's incredible."

Brett dipped the spoon back into the pot and tasted a mouthful himself. "Not bad, if I do say so myself."

"I can't believe I've known you for so long and never known you could cook like that."

She reached for the spoon but he didn't let it go, shaking his head. "Just one more taste, then you have to wait until the pasta is cooked."

Jamie made a face but dropped her hand, waiting for Brett to offer her another mouthful. He was grinning when he extended it in her direction, before pulling back and leaving her openmouthed and waiting.

"Brett!"

He just laughed and gave it to her, but she moved at the same time, meaning a few drops dripped onto her chin. Brett pulled the spoon back and reached for her face, wiping gently at her chin, his fingers sweeping across her skin to catch the sauce. He licked the sauce from his finger, and she couldn't take her eyes from him, watching his face, his mouth, his tongue.

They were standing closer than they should have been, and now they were staring way longer than they should have been, neither blinking, just watching.

Brett moved his body slightly but Jamie stayed motionless, eyes still never leaving his. She couldn't think of anything else except for Brett; suddenly he seemed to fill the room with his presence. It was like he was towering over her, his body blocking out everything, his eyes stopping her from seeing anything else, his masculinity calling out to her, making her want to close the distance between them and end up wrapped in his big arms.

"Ah, I should put that pasta on, right?" he asked.

Jamie cleared her throat, took a step backward to put some distance between them, to force a space between them that would stop the magnetic pull she was feeling toward him. Toward a man she couldn't feel like that about, not yet. Not now. She'd lost two soldiers in her life already—there was no way she was going to let a third one break her heart.

"I'll, ah, go set up the table outside," she told him, nodding her head like she was trying to convince herself. "We may as well eat alfresco."

Brett turned away and pulled out a big pot, filling it with water and setting it to boil. "This won't take long. I'll bring it all out when it's ready."

Jamie swallowed a lump of something—maybe it was just pure emotion but it felt like pure pain to her—and pulled out place mats and cutlery. She could come back for the wine, but right now she needed some space. A moment to breathe. A moment to think about what she was so close to doing.

Because if she did it, if she gave in to her feelings, then there was no going back. And she didn't want to spend the rest of her life regretting ruining the one friendship that meant the world to her, and had meant even more to her husband.

Jamie walked outside and set the table, before wandering around to the side of the house and leaning against it, out of view of the kitchen. She needed to feel the air on her face, shut her eyes and just think.

*About Sam.* About the fact that she was still wearing her wedding ring, that she still loved the man she'd married five years ago, that she didn't want to be unfaithful to him even though he was gone.

And the fact that her feelings for Brett were starting to consume her.

Because friends or not, widow or not, she wanted to know what it felt like to kiss Brett again. To be held in his arms. To have his big body pressed against hers, protecting her, *loving her.*

"You okay?"

Jamie's eyes flew open and she smoothed her hands down over her shorts.

"Yeah, fine. I just needed a minute."

She turned to find him standing by the table, not coming into her space, but concern was written all over his face. He'd brought the wine and their glasses out, along with some napkins.

"Jamie, are we okay?"

She took a deep breath. "Yeah, we're okay." Jamie paused. "We are, right?"

Brett nodded, smiling, but his eyes told a story of concern. Of not knowing what to say, of what to think about what was happening.

Because they weren't okay and yet they were, all at the same time.

"How's that pasta looking?" she asked.

"Your stomach still growling?"

She reached for the wine bottle and poured a little more into each of their glasses. "It just so happens that I'm ravenous. I can't wait."

Brett gave her one last, long look before turning around and heading back inside. "Give me two minutes. Then you can eat until you can't fit another mouthful in."

Comfort food was exactly what she needed, and if the taste of sauce she'd had inside was anything to go by, it might even take her mind off how she was feeling. At least for a few minutes.

# CHAPTER SEVEN

JAMIE LEANED BACK, glass of wine in hand, staring up at the stars. It was only nine o'clock, but the sun had gone down long ago and the only light around them was the artificial kind. She'd lit the large candle in the center of the table, and the small flame was making her smile with its constant flicker against the glass, but it wasn't doing enough to distract her entirely from Brett.

Their dinner had been amazing, and things seemed to have simmered down between them. There had been no awkward silences, no difficult conversations, just a pleasant night eating alfresco in good company. She was full and content from the huge bowl of pasta she had, the tomato taste still lingering even now. She'd never tasted homemade tomato sauce like that, and now she had, she knew she'd never be satisfied with the bought kind again.

"You know, when you're away like we were, the stars are the only constant. The one thing you can look up at, and know that someone else in another country will be staring up at that same sky."

She turned her head slightly so she could see Brett's

profile. The light was playing off his features, making him look even more handsome than usual. His dark hair looked black, shadows across part of his face making his features seem even stronger, more masculine. Jamie had always thought him handsome, but sitting out here with him tonight, watching the kind and thoughtful expressions on his face, she knew she'd never realized quite how gorgeous he really was. They'd spent so much time together over the years, but never alone like this without the other guys around.

"Did you wonder sometimes why you were there? Wish you weren't?" Jamie asked him. "I mean, it must have been hard dealing with being away so often, doing what you were doing."

He chuckled. "There were plenty of times I wished I wasn't there, but that was usually because of boredom, or missing things from home." He paused, took a long sip of his drink, clearly deep in thought. "I never lost sight of why we were there, though. And without us? So many soldiers would have been losing their lives. There would be convoys blown up everywhere without our dogs detecting IEDs. Men coming home in body bags. The young guys standing on those bloody things is enough to make you physically sick. Just kids, in their twenties, and having to have prosthetic limbs fitted just to be able to walk again." He sighed. "And besides, the army was like my family. They were all I had."

"I can't even imagine what you went through. How you could put your life and your dogs in danger…" She froze, catching her lip between her teeth. "I'm sorry, I didn't mean…" Jamie wished she could have crawled into a hole and died. She knew why they did it, she just couldn't imagine dealing with it, living it. And she hadn't meant to bring up his dog dying again.

Brett smiled, but she knew the reminder of his dog must have hurt.

"It's okay, you don't have to worry about offending me," he said. "We all know the risks when we go in, but nothing prepares you. Especially for the hatred, of how desperate they are to blow each and every one of us into pieces. It's kind of hard to understand until you're there, and once you are, you just have to stay focused on the job."

"I heard about that dog they found. The one that survived despite everything she went through." Jamie sighed. "I should be embarrassed by how much I cried when I read it."

He laughed, his smile wide. "Yeah, she was injured, survived one of the harshest winters and summers on record, and managed to be spotted by troops more than a year later. Sarbi is the poster dog for never losing hope. And better still, she's an Australian citizen."

They sat in silence for a bit, and Jamie hoped she hadn't ruined the night by bringing up war and death. She'd been trying to avoid mentioning Sam, but somehow the conversation had reverted to soldier talk, which seemed to lead straight back to her husband.

"Do you think I'm going to make it? As a dog owner, I mean?"

Brett had been leaning back, his chair on two legs, but when she spoke he pushed in closer to the table and leaned toward her instead.

"Sweetheart, Bear is in love with you and you're desperate to look after him properly. If there was ever a partnership destined to work, it's this one. And besides, you were already doing well, it was just that he was a bit confused by your signals."

The smile that spread across her face was genuine, because if Brett thought she could make it, then maybe her chances weren't so bad after all. Especially with his help to make her understand her new canine—she wouldn't have ever given up on Bear, but they sure could have struggled for a while trying to figure one another out.

"Talking of partnerships," she said, digging her fingers into her palm to force herself to continue. "Are you sure I'm not keeping you from seeing anyone? I mean, I don't want you to feel that you have to be here babysitting me."

He stared at her, face expressionless. For a moment she wondered if she'd offended him, wished she hadn't said anything, until he shrugged and grinned at her.

"I'm not seeing anyone, if that's what you're asking," he said. "And for the record, I have no plans to *babysit* you."

Jamie fought the blush that was heating her neck and cheeks, refusing to give in to it. "I didn't mean to be nosy, it's just you've been spending so much time with me, and I didn't want you to feel so sorry for me that you were missing out on seeing someone else. Someone…" *Special* was what she'd been thinking of saying. He might have said he wasn't seeing anyone, but it didn't mean he wanted to spend all his free time with her.

Now his expression was serious, completely different than before. "I'm not here because I feel sorry for you. Don't ever think that for a second."

She stared back at him, lost in his dark gaze, his eyes stormy and almost black in the half-light. She'd thought he looked beyond handsome before, but all riled up he looked even more irresistible.

"Don't get me wrong, I love having you here, but I feel guilty about keeping you from what you want to be doing," she said. "I know I need to stand on my own two feet, learn how to be alone." Just because she knew it, didn't make it any easier.

"Jamie, I only came back to Sydney for you."

She swallowed, not quite sure what to say. He wouldn't have come back to his home city if it hadn't been for her? Maybe she'd heard him wrong.

"I'm the one who should be feeling guilty, for taking so long to get back here. For not being here for you when you needed me," he said. "I've been beating myself up about deserting you for months, so believe me when I say that this is exactly the place I want to be. Sam was family to me, and that makes you family. I should have been here sooner."

"Oh, Brett, you were injured and you'd lost your best friend and your dog. You have nothing to apologize for," she told him. "I just appreciate seeing you again, having you here, but I wouldn't have judged you if you'd decided not to come home at all."

He cleared his throat, leaned across the table toward her and then seemed to change his mind, clasping his hands and staring back up at the sky.

"I didn't come back for no reason, Jamie."

When he looked back at her, she had to force herself not to hold her breath. Because she had a feeling that what he was struggling to tell her was something that would change *everything* between them. More than a touch or a drunken kiss ever could, which meant this was something she wasn't sure she wanted to hear.

Just because she was having feelings for him, knew that the way she felt about him had changed, didn't mean that she was ready to hear him admit the same to her.

"You don't need to tell me," she heard herself say, afraid..

"You know when we met, all those years ago? Before you had even met Sam?"

She did remember, well. It wasn't something they'd ever really discussed, but it wasn't something she'd ever forgotten, either. "You were dating that gorgeous blonde."

"She *was* gorgeous, but I finished with her that night."

Jamie felt her eyebrows pull together. "Why?" Now she *did* want to hear what he had to say. Why would any man end things with a woman that beautiful?

"Because after I met you, you were all I could think about. I didn't want to ask you out while I was involved, because I wanted to do it right, but by the time I found you…"

No, he couldn't have. Jamie gulped. "I was already with Sam," she finished for him.

"You were already with Sam," he repeated, "and he

was happier than I'd ever seen him in his life, so there was no way I would have ever stepped in, even at the start. Sam was like my brother, and I'd have sacrificed anything for him. *And I did.*"

"But you were looking for me?" she said, voice low, almost a whisper. "You actually came looking for me after that night?"

"Yeah." He chuckled. "Kind of ironic, huh? It all just blew up in my face like I'd never even met you, like that night had never even happened."

"And you never told Sam? You just let us…" She didn't even know what to say.

The night she'd met Brett, at a party where she'd hardly known anyone, she'd been drawn to him immediately. But their flirting had been nothing more than that, because he'd had a girlfriend, although she'd be lying if she said she hadn't been thinking about him afterward. That she hadn't wished he'd been single.

*And then she'd met Sam.* Gorgeous, kind, loving Sam, who'd she fallen in love with and married within a year. Leaving Brett as a pleasant memory of what could have been.

"I told Sam that I'd never found the girl I met at that party, the one I'd talked about nonstop, because when I saw him with you, I knew he'd found *the one*." Brett blew out a breath. "I never stopped kicking myself for letting you walk away that night, and I got to see my best friend marry my dream girl. And all these years I just kept my mouth shut and never said anything, because no good could ever have come out of me being honest about my feelings, about what had happened."

She couldn't stop staring at Brett, could hardly believe what he was telling her—the words that were coming out of his mouth. She'd been insanely attracted to him, too, but thinking about what could have been wasn't something she'd ever really considered, until now. Because she'd been happy with Sam, she'd *loved* Sam, and Brett had always been his best friend. His best friend who'd loved to flirt with her and make her laugh, who she'd always thought could have been someone more to her at a different time, different place.

"So what did you come back for this time, Brett?" she asked.

Brett shrugged. "I told myself I was coming back to look out for you, to stay true to what I promised Sam, but honestly? That's not the reason I'm still here."

Jamie's hand was shaking slightly as she reached for her glass, clutching the stem to steady it, for something to do to stop herself from staring at him. For the first time in her life, she was absolutely speechless—couldn't even grasp what he was telling her. She took a sip of wine.

"So why are you still here?" Her voice was so low she wondered if he'd even heard what she'd said.

"Because I've never forgotten how I felt that night I first met you, and how I felt every time I saw you with Sam over the past six years. Every single goddamn time, Jamie."

She'd be lying if she didn't admit to always liking him, too. Because the truth was, she'd never forgotten how she felt the night they'd met, either. And they'd always been so comfortable with one another, so easy.

"And how do you feel now?" she asked, feeling brave and needing to know how he honestly felt about her right now.

He reached for one of her hands, turned it so her palm was facing up and stroked his fingers across her skin before closing his hand over hers. "Honestly?"

Jamie nodded, needing to know, to hear what he had to say.

"I wish to hell I didn't feel so damn guilty, but my feelings for you haven't changed, and I don't think they ever will. No matter how many times I tell myself that it's wrong, all the reasons I have for it *to be wrong*, I can't change how I feel."

Which meant the ball was in her court. It was up to her to decide where this conversation was going, what would happen next. And just because she wanted something to happen, didn't mean she was ready for it.

"I…" Her voice trailed off. "I don't know what to say."

"Then don't say anything," he said. "Just don't say anything, or forget I ever told you, if you need to. I don't want things to be weird between us, but I couldn't keep this to myself any longer."

"Do you ever think about what might have happened? What could have been if I hadn't met Sam, if you'd found me before then?" she asked, her voice almost a whisper. "Even the day before I met him, that could have changed everything."

"All the time," he said straight back. "I know things would have been different, but I was too slow to find you.

We can't look back, Jamie. Trust me, I've been doing it for years and it's done nothing but infuriate me."

Jamie knew he wasn't going to make the first move—to him she was still Sam's wife, *forbidden*, out of bounds. He'd as good as told her that Sam had been the brother he never had, part of his surrogate family. But this was Brett. This was a man she'd loved as a friend for years, a man she could trust, and a man who was making her heart race like it hadn't in so long. A man whose arms, *lips*, she'd dreamed of; whose touch she'd often fantasized about. It was something she'd never admitted, but it was true.

She pulled her hand away from his and stood up, then slowly walked around the table to stand in front of him. She watched as he pushed back his chair a little, so he was facing her, the expression on his face hard to read. But his body language was more than obvious, telling her that he wanted her to come closer, that he wasn't going to say no. That he was ready and waiting for her to make a move.

Jamie moistened her lips, eyes on his as she closed the distance between them, arms hanging at her sides as she stared down at the man in front of her. She was going to bend down, had intended on sitting on his lap, but suddenly her confidence was waning. She wanted to be the confident, brazen woman who knew what to do and didn't hesitate, but it wasn't something she'd ever had to do before, especially after years of being with the same man.

Brett made it easier for her. He pushed up to his feet and now stared down at her, a good head or more taller than she was. Jamie placed her hands on his chest, feeling the heat of his body, the muscles of his body, through her palms. But it was nothing compared to the heat in his gaze.

She could hear her heart beating, her breath coming out in shallow bursts, but she wasn't going to back down, wasn't going to pull away when she was the one who'd started this. Brett was standing still, arms at his sides, but when she leaned into him, tilted her face up to him, his arms came up to circle around her waist and hold her.

They both hesitated, until her gaze hit his lips—his full, tempting mouth—and she suddenly couldn't wait any longer. Jamie stretched up, on tiptoes, lips meeting Brett's in a soft, luscious kiss that had her wrapping her arms around his neck to lock him in place.

She relaxed into him as he drew her closer, tucked tight against his big, warm body. Everything he'd just told her was running through her head, sending goose pimples down her arms and back at the thought of him wanting her all these years. And if she were honest, maybe she'd always felt the same, it just hadn't been something she would have ever acted upon. Until now.

"Jamie, are you sure about this?" Brett murmured, lips brushing hers as he spoke.

She nodded, arms still looped around his neck, and gazed up at him even though she was flushing all the way to her toes at the way he was looking back at her. Just because she was nervous didn't mean she wanted to shy away from how she was feeling—she wanted to enjoy it. Ever since Sam had died, she'd been lost, sad, alone. Brett was making her feel alive in ways she hardly remembered. It was like she'd become an old spinster, and now she was…well, now there was a fire back in her belly. It might have been wrong in so many ways, but at this moment, it was also right.

Jamie moaned as Brett kissed her again, his lips moving softly and then with more urgency, making her want to rip his clothes off him where he stood. She was conflicted, part of her unsure about being with another man, but the other part…? Maybe it was the wine giving her confidence, but Jamie wanted Brett like she hadn't wanted anything in a long time. And she'd barely consumed a glass, anyway.

She pushed up his T-shirt, wanting to touch his skin, but his hands left her waist and closed around her elbows, stopping her.

"Hey," she whispered, mouth still firm against his.

"No," he said back, and she could feel his smile against her mouth.

Jamie dropped her hands, took a step back. "I'm sorry, I thought…"

He collected her hands and put them firmly back on his body, his arms looped around her waist again, and he tugged her closer.

"You thought right, I just think we need to take this slow," he said, mouth murmuring against hers. "Let's not rush into anything we could regret."

Brett tucked a finger beneath Jamie's chin, tilting it so she was looking up at him again. He could see the confusion swimming in her gaze and he didn't like that he was the cause of it.

"Sweetheart, you mean too much to me for us to ruin our friendship in one night. I'm trying to be the good guy here, and there are only so many times I'm capable of saying no."

She looked embarrassed. "You're, ah, right. I mean…"

He'd known Jamie a long time and he'd never heard her stutter, or be lost for words. But then he'd never been intimate with her, either.

"Jamie, look at me," he said, voice husky as he stared into her blue eyes.

She obliged, eyes finally locked back on his like she'd given in to the fact that she needed to watch him back.

"I meant everything I said, but I'm not even sure we should be doing this," he confessed. "I just don't want you to have any regrets."

Jamie sighed. "I know. You're right. It's just…" She blew out another breath. "Well, it's hard and confusing, but it also just seems natural. Like we're supposed to be doing this. It should feel wrong but it doesn't."

Brett smiled and dropped a slow kiss to her lips. "Don't take my being a gentleman as not wanting you, okay? Because if I had it my way I'd be dragging you to your bed and not letting you out of it until morning." He kept his lips only inches from Jamie's, teasing her. "Or maybe the next few days."

They both laughed, and he wrapped his arms around her for a proper hug, holding her tight. Brett inhaled the fresh orange scent of her shampoo, enjoyed the softness of her silky hair against his face, the feel of her slender body against his. He wasn't lying about wanting her, but he was also between a rock and a hard place.

Sam had been his best bud. He'd have taken a bullet for him, and if it had been a choice, he would have traded places with him in a heartbeat if Sam could have been alive to come home to Jamie. But now that he was here, with a lonely widow he'd been in love with for longer than he cared to admit, walking away, resisting her, was proving to be more difficult that he could have ever imagined. All he knew right now was that he was in love with a woman who should still be off-limits to him. And instead, he'd almost been at second base with her, and he'd had to stop things before they went a lot further, and fast. So much for being in control of his feelings.

"What do you say we head inside? Call it a night?" he suggested, even though it was the exact opposite of what he wanted to be doing. To what he was thinking.

Jamie nodded against his shoulder, but she wasn't letting go. Her arms were tight around him, face nestled against his neck.

"Am I a terrible wife?"

Her words were so low, such a whisper, that he wondered if she'd even meant him to hear them.

"You were a great wife, Jamie. But if you don't want something to happen here, it's your call." He wouldn't push her, and if she said no, then that would be the end of whatever had just happened between them. "I'll be here for you no matter what, okay? I want you to do what feels right for you. And I don't want us to do anything without thinking it through properly."

She didn't say anything, just kept holding on to him. When she finally stepped back, her hand came up to his face, warm against his cheek.

"You're a good man, Brett Palmer," she said, tears swimming in her eyes as she smiled up at him. *"The best."*

Brett just watched her, jaw clamped tight as he looked into her eyes. She was more than just a beautiful woman to him—she was a friend; she was Sam's widow; she was the woman he'd lusted after for weeks until he'd seen her in the arms of another man, then wondered every what-if about since. And now she was the woman he could have a chance with. *A second chance with.*

He cleared his throat, unsure of what she was trying to say. Was she letting him down softly, or the complete opposite?

"I think you're right, we need to call it a night," she said, her hand falling away as she stepped backward.

Brett nodded, but he quickly reached for her fingers before she moved too far, squeezing them before letting go.

"I'm going to stay out here a while," he told her, "clear my head a bit."

She grinned. "If you need any help with that, there's still almost half a bottle of wine sitting there."

He gave her a mock salute, smiling as she laughed and walked backward.

"'Night, Brett," she called out. "Oh, and thanks for

the most delicious dinner I've ever eaten. You would have made your mama proud."

"Good night, Jamie," he said.

He watched as she glanced at Bear sitting under the table, but she didn't call out to him.

"You keep him for company," she said. "Just make sure he comes in before you go to bed."

Brett didn't take his eyes from her figure until she'd disappeared inside the house, and once she did, he poured himself a large glass of wine and sat down on the deck beside the dog. He would have preferred a beer, but wine would have to do.

"Do you think he'd kill me?" Brett asked the dog.

Bear raised his head and whined.

"Yeah, I know." Brett gave his head a rub before using that same hand to prop himself up. "He'd probably give me a black eye."

Sam wouldn't begrudge either of them happiness, but he'd only been gone six months and already Brett was moving in on his girl. And Jamie was more than Sam's girl, she'd been his *wife*. But he'd stood back once to let them be happy, done the right thing, and now maybe it was his turn. If something happened between them, if she really wanted it, then he wasn't going to push her away. Because he couldn't. And there was a part of him that thought maybe he finally deserved to be happy after everything he'd survived, that he needed to stop blaming himself for every bad thing that had happened in his life. That maybe he needed to accept that something good could happen to him....

*The noise was deafening. The boom that hit his ears,*

*the explosion, was still echoing in his head, until it started to ring—a high pitch that seemed to get louder and louder, and it was the only thing he could hear.*

*He picked himself up, staggered backward like he'd lost his balance, and realized his leash was still hanging from his hand. Only there was no dog attached.*

*He looked around him, tried to call out to his dog, but he couldn't hear his own voice. Then he saw the fur, parts of his dog's body. He was screaming but he still couldn't hear himself, just knew his mouth was open and his throat was raw, even as tears fell down his cheeks.*

*Sam. He couldn't see Sam either. He yelled out, spinning around and staggering, feet colliding. And then he realized Sam was gone. That the men back at the 4x4 were waving to him, he could see their mouths moving, and then he saw Bear. Sam's dog. He was dragging his leg, falling over, but Brett wasn't going to leave him. Couldn't leave him.*

*Then everything went black as arms reached out to him and he crashed to the ground....*

Brett lay back on the deck and stared at the sky, trying so hard to fight the memories, to push them away and not go back to that dark place. There was nothing he could have done for Sam, he knew that. But he could do something about Jamie—he just had to figure out whether the right thing for her was having him around, or the exact opposite.

It would have been so easy for him to stop her from going to bed, to have asked her to stay with him for a while. It would be almost as easy for him to follow her, to take her hand and tell her how he really felt, tell her what he wanted, see if she wanted the same without offering her time to think about it. But something was holding him back, and he knew it probably always would.

Because no matter how good that kiss had been, no matter how much he wanted her in his arms, she wasn't his to want. She still wore her wedding ring, and she still loved her husband. So no matter what she might think or feel right now, he *needed* to give her time. Time to figure out what she wanted. He'd told her the truth, and now he just had to wait.

For some reason, he had to be the good guy around Jamie—he'd felt the same way that first night when they'd just met and spent hours chatting. There was something about her that brought out the good in him, and he liked it.

He just hoped that it was something about her house that had helped him sleep the night before. Otherwise? He'd have yet another reason to want her in his arms. It had been months since he'd been able to shut his eyes and just relax into blackness, to sleep without thinking, and he didn't want to go back to that dark place ever again. Not if he could help it.

# CHAPTER EIGHT

JAMIE SAT ON her bed, legs curled up beneath her. She didn't know what to do. Part of her wanted to march straight back out to Brett and tell him that she'd often thought of that night they'd first met. Maybe not in recent years, but after she'd first been with Sam, she'd often wondered: *what if.* Sam had been the love of her life and she'd never for a moment *not* wanted to be with him, but Brett…well, Brett was Brett. He was a man she'd been physically attracted to from the moment she'd met him, and she'd also been charmed by him, too.

Until she'd realized that he had a girlfriend. A girlfriend she now knew he'd finished with so he could seek her out.

Argh. There was nothing about this that was easy.

Sam's smiling face, from a collection of their wedding photos, was staring at her from the dresser, a reminder to a life that no longer existed. A memory that would always make her happy, but one that wasn't a reality anymore. Just like her dad had become only a memory, so, too, would Sam. Because he was gone, and nothing she could do would ever bring him back.

But Brett was real. And he was sitting outside her house, on his own, instead of with her. Waiting for her to tell him what she wanted.

She uncurled her legs, stretched, then stood. She slowly walked toward the window and parted the blinds, knowing that she'd be able to see him. Sure enough, he was sitting where she'd left him, only now his arm was slung around Bear as he stared up at the sky. No doubt looking at the stars and remembering a time when he wasn't home, when things were different. Maybe he was even thinking about her.

Jamie longed to go to him, to be with him, but she didn't want to make a mistake with a man who meant so much to her as a friend—she'd be lost without him.

She touched her forehead to the window and watched him. Just stared at his silhouette—his broad shoulders, his dark hair, his muscled forearm resting over her dog—and the coolness of the glass gave her flushed skin some relief.

But instead of going to him, she went to her bedside table and pulled out her leather-bound notebook, the one she kept close in case she had an idea for a new story or illustration.

Suddenly she knew exactly what she needed to do. Jamie pulled the cap off her pen and tucked up under the covers, pen poised. When Sam had been away, they'd always written to one another. Even though they'd been able to talk via video chat, they'd written so they had something to look forward to, something to anticipate in the mail during the months when they were parted.

She needed to write to him now. Needed to get her

feelings off her chest and tell him…how much she still loved him, but how much she needed to let part of that go so she could move on and be happy.

Dear Sam,

This is the only letter that I've ever written to you, knowing it will never reach you. But part of me believes that you're still here, in some shape or form, and if you are, I need to tell you how I'm feeling.

I know in my heart that I will never stop loving you, no matter how much time passes or what happens in my life from this day forward. I know you'd be so proud of how Bear and I are getting along, and I wouldn't give him up for anything. But there's something I need to tell you, something I never thought would even be a possibility.

You've been gone now for just over six months, and Brett came to see me. I don't know how or why, but something has changed between us. I think I'm falling for him, Sam, and I need you to know that if you were here, this would never have happened. But you're not here, and Brett is, and I believe that you would want me to be happy. We're both holding back, stopping anything from happening, *because of you*, but I don't want to be alone just to prove to your memory that I loved you.

So I need you to know that I'm falling in love with your best friend. I trust him and I know he'd never to do anything to hurt me, and I need to see if we could be happy together.

I love you, Sam, with all my heart. Not a day goes past that I don't wish that you were still here, but I've had to accept that isn't ever going to happen. I always thought you were the one, but now I'm realizing that maybe there is more than one person out there in the world for each of us. I will never stop loving you.

Jamie xx

Jamie wiped away the tears that had spilled down her cheeks and ripped the page from her notebook, before folding the letter in half. She tucked it into an envelope, sealed it, then scrawled Sam's name across the front of it.

She had no idea if Brett would still be outside or not, but she needed to go to him before she lost her confidence. Because if she didn't act now, maybe she never would. And part of her believed that she deserved to be happy, no matter what.

Brett shut the door and locked it, before flicking the switch and plunging the living room into darkness. He'd sat outside feeling sorry for himself for so long that even the dog had tired of keeping him company, and now he needed to crawl into bed and just sleep. No amount of thinking, of questioning himself, was going to help him to make a decision, and now he just wanted to crash. Otherwise he'd just let old feelings of guilt start to seep back into his mind, and he was over dealing with the emotional baggage he'd carried for the last decade.

"Brett?"

He squinted into the dark, trying to figure out where Jamie was. Then she flicked on a light and he could see she was standing in the hall, facing the living room.

"Hey," he said, not having expecting her to still be up. "Did I wake you?"

She shook her head. "I never went to sleep."

Brett crossed the room but kept his distance, not wanting to tempt himself after the hard talk he'd been giving himself outside. Jamie was out of bounds and he had no intention of crossing that line again, no matter how much he wanted to. Unless she came to him, it wasn't even something he was going to consider. The ball was firmly in her court now, and he wasn't going to budge from *that* particular resolution.

"Can I, ah, get you anything?" he asked. He knew how stupid it sounded the moment he said it—what kind of question was that to ask somebody in their own house?

She didn't say anything, just stared at him. Why was she down here when she'd gone to bed almost an hour ago?

"Jamie, what happened before," he began, not sure how to tell her what needed to be said, what he'd been thinking about. "I'm sorry if I crossed the line, because I never meant to do anything to make you uncomfortable."

Jamie shook her head. "No, Brett, you didn't cross the line and you didn't do anything that I didn't want you to do. Sam is gone. We both know that, and we both need to understand what that means."

He swallowed, wishing this was easier, wishing he didn't feel the way he did about her. Because then he wouldn't be tempted by her lips, or her hair, or the way she was watching him.

"Jamie…"

"You said you'd be here for me, no matter what," she told him.

Brett never took his eyes off her, and he also never moved, even when she started to come closer.

"I meant that if you needed me…" he began, the rest of his sentence disappearing when her finger touched his lips to silence him.

"I need you, Brett," Jamie said, standing on tiptoe at the same time as she looped her arms around his neck. "I need you now. We can't punish ourselves for how we feel, because we're not doing anything wrong."

Brett never moved, kept his hands at his sides, scared of what would happen if he let himself touch her, if he gave in to what was so close to happening. He was only a man and if she pushed him there was no way he'd be able to walk away.

"Jamie…" he murmured, but he wasn't committed to telling her no, so he never did. He'd said if it was her choice then he'd let it happen, only he hadn't expected her to act quite so soon.

"Kiss me, Brett. That's what I need you to do."

He stared into her aqua-blue eyes, knowing he was a lost man. No amount of good intentions was ever going to be enough to resist Jamie, not when her body was skimming against his, her mouth so close.

*Damn it!* Brett's hands flew from his sides to her waist, locking her in place against him as he crushed his mouth to hers. Her moan only spurred him on more, made him yank her hard to his body, one hand leaving her hips to caress her back, to feel her long hair and fist into the soft curls.

"Jamie," he forced himself to say, his mouth hovering over hers, unable to back off even if he wanted to. "Are you sure? We can't go back from this. It changes everything."

She tipped her head back and looked into his eyes, her fingers tracing down his chest, before she grabbed hold of one of his hands and led him out of the room. Jamie flicked the switch in the hallway and walked them both to her bedroom, stopping at the door and leaning against the wall.

"I've never been so sure about anything, Brett," she whispered into his ear, her hand clutching his T-shirt tight to keep him near. "Take me to bed."

He stared at her, long and hard, before reaching past her and pushing the door open. There was only so long that he could play the good guy and keep telling her no. So what if he'd made himself a promise, if she was supposed to be forbidden? Jamie was holding his hand and inviting him to spend the night with her, and he'd lost all power to turn and walk away from her. This was her choice, and he wasn't going to try to change her mind. He'd told himself all along that he wouldn't fight it if she was sure it was what she wanted, if she came to him, and now she had.

Jamie laughed and walked backward into the room, holding both his hands. When she bumped into the edge of the bed, she stopped and pulled his hands around to settle on her waist again.

"Brett," she whispered, fingers stroking up and down his face, before she held onto his shoulders and reached up to kiss him again.

He broke the kiss only to push her back onto the bed, watching as she fell back before bending to settle over her, his thighs locking her in place as he straddled her. She reached out to him, pulling him down, but he needed a moment to drink in the sight of her—to see her long hair splayed out around her, her full lips facing him, the rise and fall of her breasts as she lay on her back beneath him. For years he'd wondered what it would have been like if things had been different, fantasized about having her in his bed, and now she was sprawled out beneath him.

Brett dropped his upper body over Jamie's, careful not to crush her with his weight, and kissed her mouth, before trailing kisses down her neck and back up to her lips again. For something that was meant to be so wrong, it felt so damn good.

"Don't stop," she whispered, sounding breathless.

He chuckled, smoothing the hair from her face before stroking her cheek. "I have no intention of stopping," Brett told her.

"Good," she replied, claiming his mouth again as

she cupped his skull to force his head down, gripping on tight, fingers twisted in his hair.

Her lips moved gently, her tongue exploring tentatively at first, before becoming bolder, colliding with his.

All the best intentions in the world couldn't have made him say no to this.

Jamie let Brett push her T-shirt up and she wriggled out of it, left in only her bra and her shorts. She gulped when he immediately reached down for her button, before unzipping the denim and pulling it down her legs—slowly, as if he were trying to tease her. She pointed her toes so he could slip off the jeans completely, and laughed.

"Why do I have all my clothes off, and you're fully dressed still?" she asked.

He grinned and shrugged, but she wasn't going to let him sit there in his jeans and T-shirt while she was left in only her underwear.

"Off with it," she ordered, pushing his T-shirt up, eyes feasting on his stomach and chest muscles.

Brett obliged, taking it off and then standing to shed his jeans, too.

She sucked back a big breath as she watched him, looking at his big body, eyes glued to him as he lowered himself back on the bed. Jamie reached out to touch the tattoo on his left arm first, and then his other shoulder, fingers tracing over both of them. Years ago, she'd hated tattoos, but she'd grown to appreciate them now. And Brett's ones meant something to him, told a story of who he was and what was important to him, and the ink stretched over his muscles gave him a tough edge that was at odds with how gentle and kind he'd always been to her. If ever she needed reminding of the soldier he was, of how he could protect her if ever she needed it, his tattoos made that crystal clear.

Jamie slipped her hands onto his shoulders to stroke her nails down his back, but his whole body tensed, went rigid.

"What's wrong?" she asked, dropping her hands, knowing that he hadn't even remotely liked the way she'd just touched him.

Brett gave her an unconvincing smile. "My back's kind of off-limits," he said.

"You mean because of your injuries?" she asked, voice soft, knowing how difficult it must be for him to talk about.

"Yeah."

"You don't have to be embarrassed, Brett," she said, leaning up to press a kiss to his shoulder, gently touching his lower back this time and avoiding where she'd almost touched before.

"Jamie…" He said her name as if it were a warning.

But she wasn't going to take no for an answer, not after all they'd been through together. She wanted to touch every part of Brett, and she wasn't scared of what had happened to him or the marks that had been left on his skin. It wasn't like they'd just met and he had to hide who he was from her.

"Let me see you," she whispered, pushing him gently back down to the bed. "There's nothing I could see right now that could change the way I feel about you."

# CHAPTER NINE

CHILLS RAN UP and down Brett's body just at the mention of his scars, of her seeing them. He hadn't let anyone other than the medical team that had worked on him see how he looked now, to really see what had happened to him. Jamie looking at the mess that was his skin wasn't something he ever wanted to happen, but the way she was staring at him, like he was doing something to hurt her by not just opening up, was telling him that he may not have a choice. He didn't want to hurt her, had no intention of pushing her away, but this was something that he needed to prepare for.

"I can't," he muttered, rolling firmly on to his back.

Jamie tucked her knees up to her chin and wrapped her arms around her legs. The mood had changed, was no longer about sex and suddenly included a whole lot of stuff that Brett wasn't ready to face. Gone was the fun, flirty vibe they'd had happening between them, replaced by a serious, we-need-to-talk session.

"You've never talked about…"

"And I don't want to," he said, voice firm as he interrupted her. There was no way he was going to start talking, not now. That he was going to ruin what had been an otherwise perfect evening by dredging up exactly how his skin had become so disfigured.

"Can we just pick up where we left off?"

"You don't need to tell me, Brett, but let me see. *Please?*" she asked.

He shut his eyes, not wanting to get angry with this woman who'd been through so much, who he so genuinely cared about. Who was being so brave in another way that he knew must be beyond difficult for her. It shouldn't be so impossibly hard, but it was. Opening up had always been difficult for him, yet he'd told her openly about the truth of his past, about his parents and how he still felt responsible for their deaths. This, though…this was different. The pain was too fresh.

"I'm embarrassed," he admitted, opening his eyes and looking straight into hers. "I'm no longer the guy who can go to the beach and just take off his top without thinking about it. It's not something you want to see or hear about. It's not who I am. And it's not how I want you to see me."

Now it was Jamie shaking her head, telling him he was the one in the wrong. "No, Brett," she told him, voice low and husky. "You *are* still that guy, because you're still handsome and you're still *you.* I don't care what your skin looks like, but we can't do this without you opening up to me. We can't take this further if there's any secrets between us."

He knew he was being stupid, that there was no point in delaying the inevitable, but letting Jamie see what he'd been through, what he was *still* going through, was like giving up a piece of his soul that he'd never intended on letting anyone be witness to. His skin had always been tanned and blemish-free, he'd always been the one to whip his shirt off on a hot day, but everything had changed the day he'd been burned. And not just his body, but his mind, too.

"It's ugly," he said, voice flat, knowing he was fighting a losing battle.

"I don't care," she said straight back, her gaze unwavering. "I just want you to let me in, Brett."

Jamie dropped her arms and moved closer, hands on his shoulders as she gently motioned for him to move. She couldn't have made him budge an inch if he hadn't wanted to, but he knew that the only way Jamie was going to trust him, that they were going to move past this, was if he let her in. If he trusted her to see what scared him the most.

Brett took a deep breath and reluctantly rolled over onto his stomach, hands under his chin as he lay there for her to inspect him. He was expecting a gasp, something to tell him what a shock it was for her seeing him like that, but all he could hear was silence. A long stretch of silence that had him holding his breath, wishing he'd refused.

*And then she touched him.* Brett dropped his head into the pillow. He'd been waiting for her to make a noise and now he was the one forcing back a groan. Or maybe it was a cry for help, he didn't know—all he knew was that Jamie was touching him in a way that was making him want to scream at her to stop, and at the same time beg her never to take her hands off of him. Because now she'd seen it, there was no going back, and all of a sudden he wanted her to see the real him. Needed her to see his pain and help to heal him, because he didn't want to be broken anymore.

Her fingers traced his entire back, dipped into the tender areas where he'd almost been burned alive, before she caressed the smooth parts of his back that reminded him of what all his skin had once looked like. What his body had once been.

Then she started to trace down his leg, too, the leg that he was so lucky to still have attached to his body, but that was disfigured from the skin grafts he'd painfully endured in recovery.

"Stop," he commanded, head rising off the pillow. His back was one thing, but she was taking things too far.

"No," she whispered, pushing him back down and straddling his buttocks instead. He still had his boxers on, but he could feel the heat of her as she sat on him. "Don't move a muscle."

Jamie put her palms over Brett's arms as he spread them out on either side of him. At the same time she dipped her head until she could press a soft, warm kiss to his back, between his shoulder blades. Here, the skin was still smooth and tanned, like his back had always been, and she wanted to start here before she moved lower.

"Jamie…" She heard him mumble her name.

She continued undeterred, moving her mouth slowly down his back. When she reached the first of the jagged edged lines that crisscrossed down his entire lower back, she made her kisses even lighter, only just letting her lips touch him, as soft as she could make them. His skin was still pink where he'd been burned, the marks a blazing reminder of what he'd been through, and she needed to show him that she didn't care, that she could deal with the wounds he'd come home with, the wounds that he'd be forced to live with forever. That she accepted the man he was today as much as she would have accepted the man he'd been before the explosion—that in her eyes he was no different.

Her hair fell forward and splayed across his back as she started to move lower again, making her way down his leg now, shuffling her body farther down the bed. His right leg was impossible to compare to his back—the scars extended all the way down his thigh and calf, enough to make her want to gasp, at least when she'd first seen them. But now she focused on the shape of his leg, the muscles still bulging from his calf, the thickness of his thigh that told her how fit he was, how determined he'd been to stay strong even through what must have been a painful recovery. Brett was a fighter, she knew that, and he'd endured what might have broken others.

"They're just marks, Brett," she told him as she wriggled back up his body and sat on his buttocks again, hands spread out over his back as she gently massaged his shoulders.

"They're marks I'll have forever," he muttered.

When he went to move, she pushed herself up on her knees so he could flip onto his back beneath her. Jamie lowered herself when he looked comfortable, staring into his eyes as she leaned forward. She tucked her long hair behind her ears to keep it out of the way.

"You're still the same, handsome Brett you were to me before I saw them," she said. "It's part of you now, and they don't scare me."

"You have to say that now," he told her. "You can't exactly be honest with me about how much they disgust you."

Jamie frowned. "Of course I can be honest with you." She paused, touching his cheek with the tips of her fingers because she needed to connect with him, needed him to know that she was telling the truth. "Do your scars terrify me and remind me of what we've both lost? Sure. But they're just marks, Brett, and they're *your* marks, so there's no point in pretending like they're not there. Now that I've seen them, I've seen them. You don't have to worry about hiding them from me, or how I'll react."

"I hate that I have a constant reminder on my skin," he admitted, reaching up for her and stroking a hand down her hair until he reached the ends of it, skimming the center of her back.

"At least you're alive to be reminded of it," she whispered. "At least you're here, right now, in my bed."

Brett groaned, his hand falling from her hair. "I'm sorry, I…"

"Shhhh," she said, leaning down on to him, her elbows on either side of his head to prop herself up, bodies pressed together. "Stop talking."

"And what?" he asked.

"Kiss me again."

Jamie didn't wait for Brett to act, because she was already hovering above him, lips aching to close over his and feel what it was like to be almost naked and this intimate with a man she'd been attracted to for so long. *And he didn't disappoint.* Brett's mouth was firm against hers, his lips warm and soft. His hands were in her hair as she pressed herself even tighter against him, her body tight to his.

She could feel how much he wanted her, and it only made her sure in her decision. Brett wasn't just some rebound guy to her, someone to fill the bed with to keep her warm. He was a man she already cared so much about, only now…

"Jamie, I think we need to slow this down," he said, hands still tangled in her long hair as he yanked her back a little.

"No," she told him, wriggling against him until he groaned, fighting him. "Don't stop."

Jamie was being cruel to him, she knew she was, because he was trying to be the good guy and she was the one lying on top of him, forcing him into compliance. Making him be bad. But she didn't want him to be the good guy right now, didn't want him to think at all, she just wanted him to act.

"Are you sure?" he mumbled in between kisses.

"I've never been so sure about anything in my life," she whispered, before claiming his mouth again and teasing him with her tongue. There was no way she was going to let him stop.

Brett's moan was all she needed to spur her on, to make her reach behind her back and fumble to unhook her bra. His expert hands came to her assistance, and all of a sudden they were completely skin-to-skin, her breasts against his warm chest, almost as close as two people could be.

"This feels right," she told him, pulling back so she could look into his eyes. "Don't you think?"

From the way he was staring back at her, she knew he felt the same. It was different, it was terrifying, and it was exhilarating, because it was the first time she'd been intimate with a man who wasn't her husband in six years, *but it was Brett.* And if there were ever going to be another man besides Sam she made love to, she knew in her heart that it was right that man was him.

# CHAPTER TEN

JAMIE WOKE UP and reached out an arm, feeling for Brett, but she opened her eyes instead because there was no warm body beside her. She sat up, pulling the sheet up with her to cover her breasts, and she spotted him straight away. He was sitting in the big armchair she had beside the window, his T-shirt and boxers on, staring at something that she couldn't see. Or maybe he was just staring at nothing.

"Hey," she said.

Brett turned, his big body filling the entire chair that had always seemed so roomy to her when she tucked her legs up and read a book in the sun.

"Morning," he replied.

Jamie watched the way he looked at her, like he wasn't sure, like something was troubling him. His expression was nothing like the one she'd witnessed before they'd fallen asleep.

"Brett, what's wrong?"

He shoved a hand through his hair. "You want me to be honest?"

She knew there was only one answer she could give to that question. "Yes."

He sighed. "Everything."

Tears pricked her eyes and she blinked them away, refused to let them even come close to spilling. After last night, she'd expected to wake up in his arms, thought what they'd shared was special, that they'd just pick up again where they'd left off, but the way he was looking at her...

"I don't understand," she managed to say, eyes never leaving his.

She watched as Brett stood and crossed the room, moving to the bed beside her. A low moan from Bear made her gaze flicker for a second, but the dog was still in his own bed.

Brett took one of her hands, the other still clutching the sheet and keeping her covered. All of a sudden she felt vulnerable being naked, whereas before she'd been completely comfortable.

"I feel guilty," he admitted, fingers stroking the back of her hand as he held it. "I don't want to, but I can't help it."

She understood the guilt, but if he was having second thoughts about what they'd done... "Brett, I don't regret last night, if that's what you're worried about. Not for a moment."

He moved closer, his thigh pressed to hers as he faced her. "I don't regret it, either, but what we did, what happened, it's changed everything."

"Is that the worst thing in the world?" she asked.

He smiled, but the sadness in his eyes scared her.

"If I'm honest with you, I can't think of anything I'd rather do than be with you. For the first time since the explosion, I've slept through the night, like I'm protected in your arms from the worst of my memories. And then I wake up and realize that I've taken Sam's place, that I've taken something from him, and it scares me."

She took a deep, shuddering breath. "If Sam was here, this never would have happened, Brett," she told him, her voice barely more than a whisper. "But we are here, together, and somehow we're helping each other through. Can't we just enjoy being together without feeling guilty?"

He nodded. "I've always thought of you as part of my family, Jamie. I guess I just don't want to be responsible for losing another family member."

Jamie touched his cheek, let the sheet fall away to her waist. "You're not going to lose me, Brett. I promise. But I'm also not going to lie to you and say that I don't love Sam still, because I do. So much. But the way I feel for you…"

"We can't," he insisted.

"We can," she said firmly, not about to let them ruin what had happened because they were afraid. Because he was scared of losing something that he wasn't even in danger of losing.

They stared at each other, and she knew how hard it was for him because it was just as hard for her.

"You're not betraying Sam."

"If sleeping with his wife isn't betraying him, then I don't know what is."

"Come here," Jamie said.

He looked like he was going to resist, but he obeyed, moving closer. It wasn't that he didn't want to be with her, she knew that, but she also understood that his morals could ruin what was so fragile, so new, between them right now.

"Take off your top and get under the covers."

Brett went to protest but she shook her head before he could say anything. "Just do it for me, please."

He followed her instructions and pulled the covers up over them both, but he still looked awkward. Jamie pushed him down on the pillow then lay her head on his chest, arm around him.

"I need this, Brett. After last night, I can't deal with arguing or not having you here beside me. Because then I might start to feel guilty about what we did, and I've accepted the decision I made."

She listened to his breathing, focused on the inhale and exhale of air and the way it made his chest move.

"I don't want to hurt you," Brett told her.

She traced circles on his skin, fingertips needing to touch. "You won't hurt me, Brett, and I won't hurt you. But if you walk out on me? That will hurt. Because I don't want last night to have meant nothing. If we're talking about betraying Sam, then that would be it."

"As in you don't want what we did to be a one-night stand."

"I don't want it to be a one-night anything," she admitted, moving so she could rest her chin on his chest and stare at him. "What we did wasn't because of loneliness or selfishness, it was because it felt right, and I know you feel the same."

Brett reached for her hair, stroking it. "I just don't feel right, being in this room, seeing the photos of him, knowing that I've just stepped in and somehow taken over his life. Slept in his bed with his wife. It's not okay."

Jamie smiled at him, needing him to be honest with her, needing to hear the words that he'd been holding trapped inside.

"You stepped in to look after me, and what happened between us? It just happened. But if you want me to…"

"You're not taking down his photos because of me."

She laughed at the seriousness of Brett's tone. "I'm not taking down any photos, but what I was going to say is that we can always stay in the other bedroom. If you need to, I mean."

Brett groaned. "Can we just go out for breakfast? Walk somewhere?"

"You bet," she said, leaning forward to kiss him.

What started as a light peck became deeper, their lips moving softly, brushing together, before Brett cupped the back of her head so she couldn't get away, mouth more insistent.

"It doesn't seem to matter what I tell myself," he muttered, breaking the kiss, "I just can't get enough of you."

"Breakfast," she told him, pushing herself up and dragging the sheet with her so she could escape to the bathroom without him seeing her naked in the bright light. "Before we end up staying in bed all day."

It wouldn't have been a bad thing, but they both

needed to get out of the house. There were too many memories in this room that were haunting Brett, and if she were perfectly honest, in the full morning sunshine, there was something not so easy to ignore about being with another man in the room she'd shared for years with her husband. No matter how much she wanted it to feel right, she knew that going out was exactly what they needed to do. A quick shower and a little makeup and she'd be ready to go.

She'd already been through losing her father, and then as good as losing her alcoholic mom for years at a time. So losing Sam and then losing Brett? Not something she had any intention of letting happen, especially not now that they'd spent the night together.

Brett clipped Bear's leash on and dropped to his haunches, looking the dog in the eye as he ran his fingers through his fur. He missed his own dog like crazy, was so used to having a constant companion by his side.

"You're doing pretty well with everything that's going on," he told the canine.

He received a low whine from Bear in return.

"It might not be guns and explosives, but it's still tough, huh?"

"Are you talking to yourself or the dog?"

Brett cleared his throat when he realized Jamie had walked into the room. "The dog, of course. Talking to myself would just be weird."

"He saying much in response?" she teased.

Brett looked her up and down, knowing there was no way he'd ever be able to resist her so long as he was staying in the house with her. When he wasn't with her, he was thinking about her, and when he was with her... *damn*. No amount of good intentions would ever help him when they were together.

"Let's go," he said, before he had any longer to think about Jamie and the way she was making him feel.

"Are we going to walk all the way there?"

He laughed. "You make it sound like it's a hike."

"I'm the girl who always takes a car. You seem to keep forgetting that."

"You have a dog now, and a guy with you who likes to feel like he's earned a cooked breakfast. So Bear and I vote for the walk, that's you outnumbered."

Jamie sighed and took Bear's leash from him, smiling as their hands collided. "My dog, remember? I'm the one who's supposed to be up for walking all the time."

Bear was looking up at them, studying them each in turn, and he felt sorry for the poor dog, listening to them banter. There was no chance he'd ever figure out what they were saying, and he'd been so used to understanding commands when he'd been on the leash for work.

"He's all yours, let's go."

Brett waited for her to shut and lock the door behind them, before walking slow to match her pace. The sun was shining down on them already, another hot Sydney day. He'd spent days and weeks out under the scorching sun, working with his dog and the other guys, patrolling for explosives constantly, but that sun had never been enjoyable. It had drained them all and made them grumpy, made their skin dry and their throats burn. This sun made him feel free. *Alive*.

"Brett, I know you don't want to talk about what happened…."

He glanced sideways, seeing the frustrated look on Jamie's face as she clearly tried to figure out how to talk to him about something she was obviously so desperate to know more about. It wasn't that he didn't want to talk to her, it was just that dredging up the past wasn't always worth the pain, or the reality. He'd been in a black hole that could have swallowed him alive, his thoughts so dark they'd almost consumed him, and going back wasn't good for him or her.

If he shut his eyes, he could still smell the burned flesh, still feel the searing pain of the fire as it shot up his leg and across his back.

"I just…" She paused and stopped walking, arms crossed like she didn't know what to do with them. "I just want to know if it happened fast? If he suffered. I'm sorry." She blew out a big breath. "I've been wanting to ask someone that question for so long, and I think you're the only one who can answer it because everyone else just wants to fob me off and pretend like it wasn't anywhere near as horrific as I know it was."

Brett started walking again, because if he was going to talk then he needed to keep moving, needed something else to focus on to help him say the words. He'd thought she wanted to know about his experience, what he'd been through, but she wanted to know about Sam and he could hardly hold that back from her. She deserved to know.

"When we were working that day, it was just like usual," he began, wondering how the hell he was going to say what he needed to say, but continuing anyway. It wasn't something he'd ever talked about, but it was a scene that had run though his head constantly ever since it had happened. He could see it as if it were yesterday—shut his eyes and pretend like it was that day all over again. "We were with a unit of SAS guys, providing support, and I was working with Sam. We both got our dogs out and started doing our drill, but we knew there was something off almost immediately."

He was staring straight ahead when Jamie slipped her hand into his, and he didn't resist. Because talking about that day was beyond hard, and it was something he'd never done before. Brett needed her strength.

"His dog identified the explosive immediately," he continued, ignoring her because now he'd started talking he needed to get it all out. "His dog went dead still, and for a split second we looked at one another, because we knew it was bad, that we were in a hot spot, that Bear had only frozen like that for one reason. We called out to the guys not to move, and then Teddy indicated another one." He paused. "You have to understand that sometimes, most of the time, our dogs just raise their tails slightly, move differently, in a way that only their handler would ever notice. But we all knew what Bear had detected that day, and we all knew how badly things could end. That we might never see another day."

Brett swallowed down the lump of emotion choking his throat and blinked to force the tears back. He didn't want to cry, didn't want to *feel* again, but the memories were crashing into him like they'd only just happened.

Jamie was squeezing his hand tight, like she wanted

to take some of the pain for him, but he knew she already had enough pain of her own to deal with. He just wanted to tell her like it was, explain to her what had happened so they could both move forward and never have to talk about it again.

"From that moment, it was like everything moved in slow motion, before becoming such a fast blur that I don't even remember the details." He looked at her, saw that Jamie's eyes were filled with tears, just like his were from going back in time to that day. "All I know is that I was blown back so far my body was slammed down close to the 4x4, and Sam was gone. So was Teddy. To this day, no one can understand how Bear managed to survive the blast, or how either of us didn't lose limbs. But it was fast, so fast that I don't know how or why I ended up so far from the bomb."

Jamie's hand in his stopped him from moving as she pulled him to a halt. She had the leash in her other hand, and she let go of Brett's hand for a second so she could loop her arm around his neck and draw him into an embrace so warm, so loving, that he was powerless to pull away. *And he didn't want to pull away.* Because no matter how guilty he felt, this felt so right, too. He needed Jamie as much as she needed him. He liked that he could be honest with her when he needed to be, that they understood what the other had gone through, on some level at least.

"Thank you for telling me," she murmured, pressing a kiss to his cheek. "Thank you, for being honest with me when no one else could."

Brett shut his eyes. Sam's blood covered him, bits

of his best friend burning and blasted all around them. There were so many pieces of him, so much flesh that when Brett had woken up, he'd vomited until there was nothing left in his stomach. And his dog, his beautiful dog had been killed on impact, too.

But they weren't memories he was ever going to share with her. If he ever needed to get them off his chest, he could tell Logan, a fellow soldier who'd seen enough on his tours to cope with what he'd hear. He'd never let Jamie suffer through those particular memories with him, the blatant truth of that day. There were some things she needed to be protected from, and that was top of the list.

Jamie pulled back then, looked into his eyes and didn't break contact even as she kissed him.

"I need you to know that I want you here, Brett. It might be weird, that we're together and all that, but all I know is that this is right. That having you in my life seems right and I don't want to lose you."

He nodded, but he still wasn't convinced that what they were doing was any part of okay or right. It wasn't that he didn't have feelings for Jamie, because he did. His problem was that he felt too much for her, and he knew that he'd never, ever want to walk away. That this wasn't just about comfort or friendship.

"When you say you want me here, do you mean that we keep this just between us, or…?"

She ran her hand down his arm before looping it through so they could walk arm in arm. "I think we should tell Logan. I mean, I don't want to lie to him and I don't want to come between your friendship. We need to be honest with him."

Brett blew out a breath. "Logan is not going to be okay with this."

"I know, but we need to tell him. *I'll tell him.* I just don't want this to be any more awkward than it needs to be, and the longer this goes on, the harder telling him will become, because he'll think we've been lying to him all along if we don't come clean."

"Maybe we should text him, tell him to meet us for lunch or something after our walk tomorrow?" Brett suggested. "He might take it better if there's a lot of people around. You know, so he can't knock out every tooth in my mouth." After the way Logan had warned him off the other night…it wasn't going to be pleasant, no matter how or where they did it. Logan was going to be furious, not with her, but with him.

Jamie laughed but he shook his head.

"What?" she asked.

"I don't think you know Logan like I do," he said. "There is nothing about this that's going to be easy. He's like a teddy bear around you, acts like he wouldn't hurt a fly, but the Logan I know isn't going to deal with this well."

"I lost my husband, Brett, and now something has happened between us. I'm not intending on acting like you've taken advantage of me, if that's what you're worried he'll think."

Logan was going to kill him. Actually kill him.

Jamie couldn't stop laughing as Bear ran after the stick she'd just thrown like his life depended on it. Having fun with him had changed the dynamic between them, and she was pretty sure her dog was enjoying it as much as she was.

"I told you, he made the squad based on his determination with balls and sticks," Brett said, grinning straight back at her.

"Why did I never realize how much fun he was before?"

Brett came up and put his arm around her. "Because you were both trying to figure the other out, and everything had become too serious. It was like a child living with you who wasn't allowed to have fun, so he was bored and didn't understand what was being asked of him."

Jamie gave Bear a hearty pat when he dropped the stick at her feet for the umpteenth time. "Good boy," she praised, before throwing it again.

"We used to call Bear the branch manager and my dog the deputy branch manager," Brett said, pressing a kiss to her cheek. "The two of them used to have a blast when we let them play."

Jamie leaned into Brett, enjoying his arm around her and the sun beating down on her shoulders. She moved only when he had to reach into his back pocket to retrieve his mobile.

"Is it Logan?" she asked.

Brett tapped a message into his phone before turning his attention back to her. "Yeah. He's said yes to lunch tomorrow."

"What do you say we just grab something to take away this morning?" she asked him, shaking her head at

Bear as he faithfully retrieved the stick again. He looked disappointed that their game was over, but it wasn't like they hadn't let him have a heap of fun. "I know a place nearby where they do a mean bacon-and-egg sandwich, and we can sit in the sun and relax."

Brett's gaze met hers. "That's exactly what I need to take my mind off things."

"You mean Logan?" she asked, tucking under his arm and pulling him along with an arm around his waist.

"Yeah." He hugged her back as they walked. "So where is this amazing food place?"

"Ah, it's more like a food shack, but I promise you it's good. They do great coffee, too."

"So it'll kind of be like our first actual date?" he asked, raising an eyebrow when she looked at him.

"Yeah, I guess it will be. That okay with you?"

"Sure is. But I'm guessing we might have to buy for Bear, too. I doubt he's going to tolerate us eating greasy food in front of him without sharing."

Brett knew he needed to just shut his mind off, but it was easier said than done. Meeting Logan was seriously playing with his head, and he knew better than Jamie how tomorrow was going to go down. But there was nothing he could do about it right now, so he needed to shake off his worries.

"My shout. Want the same as me?"

Brett returned her smile, not wanting to ruin her happiness. "Whatever's good, but order me two."

"Typical boy," she muttered, spinning around to go in and order.

He watched as she disappeared then came back with a number on a piece of brown paper.

"Oh, this is a really classy place, isn't it? I was thinking of taking you somewhere nice for our first date, not to a takeaway joint."

She giggled. Jamie actually giggled, and the noise was infectious enough to make him laugh straight back at her.

"Trust me, it's worth overlooking the surroundings for the food. And the coffee. Did I mention the coffee?"

"I think you're being paid to do PR for this place," he said to her, grabbing her hand and pulling her in against his body. "I don't believe you for a second."

"Well, you should," she whispered, tipping her chin up and brushing her lips against his.

She jumped away when their number was called. Brett couldn't take his eyes off her as she walked away—and he couldn't have forgotten her smile even if he walked away and never returned. Jamie was getting under his skin, and there was nothing he didn't like about it.

"Here you go," Jamie announced as she emerged once again. "Coffee for you, and the food is wrapped up in here. Let's go find a spot somewhere nice."

They walked the five minutes back to the park and sat on the grass, Bear sprawling out beside them. Jamie reached into the bag and pulled out massive sandwiches wrapped in paper, passed one to him, then unwrapped one for Bear and put it on the ground, before taking one for herself.

"Well, it at least smells good," he told her, taking his first bite.

She did the same, watching him, like she was expecting a reaction. He took another bite, and ketchup and sauce oozed out down his hand, along with runny egg yolk that tasted incredible.

"Amazing or what?" she asked, eyebrows raised as she kept eating hers, hands tilted up to keep the sauce from running onto her skin.

"You win, it's amazing," he told her, mouth full as he tried to talk. He kept eating, not able to stop for the juice running out of it.

When they'd both finished and cleaned up as best they could, using only paper napkins, Brett lay back on the grass beside Jamie, his elbow propping him up. He looked at Jamie, and she at him, both nursing their coffees.

"Thanks for this," he said, reaching out to run his hand down her hair, tucking a few loose strands behind her ear.

"For greasy food and damn good coffee?" she teased.

"No, for showing me that we can just hang out and enjoy being together. That it's simple things like this that are important, just..." He didn't even know what he was trying to tell her. "I guess what I'm really badly attempting to say is that being with you isn't easy for me, but it's worth it. It's worth the pain just to have you with me."

Jamie brushed the back of her fingers against her

eyes, and it was only then he realized that she was trying to disguise her tears.

"Don't cry, Jamie. Please don't cry," he murmured,
taking her hand and squeezing it tight.

"Just ignore me, I'm all emotional," she said, smiling and squeezing his hand back. "I'm happy, Brett, I
promise you I'm happy."

"Good. If you're happy, then I'm happy."

And it was true. He might be finding being with
Jamie hard to wrap his head around, to deal with, but
her being happy was what was important.

# CHAPTER ELEVEN

THE SUN SHONE brightly through the window and onto Jamie's face as she struggled to open her eyes. She reached out a hand and found an empty space beside her again, which was the only reason she forced herself to sit up, to see if Brett was sitting across the room in the chair again.

He wasn't. But when she glanced toward the door, he was standing there watching her.

"What are you doing up so early?" she mumbled, dropping back down into the pillows but not taking her eyes off of him.

He laughed, crossing the room and carrying a large tray. "First of all, it's almost nine o'clock, so it's not early, and second, I was getting you breakfast."

She pushed herself back up again and flattened the bedding out so he could put the tray down.

"Did you make this?"

Brett chuckled again. "No, I took Bear for a run and picked it all up at that place down the road. Turns out they do fresh fruit salads and muffins for people like me. All I had to do was put them on a plate and walk them upstairs for you."

She leaned in for a kiss. "Well, it's the thought that counts. And I'm starving."

Brett carefully settled himself across from Jamie, obviously trying not to tip the tray, and reached for a bowl of fruit. "It scares me to even say it, but I could get used to this. Being with you, the whole domestic bliss routine."

When she smiled he grinned straight back at her. "Me, too," she said. "But maybe you'll feel differently when you realize I'm not *that* domestic."

"When I say domestic, I wasn't exactly referring to housekeeping."

Now it was Jamie laughing at him, waving a piece of fruit on a fork in his direction. "So you mean you like bedding me and dining with me?"

Brett shrugged. "Well, when you put it like that…"

She grinned and settled back against the pillows to devour her fruit, before reaching for the coffee and muffin he'd brought for her.

"So we still on to meet Logan today?" she asked.

Brett wished they could have just stayed in their nice little bubble without involving Logan, but he knew there was little he could do to get out of it now. Trouble was, it wasn't so much how Logan would react that was troubling him, it was that he knew what he would say. And Brett knew that every word that came out of his friend's mouth would be the truth, exactly what he'd already struggled with, and he didn't want to second-guess what he was doing with Jamie when it already felt so fragile.

"How about we finish breakfast, you get yourself ready, then we take a walk before we meet him."

Jamie took a sip of her coffee. "Deal."

Jamie looked at Brett. He was staring into the distance.

"Everything okay?" she asked.

He turned to meet her gaze and smiled, but she could tell he had something on his mind. The kiss he dropped to her lips told her the problem wasn't her, but she still wanted to know. She was pleased they'd decided to walk Bear before meeting Logan for lunch—it gave them time to relax and just enjoy being together.

"It's Logan, isn't it? You're worried about telling him," Jamie stated as soon as he pulled away.

"It's not that I don't want to tell him, I can just see how this is going to go," he said, his hand stroking her hair as he looked into her eyes. "Part of me thinks we should just pretend like everything is normal, then go back to this when we return to your place."

Jamie sighed. On some level she agreed with him, but she didn't want to lie to Logan, and she didn't believe he was going to take it that badly. Not if they were honest about how everything had happened between them, that it wasn't something they'd ever have acted upon if the circumstances had been different.

"Let's just see how it goes. Maybe we're overthinking it."

He didn't look like he agreed, but he took her hand

and tugged her in the direction they needed to head in. "For my sake, I hope you're right."

"Your sake?" she queried.

"Yeah, my sake. Because he'll never believe you could do any wrong, which means that I'll be the villain. He'll hate me and he'll feel sorry for you."

Jamie hoped he was being dramatic, even as her heart started to race at the thought of things going bad. Was she being naive to think Logan would behave like an adult and hear them out?

"Come on, Bear. Let's go," she ordered, giving him a hand signal to run on ahead. He bounded off, cheerful and content, just like she'd been before they'd started talking about Logan.

"Why don't you take my mind off everything by telling me about your book project," he said.

Jamie giggled. "I thought you were going to suggest something else entirely."

He pretended to look horrified. "We're in the middle of a public park, Jamie. Shame on you."

She just kept laughing and he wrapped his arm around her so she could loop hers around his waist. "I'm writing about happy things. Fairies and flying ponies, and little girls who can achieve whatever they dream."

"Sounds good."

"I just wanted to write about a fun little world that was a happy place. So I could escape each time I sat down at the computer or sketched the illustrations. Although I can't say the topic of the book has compelled me to work on it for any decent stretch of time."

"There's nothing wrong with wanting to escape

reality," Brett told her, kissing the top of her head when she leaned her cheek against his shoulder. "We all have to do what we have to do."

"Which is why you didn't want to tell Logan," she remarked.

"Look, we can deal with Logan. Let's just not let it ruin this, okay?"

"I couldn't have said it better myself," she said. Because she had no intention of letting anyone or anything ruin what was happening between them.

Jamie stood up when she saw Logan enter the restaurant. They were sitting outside so Bear could be with them, and she didn't think he'd see them. Brett hadn't bothered to stand—he seemed more interested in shredding his sugar packet into a thousand pieces than looking out for his friend.

"Hey!" she called out when she spotted Logan.

He wrapped her in a big bear hug, holding on tight. "We don't see each other in months and now twice in a week. How lucky am I?"

She gave him a kiss on the cheek and stood back as Brett rose and the boys did some handshake-backslap ritual.

"You two hanging out a bit?" Logan asked.

Brett cleared his throat and she jumped in to answer for him. She'd hoped for a relaxed coffee first, that they could just hang out and enjoy catching up, but it seemed they were diving straight into it.

"Brett's actually staying with me, keeping me company," she said. "It's nice to have someone in the house again."

"Oh, yeah?" Logan answered, waving over a waitress and ordering a latte before picking up the menu.

"So you've been working? How's your dog?" Brett asked. "Jamie's doing really well with Bear."

Jamie frowned at him, not wanting to change the subject yet. She just wanted to get everything out on the table, deal with the two most important men in her life by being honest. Then they could get back to chitchat and food, but they needed to get this out in the open now, especially since they were already on the topic.

"We should let the dogs get together for a play, take them to the beach or something," Logan said, before turning to Brett. "And you can stay with me if you need a place to crash once Jamie kicks you out, because we both know she'll be sick of you soon, right?"

Both guys laughed, but she didn't. Jamie tapped her fingers on the tabletop, trying to figure out how to get what she needed to say out there without Logan completely losing the plot.

"I thought you'd be staying at the barracks?" Brett asked.

"I've rented a place not far from there, and no one seems to mind me living off-site. They're putting me on some local work, security and bomb checks for the celebrities they have coming in over the next few months as part of the Visit Australia tourism campaign."

"Logan, there's something we need to tell you," Jamie blurted, interrupting their talk about Logan's work. It wasn't that she wasn't interested in what he was saying, about what he did, but she couldn't sit here pretending like they didn't have something major to discus with him.

He put down his menu, looked from her to Brett and back to her again. "Is everything okay? It's not Bear, is it?" he asked, diverting his gaze to study the dog sitting at her feet, before reaching down to pat him. "You look good, boy. Jamie looking after you, huh?"

"We didn't mean for this to happen, especially not so soon after Sam passing away, but Brett and I are, well, we're close. We're, um, well we've become more than friends, and we wanted you to be the first to know." Damn it! That hadn't come out well at all, not as she'd planned, not like she'd practiced in her head. She didn't want to stuff this conversation up, and that was exactly what she'd managed to do.

Logan's fists had clenched on the table and she could see a tick at his temple.

"Logan, I can explain…" Brett began, before Logan cut him off straight away.

"Our friend dies, and instead of looking after his wife, *like we both promised to do,* you decide it's okay to sleep with her? To just slot into Sam's life like you can take his place?"

"It wasn't like that," Jamie told him, reaching for Brett's hand. "This wasn't planned, it's just…"

"So you *are* sleeping together?" he demanded.

"Logan, I can explain," she stuttered, emotion clogging her throat and making it near impossible to speak.

"Jamie, this is between me and Brett. You're a widow

and we promised Sam we'd look after you, and instead he's has taken advantage of you?"

Her hands were wet, clammy from the tension at her table, and she was starting to flush hot. *This was not good.* There was no part of this that was good. Brett had been right, they should never have told Logan, they should have just stayed in their own little bubble of happiness.

"Logan, I didn't want to tell you, but we..."

Logan laughed, but it was a harsh sound that made Jamie cringe. "Please don't insult me or Sam by using the word *we* when it comes to Jamie, Brett."

Jamie didn't know what to say, hated that they were starting to have a conversation about her as if she weren't present, as if she couldn't hear every single word they were saying. She'd known pain, plenty of it lately, but this cut straight to the bone.

"Logan, why don't we go and talk about this some-where private?" Brett asked. "Leave Jamie out of this."

"Oh, I have every intention of leaving her out of this," he said, seething.

Jamie watched as they both stood. They were big men, tall and muscled, and the testosterone surround-ing her was enough to make her head spin. She knew this wasn't looking good, that at least one of them was about to explode, but she'd never seen either of them be violent before. Surely they wouldn't...

Jamie's mouth went dry. She swiveled in her chair to watch them as they walked down the steps. It seemed too calm, too orderly, but the heated exchange that began when they were on the footpath was anything other than calm, and deep down she'd known it was coming. As soon as she'd seen Logan's expression, when she'd told him, she'd known. Her hand dropped to Bear, kneading his fur as she stayed seated.

Logan was in Brett's face, and he wasn't doing anything to stop him. Until he said one sentence. One sentence that Jamie heard even from where she was sitting, her hand now resting on Bear's head as she stared at the pair of them arguing. Her heart was thumping so hard she could hardly concentrate, a ringing in her ears making her head pound.

*"I love her, Logan."*

She froze, her hand stopping its back-and-forth stroke of her dog's head. There was nothing that could have prepared her for that moment, the second that she heard Brett say those three little words that sent her mind spiraling, that made it almost impossible for her to breathe.

*He loved her.*

Only the moment was shattered by the crack of Logan's fist hitting Brett square in the jaw. Jamie screamed, or at least she thought it was her because all she could hear was the ringing of a scream in her ears as she watched Brett stagger backward and Logan stand there, staring down at him, disgust written all over his face. Brett stood, not moving even as Logan raised his fist again, obviously deciding he wasn't going to engage, that he didn't want to fight his friend. In less than a minute, Logan stormed off down the footpath without a backward glance, disappearing before she even thought to call out to him. Before she was even capable of acting. Before she could do anything to right the wrong that had just happened because of her. Because she was as much in shock from what Brett had said, not just because of what Logan had done.

She flew down the steps and reached for Brett, gasping at the blood pouring from his nose and dripping into his mouth.

"Brett? Oh, my gosh…" The words came out like they were all connected, a complete jumble. "I don't, are you…?"

This couldn't be happening. Her hands were fluttering in the air with no idea what they should be doing to help him. And she still couldn't stop thinking about how it had felt to hear those words—*he loved her*.

"I'm fine," he insisted, wiping at his face then cursing when he covered his shirtsleeve in blood.

"No, you're not fine," she managed to say. "I'll cancel our lunch and then we can…"

"No," he said, staring down at her with a coolness in his gaze that sent shivers down her spine. This was not the same man she'd made love to, the same man whose hand she'd held as they strolled through the park earlier. The man who'd just confessed his love for her. "There can be no *us*, Jamie, don't you get that now? This is why I didn't want to meet Logan, because I knew that he'd tell me what I already knew, what I've been trying to ignore this whole time."

She stood dead-still, feet rooted to the spot, unable to move even if she wanted to. "Just because Logan didn't understand doesn't mean this is wrong. He'll get his head around it, eventually. We knew this wasn't going to be easy for him to digest, Brett, we knew it was going to be tough."

"It's not about Logan accepting us or not, Jamie, it's about him being *right*. Maybe this is me taking advantage of you, doing something that is so wrong it shouldn't have even crossed my mind that any part of it was okay." He stared at her. "Sam was my best friend, Jamie, and he trusted me like he trusted no one else. Except for Logan. And now I've lost both of them, because I did something that I've known was wrong every step of the way." He stared at her, his expression empty. "It doesn't matter how I feel about you, Jamie. I should never have let this go so far between us. I shouldn't have told you about looking for you, about seeing Sam with you. None of it."

Jamie stared back up at him, digging her fingernails into her palm, determined to stay strong.

"So what are you saying, Brett?"

He looked at her then looked away, like he couldn't even make eye contact with her anymore. "I need to think," he said, walking a few steps backward, putting enough space between them that it felt like they'd never be close, that he'd never hold her in his arms or kiss her ever again. "I'll see you later."

Jamie stood and watched him—the man she'd just opened herself up to, the man who'd only moments earlier said he loved her—walk away. Instead of fighting for her, fighting for their right to be together, he'd just given up and left her. And she had a feeling that he wasn't just walking away from lunch, he was walking away from *her. For good.*

She squared her shoulders and forced herself to walk
back up the steps and into the restaurant, hating that the
other people seated outside in the courtyard had witnessed the scene and no doubt heard some of what was
being said. Bear's wagging tail made her smile, though,
and she dropped a kiss to his head before sitting back
down again, trying to stay calm. Her dog was at least
loyal, would never leave her side unless she wanted him
to. Bear was the only constant in her life right now, no
strings attached.

"Ma'am, would you like to cancel one of your or-
ders?"

She nodded bravely. "Yes, just the eggs benedict for
me, please. And another latte. Make it strong."

There was a newspaper at the empty table beside her,
so she reached for it and started scanning the articles.
She wasn't interested in reading, but she was interested
in doing anything she could to take her mind off Brett.
To try to keep things normal and pretend that everything was okay for a little while.

If that meant sitting alone with her dog to eat brunch,
then that's what she'd do. She needed to be grateful
for her life, for the fact that she was sitting here, alive,
in the sun. She could go home and cry later, but right
now she was going to eat her eggs and drink her coffee.

Because she'd put herself through enough, *been*
through enough, to just take a moment for herself and
pretend like everything was okay. Inside, she wanted to
fall apart, but her mind was strong, and she wanted to
keep it that way. Life didn't get much tougher than losing a husband, but she'd survived that, and she would

survive this. Just like she'd survived losing her dad when she was a teenager and dealt with a mom who'd been more interested in drowning her sorrows in a bottle of wine than comforting her only daughter.

She was a fighter, and she wasn't going to lose her strength, not ever.

# CHAPTER TWELVE

JAMIE WAS TIRED. She was tired of waiting, tired of thinking, tired of everything. She'd read through the final draft of her latest manuscript, played around with all of her sketches to send her editor, but nothing was inspiring her. And now here she was, curled up in her favorite chair again with a cup of coffee, staring out the window. She'd spent a lot of time sitting in the same spot and thinking after Sam had died, after the men had come knocking at her door and told her the news, and it was the only place she felt like sitting now. She didn't know why, but whenever she looked out the window it helped her to relax.

Bear's low whine broke her trance, and she smiled over at him. He'd been through so much, which made them perfect companions, but she also knew that the only reason she was doing so well with the dog now was because of Brett.

*Brett.* She couldn't stop thinking about him if she tried. He was the only person who'd made her feel alive, who'd made her feel like *her* again since Sam had died, and now he'd gone and walked away. Not to mention the wedge she'd driven between him and Logan—a wedge she was worried might be irreparable.

*I love her.* They were the words that had echoed in her head since the fight. Maybe she'd heard them wrong, maybe he'd said something else, but the way her heart picked up speed whenever she played that moment over in her mind told her that she'd been right. That there was no mistaking what he'd told Logan, before she'd heard the smack of Logan's fist against his face. How could he feel that way about her and still walk away?

It excited and terrified her in equal parts, because this was Brett. Her friend, Brett. Her husband's friend, Brett. And he was also the man she'd made love to the night before and couldn't stop thinking about. The only man other than her husband who she could ever imagine being with, and the only man she wanted to be with. But now he was gone, and she'd never have the chance to hear the words from his lips, or say them back to him.

Jamie sighed again and reached for her phone, checking to make sure she hadn't missed a call or a text. Eventually she was going to have to admit that Brett wasn't coming back, at least not tonight. She was alone, again. Just her and Bear, and what she'd shared with Brett might be over for good, just a memory.

"Want a cuddle?" she asked the dog. She moved to the sofa and grabbed a blanket to tuck around herself.

He pricked his ears and watched as she settled herself, flicked on the television and patted the spot beside her. It didn't take him long to decide to join her—he padded over and jumped up, taking up more space than she was. But she didn't care. He was a warm body and he loved her, and that was all she needed right now. Bear was her oversized cuddly blanket—not to mention her protector at night.

Her dog was someone who wasn't going to leave her, someone who was supposed to be by her side, no questions asked. Someone who'd be in her life for as long as was possible.

Someone she could love without feeling guilty about what her heart was telling her.

Brett leaned both elbows on the counter and stared down into his drink. The warm brown liquid didn't have any answers, and it wasn't a vice he'd ever indulged before, but after what had happened with Jamie, he'd decided a bourbon might help clear his head. Not that it was doing the pounding any good, or helping the purple swirl that was starting around his eye and across one side of his nose. He'd taken one look in the cracked bathroom mirror and decided that he was best not to look at the reminder on his face.

He held up the glass and took a small sip, cringing as the liquid burned a fiery trail down his throat. It was only early afternoon, and he never drank straight spirits at the best of times, let alone on an empty stomach.

Brett glanced around at the other people in the bar— all men. It was dark and dingy, an underground dive that made it almost impossible to remember that it was a bright, sunny day outside. The kind of day he should be enjoying, rather than sitting around feeling sorry for himself.

He swallowed a larger gulp of his drink this time, finding the second taste smoother than the first.

"You ready for another?"

Brett looked up as the bartender spoke to him. "Ah, no. I think just one will do me."

He received a nod in response. "I haven't seen you here before."

"And hopefully, at this time of the day at least, you won't see me again."

The bartender chuckled. "You don't exactly look like my kind of lunchtime regular. The type who only ever consumes liquid for lunch, that is."

"Heaven help me," Brett said, tipping back the rest of the glass and closing his eyes as he swallowed it down. The drink had made his stomach swirl with a heat that felt better than the cold dread he'd been experiencing earlier, but he still didn't want to be tempted by a second.

"Woman trouble?"

Brett nodded. "You could say that."

"Don't be an idiot, that's my advice. If you love her? Tell her you're sorry and make it up to her. The guys that don't do that…?" The bartender raised his eyebrows. "They're the ones who turn into my regulars, and it's a sad story from then on. Although women troubles are pretty good for business down here."

Brett stood and put his wallet into his back pocket. "Thanks for the advice. It's not quite that simple, but you're right."

He walked to the entrance, feeling like a desperate man as he stared at the light filtering through the door.

Suddenly the confines of the bar, the darkness, even the smell, were all telling him that he needed to run, and fast. Before he turned into a depressed creature who needed bourbon and darkness to deal with his life on a daily basis.

Brett's memories would forever haunt him—that last day with Sam like a scene from a movie playing on repeat sometimes—but he wasn't ever going to give in to them. He had been part of Australia's most elite special forces team, was trained in active combat, even how to deal with being captured and held by an enemy, and that training had instilled a strength in him that he wasn't ever going to let disappear from his mind.

The trouble was, that training had also taught him that there was nothing more important than his fellow soldiers, *his men*. And Sam had been his wingman, his buddy, the person he trusted with his life on a daily basis. Part of the family that he'd created after losing his parents.

So did he maintain that loyalty even in Sam's death, or did he give in to his feelings for Jamie and try to tell himself that *that* was the right thing to do? Because the broken, hurt look in her eyes when he'd walked away from her earlier might end up haunting him for the rest of his life, too. He loved her, there was no denying that, but he also had a loyalty to his family, and that meant respecting Sam even in death. What Logan had said was what had terrified him all this time with Jamie—words that he'd told himself before giving in to the way he felt. Before making love to Jamie and knowing it was so wrong, but also so right.

Brett held up his hand to shield his eyes from the bright sunlight and started to walk, because he had nothing else to do and nowhere else to be. He just followed his feet, needing the time to think. He hadn't been lying to Jamie when he'd told her how he'd felt that first time they'd met, or about how he'd come looking for her, and part of him knew that she deserved to know the truth about the past. About how he'd felt and what he would have done if she hadn't already met Sam.

That night, that first time they'd met, they'd spent hours talking. Two people at a party, not part of the crowd around them, they'd sipped champagne, laughed and talked like he'd never talked to anyone in his life before. And then his girlfriend had interrupted them, told him off for leaving her even though he'd seen her dancing and having fun without him, knew she'd been fine on her own.

He'd walked away from Jamie, tugged in a direction that he'd known had been wrong, but knowing that he didn't have a choice. The look in her eyes, the way they'd looked at one another, was a moment he'd never forgotten. His hand held by one woman, and everything else held by a woman he'd only known for less than a few hours.

Ten minutes later, from across the room, he'd watched her leave, and the next time he'd seen her, she'd been laughing and in the arms of his best friend. *Sam.*

Brett stopped walking and stared up at the sky, eyes adjusted to the sun now

He'd fallen in love with Jamie from the moment he'd met her. So what if it wasn't the right thing in everyone else's eyes? If it wasn't what he'd planned? He'd stood back and let his friend be with the love of his life, and now it was his turn, wasn't it? It was his chance at a happiness that he'd never known, his time to see if he and Jamie could be together. Did it mean he didn't love Sam like a brother, now that Sam was gone and he and Jamie had the chance to fall in love?

If Jamie wanted him, then he was a fool to walk away, he knew that. Logan might be his friend, but Jamie could be the love of his life, the woman who'd be at his side for the rest of his life. And that wasn't something anyone else had the right to tell him he should give up. Not Logan, and not Sam's memory. Because no matter how much he respected his friends, he needed to respect himself and what was important to him, too. If they were truly his family, wouldn't they want to see him happy?

The only person who had the right to push him away and end whatever it was that had happened between them, was Jamie. He just needed to tell her that before she changed her mind and didn't want him back.

He'd spent so long worrying about what other people would think was right, about being faithful to those he loved, that he'd forgotten what was most important. What was right by Jamie. What would make Jamie happy.

*What would make him happy.*

And there was only one thing that could make him happy right now, and that was Jamie, in his life, in his arms.

He wanted to give her enough time to think, to deal

with what had happened, but he didn't want to leave it so long that she thought he didn't care.

Brett headed toward a café he could see across the street and decided to have a late lunch, just sit for a while and eat, think about what he'd say to her. Because this could be the most important thing he ever prepared for in his life, and he didn't want to screw up the one chance he might get to prove himself to Jamie.

# CHAPTER THIRTEEN

BRETT CROSSED THE street and looked at Jamie's house. It was like the first day he'd arrived, when he'd been so uncertain about coming, about what he'd say to her, and now he was feeling just as awkward.

Only this time, he actually had something to be awkward about. Not to mention something to say that he couldn't even rehearse right in his mind, let alone out loud in front of Jamie.

It was getting late but the streetlights raised the canopy of darkness. She would no doubt already be asleep, but he was ready to come back and if he didn't do it now he might never do it. He'd needed to take his time, to think and be sure about the decision he'd made, and now there was no doubt in his mind that what he was about to do was right.

Brett slid his key into the lock and turned it, quietly opening the door and shutting it behind him. Jamie had given him the key, willingly invited him into her home, but he still felt weird about just letting himself in and treating it like his own place. Especially after what had happened. She'd probably hear him and think he was an intruder, not expecting him to ever show his face again, and the last thing he wanted was to fuel her memories of what had happened in her childhood home.

"Just me, Bear," he called out in a low voice, not wanting the dog to attack him thinking he was a stranger.

He walked through the house, flicked the light on in the kitchen, and it was then he heard the low growl. Brett looked around and realized the noise was coming from the sofa.

"Hey, boy, just me. It's Brett," he whispered.

The growl turned to a whine, and he stepped toward him so Bear could see him. His eyes adjusted to the half-light and he saw that the dog was snuggled up to, and protecting, Jamie. She was sound asleep, head tucked into a large cushion, blanket half over her, half over Bear. He knew better than to approach him too quickly.

Brett didn't want to wake Jamie and give her a fright, either, so he quietly moved toward the sofa, pulled the blanket up to her chin without disturbing her or the dog, then walked back to turn the kitchen light off. He made his way in the dark into the living room again and slumped down in the armchair. It wasn't the most comfortable place to sleep, but he'd experienced far worse, and he wanted to be there when Jamie woke up.

He didn't want her to think he'd spent the night somewhere else, wanted her to know that he cared enough to come home and deal with what a jerk he'd been earlier in the day. And most of all, he wanted to be near her. This last week had made him feel alive again—

being around Jamie and Bear—and he wasn't going to give that up without a fight. Not to mention the fact that he'd finally been able to sleep since he'd been in her home with her. And if she asked him to leave in the morning? At least he could tell himself that he'd tried, that it wasn't his own fear than had driven a wedge between them. He'd respect her choice no matter what she decided.

Brett was starting to be thankful that he'd had the glass of bourbon, because without it, he may have ended up sitting awake all night. But the heaviness in his eyes told him he needed to sleep, and he wasn't going to deny himself. Not with Jamie asleep on the sofa opposite him. There was nothing he could do until she woke up, which gave him a little longer before he had to pour his heart out and convince her that what he'd said earlier, the way he'd behaved, had been him acting way out of line.

The truth had been how he'd held her in his arms the night before, what he'd said to her these past few days. Today, he'd just been plain scared, and that wasn't something he would ever have admitted to in the past.

Jamie woke to the sun shining on her face and a big body pinning her down. She could hardly feel her legs. When she opened her eyes it was to a large black nose, with Bear resting his head on her chest.

"You're squashing me," she muttered, pushing the hair from her face, trying again to stretch out her legs and failing. He either didn't hear her, or didn't care, because he didn't budge an inch and she was suddenly claustrophobic.

"Morning."

Jamie's heart stuttered into a superfast beat. Brett? What was he doing here? She locked eyes on him.

"When did you get back?" She hadn't been expecting him here, let alone waking to find him in the same room as her.

"Ah, last night. But you looked so comfortable on the sofa so I left you there. Sorry if I woke you."

She pushed Bear off and stretched, making an attempt to push her hair down, knowing how terrible she must look. She'd curled up without washing any of her makeup off, so her hair was probably the least of her worries compared to her panda eyes.

"You don't have to make breakfast," she told him, standing to watch Brett as he moved around the kitchen.

His dark brown eyes met hers, and she couldn't help but smile at him. *This was Brett.* No matter what had happened yesterday, he was still the same Brett she'd always loved as a friend, and now…what? She didn't know how to describe what had happened between them, how she felt about this gorgeous, kind man cooking in her kitchen. But she did know that she didn't want to lose him from her life.

"I want to make up for yesterday's lunch disaster," he told her, cracking eggs into the pan as he spoke. "I know it's going to take more than eggs to apologize, but it's a good start, right?"

Jamie nodded, smiling back at him, but she needed

a moment to gather her thoughts, to be alone. To deal with the fact that she'd gone to bed thinking she might never hear from him again, and now she was about to sit down to breakfast with him. Thank God she hadn't woken in the night and tried to attack him, thinking he was breaking in.

"I'm just going to freshen up. I won't be long," she told him.

Jamie headed for the bathroom and shut the door behind her. What she wanted to do was sink to the floor and feel the cool of the tiles against her skin, but she also wanted to hear what Brett had to say. He was either going to tell her he wanted to go back to just being friends, or that he wanted something more, and she needed to prepare herself either way. She wanted him here so badly, but she also had no intention of forcing him.

Not to mention she was terrified of losing him as a friend.

Brett had been trying to rehearse what he was going to say, but the trouble was that he wasn't entirely sure *what* he wanted to tell her. He put the eggs and bacon on the plates and walked them to the table, before returning with the toast and then the pot of coffee he'd freshly brewed. They said food was the way to a man's heart—he was the hoping the same might be true for women. Or just one woman in particular.

"It looks great."

He looked up as Jamie entered the room, watching as she first looked down at the table, then at him, before sitting. She immediately fingered the napkin he'd put beside her plate, as if she needed something to do, something to take her mind off what was happening or what they were going to talk about.

"The scrambled eggs look so creamy," she said, taking a mouthful and fluttering her eyes shut for a second as she swallowed. "And they taste *really* good."

"The trick is to not add any milk. Just whisk them all up and straight into the pan, and turn them off as soon as they're almost cooked."

"So you know more than just pasta and sauce, huh? What happened to you being a one-trick pony?"

Brett swallowed his mouthful and reached for a piece of toast. "One breakfast recipe and one dinner, that's all." He took a bite and watched her. "Now that you've tasted this, I don't have any more hidden talents to wow you with. This is me going all out to impress."

Jamie smiled, but before she could reply he cleared his throat.

"I didn't cook you breakfast to brag about my skills in the kitchen, Jamie. I wanted to say sorry. To genuinely tell you how sorry I am for what happened and for what I said. I was a jerk and I never should have behaved like that."

She shook her head. "You don't need to apologize. I should never have insisted we tell Logan, not so soon. It was stupid and I have no idea what I was thinking."

Brett put down his fork and leaned toward her, both arms on the table. "If we hadn't told him we would have been lying, and telling him later would have been worse. He would have felt betrayed, so you were right.

I just wish it had happened differently, and if I could do anything to change that, I would."

"So what are you trying to tell me?" she asked, picking at small bits of egg as she glanced up at him.

"What I'm trying to say is that no matter how badly it went down yesterday, telling Logan was the right thing. He's been with me, with us all, through thick and thin, and I don't want to lose him. The way I reacted was unacceptable, but everything he said just kind of fueled what I'd been worried about all along."

Jamie was looking at her food, eating little mouthfuls like she wasn't really hungry, but he waited her out, knowing she'd look up eventually. What he hadn't said was that he didn't want to lose her, either, but right now he wasn't even sure she was his to lose.

He picked up a piece of bacon between his fingers and crunched on it, never taking his eyes from her, and when she looked up he was ready. Or at least he was ready for the connection. What he wasn't ready for was the bright blue of her irises, the way they looked as if they were bathed in water from the tears glistening in them, the sight of her bottom lip tucked under her teeth, like she was having to bite on it to stop from crying—it was almost enough to break his heart.

"Why did you come back last night, Brett? Was it just to tell me that, or something more?"

Brett put the piece of bacon down that he'd been holding and wiped his fingers on his napkin. This was his moment, this was the chance he'd been waiting for, and he wasn't going to blow it.

"I came back because I was a coward yesterday, and that's not the man I am."

"I know you're no coward," she told him, a smile curving her lips and taking the sadness from her face. "You're one of the bravest people I know, and the fact that you didn't punch Logan back, and that you walked away from me? Neither of those things makes you a coward, it just makes you a person who doesn't want to do the wrong thing by the people you care about."

"I deserved the bloody nose, it's not that, but walking away from you?" He shook his head. "That was the worst decision I've ever made in my life, and I need you to know that I will never walk away from you like that ever again. I was stupid to let fear stop me from doing the one thing in my life that I've never been so sure about. *How I feel about you.*"

Brett's voice was husky, a deeper tone than it usually was. He pushed his chair out and moved around to Jamie, taking her hands in his and dropping to his knees beside her instead of towering over her.

"You're the best thing that has ever happened to me, Jamie," he told her, staring into her eyes. "What we did, what we're doing, it might not have been planned, but I'm going to fight for you if I have to. I don't care who says no and stands in our way, if you want me here, then I won't ever leave you. And that's a promise I will never break."

Jamie had tears falling down her cheeks now in a slow, steady stream. "I only want you here if you want to be here," she whispered. "I need to know how you feel about me."

She reached out and touched just under his eye, where he knew he was sporting a nasty black bruise. Her fingers were feather-light, tracing across his skin.

"I've never wanted anything so bad in all my life," he admitted. "Or any*one*."

"I can't lose another man I love, Brett. I can't…" The words were low, almost a whisper.

"I'll promise in front of every single person we know if I have to, to make you believe me, but I will never, *ever* let you down Jamie. I'm here for you, for as long as you'll have me. You're my family, too, not just the guys."

Her fingers traced beneath his bruise again before reaching around to his ear, then to the back of his head. She pulled him toward her and leaned close, her face only inches from his.

"I think I love you, Brett," she whispered, tilting her mouth toward him, lips parted.

He didn't hesitate. Brett closed his mouth over hers, lips crushed to Jamie's and moving just enough, drinking in the taste of her, the warmth of having her body and mouth pressed to his.

He only pulled back because he had to, because he needed to tell her how he felt, too.

"I don't *think* I love you, Jamie," he whispered, mouth hovering so close to hers as he spoke that her plump lips just touched his. *"I know so."*

Jamie held on to the back of Brett's head, drawing him back to her again, her mouth taking his captive. He wasn't going to stop her, but he did want to make things more comfortable.

He dragged her hand from his hair, lips barely leaving hers, and slowly moved them down to the carpet, tugging her down on top of him.

"Sorry about breakfast," she whispered, as she put her hands on either side of his head to brace herself.

"Screw breakfast," he muttered as he flipped her on to her back, so he was braced above her. "I'll take you over food any day."

"Oh, yeah?" Her fingers grabbed hold of a fistful of his hair.

"Yeah."

Brett tried to growl but she just laughed at him and tugged him lower.

"Shut up and kiss me," she said.

"Yes, ma'am."

She laughed as he kissed the hollow of her neck, just above her collarbone, holding down her arms so she was powerless to move. His lips slowly moved up her neck, before settling on her mouth. His grip on her loosened as she submitted to his kiss, moaning as his tongue teased hers, lips soft one moment then rough.

Jamie pushed up his shirt, hands sliding against his bare skin, moving across his scars and up to his shoulders, then down again.

"That's a dangerous game you're playing," he muttered against her mouth.

"I know," she whispered back as she ran her hands up his stomach this time, taking her time so she could feel his muscles, exploring every inch of him.

"Do you want me to strip you naked here on the floor?"

Hmm. She did like the sound of that… "Is that a take-it-or-leave-it question?"

"No," he said, nose against hers as he stared into her eyes. "Multichoice."

She waited, his breath hot against her skin.

"The other option is that I pick you up and drag you to your bedroom. So I can have my wicked way with you there," he said, his voice deep and husky.

There was no mistaking what he wanted from her, and she wanted it every bit as bad.

"I'll take option two," she said, liking her newfound confidence, that she could tell him what she wanted without being too shy. "It just so happens that I have nothing else to do today, so my schedule's clear."

"So I'm just some toy to pass the time with?" he asked, holding her down by the wrists again and kissing her, before hauling her up and scooping her up into his arms.

Jamie slung her arms around his neck, loving that he was strong enough to just pick her up and carry her, like he was her protector. She knew she could take care of herself, but knowing she had a man in her life who'd stand by her side no matter what was something she loved.

"No, I'm saying you're my lover, and I want you to…" She didn't finish the sentence, the heat in his gaze making the words stall in her throat.

"Lover, huh?"

"Unless you don't want to be?" she asked, catching her bottom lip beneath her teeth.

"Oh, I want to be," he said, forcing her lips to his in

a kiss that left her breathless. "Just don't expect me to let you out of your room anytime soon."

Jamie pressed her face into his chest as he carried her down the hall and kicked the bedroom door shut behind them.

Last night she'd been miserable, and this morning she was so happy she couldn't stop smiling.

Brett put her carefully on the bed and stared down at her. "I love you, Jamie," he said, all hint of playfulness gone, his tone serious. "I'm *in* love with you."

"I'm in love with you, too," she said back, not hesitating, loving that she was hearing the words straight from his mouth as he looked into her eyes, rather than secondhand, as he had admitted them to Logan.

Brett lowered himself over her and kissed her again, softer this time, more gently.

It was time for her to let go of the past and make a new future with this gorgeous, kind man, and there was no part of her that wasn't sure. She wanted to be with Brett, and no one was going to take that from her. Not ever.

Sunlight was pouring into the room, and Jamie was fighting to keep her eyes open.

"You know, I don't think I've ever been in bed at this time in the afternoon before," she mused.

Brett laughed, which sounded like a weird kind of rumbling from where she had her head pressed to his chest. She was curled up beside him, the sheet half-covering them, as she basked in the way he was stroking his fingers across her skin. Jamie felt like a well-petted cat, so content she could have purred, loving that he couldn't seem to take his hands off her.

"It feels good, doesn't it?"

"What?" she murmured. "You touching me like this? Because you can keep doing it until it's dark out, or forever, for that matter."

Brett moved his hand to stroke her hair. "Just being together. Not fighting it anymore."

"You know that Sam wouldn't have been angry with us," she said, wishing she didn't have to break the intimate moment between them, but needing to say what was on her mind. Jamie pushed up and stared down at Brett. "It doesn't mean I didn't love him with all my heart, but I think we met all those years ago for a reason, Brett. Because I met two men I could have fallen for, two men I might not have been able to decide between if I'd known that you'd come looking for me, and it's our time now. It's never been right before, but it is now."

Brett had an expression on his face that she couldn't read, but she could at least tell that he wasn't angry.

"I'm not scared of facing Sam one day," Brett told her, his lips kicking into a half smile. "He knows I would have traded places with him if I could have the day that bomb went off, and by the time I do see him, he'll be able to tell that I loved you just as much as he did."

Jamie dropped a slow, casual kiss to Brett's lips. "So are we just going to live in bliss for a while and never leave the house, take baby steps?"

Brett's face turned more somber and he sat up and propped himself against the pillows. "I know it didn't go well the first time, but I think we need to try to talk to Logan again."

Her eyebrows shot up. "You do?" The thought terrified her, especially how things had turned out, what she'd gone through thinking that Brett had left her.

He ran his fingers through her hair and tucked a few wisps behind her ear, his eyes never leaving hers. "Nothing is going to scare me off or change the way I feel about you Jamie, but Logan is important to both of us, and I want to try to make amends. Make him see that this is real, that this isn't something that's going to go away just because it makes him uncomfortable. I want to explain to him why everything he said is flawed, why this is right."

She nodded, sighing as his hand cupped her cheek and she relaxed into it. "Okay. I just don't want to burst this perfect little bubble we're floating in right now. I want to stay like this forever."

"We won't ruin this, not this time," he said. "I promise."

She trusted him, but she also knew how Logan's disapproval could affect them both if it went bad again. "So if he punches you again or tries to make us feel disgusting for what we've done?"

Brett leaned forward to drop a kiss to her forehead. "Then we tell him that his friendship means a lot to us, that he's family, but that we're in love and we need him to respect that. We're not going to change who we are or how we feel for anyone."

Jamie found herself nodding. "And when exactly are you proposing we do this?" she asked.

"Tomorrow."

"And everyone else in our lives?" she asked.

"We can take telling the rest of the world a little slower, I think," he said, pulling her closer so he could put his arms around her. "Logan can be our first step, and then we'll just take it one day at a time. Do what feels right, when it feels right."

Jamie shut her eyes and relaxed against Brett's bare chest, happy that it was warm enough that they could just lie naked, with only the light sheet covering them.

"You have a plan for how we convince him to see us again?"

He tightened his hold on her. "You can organize to meet him, say you want to talk with him, take the dogs to the river or something," Brett told her. "No matter how angry he is with me, he'll never say no to seeing you."

"You sure about that?" she mumbled against his chest.

"I'm sure," he said. "When I turn up, too, he'll have no choice other than to see me, to hear what I have to say."

"If that's how you want to do it, then that's how we'll do it."

"Good," Brett said, hands stroking her back and disappearing beneath the sheets, against her skin. "Because now that that's sorted, I want to forget about everything else for the rest of the day and just think about you."

"Oh, really?" She laughed, wriggling as he held her, teased her.

"Yes, really," he said, capturing her mouth in a kiss that made her turn into liquid against him. "And that's only the start of it."

# CHAPTER FOURTEEN

JAMIE HAD A flutter in her stomach that wasn't doing anything to help her nerves. She opened the back door of her car and signaled for Bear to jump out, just like Brett had instructed her to do with him, and he obediently hopped out and waited beside her.

"Don't overthink this."

She stared at Brett over the top of the car, where he was leaning. "I'm starting to think this wasn't such a good idea, that's what I'm thinking. Why didn't we just tell him that you would be coming?"

Brett sighed and walked around the car to her, and pulled her into his arms. "Because he would have said no, and he would have been angry before he even arrived."

She held on tight to him before stepping out of his embrace and clipping on Bear's leash. "Come on then, let's go and get this over with."

"You'll be fine. Just be yourself, and I'll deal with Logan if things don't go as planned."

Jamie shut her eyes, took a deep breath, then walked off through the park and to the river where she'd organized to meet Logan. For all her talk originally about wanting to be honest, about wanting Logan to know, she wasn't feeling so confident anymore. She would do anything to protect her relationship with Brett, and this felt like doing the exact opposite of what she should be doing.

"Once bitten, twice shy," she muttered to herself.

She looked across at Bear, wondering why he'd stopped walking, why he had his head cocked to one side, watching her. Jamie dropped to her haunches to give him a cuddle.

"I'm sorry, boy. I keep forgetting that you're always trying to figure out what I'm saying." She unclipped his leash, knowing it was about time she trusted him. "Let's go find your friend, huh? Off you go," she instructed, flinging her arm out in the signal Brett had taught her.

Bear gave her a look, like he was making sure he'd understood her properly, before trotting off ahead. She might be feeling more confident as a dog owner, but her knees were positively knocking over the idea of seeing Logan.

"Jamie!"

She looked up and saw him, standing by the river, hand held up in the air. Bear paused, looked back at her, clearly asking if he was allowed to run over to the other dog.

"Go see," she told him, walking faster herself and watching as he bounded off to say hello.

*It was now or never.*

"Hey, Logan," she called out when she was near.

"Hey," he replied, closing the distance between them and kissing her on the cheek.

It didn't feel anywhere near as awkward as she'd been expecting, seeing him after what had happened, but she knew everything would change when Brett appeared.

They both watched the dogs sniffing and playing, happily getting to know one another again.

"Do you think they remember each other?" she asked.

"Yeah," Logan said, jamming his hands into his pockets. "They've spent months at a time in the same place, and I don't think they forget. They probably have better memories that we do."

"Want to take them for a wander?"

Logan nodded and gave the dogs a whistle. "Jamie, about what happened…"

"Logan, I don't want you to apologize. There was nothing about the other day that went as planned." Jamie touched her hand to his shoulder, squeezing slightly. "I'm sorry I put you in that position. It was wrong and we should have thought it through better instead of just springing the news on you."

He stopped and stared at her, like he wasn't sure what to say.

"You're going to hate me for saying this, but Brett? He deserved a black eye. I'm only sorry about the way I spoke to you."

She sighed, shaking her head. "But that's it, Logan. Brett didn't deserve it. I'm as much to blame as he is for what's happened between us. You can't not attribute some of your anger toward me."

"Jamie, sweetheart, you're a widow. You're probably lonely." His expression was kind but it also annoyed her, like the fact she'd lost her husband meant she couldn't make up her own mind about how she felt or what she did. "Brett took advantage of you, so it is his fault."

She knew she had to tell Logan the truth, now, before Brett turned up, because this conversation wasn't exactly going as planned. "Logan, Brett and I met before I even knew Sam. Pretending like us being together isn't partly my fault is just patronizing."

His eyebrows shot up and his face seemed to visibly harden. "I'm not sure I'm following you."

"Do you remember, years back, Brett telling you about a girl he'd met? A girl he spent weeks looking for?"

Logan laughed. "Yeah, and he never found her."

"But he did," she told him, voice low. "That girl was me, and I'd just started seeing Sam when Brett finally tracked me down."

"You two weren't…"

"No!" Jamie said, not wanting him to imagine the situation being worse than it was. "I remembered him, of course I remembered him, but he never said anything about looking for me, about the night we'd met. Because he could see how happy Sam was, and he took the high road and walked away. Until recently, he never even told me what had happened."

Logan shook his head. "I think we need to keep walking."

Jamie fell into step beside him, wanting desperately for him to understand what she was trying to say.

"Brett and I have always had feelings for each other, but nothing would ever have happened while I was married to Sam." She took another deep breath. "I loved Sam so much, and nothing could have jeopardized our marriage, but with him gone and Brett back?"

Logan didn't say anything, but she knew he was listening.

"The fact that something has happened between us now is okay, Logan, because we've done nothing wrong."

"Sam has only been gone…" He shrugged. "Whatever I say isn't going to make a difference, is it? You've clearly already made up your mind."

Jamie slowly shook her head, but she panicked when she saw Brett walking in their direction.

"What?" Logan asked, looking over his shoulder. "What the hell is he doing here?"

"Don't overreact, he wanted to come and make things right with you."

"I should just leave," he muttered.

Jamie looped her arm through Logan's to keep him in place. "No, you're not. Because we're all adults here, and you guys are best mates. You're not falling out because of me, and you need to promise me that you'll listen to what he has to say."

She watched as the dogs ran over to Brett, running circles around him then bounding back off to the river to inspect the ducks again.

"Hey," Brett called out.

Logan stiffened, but she didn't let him go.

"Geez, your eye really came up," Logan said.

Brett shrugged. "Guess I deserved it." He passed them each a coffee from the cardboard tray he was holding. "I just want this coffee to go better than our last attempt, so can we all keep our fists to ourselves?"

Brett had angled his body slightly to watch the dogs, and Jamie knew Logan was watching him.

"You must miss Ted even more when you're around these two," Logan said.

Brett's eyes were nothing short of honest when he turned back, the look in them enough to break Jamie's heart. "It's easy for someone else to tell me he was just a dog, but I miss him like hell. All the time. I don't think I'll ever stop thinking about the way he died, about what I lost that day."

They all stood and sipped their coffee.

"Jamie told me, about her being the girl from all those years back."

Brett took another sip of his coffee before sending a smile in her direction. "I need you to know that I would never have come between Jamie and Sam, but I love her, Logan. I always have. This isn't something new for me, it's just something I've never acted on before."

Jamie could hardly breathe, she was terrified of what was going to happen now. Of what Logan was going to say. How his reaction could change everything.

"Did you come here wanting my blessing, or do you not care either way?" Logan asked.

"If I didn't care, I wouldn't have told you the other day, and I wouldn't be standing here now," Brett told him. "I'm not going to walk away from Jamie, but then I'm not planning on walking away from you, either. Not after all we've been through. I just want you to try to understand."

Logan started to walk, slowly, and they both started to move, too. The dogs were having a ball and they followed them along the gentle curve of the river.

"I think I just need some time to get my head around all this," Logan confessed, running a hand through his short hair. "It's not that I want to be the one that comes between you two, I just need to process it. It's a lot to take in."

Jamie couldn't help the smile the spread across her face, and the wink Brett gave her made her heart race. It was a baby step, but it was a step in the right direction.

"You both mean too much to me to lose either of you. So if you need time?" she said. "Take as much as you need."

"And you really think Sam would have been okay with this? That he wouldn't want me to do everything and anything to protect you? To stop you from making a mistake?"

"Logan, you don't need to protect her, because I'm not going to hurt her," Brett said, stopping at the same time Logan did. "Me walking away? That's what would hurt Jamie. And I love her." He smiled at her, eyes connecting with hers. "I love her, man."

Logan tipped his head back, eyes closed, before shaking his head and looking first at Jamie and then at Brett. "Just give me time. I just need time to wrap my head around all this."

Jamie knew when to change the subject, and that time was now. They'd told Logan what they needed to tell him, and it had gone down without anyone having their teeth knocked out, so now they just needed to hang out.

"Want to let the dogs have a swim?" she asked.

Logan laughed. "You ever had Bear in your car, soaking wet?"

Brett was laughing, too, and she couldn't not join in. "A quick swim and then a long walk so they can dry off, then," she suggested.

The guys exchanged looks and kept laughing, even as she told Bear to jump in and he did so with a massive bound, like he was a professional lifesaver. Ranger was barking on the sidelines, glancing back at Logan, waiting for the command. When he got it, he launched into the water, too, both dogs swimming toward a group of ducks.

"What's so funny?" she asked.

Brett's cheeky smile made her glare at him. "You. For thinking for a moment that you'll ever get your dog out of the water."

"What do you mean? He's so obedient." she said, annoyed with the way they were both grinning at her. "You told me he'll obey me at all times, Brett. Was there something you neglected to tell me?"

"Even Sam couldn't ever convince that dog to get out of the water. You? Not a chance."

Jamie threw her hands up in the air. "Maybe you could have told me that *before* he showed off his dive?"

"Nah, this is going to be way more entertaining," Brett said with a laugh.

"The joke's on you, *Brett*," she told him, hands on

hips. "Because you're in the back with him if he's still dripping wet when it's time to go home."

Logan was almost rolling on the grass he was laughing so hard.

"On second thought, he won't be wet, because we'll be using your T-shirt to dry him," she said.

"I take it all back," Logan said, still smiling. "You guys are perfect together. I've never seen Brett bossed around like this—ever."

Jamie grinned, but she had to move fast when Brett burst into a sprint and hurtled toward her.

"Don't you dare!" she squealed, running as fast as she could to get away from him. "Logan, help!"

Brett grabbed her around the waist, almost knocking the breath from her, before tossing her over his shoulder and leaving her powerless to do anything other than try to kick him.

"Take me anywhere near that water and I'll kill you," she hissed.

"Oh, baby, I like it when you talk rough," Brett whispered, slapping her on the backside.

"I mean it, Brett. Logan!" she screamed for him to help her again, but he never came to her rescue. "Logan!"

"Hey, you told me not to interfere," Logan called out. "This is me not interfering."

"Bear!" she yelled. "Bear, help me. Get Brett. Get Brett now!"

The dog who was supposed to be impossible to get out of the water leaped out with as much gusto as he'd leaped in, his big bark echoing around the park.

"Good boy, Bear!" she told him, still upside down over Brett's shoulder.

Brett stopped moving and put her back on her feet, watching the dog as he wagged his wet tail and kept barking.

"Jamie?"

"Get him, Bear!"

Bear launched at Brett and knocked him to the ground, giant paws landing square on his chest before he took him down.

"Just licks," she told him. "Lick Brett."

Her dog did as he was told, and now it was her laughing, watching Brett pinned to the ground with Bear lying on top of him, soaking wet, pleading with her to make it stop.

"Who's wet now?" she asked.

Logan held his hand up for a high five, and she gave him one back. This was how it was supposed to be—Brett and Logan getting on like they always had. And she felt good. Ever since Sam had died, she'd been like a fish out of water, but all that had changed, and she couldn't have been happier.

"Come on, Bear, let him go," she commanded. "That's no way to treat your new daddy."

# EPILOGUE

JAMIE LOOKED AROUND the large table and couldn't wipe the smile from her face. A year ago, she'd been a widow, and even her friends had struggled to know what to say to her, or how to treat her. And now? Now she was married to a man she could be herself with. A man who wasn't scared by the fact that she would always love the husband she'd lost, who was okay with her wearing her old wedding ring on her other hand, because Brett had loved Sam, too. Perhaps even as much as she had.

A tap on a glass made her turn to her new husband, eyes locking on his as he grinned and leaned sideways to give her a quick kiss.

"What are you doing?" she whispered to him.

"I'm about to do my speech, unless you want to go first?"

*A speech?* She hadn't even thought about speeches, had been so preoccupied with her vows that she hadn't even considered having to speak in front of everyone at the table.

She watched as Brett stood up beside her, their

friends and family lowering their voices until they were eventually surrounded by silence.

"I guess I need to start by thanking you all for being here," Brett said, one hand holding his champagne flute, the other falling to rest on her shoulder. "This was a day we only wanted to share with those people closest to us, and there is one person that isn't here today that I would like to acknowledge."

Jamie reached for Brett's hand, her palm covering his fingers. She didn't want to cry, but the whole day had been so emotional and now she had tears caught in her lashes again.

"We all know I wouldn't be standing here today with Jamie if Sam was still alive," Brett began, taking a big breath before continuing. "Sam was my best friend, and I always promised that I would look after Jamie if anything ever happened to him. I know he wasn't meaning it quite so literally when he said that—" Brett paused as a few of their guests chuckled "—but I also know that he would have wanted us both to be happy in his absence."

Jamie stood then, needing Brett to know that she wanted to hear what he was about to say, what he was already saying, and not knowing how to. She looped her arm around his waist, holding him tight.

"Sam was the only one of us who was married, and no matter how much we teased him about marrying so young, we loved Jamie as much as he did. I just want to say, Sam, if you're up there—" Brett wiped his eyes with the back of his hand before holding up his glass

"—that I will look after this woman until my dying breath."

Jamie had tears falling fast down her cheeks, curling into her mouth. There was nothing she could do to stop them, and she also didn't want to. Because she had loved Sam with all her heart, and now she loved Brett, too, just as deeply but in a different way. And she needed to hear what he had to say.

Brett turned toward her, putting down his glass and taking both of her hands into his.

"I always told Sam he was the luckiest guy in the world, and I mean it when I say I will look after you. One day, I might have to give you back to Sam, because I don't want to be fighting him in the afterlife, but while we are here, on this earth, I will never let you down, Jamie. I will always be here for you, and I will do anything to be the husband you need me to be. I love you."

Brett wiped away the tears that had stained her cheeks, before leaning in and kissing her softly on the mouth. She put her arms around his neck and held on tight, not wanting him to stop, but the clapping and clinking of glasses around them forced the kiss to an end.

Even though her throat was choked up still and her eyes wet with tears, Jamie turned to face the table. She needed to say something, and they were *her* family, *her* friends. They were here to celebrate, and if they saw her cry it didn't matter.

"I don't have anything planned to say, and I'm sure you're all ready for dinner to be served, but I'd like to say thank you to all of you for being here today." Jamie looked at the light hanging above the table, needing a second to gather her strength and force her emotion back as best she could, so she could get the words out. Brett took her hand and squeezed, and it was all she needed to find the strength to continue. "When I married Sam, I knew I'd found my soul mate, but it seems that I'm one of the lucky ones." She squeezed Brett's hand back. "Brett was our friend for so many years, and now he's my husband. Life has a way of throwing us curveballs, some so bad that we wonder how we'll ever live through them, but Brett has proven to me that sometimes we have more than one soul mate in the world. I am so grateful to be standing here today, with the man I love."

Jamie reached for her glass and held it up. "To Brett, for being the love of my life, and teaching me that falling in love for a second time might be a miracle, but it was one that I deserved."

"To Brett." The words echoed around their table as everyone raised their glasses.

"I love you, Brett. So much," she whispered to him.

"And I love you, too, baby," he said, dropping a kiss to her forehead.

As they sat down, two waiters appeared with the main courses, but it was the tapping against a glass again that had Jamie's attention, followed by a deep *huh-hmm*. She scanned the table and realized it was Logan, sitting directly across from them.

"I'll make this quick because dinner is being served," Logan said, standing. "For the past ten years, the two most important people in my life have been Sam and

Brett. When Sam died, we were all hit hard, and thinking about Jamie being on her own was almost as hard as losing him." He gave her a wink across the table. "I might have given Brett a black eye when I first found out, but I honestly believe, now I look back on what happened, that Sam would have told me what a jerk I was being. Because looking at these two today, it's obviously they were meant to be together." He held up his glass. "And let's not forget Bear, Sam's loyal dog, who has taken up the role as Jamie's number-one protector. If anyone didn't approve, it would have been Bear, but even he seems to accept this union." Logan laughed. "To Brett and Jamie, two of my favorite people in the world."

Jamie smiled at Logan—the man who had been her first husband's best friend and was undeniably Brett's best friend, too—and held up her glass. She took a slow sip before looking at every single person seated around the long table again. The white tablecloth was set with low candles from one end to the other instead of flowers, because she'd wanted to be able to see and talk to everyone, and she loved watching the smiles and chatter as she looked at them all now.

Brett nudging her broke her trance, and she switched her attention to him.

"You okay?" he asked.

"More than okay," she assured him, looking down at the plate of food in front of her.

"Then eat up, Mrs. Palmer," he said, waggling his eyebrows and making her laugh. "Because you'll need *all* your energy tonight."

Jamie elbowed him in the ribs but he was having none of it, swiftly grabbing her arm and pulling her in for another quick kiss.

"I'm so pleased I married you," he said, his mouth hovering over hers.

"Ditto," she said, laughing as he kissed the tip of her nose instead of her lips.

She reluctantly turned her attention back to her food—king prawns, calamari and scallops tossed in her favorite linguine with garlic.

*Life didn't get much better than this.*

* * * * *

# *Darn it. Darn it. Darn it.*

He moved back to the bench. She stowed her handbag, made sure the kids had their seatbelts fastened and then moved to the driver's seat. She glanced at Mr Fairhall and bit her lip.

Blowing out a breath, she wound down the passenger side window. 'Mr Fairhall?'

He glanced up.

'We've just had a family conference.'

He stood. He wasn't terribly tall—he might be six feet—but he had a lean, athletic body that moved with effortless grace. She watched him approach—stared as he approached—and her mouth started to dry and her heart started to pound. She tried to shake herself out from under the spell, only she found she'd frozen in position. She wished now she hadn't called him over.

With a superhuman effort she cleared her throat. 'As we're...uh...all headed in the same direction we thought if you would like a lift all or part of the way...'

He blinked. Hope lit his face, making it truly beautiful, firing his brown eyes with a light that made her swallow.

# ROAD TRIP WITH THE ELIGIBLE BACHELOR

BY
MICHELLE DOUGLAS

Published in Great Britain 2014
by Mills & Boon, an imprint of Harlequin (UK) Limited,
Eton House, 18-24 Paradise Road, Richmond, Surrey, TW9 1SR

© 2014 Michelle Douglas

ISBN: 978 0 263 91265 4

23-0314

Harlequin (UK) Limited's policy is to use papers that are natural, renewable and recyclable products and made from wood grown in sustainable forests. The logging and manufacturing processes conform to the legal environmental regulations of the country of origin.

Printed and bound in Spain
by Blackprint CPI, Barcelona

At the age of eight **Michelle Douglas** was asked what she wanted to be when she grew up. She answered, 'A writer.' Years later she read an article about romance writing and thought, *Ooh, that'll be fun*. She was right. When she's not writing she can usually be found with her nose buried in a book. She is currently enrolled in an English Masters programme for the sole purpose of indulging her reading and writing habits further. She lives in a leafy suburb of Newcastle, on Australia's east coast, with her own romantic hero—husband Greg, who is the inspiration behind all her happy endings.

Michelle would love you to visit her at her website: www.michelle-douglas.com.

To my gorgeous nephew, Josh—
hero and all-round good guy

# CHAPTER ONE

'HELLO.' QUINN LAVERTY tried to find a smile for the customer service clerk on the other side of the counter. She raised her voice to be heard above the jostling crowd. 'I'm here to collect the car I booked.'

'Name, please?'

Quinn gave him her details and tried to slide her credit card free from its slot in her purse with one hand. Chase hung off her other hand, all of his six-year-old weight balanced on one leg and her arm as he stretched as far as he could reach along the counter with his toy car, making the requisite 'broom-broom' noises.

She made him straighten and stand on two legs and then grimaced at the customer beside her who'd been 'driven over' by said toy car. 'I'm sorry.'

'No problem at all.'

He flashed her a smile and she found herself smiling back. Nice smile. *Really* nice eyes. Actually...

She frowned. There was something faintly familiar about him. She stared and then shook herself and shrugged it off, turning back to the clerk. It might just be that he was the exact model of son her father had always wanted—clean-cut, professional and respectable. She did her best not to hold that against him.

Speaking of sons...

She glanced to her left. Robbie leaned with his back

against the counter and stared up at the ceiling, his face dreamy. Quinn tried to channel some of his calm. She hadn't expected this all to take so long.

Mind you, when she'd booked the car over a month ago she hadn't thought there'd be a national plane strike either.

'I'm afraid there's been a slight change to the model of car you booked.'

Her attention spun back to the clerk. 'What kind of change?'

'Ow!' Chase pulled his hand from hers and glared.

'Sorry, honey.' She smoothed down his hair and smiled at him, but a fist tightened in her chest. She glanced back at the clerk. 'What kind of change?' she repeated.

'We no longer have that model of car available.'

But she'd booked it a whole month ago especially!

The commotion in the car rental office didn't die down. Beside her she sensed her neighbour's frustration growing too. '*I have to leave Perth today!*' He didn't shout, but every word was clipped and strong.

He glanced at her and she suddenly realised she was staring. She sent him a buck-up smile and turned back to the clerk, doing her best to block out all the background noise. 'I'm driving across the Nullarbor Plain. I need a car that can go the distance.'

'I understand the reasons you booked a four-wheel drive, Mrs Laverty, but we just don't have any available.'

Brilliant.

She didn't bother correcting him on the *Mrs*. People made that assumption all the time.

She lifted her chin, preparing for a fight. 'I have a lot of luggage to fit into the car.' Another reason she'd chosen a four-wheel drive.

'Which is why we've upgraded you.'

Was that what they called it? She folded her arms. She'd chosen the car she had because of its safety and reliability rating. As far as fuel efficiency went it was one of the best too. It was the perfect car to take them across the country.

'We've upgraded you to a late model station wagon.'

'Does it have four-wheel drive?'

'No, ma'am.'

Quinn closed her eyes briefly, but all that did was underscore the scent of desperation and outrage in the air.

'I want to speak to the manager,' the man beside her clipped out.

'But, sir—'

'Now!'

She drew in a breath and opened her eyes. 'I need a four-wheel drive. The fuel consumption on that wagon will be outrageous and as I'll be travelling to New South Wales in it that's an awful lot of fuel.' She'd be driving the car for forty hours. Probably more. 'And, I might add, with none of the benefits the four-wheel drive offers.'

Driving suddenly seemed like the stupidest idea a woman had ever had. She lifted her chin another notch. 'Thank you, but I don't want an upgrade. I want the car I originally booked.'

The clerk scratched his nose and shuffled his feet, staring everywhere but at her. 'The thing is, ma'am, with the plane strike, you understand there just aren't any four-wheel drives currently available.'

'But I booked this over a month ago!'

'I understand and I do apologise. We won't be charging you for the upgrade. In fact, we'll be offering you a discount and a credit voucher.'

That was something at least. Quinn couldn't afford to stray too far from the budget she'd set herself.

'And the crux of the matter is…' the clerk leaned confidentially across the counter '…there isn't anything else available.' He gestured to the crowded room behind Quinn.

'If you don't want the station wagon we'll have plenty of other takers who will.'

She glanced back behind her too and grimaced.

'I can't guarantee when a four-wheel drive vehicle will become available.'

She bit back a sigh. 'We'll take it.' She didn't have any other option. They'd sold up practically everything they owned. The lease on their house had run out and new tenants were expected within the next few days. Their lives no longer belonged here in Perth. Besides, she'd made a booking at a caravan park in Merredin for this afternoon. She didn't want to lose her booking fee on that as well.

'Excellent. I just need you to sign here and here.'

Quinn signed and then followed the clerk out through a side door. She made sure both boys had their backpacks— they'd refused to leave them with the rest of the luggage back at the house.

'Keep the paperwork on you. You'll need it for the New-castle office. And if you'll just wait here the car will be brought around in a jiffy.'

'Thank you.'

The relative quiet out here after the cacophony in the office was bliss.

Robbie sat on a nearby bench and swung his feet. Chase immediately knelt on the ground beside the bench and 'broom-broomed' his toy car around.

'I'm sorry, Mr Fairhall, I wish I could help you. I have your card so if something comes up I'll let you know im-mediately.'

Fairhall? That was it! She'd known she'd seen him before. She turned to confirm it anyway. Uh huh, her neighbour at the service counter had been none other than Aidan Fairhall, up-and-coming politician. He'd been trav-elling the country canvassing for support. He had hers.

He had a nice on-air manner too. No doubt it was all

orchestrated as these things were, but he came across as intelligent and polite.

Polite shouldn't be overrated. In her opinion there should be more of it. Especially in politics.

She watched him slump onto a neighbouring bench as the man with the manager badge pinned to his shirt strode away. His shoulders drooped and he dropped his head to his hands. He raked his hands through his hair and then suddenly froze. He glanced up at her—a long sidelong look from beneath his hand—and she swallowed, realising she'd been caught out staring at him *twice* now.

He straightened. Her heart did a crazy little thump-thump. She swallowed and shrugged. 'I couldn't help over-hearing. I'm sorry.'

He smiled, but she sensed the strain behind it. 'It looks as if you've had more luck.'

Her lips twisted. 'Considering I booked this car over a month ago...'

He let out a breath, nodded. 'It'd be very poor form if they cancelled it on you at this late date.'

'But they're not giving us the car we wanted,' Robbie piped up.

She should've known he'd been listening. His dreamy expression lulled her every single time. 'But it's a better one,' she said, because she didn't want him to worry. Rob-bie had taken to worrying about everything.

'We're moving house,' Chase declared, glancing up from his car. 'All the way across the world!'

'Country,' she corrected.

Chase stared at her and then nodded. 'Country,' he re-peated. 'Can we move to the moon?'

'Not this week.' She grinned. Robbie and Chase—her darling boys—they made it all worthwhile.

'It sounds exciting,' Mr Fairhall said. He glanced at

Robbie. 'And if you're in an even better car now that probably means your trip is going to be lucky too.'

She liked him then. Amid his own troubles he found the time to be nice to a couple of young boys—and not just nice but reassuring. If he hadn't already won her vote he'd have had it now.

'The plane strike seems to be turning the country on its head. I hope it ends soon so you can be where you need to be.'

He must have a crazy schedule. Actually—she rested one hand on a hip and surveyed him—maybe this would prove a blessing in disguise. He looked tired. A rest from the hurly-burly might do him the world of good.

His eyes darkened with some burden that would have to remain nameless because she had no intention of asking about it. 'Rumour has it that things on that front are going to take…' his shoulders sagged '…time.'

She winced.

'Mrs Laverty?' A man bounced out from behind the wheel of a white station wagon. 'Your car.'

She nodded as he handed her the keys with a cheery, 'Safe driving.'

'Thank you.'

Mr Fairhall rose. 'You boys have a great journey, okay?' And as he spoke he lifted their backpacks into the back of the wagon.

'Can I sit back here with the backpacks?' Chase asked, climbing in beside them.

'Most certainly not,' she countered, lifting him out again. 'Thank you,' she said to Mr Fairhall as he closed the wagon.

'Where are you going when the planes work again?' Chase asked as Quinn ushered him around to the back seat.

'Sydney.'

'That's near where we're going,' Robbie said. 'We looked

it up on the map.' He pulled out the map he'd been keeping in his shorts pocket.

The swift glance her polite politician sent her then had her stomach tightening.

'You're going to Sydney?'

She shifted her weight from one foot to the other. 'A couple of hours north of Sydney.'

'You wouldn't consider…?'

He broke off, no doubt in response to the rictus of a smile that had frozen to her face.

'No, of course not,' he said softly, as if to himself.

The boys glanced from her to him and back again.

Darn it! This was supposed to be a *family* trip. This road trip was about giving the boys a holiday…with the opportunity to ask her whatever questions they wanted about this new life they were embarking upon. In a relaxed atmosphere. Another person—a stranger—would throw those dynamics out completely.

She made herself brisk. 'C'mon, boys, in the car. Seat belts fastened, please.'

Aidan Fairhall nodded at her. 'Safe trip.'

'Thank you.'

*Darn it. Darn it. Darn it.*

He moved back to the bench. She stowed her handbag, made sure the kids had their seat belts fastened and then moved to the driver's seat. She glanced at Mr Fairhall and bit her lip.

'He wanted to come with us,' Chase said.

Why did children have to be so perceptive when you didn't want them to be and so obtuse when you did?

'You always tell us we should help people when they need it,' Robbie pointed out.

She turned in her seat and surveyed them both. 'You'd like to invite Mr Fairhall along on our journey?'

Robbie stared back. 'How'd you know his name?'

'I've seen him on the television. He's a politician.'

'Would he come all the way with us?'

'I'm not sure. As soon as the plane strike ends he might jump ship at any place that has an airport.'

'He's a nice man,' Chase said.

She had a feeling Chase was right.

Robbie studied the object of their conjecture and then turned back. 'He looks kinda sad.'

'Yeah.' She tried not to let those slumped shoulders pluck too hard at her. It was just… She knew exactly how that felt—the defeat, the worry and the helplessness.

'It might make our trip luckier,' Robbie said.

She couldn't mistake the hope in his eyes. She bit her lip to stop from saying something rash. Her eldest son ached for a male role model and the knowledge cut at her. Not that she expected Aidan Fairhall to fill that role. Still…

She blew out a breath and wound down the passenger side window. 'Mr Fairhall?'

He glanced up.

'We've just had a family conference.'

He stood. He wasn't terribly tall—he might be six feet—but he had a lean athletic body that moved with effortless grace. She watched him approach—stared as he approached—and her mouth started to dry and her heart started to pound. She tried to shake herself out from under the spell, only she found she'd frozen in position. She wished now she hadn't called him over. With a superhuman effort she cleared her throat. 'As we're…uh… all headed in the same direction we thought if you would like a lift all or part of the way…'

He blinked. Hope lit his face, making it truly beautiful, firing his brown eyes with a light that made her swallow. They weren't a boring brown, but a deep amber that brought to mind blazing hearth fires, fine brandies and rich caramel.

Then the light in those beautiful eyes faded and for some reason her heart sank too. Maybe it was the unspoken judgement she recognised in those deep amber depths. She sat back a little. She swallowed. 'I'm not given to recklessness, Mr Fairhall. I recognised you and I like your public persona. I like your education policies more.'

His lips twisted but the darkness faded from his eyes. His fingers drummed against the roof of the car.

'But, as I don't actually know you, and if you do take us up on our very kind offer, I'll be informing the manager of this car hire company that you'll be accompanying us. I'll also be ringing my aunt to tell her the same.' He didn't say anything. She shrugged and forced herself to add, 'But if we can help you out in any way then we'd be happy to.'

'Why would you do that?'

'People should help each other out always,' her earnest eldest son said.

'And you looked sad,' Chase added.

The light in those amazing eyes faded again, although the lips kept their smile.

Quinn rushed on. 'Also, it'd be nice to share some of the driving…not to mention the fuel costs. I'm afraid it wouldn't precisely be a free ride.' She'd sensed that would go against the grain with him.

There was a long silence. Quinn kicked herself. 'I'm sorry we have you at a disadvantage. I'm Quinn Laverty and these are my sons, Robbie and Chase.' She fished her licence out and handed it to him as proof of both her identity and the fact she could drive. 'If you decide to accompany us I'd want you to phone someone to let them know about your plans and who you're travelling with.'

He handed the licence back to her. 'I'm not given to recklessness either, Mrs Laverty.'

She didn't bother correcting the *Mrs*. 'Quinn,' she said instead. As she had no intention of becoming romantically

involved with any man, let alone a politician—dear God!—
the *Mrs* provided her with another level of protection.

Not that she needed protection from unwanted suitors.
She could squash them flat as easily as swatting bugs.
But correcting that Mrs might give the wrong impression.

Aidan Fairhall was from her parents' world and she had
no intention of returning to that world. *Ever*.

She shuddered. Another long silence ensued. Eventually
she cleared her throat. 'I'm sorry to hurry you, Mr Fairhall, but we'd really like to get going soon.'

Aidan's gaze snapped to Quinn Laverty's. 'If it was just
work commitments I wouldn't dream of imposing on you
like this.' His father would hit the roof if he ever heard
Aidan utter that sentiment. 'But...' He hesitated.

'But?'

She had an unhurried way of speaking that was restful.

'I have a family commitment I have to meet.'

'Like I said, if we can help...'

She'd probably harangue him the entire way, pointing
out all the flaws in his proposed policies, but... He had a
sudden vision of his mother's worn eyes. He nodded. The
alternative was worse. He made his lips curve upwards
even though the heaviness in his heart made that nearly
impossible. 'I will be forever in your debt. Thank you, I'd
very much like to take you up on your very kind offer.'
He pulled his cell phone from his pocket and gestured the
manager back over.

Quinn spoke to the manager.

Aidan rang his mother.

As he expected, she fretted at the news. 'But you don't
even know this woman, darling, and it's such a long way
to drive. How do you know you'll be safe?'

He tried to allay her fears. Not very successfully. Eventually he said, 'If it will make you happier, I'll remain in

Perth until the plane strike is over.' He had to grit his teeth as he said it. He had to remind himself there were a lot of reasons for her anxieties and apprehensions.

'But you must be back in time for the party!'

Yes. He bit back a sigh. He must be back in time for the party. Still, it was a fortnight away.

'Harvey thinks the industrial action will be protracted. He's talking seven whole days. I can't get a train or bus ticket out of the place or hire a car for the next week. Everything is booked solid.'

'Oh, dear.'

He didn't need to see her to know the way her hands fluttered about her throat. 'This is my best option. As soon as the strike ends, I'll make my way to the nearest airport and be home as soon as I can.'

'Oh, dear.'

'I really don't think there's anything to worry about, Mother.' And movement of any kind beat kicking his heels in Perth.

There was a slight pause. 'Of course you must do what you think best, darling.'

And thereby she absolved herself of any responsibility and placed it all squarely on Aidan's shoulders. He tried not to bow under its weight. 'I'll call you this evening.'

He collected his overnight case and stowed it in the back. 'You travel light,' Quinn observed.

He slid into the passenger seat. 'I was only supposed to be in Perth for a single night.'

She started the car up and eased it out of the car park and onto the road. 'It's a long way to come for just a day.'

'Two days,' he corrected. 'And one night.'

He thought she might glance at him then, but she kept her eyes on the road. 'I see you're a man who knows how to make the most of his time.'

'That's me.'

Quinn Laverty had a blonde ponytail and wore a kind of crazy oversized tie-dyed dress that covered her to her ankles. She wasn't exactly a flower power child, but there was something of the hippy about her.

The longer he stared at her, the more he wanted to keep staring. Crazy. He loosened his tie a fraction and turned to the boys. 'Robbie and Chase, it's great to meet you. Thank you for letting me share your journey.'

'You're welcome, Mr Fairhall,' the elder, Robbie, said with perfect manners.

He could see the path set out for the boy now—school prefect, school captain, dux, university medal and then a high-powered job in the public service.

What a nightmare!

*Only for you.*

He pushed the thought away. 'If it's okay with your mother you can call me Aidan.'

Quinn glanced at him briefly. Her lips tilted up into an easy smile. 'That's okay with me.'

Ten minutes later they stopped at an unprepossessing house and loaded the back of the car with an assortment of boxes and suitcases. The backpacks moved onto the back seat with the boys. Aidan insisted on doing all the heavy lifting.

'See you, Perth,' Quinn said with a jaunty wave at the house.

Both boys waved too.

'Can we play our Gameboys now?' Chase asked.

'You can.'

Both boys whooped and dived into their backpacks. She glanced at Aidan and rolled her eyes. 'They were specially bought for the trip.'

Probably quite a financial outlay for a single mum. Not that he had any proof that she was single.

'And the deal was that they weren't allowed to play them until the trip itself started.'

Smart move. Those things would keep the boys occupied for hours, which, quite obviously, had been her plan. He settled back in his seat as the suburbs of Perth passed by one after the other. 'I know the clerk back at the store called you Mrs Laverty, but I also notice you're not wearing a wedding ring.' He kept his tone neutral. He didn't want her thinking he was judging her or condemning her in any way. 'Are you married or single or...'

Her brows lifted. 'Does it matter?'

He loosened his tie a tiny bit more. 'Not at all. But some people get fixated on titles so I always like to get them straight.'

'I prefer Ms.'

Which told him precisely nothing at all. When he met her gaze, she laughed. Sparkling green eyes momentarily dazzled him. 'You first,' she dared.

A question like that would normally have him sitting up straighter. Instead he found himself chuckling and relaxing back into his seat even more. 'Single. Most definitely single. Never been married; hence, never been divorced and not currently in a relationship.'

'Ditto,' she said.

'So, are you moving back home? Is Newcastle where you grew up?'

'No.'

Her face shuttered closed—not completely but in a half-fan—and he bit back a sigh. False start number one.

A moment's silence ensued and then she turned to him with a smile that was too bright. 'Is your campaign going well?'

He bit back a curse. Was that all people could think to converse with him about—his darn job? 'Yes.'

Another moment's silence. False start number two. For

pity's sake, he was good at small talk. He opened his mouth. He closed it again. The deep heaviness in his chest grew. Normally he could push it away, ignore it, but today it gave him no quarter. It was this stupid plane strike and the break in his routine. It had given him time to think.

Thinking wouldn't help anything!

She glanced at him, her face sober, and he knew then that she was going to bring up the subject he most dreaded. He wanted to beg her not to, but years of *good* breeding prevented him.

'How are you and your parents now, since your brother...?'

That was a different approach to most, but...The heaviness started to burn and ache. He rested his head back against his seat and tried to stop his lip from curling.

'I'm sorry. Don't answer that. It was a stupid thing to ask. Grieving in public must be harrowing. I just wanted to say I'm truly sorry for your loss, Aidan.'

The simple words with their innate sincerity touched him and the burn in his chest eased a fraction. 'Thank you, Quinn.'

Two beats passed. Quinn shuffled in her seat a little and her ponytail bounced. 'I'm moving to an olive farm.'

He straightened and turned to her. 'An olive farm?'

'Uh-huh.' She kept her eyes on the road, but she was grinning. 'I bet that's not a sentence you hear every day, is it?'

'It's not a sentence I have ever heard uttered in my life.'

'It's probably not as startling as saying I was moving to an alpaca farm or going to work on a ferret breeding programme. But it's only a degree or two behind.'

She'd made things good—or, at least, better—just like that. With one abrupt and startling admission. 'What do you know about olives?'

She lifted her nose in the air. 'I know that marinated olives on a cheese platter is one of life's little pleasures.'

He laughed. She glanced at him and her eyes danced. 'What about you; what do you know about olives?'

'That they grow on trees. That they make olive oil. And that marinated olives on a cheese platter is one of life's little pleasures.'

She laughed then too and he couldn't remember a sound he'd ever enjoyed more. He closed his eyes all the better to savour it. It was the last thing he remembered.

Aidan sat bolt upright and glanced around. He was alone in the car. He peered at his watch.

He closed his eyes and shook his right arm, but when he opened them again the time hadn't changed. He'd slept for two hours?

He pressed his palms to his eyes and dragged in a breath before stretching to the right and then the left to ease the cricks in his back and neck. Finally he took stock of his surroundings. Quinn had parked beneath a huge old gum tree to give him shade. At the moment she, Robbie and Chase kicked a ball around on a big oval in front of him. She'd hitched her dress up to mid-thigh into a pair of bike shorts.

His eyes widened. Man, she was…fit!

He shook his head and pressed fingers to his eyes again.

With bones that literally creaked, he pushed out of the car and stretched. Warm air caressed his skin and he slid his suit jacket off to lay it on the front seat. Quinn waved and then pointed behind him to an amenities block. 'They're clean and well maintained,' she called out.

He lifted a hand to let her know he'd heard.

When he returned he found her sitting cross-legged on a blanket at the edge of the oval beside an assortment of bags.

'Where are we?'

'Wundowie.'

He pulled out his smart phone and searched for it on the Internet. 'We've been travelling...'

'Nearly two and a half hours, though we're still only about an hour out of Perth. There was a lot of traffic,' she said in answer to his raised eyebrow. 'And there was some mini-marathon we had to be diverted around.' She shrugged. 'It all took time. Would you like a sandwich or an apple?' She opened a cooler bag and proffered its contents towards him. 'Or water? There's plenty here.'

He reached for a bottle of water. 'Thank you, I'm parched.'

'But well rested,' she said with a laugh.

His hand clenched about the water bottle, making the plastic crackle. 'You should've woken me.'

She turned from watching the boys as they continued with their game. 'Why?'

He opened his mouth. He closed it again and rubbed the nape of his neck. 'I, uh... It wasn't very polite.'

'It wasn't impolite. You were obviously tired and needed the sleep.'

She selected an apple and crunched into it. 'Please eat something. It'll only go to waste and I hate that.'

He took a sandwich. Ham and pickle. 'Thank you.' And tried to remember the last time he'd let his guard down so comprehensively as to fall asleep when he hadn't meant to.

It certainly hadn't happened since Daniel had died.

His appetite fled. Nevertheless he forced himself to eat the sandwich. He wouldn't be able to stand the fuss his mother would make if he became ill. And this woman beside him had gone to the trouble of making these sandwiches for her children and herself and had chosen to share them with him. The least he could do was appreciate it.

He and Quinn sat side by side on the grass with their legs stretched out in front of them. They didn't speak much. A million questions pounded through him, but they were all far too personal and he had no right to ask a single one of them.

But the inactivity grated on him. It didn't seem to have that effect on Quinn, though. She lifted her face to the sky and closed her eyes as if relishing the sun and the day and the air. Eventually she jumped up again. 'I'm going to have another run with the boys for a bit. Stretch my legs. Feel free to join in.'

He glanced down at himself. 'I'm not exactly dressed for it.'

She took in his tie, his tailored trousers and polished leather shoes. 'No,' she agreed and he couldn't remember the last time he'd felt so summarily dismissed. 'Oh, I meant to tell you earlier that we're only going as far as Merredin today,' she shot over her shoulder before racing off towards the boys.

He looked Merredin up on his smart phone. A quick calculation informed him it was only another two hours further on. Surely they could travel further than that in a day? He scowled and started answering email. He might as well do something useful. He made phone calls.

They stayed in Wundowie for another thirty minutes. He chafed to be away the entire time but was careful not to keep glancing at his watch. If they were only going as far as Merredin they'd be there mid-afternoon as it was. An additional half an hour in Wundowie either way wouldn't much matter.

Aidan would've liked to have kept working when they were back in the car, but he suspected Quinn would consider that bad manners.

He dragged a hand through his hair. What was he thinking? Of course it'd be bad manners. Besides, she and the boys had kept quiet so he could sleep and it hardly seemed fair to continue to expect such ongoing consideration. Especially when they were doing him a favour.

The fact his phone battery was running low decided it. He tucked it away and glanced around to the back seat. 'Do you boys play a sport?'

'Soccer,' said Robbie.

'Robbie is the best runner on his team,' Chase said.

Quinn glanced at him. 'He means fastest.'

Robbie's mouth turned down. 'I mightn't be in my new team.'

Quinn tensed. Aidan tried not to wince. He hadn't meant to tread into sensitive territory. 'Uh...' He searched for something to say.

'Do you play sport?' Robbie asked.

'Not any more.' And all of a sudden his heart felt heavy as a stone again.

'Why are you on the television?' Chase demanded to know. 'Mum said she'd seen you.'

'Because of my job. I'm a politician so I go on television to tell people how I'd run the country if they vote for me.'

Robbie frowned. 'Do you like your job?'

A bitter taste lined his mouth. 'Sure I do.'

'What do you do?'

'Well, I go into my office most days and I go to lots of meetings and...' Endless meetings. It took an effort of will to keep the tiredness out of his voice. 'I go on the television and talk on the radio and talk to newspaper reporters so they can tell all the people about the things I think would make our country run better. I have people who work for me and we draft up proposals for new policies.'

'Wouldn't being a fireman be more fun?'

'A fireman would be excellent fun,' he agreed. Lord, his mother would have a fit! He almost laughed.

'When you're finished being a politician maybe you could be a fireman,' Chase said.

'And then you could play soccer too,' added Robbie.

He didn't know how those two things were linked. He glanced at Quinn for direction. She merely smiled at him.

'Mum, can we play one of our CDs now?'

'I did promise the boys we'd play one of our CDs on this leg of our journey. We burned a few especially.'

'I don't mind.' It'd save him searching for topics of conversation.

'We sing pretty loud.'

'You don't need to apologise about that.'

For some reason that made her grin. 'You haven't heard our singing yet.'

He forced himself to smile.

She slipped a CD into the player. 'The Purple People-Eater' immediately blasted from the speakers and his three companions burst into loud accompaniment, the boys laughing throughout most of the song. That was followed by 'Llama Llama Duck' and then 'My Boomerang Won't Come Back'.

He stared at her. 'You have to be joking me?'

'Fun novelty songs are our favourite.' Her grin was so wide it almost split her face. 'If there's a doo-wop or chirpy-chirpy-cheep-cheep to be had then we love it.'

Hell, that was what this was. Absolute hell. He slunk down in his seat and stared straight out in front of him as the songs came at him in a relentless round. 'This isn't music!' He glared at the road. 'You could've warned me about this back in Perth.' No way would he have got into the car with her then.

Then he thought of his mother.

Quinn merely sang, 'I'm a yummy, tummy, funny, lucky gummy bear,' with extra gusto.

He closed his eyes, but this time sleep eluded him.

# CHAPTER TWO

THEY REACHED MERREDIN ninety minutes later. It had felt like ninety hours. Aidan had endured forty minutes of the 'Monster Mash', 'Achy Breaky Heart' and many more novelty songs, which was enough to last him a lifetime. Twenty minutes of I Spy had followed and then a further thirty minutes of the number plate game. There was only one rule to the game, as far as he could tell, and that was who could make up the silliest phrase from the letters of a passing number plate.

PHH. Penguin haircuts here. Purple Hoovering hollyhocks. Pasta hates ham.

LSL. Larks sneeze loudly. Little snooty limpets. Lace scissored loquaciously.

CCC. Cream cake central. Can't clap cymbals. Cool cooler coolest.

And on and on and on it went, like some kind of slow Chinese water torture. His temples throbbed and an ache stretched behind his eyes. He didn't join in.

He sat up straighter though when Quinn eased the car down the town's main street. He glanced up at the sky. There was another four hours of daylight left yet. Another four hours of good driving time.

Manners prevented him from pointing this out. Biting back something less than charitable, he studied the few shops on offer. Maybe he'd be able to hire a car of his own out here?

Quinn parked the car in the main street and turned off the motor. 'The boys and I are staying at the caravan park, but I figured you'd be more comfortable at the motel.'

A caravan park? He suppressed a shudder. Again, he didn't say anything. Quinn was obviously on a tight budget.

She and the boys all but bounced out of the car. Aidan found his limbs heavy and lethargic. It took an effort of will to make them move. He wondered where Quinn found all her energy. Maybe she took vitamins. Unbidden, an image of her racing around the soccer oval in her bike shorts and dress rose up through him and for some reason his throat tightened.

He glanced up to find her watching him. He felt worn and weary, but her ponytail still bounced and her cheeks were pink and pretty. She waited, as if expecting him to say something, and then she merely shrugged. 'The motel is just across the road.' She pointed. 'We'll collect you at nine in the morning.'

He snapped to and retrieved his overnight bag from the back of the wagon. 'I'll be ready earlier. Say six or seven if you wanted to get an early start.'

'Nine o'clock,' she repeated, and he suddenly had the impression she was laughing at him.

She swung back to the boys. 'Right!' She clapped her hands. 'Chase, I need you to find me a packet of spaghetti and, Robbie, I need you to find me a tin of tomatoes.'

As they walked away he heard Chase ask, 'What are you looking for?'

'Minced meat and garlic bread.' And they all disappeared into the nearby supermarket.

He'd been summarily dismissed. Again.

From a grocery trip? He shook the thought off and headed across the road to the motel.

His room was adequate. Merredin might be the regional centre for Western Australia's wheat belt, but as far as he was concerned it wasn't much more than a two-horse town and his early enquiries about hiring a car proved less than encouraging.

He strode back to his motel room, set his phone to charge and then flipped open his laptop and searched Google Maps. He frowned. What the heck…? If they kept travelling at this pace it'd take them two weeks to drive across the country!

His hands clenched for a moment. Counting to three, he unclenched them and pulled a writing pad from his briefcase and started to plot a route across the continent. He spread out a map he'd grabbed from the motel's reception and marked logical break points where he and Quinn could swap driving duties.

That took all of twenty minutes. He closed his laptop and glanced about his room. There didn't seem to be much more to do. He wandered about the room, opening the wardrobe doors and the desk drawer. He made a coffee that he didn't drink. He reached for his cell phone to call his mother, stared at it for a moment and then shoved it back onto its charger.

Flopping back onto the bed, he stared at the ceiling for what seemed like an eon. When he glanced at his watch, though, he cursed. What on earth was he going to do for the rest of the afternoon, let alone the rest of the night?

He raised himself to his elbows. He could go and find Quinn and the boys.

*Why would you do that?*

He sat up and drummed his fingers against his thighs, before shooting to his feet. He tore the page from his writing pad and stalked from the room.

It didn't take him long to find the caravan park. And it didn't take him long to locate Robbie and Chase either. They played—somewhat rowdily—on a playground fort in primary colours so bright they hurt his eyes. And then he saw Quinn. She sat cross-legged on a blanket beside a nearby caravan, and something about her sitting in the afternoon light soothed his eyes.

'Hey, Aidan,' she called out when she saw him. 'Feeling at a loose end, huh?'

He rolled his shoulders. 'I'm just exploring. Thought I'd come see where you were camped.'

She lifted her face to the sun. 'This is a nice spot, isn't it?'

It was? He glanced around, searching for whatever it was that she found 'nice', but he came up blank.

'I thought you'd be busy catching up on all of your work.'

It hit him that in amongst all of his restlessness it hadn't occurred to him to ring back into the office. They knew he was delayed, but...

It didn't mean he had to stop working. There'd still be the usual endless round of email that needed answering. He could've set up meetings for this evening on Skype.

The thought of all that work made him feel as tired as the idea of ringing his mother. When Quinn gestured to the blanket he fell down onto it, grateful for the respite.

He had no right feeling so exhausted. He'd done next to nothing all day. He shook himself in an effort to keep the moroseness at bay, glanced around as if he were curious about his surroundings. If he pretended well enough, maybe he'd start to feel a flicker of interest and intent again. Maybe. 'Are you planning to stay in caravan parks for all of your journey?'

'You bet.'

He kept his face smooth, but somehow she saw through

him and threw her head back with a laugh. 'Not your idea
of a good time, I see.'

'I wouldn't say that.' He wasn't a snob, but... Walking
to an amenity block when he could have an en suite bathroom? No, thanks.

'Only because you're incredibly polite.'

She made that sound like an insult.

'Look about you, Aidan. This place caters to children
far better than your motel does. Most caravan parks do.
Look at all that open green space over there. The boys can
kick a ball around to their hearts' content. And then there's
that playground, which I might add is fenced.'

In those eye-gouging primary colours.

'Robbie is old enough not to wander off, but Chase is
still easily distracted.'

He straightened when he realised this place gave her
peace of mind. 'I hadn't thought of that.'

'And there're usually other children around for them
to play with too.'

He watched another two children approach the playground.

'Most people here won't mind a bit of noise from the
children, but I bet you're glad we're not staying in the room
next to yours at the motel.'

He rolled his shoulders. 'It's not a bad noise. It's just a
bit of laughing and shouting.'

She raised her eyebrows.

'But I take your point.'

'It'd be hard to get any work done with all that noise.'

There she was, talking about work again.

He promptly pulled the itinerary he'd plotted out for
them from his pocket along with the map and smoothed
them on the rug between them. 'I thought that tomorrow
we could make it as far as Balladonia. If we wanted to
take two-hour shifts driving, which is what all the driver

reviver and driving safety courses recommend, then we could change here, here and here.' He pointed out the various locations on the map.

Quinn leaned back on her hands and laughed. 'I've seen this movie. In this particular scenario you're Sally and I'm Harry, right?'

He stared at her. What on earth was she talking about?

'*When Harry Met Sally*,' she said when he remained silent. 'The movie? You know? Sally who's a bit uptight and super-organised and Harry who's casual and laidback?'

He searched for something to say.

'There's a scene early in the movie when they're driving across America together and…' Her voice lost steam. 'You haven't seen the movie?'

He shook his head.

Her face fell. 'But it's one of the classic rom-coms of all time.'

For some reason he felt compelled to apologise. 'I'm sorry.'

And for some reason he couldn't fathom that made her smile again, only it wasn't the kind of smile that reached her eyes. She touched his map and shook her head. 'No.'

He blinked. 'No?' But…

She laughed and he could see it was partly in frustration with him, but she didn't do it in a mean way. She rested back on her hands again. 'Aidan, you really need to learn to relax and chill out a bit.'

And just like that she reminded him of Daniel.

It should've hurt him.

But it didn't.

'I…'

He stared at her as if he'd never seen her before. Or as if no one had ever told him to slow down and smell the roses. He stared at her as if that very concept was totally alien.

She bit back a sigh. This trip—spending time with her boys and doing all she could to make this transition in their lives exciting and easy—was important to her. Taking pity on Aidan and inviting him to join them had thrown the dynamic off more than she'd anticipated. She'd promised the boys a holiday and she wasn't going back on her word.

And eight hours a day driving wasn't a holiday in anybody's vocabulary.

'We probably should've compared notes about the kind of travelling we were expecting to do before we left Perth.' How could he know she meant to take it slow if she hadn't explained it to him? He was obviously in a hurry, but… 'It didn't occur to me at the time.' She moistened her lips. 'But we're obviously working on two different timetables here.'

Her stomach churned. He was probably used to everyone rushing around at a million miles an hour. That was what people from his world—her parents' world—did.

*Don't hold that against him. It doesn't make him like your parents.*

'I made enquiries in town to see if I could hire a car of my own.'

She swallowed. It'd be one solution to the problem. 'And?'

'No luck, I'm afraid.'

'I see.'

'You're regretting taking me on as a passenger.' He said it simply, without rancour, but there was such exhaustion stretching through his voice it was all she could do to not reach across and clasp his hand and to tell him he was mistaken. Only…

She glanced across at her boys, now happily playing with the newcomers to the playground. A fierce mixture of love and fear swirled through her. Pushing her shoulders back, she met his stare again. Pussyfooting around would only lead to more misunderstandings. 'Aidan, you've been unfailingly polite, but you haven't really been all that friendly.'

'I beg your pardon?'

He gritted his teeth so hard his mouth turned white. She hated being the reason for that expression, but she soldiered on all the same, hoping she wasn't punishing him for the reminders of the past that he'd unwittingly brought rushing back to her. 'You didn't join in on our singalong. You didn't play I Spy or the number plate game.'

He stared at her. For someone groomed to project and maintain a certain image, he looked all at sea. 'Please don't tell me you want to part company here in this two-horse town.'

'Of course not!' How could he think she'd abandon him like that?

'Once we reach Adelaide I'll make other arrangements.'

'Okay.' She bit her thumbnail for a moment, unable to look at him. Adelaide was still six or possibly seven days away yet. If she could make him see how important this trip was…well, then, he might make more of an effort to fit in. Maybe.

She stretched her legs out in front of her. 'You know what I think? I think we should break the ice a little. I think we should ask the questions that have been itching through us and get that all out of the way.'

He looked so utterly appalled she had to bite her lip to stop from laughing. This man took self-contained to a whole new level. 'Or, better yet, why don't we tell each other something we think the other wants to know?'

His expression didn't change but she ignored it to clap her hands. 'Yes, that'll be much more fun. I'll go first, shall I?' she rushed on before he could object. She crossed her legs again. 'I'm going to tell you why Robbie, Chase and I are on a road trip across the continent.'

He shifted, grew more alert. She could tell from the way

his eyes focused on her and his shoulders straightened. Oh, he was appalled still, of course, but she hoped his curiosity would eventually conquer his resistance.

'The olive farm is in the Hunter Valley wine district and it belongs to my aunt. She's the black sheep of the family.' She rolled her eyes. 'And I happen to take after her.'

'Your family consider you a black sheep?'

A question! She schooled her features to hide her triumph. 'Actually, in all honesty, I'd be very surprised if my parents thought about me at all these days. They're from Sydney. I became pregnant with Robbie when I was eighteen. They wanted me to go to university and carve out some mythically brilliant career. When I decided to have my baby instead, they cut me off.'

His jaw dropped. He mightn't be 'friendly' in a traditional sense, but he didn't strike her as the kind of man who'd walk away from his family when they needed him.

*And you're basing that on what—his pretty smiles and earnest eyes in his television interviews?*

Hmm, good point.

'Siblings?'

Another question! 'None. So, after my parents handed me their ultimatum, I packed my bags and moved to Perth.'

'Why Perth?'

'Because it was about as far away from Sydney as I could get while still remaining in the country.'

He stared at her for a long moment. She held her breath and crossed her fingers that he'd ask a fourth question.

'Did Robbie's father go with you?'

She wanted to beam at him for asking. 'Yes, he did.' But she didn't want to tell him that story. 'When I had Robbie my Aunt Mara—'

'Of black sheep fame?'

He was totally hooked, whether he knew it or not. 'The very one. Well, she came across to Perth to help me out for a couple of weeks. I was barely nineteen with a new baby. I appreciated every bit of help, advice and support she gave me.'

He plucked a nearby dandelion. 'That's nice.'

'She didn't have to. We'd had very little to do with each other when I was growing up.' Her parents had made sure of that. 'But those two weeks bonded us together in a way I will always cherish. We've been close ever since.'

'You're moving to be nearer to her?'

A little twist of fear burrowed into her gut. She shifted on the blanket. She was turning all of their lives upside down. What if she was making a mistake? They'd had a perfectly comfortable life in Perth.

*You weren't happy.*

Her happiness had nothing to do with it. She scratched her nose and stared across at Robbie and Chase.

'Quinn?'

She shook herself and pasted on a smile. 'Mara is only fifty-two but she's developed severe arthritis. She needs a hip replacement.' She needed help. 'My boys don't have any family in Perth. I think it'd be nice for them to know Mara better.'

Comprehension flashed across his face. 'You're moving there to look after her.'

'I expect we'll all look after each other. Like I said, she owns an olive farm and her second-in-command recently married and moved to the States.'

'And you're going to fill the position?'

He didn't ask with any judgement in his voice. She shouldn't feel as if she'd been found so...lacking. 'Yes.'

She tossed her head. Besides, she was looking forward to that challenge. Her admin job in the Department of Chemistry at the University of Western Australia had palled years ago. Not that it had ever had much shine.

Still, it had provided them with the security of a fortnightly pay packet. It had supported her and the boys for the last five years. It—

She slammed a halt on the doubts that tried to crowd her. If worse came to worse, if things didn't work out at Aunt Mara's, she'd be able to pick up an office job in no time at all. Somewhere.

She bit back a sigh and then straightened her spine. There was absolutely no reason why things wouldn't work out. She loved her aunt. So did the boys. The Hunter Valley was a beautiful place and the boys would thrive in all of that sunshine and the wide open spaces. They'd go to good schools and she'd get them a dog. They'd make friends fast. And so would she.

She crossed her fingers. The change might even help her overcome the ennui that had started to take her over. She'd learn new skills and maybe, eventually, she'd stop feeling so alone.

Win-win for everyone. Perfect!

She turned back to Aidan and pressed her hands together. 'This is such an exciting time for us.'

'And a scary one too, I imagine.'

She didn't want to admit that. Not out loud.

'I mean you're turning your whole life on its head.'

She sucked her bottom lip into her mouth and concentrated on keeping her breathing even.

He stared across at the playground. 'And it's not just your life that this decision impacts either so—'

'Are you trying to make me hyperventilate?' she demanded.

His jaw dropped. 'Heck, no! I just think it's amazing and courageous and...'

She gritted her teeth for a moment before pasting on another smile. She suspected it was more a grimace from the way Aidan eased back a fraction and kept his eyes trained on her. 'Which is why this road trip of ours is so important to me. I've promised the boys that we'll treat it as a holi-day. I'm determined that we'll take our time and that ev-eryone will be as relaxed as possible so I can answer any questions about this new life of ours, help ease any fears and apprehensions that might come to light, and to just...'

She reached out as if to grasp the words she sought from the air. 'To help us all look forward to this new beginning and be excited about it.' She turned to him, willing him to understand. 'It's the reason I've been chirpy-chirpy-cheeping with all of my might.'

Beneath his tan, he paled. 'And I'm screwing that up for you.'

'No you're not. Not exactly. But now that you know, maybe you can ease up a bit.'

'And part company with you at Adelaide.'

She slapped a hand down on the blanket between them and leaned in closer. He smelled of something spicy and sharp like eucalyptus oil or crushed pine needles. She breathed him in and the constriction about her lungs eased a fraction. 'By going with the flow and relaxing,' she cor-rected. 'You're obviously stressed about this plane strike and getting back home to Sydney, but...'

He latched onto that. 'But?'

'We're all stuck with each other for the six days or so, right?'

'Six days!' He swallowed. He nodded. 'Six days. Right.'

'So can't you stop chafing at the constraints and just... just look at this time as a bit of a gift? Embrace it as an unexpected holiday or a timeout from a hectic schedule?'

He stared at her. 'A holiday?' He said the words as if testing them out. Very slowly he started to nod. 'Fretting about the delay isn't going to change anything, is it?'

Precisely.

'In fact, it would be making things harder on you and the boys.'

'And on you.' She shook her head. 'I hate to think what your raised cortisol levels are doing to your overall heath.'

'Cortisol?'

'It's a hormone that's released into our bloodstreams during times of stress. It's not good for us in large constant doses.' It took an effort of will not to fidget under his stare. She waved a dismissive hand. 'I read about it in a book.'

This man would benefit from regular meditation too, but she didn't suggest it. She'd suggested enough for one day. She leant back on her hands and lifted her face to what was left of the sun and made herself laugh. 'We're certainly getting holiday weather.' Summer might be over officially, but nobody had informed the weather of that fact.

He glanced around and nodded.

'Look at how blue the sky is and the golden haze on the horizon. This is my absolute favourite time of day.'

His shoulders loosened.

'I love the way the shadows lengthen and how stands of trees almost turn purple in the shade, like those ones over there,' she murmured.

He pulled in an audible breath and let it out in one long exhalation.

'I just want to drink it all in.'

They were quiet for a few moments. She hoped he was savouring the afternoon as much as she was.

'You remind me of someone.'

It was the most relaxed she'd heard him sound. 'Who?'

He swivelled to face her. 'My turn.'

She blinked. 'For?'

'For sharing something I think you want to know.'

It took all her willpower to not lean forward, mouth agape. She hadn't expected him to actually take part in her 'you tell me yours, I'll tell you mine' strategy. She'd just wanted to impress upon him the importance of this trip. Not that she had any intention of telling him that now, though.

'Okay.' She forced her eyes back to the hazy horizon, careful to not make him feel self-conscious.

'Daniel's death has devastated my family.'

His brother had died in a car accident eight months ago now. It had made all the headlines. She gripped a fistful of blanket, her heart burning for Aidan and his family.

'He was the apple of my parents' eyes. His death shattered them.' He stared down at his hands. 'Hardly surprising as he was a great guy.'

He didn't have to say how much his brother's death had devastated him. She could see it in his face. A lump ballooned in her throat.

'Ever since Danny's accident my mother has lived in mortal fear of losing me too.'

The poor woman.

And then Quinn saw it, what Aidan wasn't saying. With an effort, she swallowed and the lump bruised her all the way down until it reached her stomach. 'So this plane strike and your road trip across the country, it's going to be a real…worry for her?'

And that was what had really been chafing at him. Not the interruption to his political campaigning or the fact he was missing important meetings.

'What did you call it? Cortisol?'

She nodded.

He pointed skyward. 'Hers will be through the roof.'

And Aidan wanted to do whatever he could to ease his mother's suffering. Her heart tore for him.

'My parents' thirtieth wedding anniversary is soon and—'

'When?' Good Lord! She had to make sure he got home in time for that.

'Not until the twenty-fourth of the month.'

She let out a breath. She was hoping to be at Mara's no later than the twenty-second. He'd get home in time.

'I should be there helping with all the preparations. There's a huge party planned. I encouraged them to have it. I thought it might help.'

That was when she started to wonder how much of his life he was putting on hold in an effort to allay his parents' grief. And what of his own grief?

She surveyed him for a long moment. When he turned to meet her gaze the rich brown of his eyes almost stole her breath. She swallowed, but she didn't look away. 'Aidan, I am truly sorry for your loss.'

He looked ragged for a moment. 'Thank you.'

The silence gathered about them and started to burn. 'May I say something about your mother?' she whispered.

He stilled. He turned back. 'Only if you say it gently.'

Gently? Her heart started to thump. She moistened her lips and stared across to the playground with its riot of happy laughter. 'I can't imagine how bad it would be to lose one of my boys.' Her voice wobbled. 'I can't actually imagine anything worse.'

He reached out and squeezed her hand.

'In fact, I can't actually comprehend it, and I'm utterly and probably somewhat selfishly grateful for that.'

'It's not selfish, Quinn,' he said quietly.

'Your poor, *poor* mother, Aidan.' She clasped his hand tightly. 'God forbid if I should ever lose Robbie, but...I can't help feeling that wrapping Chase up in cotton wool would not be a good thing to do. For him or for me.'

He met her gaze, his face sober. 'She can't help her grief.'

'No.' But tying Aidan down like this was hardly fair. 'You will get home safe and sound and in one piece.' It was probably a foolish thing to say because neither one of them could guarantee that. But she couldn't think of anything else to say.

'Of course I will.'

'And there's nothing you can do for your mother at the moment except to give her a daily phone call to let her know you're okay.'

'No,' he agreed.

'Can you live with that?'

'I guess I'll have to.'

'You know,' she started slowly, 'this might be a good thing.'

'How?'

'Maybe it'll force her to focus beyond her fear, especially if she has the party to turn her attention to. And once she does that she might realise how irrational her fear is.'

His face lit up. 'You think so?'

Oh, heavens, she'd raised his hopes. Um… 'Maybe.'

He stared at her for a long moment and then he smiled. 'That person you remind me of?'

Her heart started to thump. 'Uh-huh?'

'It's Daniel. Quinn, you remind me of my brother.'

# CHAPTER THREE

AIDAN TOOK THE first driving shift the next day. He'd thought he might have an argument on his hands about that but, after subjecting him to a thorough scrutiny, Quinn merely handed him the keys and slid into the passenger seat.

He surveyed her the best he could without alerting her to that fact. She looked a little pale, a little wan.

'Okay, boys.' She turned to Robbie and Chase in the back. 'You have one hour of Gameboy time.'

Both boys whooped and dived into their backpacks. She shrugged when she caught Aidan's eye. 'I know it'd make things a whole lot easier and simpler, not to mention quieter, if I just let them play with their Gameboys all day, but I don't think that's good for them.'

'I don't either.'

Her brows shot up. 'It's something you've thought about?'

He might not have kids, he might not really know any kids, but it didn't make him totally ignorant. 'Only in the abstract.' Besides, he hoped to have kids one day. 'The rise in childhood obesity is worrying. I've been part of a government task force that's been looking at strategies to combat it.'

'That's good to know.' Yesterday she'd have asked him all sorts of questions about it. Today she stifled a yawn and stared out of the window with a mumbled, 'Glad our taxes are being put to good use.'

Aidan had set their course on the Great Eastern Highway and the scenery grew browner and drier by the kilometre. All that was visible from the windows was low scrub, brown grass and brown dirt. For mile upon endless mile.

He glanced across at her again. 'Rough night?'

She straightened and he wished he'd kept quiet and just let her drift off for a little while.

'The bed was hard as a rock.'

She smiled but it left him vaguely dissatisfied. Quinn might spout assurances that this move across the country was the greatest idea ever, but he sensed a certain ambivalence in her.

*That she doesn't want to talk about.*

Yesterday's disclosures didn't give him the right to pry.

'I'll sleep very well tonight, though.' She sent him one of her buck-up smiles. 'Whether the bed is made of rock or marshmallow.'

He determined in that moment to let her rest as much as he could. 'Mind if I turn on the radio? I'll keep the volume low.'

'Sounds nice.'

Although he willed her to, she didn't fall asleep. She merely stared out of the window and watched the unending scrub pass by. At the one hour mark she snapped to and turned to the boys. 'Time's up.'

There were groans and grumbles and 'let me just finish this bit' but within five minutes they'd tucked their Gameboys back into their bags. Quinn then asked them what games they'd been playing and received blow-by-blow accounts. She spoke her children's lingo. She connected with them on every level and he suddenly and deeply admired her.

She was a single working mother, but she'd evidently spent time building a solid relationship with her children. It couldn't have been easy, she'd have had to make sacrifices, but he suspected she hadn't minded that in the least.

Robbie stretched out his arms to touch the back of Aidan's seat. 'How long is Aunt Mara going to be in hospital for?'

'If all goes well, just a few days. But she'll have to take it easy for weeks and weeks. Don't forget, though, that her surgery isn't scheduled until later in the year.'

'I'll read to her.'

'She'll like that.'

'And I'll play cars with her,' Chase piped up, evidently not wanting to be left out.

'Heavens! She'll be back on her feet in no time with all of that attention.'

Robbie stretched to touch the roof. 'What are we going to do for a car if we have to give this one back?'

'We're going to share Aunt Mara's car for a while and there's a farm ute we can use too. But we'll buy a new one eventually. What do you guys think we should get?'

A lively discussion followed, mostly based on television ads that the boys liked. It made Aidan smile. And then he remembered Quinn's words of yesterday and how she'd thought him unfriendly and the smile slid straight off his face. He had to do more than just listen. 'What about a minivan?' he suggested. 'One of those bus things that can practically carry an entire football team.'

The boys thought that a brilliant idea. Quinn accused him of harbouring a secret desire for a shed on wheels, which made him laugh.

'So,' he asked when silence reigned again, 'are you boys looking forward to the move?'

'Yes,' said Chase without hesitation.

In the rear-view mirror he saw Robbie frown and chew

the side of his thumb. 'I'm going to miss my friends Luke and Jason.'

Quinn's hands clenched. He flicked a glance at them before turning his attention back to the road. 'I know it's not precisely the same, but you'll be able to Skype with them, won't you?'

Robbie frowned more fiercely. 'What's that?'

'It's like talking on the phone only on the computer, and you get to see each other.'

He stopped chewing his thumb. 'Really?' His face lit up. 'Can I, Mum? Huh, can I?'

Quinn's hands unclenched. 'Sure you can, honey.'

She sent Aidan such a smile he was tempted to simply sit back and bask in it. But then he remembered yesterday's impression. Unfriendly? He wasn't having a bit of it.

'And can I Skype with Daddy too?'

He swore every single muscle Quinn possessed bunched at that. 'I...' She cleared her throat. 'I don't see why not.' She flashed Robbie a smile. For some reason it made Aidan want to drop his head to the steering wheel. He kept both hands tight about it, though, and his eyes glued to the road ahead. 'You'll have to ask him the next time he rings.'

''Kay.'

'Look, kangaroos!' Aidan hollered, pointing to the right and blessing Providence for providing them with the perfect distraction.

Both boys strained in their seats, their mouths open and their faces eager as they watched four large grey kangaroos bounce through the scrub beside the car.

Quinn leant her head back against the seat and closed her eyes.

Aidan pulled in a breath. 'Okay, Robbie and Chase, I think it's time I taught you a song.'

'Is it a fun song?' Chase demanded, as if that was the only kind of song he was interested in.

He scrubbed a hand across his chin. 'It has a yellow submarine. Does that make it fun enough?'

'Yes!' the boys chorused.

Besides, it was a classic. If they were all so hell-bent on novelty songs they might as well learn the best. So he taught them the Beatles' 'Yellow Submarine'. By the time they'd finished they'd reached their first rest stop. While Quinn spread out the picnic blanket in the park area behind the lone roadhouse, Aidan grabbed his laptop and downloaded the song so the boys could listen to the original version. The three of them sang along at the tops of their voices.

When they'd finished, Aidan turned to find Quinn curled on the blanket, fast asleep. He thought of his exhaustion of the previous day. He thought about how she was turning her whole world on its head. He swung back to the boys. 'How about we kick a ball around and let your mum sleep?'

'I'm tired of kicking a ball around,' Chase grumbled. 'I wanna play hopscotch instead.'

Hopscotch?

Without a murmur, Robbie went to the boot of the car and pulled out a plastic mat which, when unfolded, formed a life-sized hopscotch…court, shape or whatever one called it.

'Uh, guys…' Aidan glanced at Quinn. He shook his head. 'Never mind.'

So they played hopscotch.

And darn if it wasn't fun!

'Are you guys worried about making friends in your new home town?'

Chase hopped. 'Mum said it'll be really easy to make friends in school.'

'I expect she's right.' Aiden patted Chase's back. 'Well done, buddy; that was a big hop to end with.'

Robbie took his turn. 'Mum said I can play Saturday morning soccer in Pokolbin, just like I did in Perth.'

'Sport is a great way to make friends.' He stepped back to give Robbie plenty of room to finish his turn. 'You're quick at this.'

'I know.' Robbie nodded, but as Aidan took his turn he could tell the boy was pleased with the praise.

'You'd be quicker if you had play clothes.'

Aidan puffed over the finish line. 'Ain't that the truth? I'll have to buy some when we get to Norseman this afternoon.'

Robbie squinted up at Aidan, chewing his lip. Aidan mightn't have a kid of his own, he mightn't have friends with kids, but it didn't take a rocket scientist to work out that Robbie had something he wanted to ask. 'Out with it, buddy,' he advised.

'You gotta promise to tell me the truth.'

Jeez! He rubbed a hand across his jaw. 'I'll do my best.'

'Is hopscotch a girls' game?'

Aidan automatically went to say no, that anyone was at liberty to play hopscotch, which wasn't really a lie, but... He closed his mouth. Kids could be cruel and, as far as he could tell, political correctness wasn't high on their radar, regardless of what their parents tried to teach them.

He squatted down in front of Robbie and Chase, a glance over his shoulder confirming that Quinn still slept. 'Okay, it shouldn't just be a girls' game, but it kinda is.' He didn't want these kids getting bullied. 'So I wouldn't play it at your new school.'

'Right.' Robbie nodded, evidently glad the question had been settled.

Chase leant against Aidan and the rush of the child's heat against his arm did something strange to Aidan's stomach. He had a sudden primeval impulse to take out anyone who tried to hurt these kids.

'But,' Chase whispered, 'I like playing hopscotch.'

And nobody should be allowed to prevent these kids from enjoying such an innocent diversion. 'That's why I think you should play it at home whenever you want. If anyone finds out about it and gives you a hard time, tell them your mum makes you play it with her. In fact—' a grin built through him '—when you have friends around, tee up with your mum beforehand to make you all play it.'

They'd all love it. He'd tell Quinn to make cake...or chocolate crackles. Kids would forgive any eccentricity for chocolate crackles. They might groan to their parents or other kids that Ms Laverty made them play hopscotch, but then they'd remember the chocolate crackles and still think she was great.

It'd be a win all round.

He beamed at the boys. They beamed back. 'C'mon, who's up next?'

Quinn woke to find Aidan playing hopscotch with Robbie and Chase. She blinked. She sat up and then had to blink again. He actually looked as if he was having fun!

She suddenly grinned, all trace of her thundering headache gone. The sun, the clear blue sky and the dry dusty smells of the rest area seemed filled with a promise they'd all lacked earlier.

She lifted her chin and pushed away the doubts that had spent the night harrying and hounding her. This new beginning should be savoured, not dreaded. Mindless worrying wouldn't help any of them.

Aidan glanced around as if he'd sensed her gaze. Her heart did a silly little flip-flop. Actually, maybe it wasn't so silly. Perhaps it was entirely understandable. Aidan looked a whole lot more...uh, personable without his jacket and tie...or his shoes and socks.

'You lot must be ready for a drink and a snack,' she

called out, but her voice came out a bit higher and threadier than it usually did. She blamed it on the dust in the air. The boys raced over, full of reports of their game, but she only heard every second word. Her eyes never left Aidan. He packed up the game and then ambled over—practically sauntering—and it highlighted the leanness of his hips and the power of his thighs.

And it made her throat as dry as a desert. An ancient hunger built through her. Ancient as in primeval. And ancient as in she hadn't experienced this kind of hunger in over five years. She dragged her gaze away, refused to let it dwell on a body that interested her far too much. Bodies were just bodies. Hormones were just hormones. And this was nothing more than a hormone-induced aberration. She handed out sliced apple, carrot sticks and bottled water and kept her eyes to herself as best she could.

Aidan fell down onto the blanket beside her, slugging her with his heat. The scent of his perspiration rose up, making her gulp. She tried telling herself she loathed man sweat. But it was clean sweat earned in the service of playing with her children and she couldn't hate it. Beneath it threaded that woodsy spice that she'd like to get to know a whole lot better.

'How are you feeling?'

His words rumbled against her. She grabbed an apple slice and crunched it, nodding her head all the while. 'Much better. Thank you for letting me sleep—' she glanced at her watch '—for a whole hour!' He'd taken care of the boys for a whole hour? 'Oh my word! What kind of irresponsible mother you must think me!' What kind of mother just fell asleep in a strange place and—?

'I think you're a brilliant mother, Quinn.'

She had to look at him then. Her mouth opened and closed but no sound came out.

'So do we,' Robbie said.

Chase nodded.

She had to swallow a lump. 'Thank you.' She cleared her throat. 'All of you.'

'I'm going to run now,' Robbie said gravely, and then proceeded to do precisely that. Chase followed at his heels.

She turned back to Aidan to find those molten amber eyes surveying her. 'Thank you for keeping them entertained.'

'It was no big deal.'

He lifted a shoulder, which only alerted her to the fact that while he might not have the physique of a bodybuilder, his shoulders had breadth and his chest didn't lack for depth.

*Oh, stop it.* She dug fingernails into her palms. A man let her sleep for an hour and she became a sex maniac? *I don't think so.*

'The boys and I had fun. You obviously didn't sleep well last night and I expect the last few weeks have been hectic with the preparations for the move. You're entitled to some downtime too.'

And for the first time in a long time she caught a glimpse of what it must be like to co-parent rather than having to do it all on her own. The vision was unbelievably beguiling.

A man let her sleep for an hour so she built family fantasies about him? She bit back a snort. *I don't think so.* Those fantasies were nothing but a big fat lie. In her experience, most men couldn't be trusted to stick to something as important as fatherhood and even if Aidan proved to be one of the exceptions he never would with her.

And she sure as heck wouldn't with him! Nothing— *nothing*—would ever induce her back into his world and that privileged circle again. She could see it already—the claims of his job would eventually take precedence over his wife and any children he might have. In effect, his wife would be a single parent. Mind you, she'd have the money to hire nannies, but what were nannies to a parent's love? Quinn refused to raise her children in a world where social status and professional prestige were more important than the warmth and intimacy of family ties.

She bit into another slice of apple and glared at a nearby stunted tree, grateful Aidan hadn't connected her with the Sydney Lavertys. It wasn't something she publicised and it certainly wasn't something she wanted to talk about.

But the memory of his world brought her back to herself. It reminded her of all of his responsibilities and duties. 'How was your mother when you rang her last night?'

He grimaced.

This was one of the many things she'd considered in the wee small hours when sleep had refused to come. 'I thought about her last night.'

He lifted a brow. 'And?'

'I think you need to give her a task, something concrete to do.'

'To take her mind off...other things?'

'It's hard to brood when you're busy.'

He considered her words and very slowly the line around his mouth eased. 'I could get her to double check the arrangements with the caterers and—'

'I was thinking—'

She broke off and flushed. 'Sorry, that was rude of me. I have no right stomping on your ideas with my big fat hypothetical work boots.'

'I'd like to hear your idea.'

He would? She glanced up to find him watching her closely and it occurred to her that he wouldn't have been nearly as open if he'd known her. But as they'd never clap eyes on each other again—well, she might see him on the television but that didn't count—after the next few days it was almost as if they were in a bubble. A bubble that had no impact or relevance on their real day-to-day lives. And when they returned to those real lives there'd be barely a ripple of this time to ruffle the surface.

It was unbelievably freeing. She understood that.

It was also unutterably sad, which she didn't understand at all.

She shrugged that off and dragged her attention back to the conversation. 'I just think you need to give your mother something to do that she can't shrug off as unimportant or that she can delegate to someone else.'

'You think she considers the party unimportant?'

Yikes! She'd need to tread carefully. Aidan had been through enough and she had no wish to hurt his feelings. Before she could roll out a tactful response, though, he said, 'You think the party is making me feel better, but not my mother.'

'I don't know your mother, Aidan, so I can't possibly comment on that.' He leaned away from her. Lines of strain fanned out from his mouth and it made her heart clench. 'I bet it's making your father feel better.'

His head snapped up, confirming her suspicions. She made herself smile. 'And that's no mean feat, surely?' The man had lost his child too.

Air rushed out of him. 'Dad and I concocted the party idea between us.' He lifted a hand as if to push it back through his hair, but he let it drop as if he didn't have the energy for it. 'It's given us something else to focus on.'

Her heart thumped. 'Aidan?'

He looked up.

'A party, no matter how ritzy and beautiful, or how well-meaning, won't…'

'Won't make up to my mother for losing a son,' he said, blunt and emotionless.

She tried not to flinch.

'You must think I'm an unbelievable idiot, and shallow to boot, to think a party would help.'

'I think you're worried about your mother and want to see her happy.'

He met her eyes.

'But I think you might be better served giving her something to do that *she* thinks is important. I mean as important as your desire to cheer her up is to you.'

He mulled her suggestion over for a moment. She could see his mind ticking over, but she had no idea what conclusion he came to. 'You make a good case.' The faintest of smiles touched his lips and something inside her unclenched a fraction. 'I take it you have had a thought or two on that head as well.'

'Well…yes.'

The smile grew a millimetre or two bigger. 'C'mon then, out with it.'

She pulled in a breath. 'I asked myself what your mother would consider important and I didn't have to go far to find it—you. She's invested in your happiness and your welfare, yes?'

His lips twisted. 'Yes.'

'Therefore, I expect your career is of prime importance to her.'

He closed his eyes and just like that any trace of a smile vanished. Her throat tightened as if a fist squeezed about it. She wasn't sure what she'd said wrong, but she had no intention of adding to her travelling companion's heartache. She straightened and eased back. 'I'm sorry. Like I said before, this is none of my business and I have no right—'

'I would like to hear what you have to say.'

She bit her lip but his gaze held hers so steadily that eventually she nodded. 'I was thinking that you should ask her to go into your office to oversee the daily operations of your campaign while you're not there.'

'I have staff to do that!'

'You could tell her that you respect your staff, but that you trust her rather than them to have your best interests at heart.' She rubbed her right hand back and forth across her left. 'You could tell her that you believe she was one of the reasons your father was elected when he ran for office back in the nineties. You could tell her that if she can find the time and has the heart for it, that it would mean the world to you if she would help you run your campaign.'

He'd gone grey. 'It's the one thing I've been avoiding.'

She bit her lip but the question slipped out anyway. 'Why?'

He stared up at the sky for a long moment. 'Selfish reasons.'

She bit her lip so hard then that nothing could slip out.

He straightened and pushed his shoulders back. 'You're right, though. That's precisely the kind of thing that would give her another focus. Dad and I have been wrapping her in cotton wool and that's the last thing she needs right now. What she needs is to be busy with some project close to her heart.'

'It's not selfish to want to protect the people we love. It's natural.'

He reached out to grip her shoulder, squeeze it, but his smile didn't reach his eyes. 'You're wise beyond your years. Thank you.'

She frowned. 'You're welcome.'

His hand remained on her shoulder and every nerve in her body sprang to life, making her breath hitch. He stilled and then his gaze speared to hers. He took in the expression on her face and that hot caramel gaze of his lowered to her lips. Something inside her started to tremble and gasp and her blood quickened in a sweet rush of need.

His eyes darkened. Hunger flared in their depths. His gaze locked to hers. 'Quinn?' He leaned towards her.

She tried to shake her head, to negate the question in his eyes, but her body refused to cooperate with her common sense. Her lips parted. If she leaned towards him...

A stream of childhood laughter reached her and it gave her just enough strength to close her eyes and lower her chin. Aidan removed his hand and eased back, but his scent—all spice and woods—wove around her, and she started to ache. She heard him climb to his feet. If she just whispered his name...

'Probably time for us to hit the road again.'

She snapped her eyes open and steeled her spine. She gave a swift nod of agreement. Excellent idea. She didn't say the words out loud, though. She didn't trust her voice not to betray her.

They reached Norseman at five o'clock.

Norseman had a population of sixteen hundred and was one of the few towns on the Nullarbor Plain with decent facilities. Quinn had called ahead to book her and the boys a caravan for the night. Tonight, regardless of how hard her bunk might prove to be, she'd be asleep by the time her head hit the pillow.

She and the boys had hamburgers for dinner. She allayed her guilt by telling herself they were on their holidays.

She didn't know where Aidan ate. Or when. Her efforts to avoid him had met with spectacular success. She suspected that was due to the fact that she had his full cooperation on that front.

She thought of that moment again—the moment when they might have kissed—and her breath jammed. How much she'd wanted to kiss him! But kissing Aidan was out of the question. The world he belonged to had betrayed her before. She wasn't giving it a chance to hurt her again.

Thank heavens for Robbie and Chase. They kept her

busy, claiming most of her attention and giving her little time to brood. However, they both fell asleep before seven o'clock. Quinn might be tired, but seven o'clock was far too early for a grown woman to go to bed.

She glanced around the caravan, rubbed her hands together a few times, picked up a magazine and then put it down again. She was too wired. With a glance at the sleeping boys, she eased the door to their caravan open and slipped outside. If the insects weren't too fierce she could sit out here at one of the picnic tables for a bit and lap up the quiet.

And the quiet was amazing. So was the dark. It had never been this dark in her suburb in Perth. She glanced up and her jaw dropped. She took a few steps forward. Stars, magnificent in their brightness and multitude, stretched across a navy dark sky and she wasn't sure she'd ever seen anything so spectacular in all her life.

'It takes your breath away, doesn't it?'

Aidan! She half turned but kept her gaze firmly fixed on the stars. *He* stole her breath. 'They're amazing.' And if her breath came out a tad husky she'd blame it on the night air and the majesty of the sky.

'I was hoping you'd be out here.'

That made her look at him.

He held a bottle of wine in one hand and two wine glasses in the other. Her mouth dried. 'Aidan,' she croaked. 'I—'

'It's just a glass of wine, Quinn. That's all, I promise.'

Without another word, she took a seat at the table he gestured to and accepted a glass of wine with a murmured, 'Thank you.' She couldn't help it. There was something about this man she trusted.

'Cheers.' He raised his glass. She raised hers back. They both sipped...and grimaced. 'Sorry,' he murmured. 'There wasn't a whole lot of choice at the hotel.'

'Don't apologise. This is nice.' She gestured to the bottle. 'Makes me feel like a grown-up.'

Which, perhaps, wasn't the message she should be broadcasting. 'I mean it's such a change from sitting holding a toy car or a super-soaker or someone's crayon that—'

'I knew what you meant.'

His words, soft and warm in the dark, skimmed the bare surface of her arms and neck and she had to suppress a shiver. A *sexy* shiver. For heaven's sake, she had to find a way to get over this stupid awareness. She glanced at Aidan. And this stupid awkwardness. She'd been fine before she'd started lusting after him. She'd been fine when they'd been talking about his mother.

Speaking of which…

'Have you spoken to your mother tonight?'

'Yes.'

He didn't elaborate. She bit the inside of her cheek and then took a hasty sip of wine. 'It improves on a second tasting,' she offered.

He suddenly laughed. 'You're minding your manners beautifully. To answer the question you refuse to ask, your little suggestion has worked a treat. My mother is racing into my office first thing tomorrow to make sure everything is shipshape. And heaven help my staff if it's not.'

'Have you warned them?'

'Oh, yes.'

'And your mother seemed…' Happy was too much to hope for. 'Engaged?'

'Yes,' he murmured. 'Yes, she did.'

'Well, that's good isn't it?' He sounded pleased and not pleased at the same time.

'Of course it's good.'

He didn't add anything else.

Okay. Um…

Quinn went back to staring at the stars until the silence

chafed too badly. She risked a glance at her travelling companion and found him staring into his wine glass with pursed lips.

'So…uh…are you staying at the caravan park too?'

'I'm staying in one of the cabins here.'

He didn't say anything else. It took all her willpower to stop from jiggling her legs. Tonight this silence with Aidan was too fraught. She wanted the distraction of conversation. 'So…' She decided against asking if his cabin was nice or not. It might be a step up from a caravan, but she expected it would still be fairly basic. 'Have you always wanted to be a politician?'

'No.' The word shot out of him. A moment later his head snapped up. 'I mean, I know that's what the Fairhalls do and what we're known for, but it was always Daniel's passion, not mine.'

A sliver of ice traced a path down her back. 'What were you doing before you made the move to politics?'

'I was a lawyer.'

'Oh?' She injected every ounce of curiosity and interest that she could into that single syllable.

'I worked for a big firm in Sydney that prided itself on its social conscience.' He named the firm.

'I've heard of them!'

'Yeah.' He grinned crookedly and it flipped her heart right over. 'We made the news a lot. We'd take on high profile cases and charge through the nose so we could afford to subsidise the cases we were really interested in.'

'You guys did great work.'

'We did.' He sobered. 'They still do.'

Without him. And that was the moment she realised what he wasn't saying. 'You're keeping the family tradition alive by giving all of that up and going into politics.'

He glanced up as if he'd heard the censure in her voice. 'I will do good work in politics too, Quinn.'

'I don't doubt it.' But at what cost to himself?

The silence between them stretched. Eventually she cleared her throat. 'You know what you said to me yesterday afternoon about who I reminded you of?'

He stilled.

'Is that a good thing or a bad thing?' Did it bring him pain to spend time in her company?

His lips lifted. It was as if she'd removed a weight from him. He met her gaze. 'A good thing.'

She didn't know what to say after that.

He went to top up her glass but she snatched it up and shook her head. 'I really should go to bed now.'

'It's not even eight o'clock.' He set the wine bottle down with an audible thump. 'What are you afraid of, Quinn? That I'm going to make a pass at you and pressure you to have sex with me?'

The thought filled her with a heat almost impossible to ignore, although she did her best to do precisely that. 'I don't want to give you the wrong impression.'

'You're not.'

She leaned towards him. 'I haven't done anything impulsive in a very long time. To be honest, me and impulsive are barely on speaking terms these days. But this trip, and you, it feels as if...'

'What?'

He'd stilled but she recognised the hunger burning deep in his eyes. 'This trip feels like a timeout from the real world, and it feels as if what happens now couldn't possibly affect the future.'

'And that scares you.'

'You're darn tootin' it scares me. I know it's an illusion, a lie. How on earth do you think I ended up single with two children?'

Even in the dark she could see the way he paled.

'Aidan, we're from two different worlds.' Which wasn't

precisely true. 'And we're on two different paths.' Which was. 'You're a politician who certainly doesn't want to blot his copybook by doing something reckless. And I'm a single mum who can't afford the luxury of recklessness.'

She stared down at her hands. 'I've turned my whole world upside down and there's a part of me that's screaming in panic. I like you, you're a very attractive man, but I don't want to go looking for comfort and reassurance where I shouldn't. Experience warns me it will only get me into trouble.'

'I don't want to cause you any trouble, Quinn.'

'I know that.' She rose. 'Which is why I'm going to bed. I'll see you in the morning. Thank you for the wine.'

He didn't say anything, but she could feel the weight of his gaze and it slowed her steps. But it didn't stop them.

# CHAPTER FOUR

AIDAN MADE COFFEE—instant—from the complimentary jug and tiny sachets in his cabin. The cheap shorts and T-shirt he'd bought at a discount store in Norseman's surprisingly adequate shopping strip yesterday scraped scraped against his skin with an unfamiliar stiffness. That said, they were strangely comfortable, even if they didn't fit as well as the closetful of designer clothes he had in his apartment in Sydney. He slid on his brand new tennis shoes and, mug in hand, headed outside.

The harsh Outback light bouncing off caravan windows made him blink and he had to squint until his eyes adjusted. He'd slept later than he'd meant to, but with the easy, unhurried hours Quinn kept he didn't think that'd be a problem. He glanced around and something tugged at him, something off-key that he couldn't identify. Stifling a yawn, he shrugged it off. This whole situation was strange and off-key.

He ambled up and down the line of cabins and caravans for a bit, reminding himself to get what exercise he could. Mind you, they were only going as far as Madura today—less than six hours of driving. He spent twice that long in his office chair most days.

For pity's sake, they were still only eight hours from Perth! They had another twenty to go before they reached Adelaide. That was what was off-key—this plodding, leisurely pace. He sipped coffee and then frowned. No, what was off-key was his easy acceptance of it.

He closed his eyes and shadows danced behind his eyelids as he acknowledged his utter disinterest in returning to Sydney and his wretched campaign.

But the way his mother's voice had quickened on the phone last night. He forced his eyes open again. Her immediate interest and concern had pulled her out from beneath a morass of apathy. Just like that.

It was why he'd bought the wine. It was why he'd sought out Quinn's company. He'd been searching for solace and reassurance.

*Liar.*

He blinked.

*You wanted her. You still want her. You hoped—*

No he didn't! His head reared back. He…

His brain synapses slowed to the consistency of cold treacle. Realisation spread like a toxic chill. He *did* find Quinn attractive. *Very* attractive. From the moment when he'd nearly kissed her yesterday he hadn't been able to get the thought of what she'd taste like out of his mind.

He scratched a hand through his hair and scowled at his feet. Why had he hidden his motives behind a barricade of petty justifications and oh-woe-is-me excuses?

His lungs suddenly cramped. Because of Danny? Because Danny was no longer around to pursue and woo a pretty woman?

For a moment he thought he might throw up.

And then, out of all the spinning chaos in his mind, one tiny shard of comprehension detached itself. That sense of wrongness when he'd stepped out of his cabin…

He spun, coffee flying out in an arc around him. Her car was gone. Quinn's car was gone. She'd left him. *Abandoned* him!

Air punched out of his lungs. He bent at the waist, resting a hand against his knee, while he fought to get oxygen back into his body. He'd screwed up. *Royally.* Quinn's every instinct last night had been spot on. He might've lied to himself, but she'd seen through him. He'd gone looking for temporary respite in its nearest available form—Quinn.

Why? Because he'd felt backed into a corner after that phone call with his mother? What on earth did that have to do with Quinn? *Nothing!*

He straightened. Taking, that was all he'd been interested in. He deserved this. Totally deserved it. But…

He braced an arm against the side of Quinn's caravan—Quinn's *empty* caravan—and rested his head against it.

'Aidan?'

He lifted his head.

'Aidan?'

He jerked around.

Quinn!

'What's wrong?' Her brows drew together.

He glanced beyond her to see the station wagon parked on the other side of the caravan. Robbie and Chase loitered nearby. 'I, uh…just waking up. Where have you been?' His voice came out on a croak.

'Just into town to grab some supplies. This is the last decent-sized town now until we reach Ceduna or Port Augusta.' She shrugged. 'On impulse we popped out to the Beacon Hill lookout.' She shifted her weight. 'I left a message for you at reception in case you were looking for us.'

Of course she had!

She frowned then and planted her hands on her hips. He didn't want her to question him too closely. 'What time do you want to set off?'

'Within the hour.'

'I'll…um…go get packed up.'

He stumbled back into his cabin and collapsed onto the sofa and dropped his head to his hands, his coffee mug still dangling from his fingers. He'd been given a second chance.

*Don't mess it up*!

Aidan intended on being the best darn travelling companion Quinn and her kids had ever had.

With his encouragement, the boys spent most of the first hour telling him about the Beacon Hill lookout. They'd seen salt lakes and giant mine tailing dumps. The view obviously hadn't been pretty, but it had certainly left an impression. He tried to squash the sense of having been left out. Instead he recalled his gratitude when he'd lifted his head to see Quinn standing in front of him this morning.

The talk moved from that lookout in particular to lookouts in general and Aidan found himself trying to describe the view from Corcovado in Rio de Janeiro.

And to then explaining that there weren't any tigers in South America, other than in zoos. Which in turn led to a discussion about zoos. The boys loved zoos—no surprises there. 'You should get your mum to take you to Taronga Park Zoo in Sydney once you've settled in. It'll only be a couple of hours in the car.'

'You live in Sydney,' Robbie said. 'You could come too.'

'If I'm free it's a date,' he promised.

Quinn glanced at her watch. 'Okay, you have an hour of Gameboy time if you want it.'

The boys were soon immersed in their games. She glanced at him, their eyes clashed for the merest fraction of a second before she whipped her gaze back to the road. Damn it! He didn't want her feeling tense around him. He wanted her relaxed and happy. Not because he wanted to seduce her, but because she was a nice woman who'd helped him out and she deserved good things in return.

He shifted on his seat, cleared his throat. 'I've gotta

say the variety and splendour of this scenery is something to behold.'

'Uh-huh. Dirt and scrub for as far as the eye can see. You could go a long way before seeing something so…'

'Appealing? Engaging? Captivating?' All words that could describe her. He cut off further musings in that direction. It wasn't going to happen.

'It's amazing, though, isn't it?' she said. 'It's so unvarying, so…unrelieved.'

'I think it's amazing anyone can eke a living out here.'

She puffed out a breath. 'I don't think I could live so far from civilisation.'

Polite chit-chat. Nothing threatening. He excelled at this stuff. He bit back a sigh.

From the corner of his eye he saw her glance at him again. He lifted his chin. 'Do you know we're now on the single longest piece of straight road in Australia?'

'A hundred and forty-six point six kilometres.'

She did know.

'Aidan, you're being great with the boys and I appreciate it, but I don't want you to feel as if you have to make promises to them.'

The change in topic threw him. 'I don't. I…' He stared at her. 'You mean the zoo?'

She nodded.

He rolled his shoulders and stared back out to the front. 'If you want the truth, I'd love to spend the day with you and the boys at the zoo.'

Her knuckles whitened around the steering wheel and he snatched back a curse. 'I've not had much to do with kids. I didn't know…'

She didn't look at him. 'What?'

'I didn't know how much fun they'd be or how much I'd enjoy their company.'

Her knuckles returned to their normal colour. 'Really?'

'I always figured I'd marry and have kids one day. I mean, it's what you do, isn't it?' He scraped a hand across his jaw. 'But… Now I *know* that's what I want.'

The softest of smiles touched her lips and an ache started up deep inside him. An ache that stretched and burned and settled in his groin. He shifted on the seat and did what he could to ignore it. 'I gotta tell you the conversation I had with the boys over hopscotch yesterday.'

He proceeded to tell her about Robbie's question and the plan they'd concocted between them, embellishing where he could until she was laughing so hard he had to reach out and help her steer for a moment.

'Oh, that's priceless.' She dabbed at her eyes—first with her left wrist and then with her right.

She had colour in her cheeks. She'd stopped biting her lip every other minute. He settled back into his seat and listened as she hummed along to a song on the radio. The view outside hadn't changed—still an unending expanse of sand and scrub—but it somehow looked brighter and more inviting than it had earlier.

They reached Madura late afternoon. They'd had what Chase quaintly phrased 'pit stops' at Balladonia and Caiguna. Settlements that were mere specks on the maps. Balladonia had a population of nine. Nine! That put the concept of isolation into perspective. The boys had a lot of fun choosing the nine people they'd most like to have in town…and the nine they'd least want.

Like the rest of the Nullarbor Plain, they were dry dusty places with that same endless low scrub. But they did have roadhouses and accommodation.

Madura was a little larger and some would say a little more scenic, situated as it was at the base of the Hampton Tablelands. As far as Aidan could tell, that just meant that the land undulated a bit more. They booked rooms at the motel and the boys were over the moon to discover it had a pool.

Which was how Aidan found himself wandering around outside the pool fence with Quinn while the boys splashed and whooped inside. Out of the corner of his eye he saw Robbie race from one end of the pool enclosure to the other as a run-up for a big jump into the water. It had been a long time since he could remember running for the sheer joy of it. He wouldn't mind running now.

He ran a finger around the collar of his T-shirt and reminded himself he was a grown man. 'Quinn, about last night…'

She tensed. She tensed so much she stopped walking.

He squinted at the sky. 'Last night I was feeling at a bit of a loss. I didn't know what to do with myself.'

She started a jerky forward motion again. 'Because of your conversation with your mother?'

'Do you think it's crazy of me to worry about her?'

'No.'

His collar stopped trying to strangle him.

She glanced at him. 'Do you read?'

'Sure I do. Not that I get much time for it.' When she raised an exaggerated eyebrow he had to nod. 'You're right, there's plenty of time for it at the moment.'

'If you're interested, I have a few books in the back of the car.'

Reading for pleasure had become a rare treat. He straightened. 'I'd love to borrow one.'

'C'mon, then.' She hitched her head in the direction of the car.

She moved with the grace of a gazelle, dainty and elegant, though neither of those things hid her supple strength. He had to force his gaze from the long length of her legs and back to his surroundings before he betrayed himself.

She shifted a couple of boxes in the wagon and then pointed. 'That box there, can you drag it out?'

He did. When he peered inside it his lip started to curl. 'Science textbooks?'

Her grin was sudden and swift and he thanked heaven he was leaning against the car or he might've fallen face first into the dirt. 'I worked in one of the science departments at the University of Western Australia and one of the professors had a clean-out of his bookshelves last week. I helped myself to a couple.'

Good Lord, why? He didn't ask, but she must've seen the question in his face. 'If you find such things dull and dry, they're guaranteed to put you to sleep in five minutes flat.'

She didn't find them dull or dry, though, did she? What had she meant to do with her life before fate had intervened in the shape of an unplanned pregnancy? He stared at the textbooks.

'Dig deeper.' She nodded at the box. 'There's quite a selection in there.'

He chose an autobiography of a famous actor. He turned it face out to show her. 'Do you mind? I've been wanting to read this for ages.'

'Help yourself.'

He packed the box back up and stacked it in its original position. When he finished he turned to find her leaning against the car with her eyes closed and her face lifted to the sun.

A breath eased out of him.

Her eyes sprang open. 'What?'

*Stop staring!* He shut the trunk. 'I was just thinking how much more relaxed you look today than you did yesterday or the day before.'

'Oh, that.' She blinked and then she smiled and it was such a beautiful smile the breath punched out of him all over again. There were moments when this woman smiled with her whole being, the way Daniel used to. It made him crave something he had no name for.

'When we set off from Perth I started having panic attacks wondering if I was doing the right thing or not.'

'And now?' His heart pounded though he couldn't have explained why.

'Now I've decided to embrace what's ahead of me—to enjoy it and make the absolute best of it.'

'Bravo!' No sooner had the word left his mouth than his mind started to whirl. Could he take a leaf out of her book, follow her example? Could he find a way to embrace the course set before his feet—the political life?

His legs and shoulders grew heavy. The day darkened, even though the sun remained high and warm above them.

They started walking again because their only two options were walking or sitting and they'd both had enough of sitting.

He supposed he could excuse himself and retire to his room with the book. He didn't want to, though. There'd be enough time for solitude later. He rolled his shoulders and tried to throw off his funk. 'What are you hoping to gain from your move, Quinn?' Considering her future—and the boys'—was a more promising option than trying to make sense of his. Still, he intended to retract the question if it made her look the least bit uncomfortable.

A breath eased out of him when it didn't.

She nodded towards the boys and he had to remind himself not to hold her gaze for too long. *Don't let her see how much you want to kiss her.*

He watched the two boys dive simultaneously into the pool. He clapped his hands and shouted praise.

He glanced from them and back to their mother. Steel flooded his spine. He was not going to mess with her. Him and her, they were on different courses and he had no intention of dragging her or her boys into his own private hell.

*What are you hoping to gain from your move?*

Aidan's words scored through her. Quinn twisted her hands together and watched her boys. They were so absorbed in their splashing and diving, and her heart filled with so much love it almost hurt.

She pointed a finger at Chase, who looked as if he was about to tear off down the other end of the enclosure. 'No running,' she said for the second time. 'Wet feet and wet concrete are not a good combination.' Her second son had a tendency to learn his lessons the hard way.

She glanced back to find Aidan watching her with a queer light in his eyes. She didn't know what it meant. Today he'd been so *friendly* that she'd started to think she'd been mistaken about the vibes she'd sensed last night.

*He might not want you, but you still want him.*

He must know lots of beautiful polished women. The idea of him being attracted to a single mother who wore next to no make-up and didn't give two hoots about designer outfits was laughable.

She tried to push that thought aside, tried to shake off the heaviness that threatened to descend and to concentrate on what really was important—her move across the country.

*What are you hoping to gain from your move?*

'Family,' she finally said. 'I'm hoping to give my boys, my aunt and myself a family.'

'Family,' he repeated, annunciating each syllable in a kind of slow homage to the word.

'You're close to your parents.' She wasn't sure if she was asking or stating.

'I guess.'

But he'd become guarded, wary, and her heart burned

for him. She refused to pry, though. He and his parents had suffered so much. She dredged up a smile and a shrug. 'I found myself watching my friends in Perth over the last year and seeing what a source of strength their families were to them. I'm talking about extended families—parents, grandparents, siblings, cousins, aunts and uncles—and I started to envy them.'

Somewhere along the line she'd stopped walking. She kicked herself back into action, forced one foot in front of the other. Aidan's long legs kept easy pace beside her. The sun had started to lower in the west and the scrub, low trees and sand all glowed orange and khaki. A sigh eased out of her. 'I know their families were occasionally—even often—a source of frustration, but they were a source of happiness too.' A source of belonging.

'And you want that?'

'Yes.' With all her heart and she wasn't ashamed to admit it. She knew her own strength. She knew she could continue to go it alone. But if she didn't have to...

'And as I only have one relation who is the slightest bit interested in wanting to know me...' She'd made her voice tongue-in-cheek, but Aidan didn't smile.

She reached out and pulled him to a halt. His arm flexed beneath her fingers and she sensed its latent strength. Reluctantly she released him. 'I'm tired of feeling alone, Aidan.'

She didn't know what it was about this man that made her so ready to confide in him. Maybe it was the innate 'ships passing in the night' nature of their association. It had broken down the usual barriers of reserve.

His face became gentle. He reached out as if to touch her cheek, but he drew his hand back at the last moment. The usual barriers hadn't broken down that much.

'Don't get me wrong.' She forced herself to start walking again. 'I'm not lonely. I have friends, colleagues, not to mention my boys. I'm not unhappy. It's just when I have to make a decision about one of the boys—should I go up to the school and make an issue about Chase's appalling handwriting or another child's constant use of a bad word, or should I let Robbie stay up late on the occasional Saturday night so he can watch a rugby test match, or any number of things like that. To be able to talk it over with someone who's also invested would be such a comfort. Even if we didn't agree.'

'Wow,' he eventually breathed.

She immediately cringed. 'Sorry, that was probably way more information than you wanted and—'

'Mum!'

Chase's scream and Robbie's shout had her spinning around, adrenaline flooding her every cell. Heart pounding, she raced for the gate, all instinct and fear.

Blood.

Blood in the water.

Chase in the water.

She tugged and tugged on the safety latch on the gate, but her fingers kept slipping and finding no purchase, as if she'd forgotten how to use an opposable thumb. Her breath came hard and short in little sobs. *Please, gate. Please open.*

It wouldn't open!

In one easy vault, Aidan cleared the fence and, without breaking stride, dived into the water and pulled Chase into his arms. 'He's okay,' he called to her.

Okay meant he wasn't drowned. It didn't mean he was *okay*.

Magically the gate opened and she flew to Aidan as he emerged with a howling Chase from the shallow end. There was so much blood!

She reached for him and Chase reached for her, but Aidan pushed her down onto the banana lounge that held the boys' towels and shirts before setting Chase onto her lap.

She held him close and rocked him, murmuring nonsense in an effort to quiet him, while Aidan tried to stem the blood from the cut above Chase's eye. She handed him one of the shirts she half sat on. They could replace a shirt, but she would never be able to replace one of her beautiful boys.

Her heart thunderstormed in her chest as she watched Aidan's face, trying to gauge the extent of the damage by his expression, but he kept his face carefully schooled and she couldn't read it at all.

Fear gripped her by the throat. If Chase were badly hurt…way out here in the back of beyond, it'd be her fault. *Please God. Please God. Please God.*

She glanced up to find Robbie staring at her with fear in his eyes. She did what she could to swallow her own. 'What happened, honey?'

Robbie scuffed a toe against the cement. 'He, um… slipped and hit his head on the side of the pool before falling in.'

They'd been running! She should've been keeping a closer eye on them! She should've been watching them properly, not pouring her heart out to the first man who'd shown a modicum of interest in her in months!

Aidan straightened and her gaze flew back to him. 'What?' She couldn't push anything else out.

'He's going to have a heck of a lump and a shiner tomorrow, and probably a corker of a headache tonight, but the cut's not deep and it won't need stitches.'

She closed her eyes and sent up a prayer of thanks. 'There was so much blood,' she whispered.

'Head wounds bleed a lot.' He sat back on his heels, a smile touching his lips. 'With two young sons, I'd have thought you'd have known that.'

Crazily, she found herself almost smiling back.

Chase's sobs had eased and Aidan gestured to him. 'I'd like to check him for concussion.'

'Hey, baby,' she crooned. 'Can you look at Mummy?'

Chase sat up a bit and touched his head. 'It hurts,' he hiccupped.

'I bet it does. That was a heck of a tumble,' she soothed, smoothing his hair back.

'There was blood.' His lip wobbled.

'You're not wrong about that, buddy.' Aidan crouched down in front of them. 'We're going to play a quick game.' He hurried on before Chase could refuse and bury his head in her shoulder again. 'How many fingers am I holding up?'

'Three.'

'What's my name?'

'Aidan.'

'And what comes after D in the alphabet?'

Chase started reciting the alphabet under his breath. 'E.'

'Excellent, Chase, you got a perfect score.'

Chase snuggled into her and started to shiver. Aidan grabbed a towel and wrapped it around the child. 'We need to get him warm and dry.'

'How do you know so much about this?' Aidan seemed so calm and professional—utterly unfazed, unlike her. Besides, talking kept the demons at bay.

'I did a St John's Ambulance course six months ago.'

She struggled to her feet. In another year Chase would be too big for her to carry. But she could still manage it at the moment. 'What made you decide to do that? Not that I'm not grateful, of course, but—'

She broke off. Daniel. The car accident.

Right.

In his grief, Aidan had chosen to do something positive rather than negative. Good for him.

'Thank you,' she murmured when he opened the gate for her.

'You're welcome.'

And then he draped a towel around the shoulders of a too quiet Robbie and rested his arm across her eldest son's shoulders in a gesture of comfort and companionship and walked them back to their room.

It didn't make her knees weak. It didn't make her pulse quicken. But it did make her heart tremble.

Aidan was sitting to one side of her door in a camp chair when she slipped out of her room that night. He rose and set another chair out for her.

And then he handed her a can of beer.

And a chocolate bar.

Tears pricked her eyes. A big lump lodged in her throat, making it impossible to squeeze out so much as a thank you. She sat.

'Thought you could do with a pick-me-up.'

She nodded, sniffled and pulled in a breath that made her entire frame shudder. And then she opened her beer and took a gulp. She tore open the wrapper of her chocolate bar and took a big bite.

She closed her eyes, sat back and let the tension drain out of her. She drank more beer. She ate more chocolate. It was a disgusting combination and she relished every single mouthful.

Aidan sat with his legs stretched out and eyes to the front, quietly surveying the night. No rush or impatience or expectation. His stillness slowly eased into her. She finished both the beer and the chocolate bar. 'That's exactly what I needed.'

'Good.'

'Thank you.'

'You're welcome.'

She turned to him as much as her tired limbs would allow. 'I want to thank you for springing into action so quickly today.'

'It was no big deal.'

'It was a huge deal to me. I couldn't even get the rotten gate open.'

'You would've eventually.'

She shuddered. 'Chase could've drowned by then.'

'Stop exaggerating,' he chided. 'He was holding his head out of the water when I got to him.'

He had been? A little more of the residual fear eased out of her.

'He was just a bit dazed and in pain. How is he now?'

'Asleep, thankfully. They were both exhausted.'

'And how are you?'

She sent him a wan smile. 'Well, I've slowed down on the blame game and I'm slowly recovering from the fright.' She stared out towards the scrub beyond the circle of light cast from the motel, but she couldn't see a thing. It was all deep blackness. 'I never knew I could feel so afraid until I had children.'

'Did I really say earlier that I wanted them?'

She laughed. 'It's worth it.' But not if you worked in excess of eighty hours a week. She glanced at him. She opened her mouth. She closed it again. *None of your business.*

They were both silent for a while. 'Funny, isn't it?' she eventually said. 'How love and pain can be so closely linked. Not just romantic love, but love for one's children and parents and friends.'

Though this man knew more about that than most. 'Still—' she pulled in a breath '—life's not worth living without it.'

'Which makes the human race either incredibly stupid or incredibly brave.'

'I'll go with brave if they're the only two options on offer.'

She was rewarded with a lopsided grin and a shake of his head.

'I thought you were very brave today. I'm in your debt, Aidan. I doubt I'll ever be able to repay you, but if there's anything I can do…ever…'

He turned to her and behind the tempting brightness of his eyes she sensed his mind racing. 'There might be one thing you could do…'

The look on his face made her breath catch and her stomach do slow loop the loops.

He wouldn't!

He rose. 'I'll give it some thought and let you know in the morning. Goodnight, Quinn.'

She could only stare after him, wondering what on earth he was playing at. Or if he was playing at anything at all.

# CHAPTER FIVE

THE NEXT MORNING Quinn and the boys enjoyed a picnic breakfast at a table near the pool. It wasn't fancy—cereal and toast. Quinn had lugged cereal and long-life milk with her from Perth. She'd bought fresh bread from the road-house that morning.

While it might not be fancy, the warm morning and the novelty filled the boys with glee and took their minds off eating in the roadhouse restaurant. It wasn't that she needed to count every penny, but she did want to be careful. Besides, she wanted them to eat as healthily as she could manage whilst on the road.

She was blowing on her coffee when Aidan sauntered into view. The steam floated up into her face, haloing him in a smoky soft focus. He looked like a mirage, like a man walking out of the desert. A sigh breathed out of her and more steam drifted upwards.

She shook herself and then blew on her coffee until the steam blinded her. When he reached the table, she smiled in his direction, but took a moment to hand Robbie a paper napkin so she didn't have to address him. Of course, that didn't block his scent when he sat beside her. She breathed him in, and the knot in her chest unwound.

'Morning, troops.'

The boys sing-songed their greetings back to him through mouthfuls of Vegemite toast.

'Have you eaten?' She sort of half glanced at him. His hair was damp as if he'd just showered and he wore a different T-shirt than he had yesterday. The T-shirt had obviously come in a packet and two creases bisected his chest and another his stomach. He looked utterly different from the man who'd begged her for a ride. Her father wouldn't have approved. She did, wholeheartedly.

'Help yourself.' She gestured to the cereal boxes and pile of toast. 'There's another cereal bowl in our room if you'd like it.'

He nodded behind him to the roadhouse. 'I've already eaten.'

She hoped his breakfast had been healthy. She opened her mouth. She closed it again. *None of your business*.

He glanced at their table. 'But this looks nice.'

She couldn't mistake his wistfulness, though it was harder to explain the burn in her heart. 'Well, you're absolutely welcome to join us for soggy cereal and cold toast tomorrow.'

He laughed as she'd meant him to, but the burn in her heart only intensified.

He glanced at Chase. 'How's the head, buster?'

'It's better.' He glowered at Quinn. 'I keep telling Mum I'm all better and that I can go swimming in the pool again, but she won't listen.'

She had to bite back a smile. Both of her children would need to be seriously under the weather to resist the lure of a swim.

'Your mum is probably right. A quiet day could be just the thing.'

Chase heaved a sigh, evidently exasperated with clueless adults.

'Which is why I want to run a proposal by you all.'

Aidan ran a hand down his shirt as if to smooth out the

creases and she suddenly realised she'd been staring. She shook herself. 'Proposal?'

His look told her he was thinking of last night and her 'returning the favour' remark. The boys glanced to her and she sat up a little straighter. 'We're all ears.'

'I was thinking we could all do with a day off from driving.'

She'd been working on the theory that it'd take them ten days to reach Aunt Mara's, longer if they decided to tarry somewhere. With the NSW school holidays currently operating, the boys weren't missing any school. This was only day four of their great 'across the country' expedition, so they weren't even halfway through their journey yet, but she didn't say anything. She was too curious to see what Aidan meant to propose.

In the morning sunshine his eyes twinkled. It could've been the reflection cast up from the pool, but she didn't think so. She had a feeling it came from within. She hadn't seen him fired up with enthusiasm before, except for that moment when he'd talked about his law firm. Now, though, he smiled and twinkled and she could barely drag her gaze away. An answering enthusiasm built through her. 'A day off?'

He leaned in towards her, his smile growing and she pulled in a great breath of him. 'I know you don't want to drive longer than five hours a day if you can help it…'

They'd had to drive five and a half yesterday. It made the boys restless. And look at what had happened at the pool afterwards.

'But if we drove to Penong today—'

'How long?'

'A bit over six hours.'

She grimaced and gestured for him to continue. 'The thing is, Penong is close to a place called Cactus Beach.'

'A beach!' Robbie and Chase gazed at her as if pleading for her to accept any proposal that included a beach.

'Cactus Beach is well known in surfing circles.'

Aidan was a surfer? Really?

'If we drive to Penong today, we could spend all of tomorrow at the beach.'

'So…we'd spend two nights at Penong before heading for Port Augusta?'

'That's right.'

The lure of not having to pack up everything for a whole day spoke to her. Loudly.

The boys started shouting out their excited endorsements of Aidan's plan, interspersed with lots of pleading and assurances that Chase was better and that they'd be extra good.

A whole day at the beach? It sounded wonderful. This was exactly the kind of adventure she'd hoped for on their journey. Her boys' excited faces almost sealed the deal, but she forced herself to pull back. It was harder than it should've been. 'What about your burning need to get to Adelaide asap?'

Robbie scowled at Aidan. 'Why you wanna do that? Aren't you having fun with us?'

'I'm having the best time,' Aidan assured him. 'And I have another song to teach you later.'

Robbie's scowl vanished.

Aidan ran his hand down the crease in his T-shirt again. She tried not to follow his hand's progress. 'I think my absence in the office for another couple of days could be a…' The happy light in his eyes faded a little. 'A good thing.'

Why should that leach the happiness from him?

She glanced down at her toast. She'd had a thought or two on that head, but… *It's none of your business.* Then she recalled the way he'd vaulted the pool fence and the way he'd lifted Chase into his arms.

She could make it her business.

At the beach.

'It sounds like the best idea ever.' She crossed her fingers. Aidan grinned. The boys cheered.

She turned to Robbie and Chase. 'It does mean a long time in the car today.'

'We promise to be good.' Robbie nudged Chase, who nodded enthusiastically. 'If we get grumpy we'll just think of the beach and we'll be happy again. It'll make it all worth it.'

Oh, how she wished she could've given them more fun, more outings and holidays in their short lives. She swallowed a lump. 'Okay, then. Let's get this mess cleaned up and start packing.'

They reached Cactus Beach at the end of a long dirt road. The landscape surrounding them amazed Quinn. Nullarbor translated from the Latin to mean no trees and today it definitely lived up to its reputation. Rocks, low scrub and amazing sand dunes stretched out on all sides. When the beach came into view, nobody uttered a word.

A crescent of white sand with rocky outcrops at either end and a sea of jewelled blues and greens spread out before them like an ancient Mecca. It was utterly deserted. And it was utterly beautiful.

The boys just stared at it with their mouths agape. Aidan folded his arms and grinned. She let out a long, low, pent-up breath.

Aidan swung to them, his grin widening. 'Cactus Beach has three perfect surfing breaks—Castles and Cactus which are both left-handers and Caves which is a powerful right hand break.'

'And that's good?'

'It's epic!'

Right. 'I hate to rain on your parade, but you, uh, don't have a surfboard with you.'

He shook his head. 'Doesn't matter. I can now say I've been here.'

Robbie and Chase broke free from their enthralment long enough to tug at her, their excitement palpable. 'Can we, Mum? Huh, can we?'

She'd already slathered them both in sunblock back at their on-site van in Penong. It might be late March, but the sun shone with all of its usual enthusiasm and the faint breeze was warm with the memory of summer. 'Okay, give me your shirts and off you go.'

Both boys raced straight for the water.

She could tell Aidan itched to hit the waves as much as her children did. Still, he waited for her to choose the perfect patch of sand before setting down the cooler bag that practically burst with their supplies for the day. She'd packed sodas, water, sandwiches and fruit. She'd even splurged on cheese and crackers.

'Go on.' She gave him a playful push. 'I can tell you're as eager to be out there as Robbie and Chase.'

She glanced at the boys. For all of his talk of big breaks, the surf was remarkably gentle today.

He flashed a grin that made her heart stutter before dragging his shirt over his head and revealing a perfectly toned torso. Wind instantly rushed in her ears, filling her head with noise. She stared, pressing hands to cheeks that had grown red-hot. With a start she pulled them away and pushed them into the small of her back instead and pretended to stretch, praying he hadn't noticed her heat and confusion...her desire.

She sent up a prayer of thanks when she finally managed to make her eyes focus. He just stood there as if relishing the feel of the sun against his bare skin. She glanced away, having to fight the urge to reach out and touch him.

For all his talk of castles and caves and whatnot, he wasn't what she'd call tanned for this time of year. Exactly how many hours was he putting in at that office of his?

Her lips twisted. At the moment she'd bet eighty-hour weeks were a conservative guess. The thought made her shudder. It eased the burn threatening to consume her too. He might have a hot body—the hottest she'd seen in a very long time—and he might be a nice man—the nicest she'd come across in a very long time—but his lifestyle was repugnant to her. Why would someone embark on a relationship with a man like him? You'd never see him long enough to enjoy the hot body or to indulge in long, intimate conversations.

Why? Her lips twisted. Status, standing and prestige, not to mention wealth. That was why. And none of that could tempt her.

He took a step towards the water. 'I hope you're wearing sunscreen.' As soon as the words left her mouth, she realised how ludicrous they were. The man had been trying to get a flight out of Perth. One thing he hadn't been doing was planning a beach holiday.

He turned back and his grin when it came was low and wicked. She wanted to respond. She wanted to take the bottle of lotion from her bag, amble over to him with a sinuous swing of her hips and slowly rub lotion into his shoulders, his back and his chest. She'd like to—

She snapped herself out of her fantasy—reminded herself about eighty-hour working weeks—seized the bottle of sunscreen and tossed it to him.

'Are you coming in?' he asked when he was done, handing the bottle back to her.

He hadn't been able to reach all of his back. *Not your problem.*

With a sigh she took the bottle from him and poured lotion into her hand. She didn't need a travelling companion with a serious case of sunburn. Or sunstroke. She slathered it on his back with as much cool efficiency as she could muster. Reciting the periodic table in her mind helped.

'Would you like me to return the favour?'

She recapped the bottle a little too vigorously. 'Uh, no thank you. Robbie and Chase took care of it earlier.'

'So, are you coming in?'

That was when she realised she'd been biting her lip the entire time. She released it. 'Sure I am. In a bit.' She couldn't explain why, but she didn't want to pull her sundress over her head to stand in front of him in nothing but her birthday suit.

*Bathing suit!* Lord, talk about a Freudian slip.

She was a mother. She had responsibilities. Ignoring Aidan, she walked down to the shore to paddle and keep an eye on the boys. She was no longer that impulsive girl who'd let passion rule her head. Even if a remnant of that girl remained in the woman she'd become.

Eventually, though, the lure of the water became too much and she tossed her dress to the sand. She splashed with the boys. She laughed and relaxed and forgot to worry about anything for a while.

Chase didn't have Robbie's confidence in the surf, but he begged her to take him out to the deeper water. Robbie wanted to go out too. He was a good swimmer, but if either one of them got into trouble she'd be hard pressed to deal with the both of them. She was about to suggest she take them out one at a time, but suddenly Aidan was there with a summer grin and holiday eyes.

'Hey, Robbie, you wanna learn how to body surf?'

'Yes!'

So they all moved into the deeper water beyond the break of the waves. The gentle rolling of the swell rocked them and it eased the frenetic craziness of the last few weeks. She gave Chase a swimming lesson, and then they both floated for a while. She turned her head to watch Aidan and Robbie.

A laugh spurted out of her oldest son and then he looked up at Aidan as if...

She straightened. Her heart caught and then vibrated with sudden pain. Aidan was all kindness and attention and her eldest son was blossoming under that influence. In fact, Robbie lapped up every scrap of Aidan's attention like a starving dog.

Her eyes stung. She knew he hungered for this kind of male bonding. If only Phillip would spend more time with his sons!

'Ow, Mum, you're hurting my hand!'

She immediately relaxed her grip on Chase's hand. 'Sorry, honey.'

'Can we go in so I can jump over the waves again?'

'Sure we can.'

She and Chase jumped waves, but the entire time she could see her eldest son's hero worship growing—it was reflected in the way he laughed too loudly, the way he gazed up at Aidan, and in his absolute lack of self-consciousness as he came out of his usual reserved shell.

Damn it! Why couldn't she be everything her sons needed? Why couldn't she be both mother and father to them? She didn't want them to lack for anything and it wasn't right that they should.

She re-tied her ponytail. She only had one set of arms and one set of legs, though, and there were two of them and some days she was spread too thin as it was.

'Are you okay?'

She jumped to find Aidan beside her, staring down at her with narrowed eyes. She spun and located both Robbie and Chase. 'Yes, I'm perfect.'

'I'll second that.' He grinned down at her and it snapped her out of her funk in an instant. The remnant of the reckless girl she'd once been gave a long, low stretch. Her common sense raised an eyebrow. She had to bite back a groan. If she weren't careful she'd end up with a serious case of hero worship too.

Robbie insisted on sitting next to Aidan when they had lunch. He argued about putting his shirt and hat back on, until Aidan put his shirt on too.

She liked Aidan. She liked him a lot, but it would do Robbie no good to become too attached to him. They'd see neither hide nor hair of Aidan once this adventure was over.

Aidan would return to his relentless workload and his social position and his prominence on the political landscape and he'd have no time for surfing with young boys.

She rested back on one hand and bit into an apple. 'I guess we'd best make the most of your company while we have it, Aidan. I mean in another two days we'll be in Adelaide.'

Robbie stared from Aidan to her. 'What happens in Adelaide?'

'The plane strike ended today so I guess Aidan will catch a plane back to Sydney.'

'But we could drop him off in Sydney in the car.'

'We could,' she agreed. It took an effort to keep the smile on her face and her voice breezy. 'But it'll take a few days longer and Aidan can't afford any more time off work.'

Aidan looked as if she'd slapped him. *Oh, Aidan…* She ached to reach out and hug him.

'Aidan could come visit us at Aunt Mara's.'

''Course he can,' she agreed. 'Just as soon as he has some free time.'

Robbie's face fell and she knew he was thinking of his father's endless litany of excuses for why he couldn't visit.

*Oh, Robbie…* She wanted to hug him and never let him go. But that wouldn't help him either, not in the long term.

'Hey, who wants to go and explore the rock pools over there?'

That distracted both of the boys. She packed up the remnants of their lunch before grabbing the can of soda she hadn't finished yet. The boys raced ahead.

'Are you looking forward to getting rid of me?'

The bluntness of Aidan's question shattered her carefully constructed veneer. 'Oh, Aidan, no.' She reached out to grip his arm. 'I don't know if you realise this or not, but Robbie is developing a serious case of hero worship where you're concerned.'

'I…' He blinked.

'You're being great with him. I don't want you to change the way you are…'

'But?'

She realised she still held him. She let him go. 'These aren't waters I've had to navigate before.' Adelaide loomed ahead like a dark cloud. 'I just want him to be prepared for when we do part company, that's all. I wasn't trying to make you feel unwanted.'

He grimaced and scratched a hand through his hair. 'Sorry, I'm not usually so touchy.'

But they'd been having the most perfect day and her words had obviously taken him off guard.

'I'm clueless—' he waved towards Robbie '—about the whole kid thing.'

'So am I some days.'

'What about their father? Where's he?'

'In London at the moment. When he's in Australia he's mostly in Sydney. His contact with the boys is erratic.' It was the politest way she could put it.

Aidan called Phillip such a rude name she snorted soda

out of her nose. Not that she disagreed with him. 'That's one way of putting it.'

'Sorry.'

'You are not.' But she didn't mind in the least. 'He claims that our living in Perth makes it difficult for him to visit. But now surely a two-hour drive north isn't too much of an effort when he is in the country. I'm hoping this move means Phillip will start spending more time with Robbie and Chase. God knows they crave it.'

He stopped and fixed her with those fiery amber eyes. 'That's the real reason you're moving, isn't it?'

He said it as if it were the most amazing thing. She wrinkled her nose and rolled her shoulders.

'It is, isn't it?'

It was part of it. So what? 'There are a whole host of reasons.'

He caught her hand, pulled her to a halt, turning her to face him. 'It is, isn't it?'

The warmth and sympathy in his eyes had a lump wedging in her throat. She wanted to fling herself into his arms and soak up some of his strength and goodness. But that way lay ruin, as her mother would so quaintly put it.

Instead she very gently disengaged her hand from his. She swallowed. When she was sure her voice would emerge normally she said, 'You know what I hate? That a vast section of our society still looks down on single mothers, thinking they're only out for what they can get. Phillip pays child support, yes. When he first left a part of me wanted no contact and no links, but that's not my decision to make. I have no right putting my pride before my children's welfare.'

Shading her eyes, she turned to survey the boys, who were both clambering over the rocks, safe and occupied. She swung back. 'Another woman once told me she thought it a form of child abuse for a woman to refuse child support from her child's father. She said it'd be depriving the child of a better financial future. And she's right.'

'And now you feel you owe Phillip?'

'No! I owe Robbie and Chase. I owe them a good future. It's my responsibility to ensure they have all the things they need.' And at the moment they ached for their father. At least, Robbie did, and in a couple of years so would Chase.

'But it seems to me that society doesn't commend women for making those kinds of sacrifices. And it seems to me that in the vast majority of cases it's women who do actually make the real sacrifices.'

He stared down at her, his eyes soft. Aidan would never abandon a child. She didn't know what made her so sure, only that she was.

'I think you're amazing. I think you're wonderful.'

She had no hope of hiding how much his words touched her. 'Thank you.'

'I—'

'No,' she warned, keeping her voice crisp. 'Don't lay the compliments on too thick or you'll spoil the effect.'

He laughed. It was a good sound.

'C'mon, let's see what the boys are up to.'

They'd walked five steps when he asked, 'What happened between you and Phillip?'

A sidelong glance told her he wasn't looking at her. In fact he was looking suspiciously nonchalant. Her pulse leapt. She tried to stamp on it. 'That's a story for another day when the boys are in bed.' And while she didn't mean them to, the words emerged as a pledge.

The rest of the day lived up to its perfect promise. They explored the beach. There was more swimming and eating. The boys built sandcastles and as the tide came in the surf built up into the perfect breaks that Aidan had spoken about earlier.

His eyes lit up. 'I'm going to come back here one day with a surfboard.'

The afternoon waned and the sun had started to sink into the sea to the west when she and Aidan drove two very tired boys back to Penong.

After showers and a makeshift dinner of beans on toast, Aidan built a campfire in the pit in front of their on-site vans—he'd chosen to hire the one beside hers rather than stay at the motel—and then produced a bag of marshmallows.

They sat around the fire and toasted marshmallows as if they were a real family. Her heart wanted to spring free to dance and twirl but she wouldn't let it.

'It's been the best day in the world,' Chase said, leaning against her.

'The very best,' Robbie said, leaning into her other side.

They both grew heavy with sleep. 'Bedtime, I think,' she murmured to Aidan.

Without asking, without even apparently thinking about it, he rose and lifted Robbie into his arms, waited until she'd lifted Chase into hers, before following her into the van and helping her put them to bed. Both boys were asleep before she and Aidan left the caravan.

It made the task so much easier with someone to help. If only... She shook her head. She shook her whole body. 'Soda?'

'I bought a bottle of wine.' He rubbed the back of his neck. 'I thought...'

He looked delightfully nonplussed. She shifted from one foot to the other and then finally nodded. 'A glass of wine would be lovely.'

They sat beside the dying embers of the fire and sipped wine, staring up into the majesty of a glittering sky. She knew he was still curious about her and her history, but he'd be too polite to ask again. Well, she had questions of her own, and if she talked first maybe he'd open up to her too.

She crossed her fingers.

'I discovered I was pregnant in the time between graduating high school and the start of the university academic year.' Though he didn't move, she sensed she had his full attention. 'To say it was a shock is an understatement. For everyone.'

'You didn't consider an abortion?'

'Sure I did. I was only eighteen. I was supposed to have my whole life in front of me. I had plans. Plans a baby would interfere with.'

'But?'

With his non-judgemental attitude, Aidan would make a very good politician. She wondered if he realised that. 'But my parents and Phillip's parents insisted I have an abortion.'

'And that got your back up?'

'Oh, yes. I sometimes wonder if I only went ahead with the pregnancy just to spite them.' She glanced at him. 'That's not a very edifying thought, is it?'

'And not something I believe for a minute.'

She smiled at the fire. Maybe not. There'd been a part of her that had started loving the child inside her the minute she'd found out she was carrying it. A part of her she hadn't been able to ignore.

'Did Phillip want you to have an abortion too?'

She sipped her wine and then leaned back on one hand. 'Actually, he was really good. He didn't pressure me at all. He was a reasonable human being back then.' She had hopes he'd become one again. 'He said he'd stick by me whatever my decision. I didn't find out for another three years that he'd hoped I'd choose the abortion.' That had been the same night he'd accused her of ruining his life.

'As I believe I mentioned before, my parents cut me off

completely when I refused to obey their ultimatum. They thought it'd bring me to heel, but it didn't. Phillip's parents weren't quite so harsh, but they counselled him to go to university as planned and to have minimal contact with me and the baby.'

'Nice.'

His sarcasm wrung a smile from her. 'They didn't cut him off, but they refused to acknowledge me and I wasn't welcome in their home.'

She crossed her legs. 'So we moved to Perth. He got a job in a bank as a teller. I did a short office admin course and picked up some temp work until the baby came. Robbie was three months old when I picked up some part-time work as an administrative assistant at the university and we put him into childcare two days a week.'

'It sounds tough.'

'Thousands of people do it every year.' She shot him a smile. 'It was a challenge to make ends meet, but we were young and…I loved him.'

Aidan didn't say anything. She glanced at him. 'Have you been in love?'

He shook his head.

'It's wonderful. It gives you wings. It gives you hope. And it can make you very determined. It makes the tough times worthwhile.' She sipped her wine—a cool, crisp Sauvignon Blanc that slipped down her throat smoothly. 'But when love goes bad it's terrible.'

'I'm sorry it went bad for you, Quinn.'

He earned a big fat Brownie point for not asking why it had gone bad. Her fingers tightened about her glass. If she shared that with him, though, maybe he would share with her. She could only try. 'Things were going fine until I fell pregnant with Chase. It sounds dreadfully irresponsible, doesn't it, but we'd used birth control both times I fell pregnant. I'm obviously disgustingly fertile.'

A low rumble left Aidan's throat. It eased the heaviness that threatened to settle over her.

'It was too soon for us to have another child.' And yet she'd felt the same love for it as she had for Robbie.

'Much too soon for us to have another baby,' she whispered again, almost to herself.

'What happened?'

'Phillip panicked.' She shrugged. 'He panicked throughout my pregnancy about how we'd make ends meet. He asked me to have an abortion. I refused. I wanted Robbie to have what I'd never had—a sibling.' A friend. 'Phillip kept right on panicking after Chase was born and he never connected with him the way he had with Robbie. I cut back on our expenses as much as I could, but…'

The fire blurred for a moment. Aidan reached over and took her hand. And bless him. He just waited. He didn't try to hurry her.

'I discovered his secret bank account. He told me it was his university fund. He hadn't been panicking about how we'd make ends meet at all. He was panicking that he might have to dip into his university fund.'

Air hissed from between Aidan's teeth.

'And then his parents pounced when Phillip was at his weakest.' She pulled her hand from his. 'They offered to pay for him to study in London.'

The night wasn't really silent—there were the chirrups of night birds and insects, and the occasional crackle from the dying embers, but the night pressed in hard around them. Aidan stared at Quinn and ached for her.

'So when Chase was four months old, Phillip left.'

Phillip had left her with two small children? One of them just a baby? The jerk had turned his back on his own flesh and blood? 'The low-life rat scum!'

She gave a small laugh, but the thread of tiredness that stretched through it caught at his heart.

'So there you have it, Aidan, my sordid little story.'

His chin jerked up. 'I don't think it's sordid.' Not on her part at least. Phillip was another matter. And so were her parents. The people who were supposed to love her had all let her down, abandoned her. He made a vow to himself then to check out her Aunt Mara. He wasn't letting anyone else take advantage of Quinn.

*That's not your decision to make.*

He ground his teeth together. She was his friend. He'd make it his business.

He started when he realised her glass was empty. He lifted the bottle towards her in a silent question.

She hesitated and then held it out. 'Half a glass would be lovely.'

'I think you've done a great job with Robbie and Chase, Quinn. They're great kids. You should be proud of yourself.'

'Thank you.'

When she smiled at him he had to fight the urge to reach across and place his lips on hers. He closed his eyes and hauled in a breath. Kissing her wouldn't help. He forced his eyes open again. 'Do you ever regret the path you chose?'

'No, I don't. And I'm sure that's made things easier.' She turned to him more fully on the blanket. 'Remember how I said love makes everything easier?'

He nodded.

'Well, that goes for all love, not just romantic love. I love the boys with everything I have. They make it all worthwhile.'

Had she had to sacrifice all her dreams, though? 'What were you going to study at university?'

'Science. I was a major science geek.'

He recalled the science texts in her car. 'Is that why you chose to work in a science department at the university?'

'You bet. It meant I got to live vicariously through the research going on there. It was fun.'

His heart ached at the fierceness of her smile.

'But enough about me.' She dusted off her hands. 'I have a couple of questions of my own.'

He swallowed and shrugged. 'Ask away. After everything you've just shared, the least I can do is answer a couple of questions.'

She laughed and it flowed through him like some kind of energy drink. 'Careful, you might regret that impulse.'

What was it about her that could lift his spirits so instantly and comprehensively? 'Do your worst,' he dared on a laugh.

Slowly she sobered. She leaned in towards him. 'Aidan, why are you standing for office if you don't want to be a politician?'

# CHAPTER SIX

AIDAN STARED AT Quinn and reminded himself to keep breathing.

*How did she know?*

His heart thumped. Perspiration prickled his scalp. He forced himself to sit up straighter and to lean away from her and the temptation of warm lips…of warm woman. 'Of course I want to be a politician.'

The sparkle in her eyes faded. 'Uh-huh.' She set her half glass of wine to one side and started to rise. 'It's been a lovely day, but a long one.'

She was going to leave? But she hadn't finished her wine! He didn't want the day to end, but he had no intention of talking about this.

'I hadn't thought it through properly, but of course you'd be worried I'd take such a story to the papers.'

'I think no such thing!'

Her face was a study in scepticism. 'Goodnight, Aidan, sleep tight.'

He scowled. He'd given her and her children a lovely day. Why did she have to push this?

*Oh, so this day was more for their benefit than yours, was it?*

He scowled harder, but Quinn didn't see. She was halfway back to her van by now.

And he didn't want her to go.

'When my brother died…'

She didn't turn, but she stopped. She didn't come back. She waited. He swallowed and tried to match his voice to the quiet of the night. 'I already told you that Danny's death devastated my parents.' A beat passed. 'Everything changed!'

She came back and sat on the blanket. She didn't pick up her wine glass. She didn't touch him. She didn't say a word.

He wanted her to say something—needed her to —because a lump had lodged in his throat and he couldn't push past it.

'What about you, Aidan? You must've been devastated too. You obviously loved your brother.'

The warm cadence of her voice helped him to relax, eased his throat muscles. 'I…' He ignored his wine to seize a bottle of water. He knocked back a generous swig. 'You have to understand that Danny was full of life, full of fun. If you were feeling low you could rely on Danny to cheer you up. You always found yourself laughing around him. He was the life of the party without being a party animal.' He capped the water bottle. 'When he died it felt like the light had gone out of the world.'

He hadn't said that out loud before. It wasn't something designed to cheer his mother or father, or anyone else for that matter. Quinn shuffled closer until their arms and shoulders touched. She took his hand. Strangely, her warmth did give him a measure of comfort.

'I always wanted a brother or sister. I can't imagine what it would be like to lose one I loved.'

Lost? They hadn't lost him. He'd been taken from them. Stolen. But it occurred to him then that he had memories Quinn would never have. Memories he could hold tight for the rest of his life. Something inside him shifted and changed focus by several degrees. He wanted to put his arm around her and hug her. He'd lost a brother, but he'd never been alone the way she had been.

'I was at a loss how to console my parents. Daniel wouldn't have been.'

She pulled herself up to her full sitting height. He'd slumped so the top of her shoulder almost came to the top of his. Although he should be focusing on other things, he couldn't help but enjoy the warm slide of her against him.

'Aidan Fairhall, you can't know that! You cannot possibly know how much Danny would've been affected if circumstances had been reversed. He might've gone completely to pieces.'

He shook his head. Danny would've known exactly how to comfort their parents. Besides, although none of them had said it out loud, they all knew his parents wouldn't have needed as much consoling if his and Danny's positions had been reversed.

That fact could still make him flinch.

Quinn's hold on his hand hauled him back. 'What does Danny's death have to do with you giving up a career you love and becoming a politician?'

He'd been foolish to think this woman had been fully preoccupied with her cross-country move and her two energetic sons. She'd picked up on a lot. Probably too much. 'Danny was always going to be the politician.' He moistened his lips. 'As you probably realise, Fairhalls always stand for office.'

'Your father, his father and his father before him, yes, but nobody could've foreseen what happened to Danny.'

He met her gaze. The light of the fire glimmered in her eyes. 'The only thing that brought my parents a moment of respite and consolation was my promise to stand for office in Danny's place.'

Her lips parted. Her eyes and their sympathy burned

through him. 'Oh, Aidan,' she whispered. 'Would it have been such a bad thing if it skipped a generation?'

He set his jaw. 'It might not be my first career choice, and I realise I'm probably going to make a dreadful politician, but—'

'No you won't! You'll be very good at it.'

He closed his eyes.

'But it'll be such a tough job if your heart isn't in it.'

He opened his eyes again. 'So I'm left with a choice that's really no choice at all. Either quit politics and break my parents' hearts all over again or reconcile myself to a job I have no real passion for.'

She swore. It was low and soft, but he caught it all the same and it made him swing towards her, his eyebrows lifting.

'Sorry,' she murmured. 'I just realised I'd made things ten times worse when I suggested you drag your mother into the office to help out with your campaign.'

That had sealed the deal. Not that there'd been much hope of pulling back now anyway. None of that was Quinn's fault.

'I think you're making a big mistake, Aidan.'

He shrugged. When a person got right down to it, what did his happiness count in the greater scheme of things? Besides, he wouldn't be miserable. He just wouldn't be following the path he'd choose for himself. It was no biggie.

His shoulders slumped.

'It wouldn't all go to hell in a hand basket if you were to retire from the campaign,' she argued, squeezing his hand. 'There are people who could step into your shoes, like your second in command.'

He appreciated her efforts, but she didn't understand how fragile his parents were.

'And you're not being fair to Daniel.'

Every muscle he possessed stiffened. He swung to her,

a snarl rising up inside him. 'Not fair to Daniel? When I'm keeping his memory alive?'

She stared at him with wide eyes. She dropped his hand and it left him feeling strangely adrift. 'We keep our loved one's memory alive by remembering them and talking about them. Not by making a mockery of what they held dear.'

He bared his teeth. 'A mockery?'

'Well, what would you call it?' Her eyes flashed. 'He loved politics, yes? While you…you're just going to grit your teeth and force yourself to go through the motions. How do you think he'd feel about that, huh?'

Bile rose up through him.

'On a personal level, if he was any kind of brother at all, I bet he'd tell you to do whatever made you happy. On a professional level he would kick your butt for using the job he loved to make yourself and two other people feel marginally better.'

His jaw dropped. His stomach churned.

'Because he'd know politics is more important than that. Or, at least, that it should be. And he'd also know that you stepping into his shoes wouldn't bring him back.'

His head rocked back. Wind roared in his ears. His every last defence had been ripped away in one scalding wrench. He struggled to his feet, but he didn't know what to do once he'd reached them.

Flee?

Stand and fight?

*Won't bring him back.*

What he wanted to do was punch something and then hide in the dark and bawl his goddamn eyes out!

He backed up to lean against a nearby boulder outside the circle of light cast by the dying embers of the fire. Bracing his hands against his knees, he tried to pull air into lungs that didn't want to work.

He didn't hear her move, but suddenly she was there, insinuating herself between his legs, her arms going about his shoulders.

He couldn't help it. His arms went about her and he pulled her against him tight, his face buried in her shoulder.

*Won't bring him back.* But he wanted Danny back. He wanted it with his every aching atom, with every single, secret part of himself.

'You don't know what it's like, Quinn.' His voice came out raw and ragged. 'The pain…it tears at you from the inside out and you make deals with a God you don't believe in any more just to make it stop for five minutes. You'll do anything to try and get it to stop, to ease it a little bit, but…' Nothing worked. Not for long.

'I know, baby,' she crooned, cradling his head against her as she would if he were Chase or Robbie.

*Won't bring him back.*

He started to shake. A great hulking sob tore at his throat. Claws, cruel and vicious, raked at the parts of him he'd tried to protect, savage jaws closing about tender flesh as teeth, keen and sadistic, bit at him. A black pit opened up. A great scream roared in his ears. And all he could do was groan in grief and denial as night enclosed him, inside and out.

He didn't think he would ever be able to find his way out of it—out of the darkness—but faintly, ever so faintly, he heard Quinn's voice and he tried to focus on it, tried to move towards it. And eventually the shaking eased and the pain moved back a fraction and he could breathe again.

Slowly, the warmth of Quinn, the comfort of holding someone close, of having them hold him close, seeped through, pushing the darkness back further and further.

Finally he lifted his head. He wiped his eyes and said

the rudest word he knew. Quinn didn't flinch. Beyond her, in the sky, he could see a thousand stars.

He swore again. 'I just bawled like a great big baby, didn't I?'

'Oh, for heaven's sake.' She moved to sit beside him. He missed her warmth but he realised then that he'd been the first to let go. 'You're not going to come over all macho and tell me real men don't cry, are you?'

He blinked.

'For heaven's sake, how outdated are you? That is one message I won't be passing onto Chase and Robbie. You're human, right? Men feel just as deeply about things as women. Or are you going to tell me all men are shallow brutes?'

Nope. They weren't. Well, not most of them anyway, though he had serious doubts about Phillip.

'Bottling up grief like that makes everything bad. It doesn't let us keep hold of the stuff that's good.'

'What's good to be had from crying like that?' he muttered.

Even in the dark he could tell she'd fixed him with a 'look'. He found himself having to fight a smile.

She jumped up, refilled their glasses and handed him one. 'You told me Danny was full of life, the life of the party and all that. Give me a specific example.'

He blinked. He opened his mouth and closed it again. He took a sip of wine and found it soothed his throat. A sigh sneaked out of him. One example of Danny's funness, huh?

The first memory hit him. Then a second. And then they flooded him, one after the other. Nights at the local with their mates. Fishing trips. Surfing. Lots of laughing. Fights that had ended in laughter too. Barbecues. Late night talks sitting over a nice bottle of single malt.

He glanced at Quinn. She smiled and he found he could

smile back without any effort at all. He knew then that he didn't have to relay a single one of those memories—she knew. How? He thought about all she'd been through and promptly stopped wondering.

'You must be tired.'

Her words were a caress in the night. 'You'd think so.' She'd barely touched her wine. He suspected she wasn't used to drinking. 'But I'm not.' He felt oddly invigorated. Besides, it couldn't be much more than nine-thirty. 'Danny and I used to have these late night talks. We'd discuss how we were going to save the world—him the politician and me the human rights lawyer.'

*The human rights lawyer.*

'Sounds nice.'

His chest clenched. So did his hand. 'You're right, you know? He wouldn't want me living his dream.' Danny had possessed a heart as big as the Great Australian Bight. 'He'd have wanted me to follow my own dreams.' Danny had always cheered him from the sidelines.

'I wish I'd known him. He sounds like a great guy.'

It was the perfect thing to say. They stared at the stars for a while. 'My parents won't see it that way, though.'

'No.'

It was half-question, half-statement.

She leant against him, shoulder to shoulder. 'Are you going to try?'

'I think I have to.' But how? His mother's pale, haggard face and haunted eyes rose in his mind. Who did he most owe his allegiance to—his parents or Danny?

'You owe it to yourself,' Quinn said quietly, and he re-alised he'd spoken his thought out loud.

He didn't trust that, though. Following his dream, doing what he wanted seemed wrong and selfish in the circum-stances. Yet it was the path Danny would have urged him to take.

'I take it your mother has been depressed, lethargic, hard to rouse?'

He nodded, his heart heavy again. Helping out on his campaign had certainly roused her, though.

'Have you ever considered the idea that behaving badly might rouse her more effectively than toeing the line?'

His glass halted halfway to his mouth. He slanted her a sidelong look. 'What are you talking about?'

She lifted one shoulder. 'If your mother thought that in your grief you were going off the rails...'

'It'd only add to her worries.' Surely?

'Or it might give her something different to worry about—something she could actually act on and make a difference to.'

She couldn't do anything about Danny's death, she couldn't bring him back, but she could certainly pull Aidan back into line.

'There's a thread of deviousness in you, isn't there?'

'I know.'

She puffed out her chest and it made him laugh. 'What did you have in mind?'

'Well, I was thinking that maybe when you reach Adelaide, rather than catch the first available flight back to Sydney, what if you were seen out on the town, gambling and drinking? I'm not saying to actually do those things, but if it appeared as if you were...'

Quinn watched the implication of her idea ripple behind the smooth dark amber of Aidan's eyes.

'She'd be livid.'

'Livid could be good,' she offered. 'It's better than apathy.'

'If I could somehow help her remember the good stuff too...'

He turned to her and his face was so vulnerable in the

starlight she wanted to hug him. He was such a good man. 'She won't forget her grief, Aidan. Just like you won't forget yours.' They'd carry it always and there'd still be bad days. She hoped he knew that. 'But hopefully she'll learn to live with it.'

'You helped me get rid of something dark and heavy inside me, Quinn, that I didn't even realise I was carrying around.'

'You'd been pushing your grief back to focus on your parents' needs instead.' No wonder he'd been ready to explode. Who'd been looking after his needs?

'And you think if I force my mother to focus on me instead of her grief, that it might help her?'

'I don't know. I don't know your mother, but I thought it might be worth a try. What do you think?'

He stared at the fire. 'I think it might be worth a try too.' He cocked an eyebrow at her. 'Going off the rails, huh?'

He grinned. It made her heart chug. She set down her glass. The wine was obviously going to her head.

'You left out one important element in your little "going off the rails" scenario, Quinn.'

'What's that?'

'An inappropriate woman draped on my arm.'

His grin deepened and she knew she was in trouble. She did what she could to swallow back a knot of excitement. 'Do you really think that's necessary?'

'Absolutely! Drinking, gambling and carousing with wild women won't do my campaign any good.'

She stared at him.

'What?' he eventually said.

'You seem to think your mother will only be worried about your campaign and the damage you might do to it.'

He glanced away.

Didn't he think his mother would be worried about him on a personal level? She understood that some people found it hard to separate the personal and professional, but what did a job matter when it came to a loved one's mental and emotional health and their—?

She broke off, remembering the world he came from—a world where duty and position and prominence were more important than loving your family.

'If I'm going to do this, Quinn, I mean to do it big.'

So he couldn't turn back? She understood that—way down deep inside her in a place she didn't want to look at too closely. He wanted to give his mother an almighty jolt *and* he wanted to sabotage his campaign at the same time. Two birds. One stone. She felt suddenly uneasy, though she couldn't explain why.

'Will you help me?'

'You want me to be that wild woman on your arm?'

'Yes.'

She wasn't opposed to helping him. She and the boys had plenty of time to dilly-dally. 'Tell me what it would entail.'

He drummed his fingers against his thigh. 'It'd mean spending a couple of nights carousing on the town. So... three nights all up in Adelaide.'

'Okay.' That was manageable. 'What about the boys? I don't want them in the papers.' She and Aidan wouldn't make front-page headlines, but they'd make the social pages.

'We can shield them. And we can do fun stuff with them through the day too,' he added, unprompted. It turned her heart to jelly. 'There's a zoo. And I bet they'd love the Adelaide Gaol Museum, not to mention the Haigh's Chocolate visitor centre. And there's this fabulous aquatic centre with slides and caves and all sorts of things.'

He cared about making her boys happy. She knew then that she wouldn't be able to refuse him.

*Not that you ever intended to.*

'We'll stay somewhere upmarket that has a babysitting service.' He straightened and pinned her with his gaze. 'And I'll be covering all the expenses in Adelaide. That's non-negotiable.'

She rolled her eyes. 'I'm not exactly penniless, you know? I have enough to cover it.'

'You might not be penniless, but you're understandably careful with your money. Besides, given the choice, you wouldn't stay in an upmarket motel. Also, you're doing this as a favour to me so I'm paying.'

She planted her hands on her hips. 'On one condition.'

'Shoot.'

'That you don't pay for my car rental.' He'd paid for all of their fuel so far and she'd figured that was a good enough deal.

He'd started to turn away but he swung back. 'How'd you know I was going to do that?'

'Oh, Aidan Fairhall, you are as see-through as glass.'

He thrust his jaw out. 'I am not!'

She just laughed.

His jaw lowered. 'All right then, *you* might see through me but most people don't.'

She'd give him that. Most people, she suspected, only saw what they wanted where Aidan was concerned.

'Okay,' he grumbled. 'You have yourself a deal.'

He held out his hand. She placed hers in it and they shook on it. He didn't release her. 'Thank you, Quinn. I can't begin to tell you how much I appreciate it.'

She opened her mouth to tell him to try, but realised that might be construed as flirting. Her reckless self lifted its head and stretched. She cleared her throat. 'You're welcome.'

One side of his mouth hooked up in a slow, slightly wicked smile. He still held her hand. 'I'm looking forward to hitting the town with you.'

She should pull her hand free. 'Why?'

He tugged her a little closer and her reckless side shimmied. 'Do you dance?'

Her breath caught in her chest, making her heart thud. 'Like you wouldn't believe.'

'I'm better,' he promised.

'We'll see about that.'

'What's your favourite cocktail?'

'A Margarita. Yours?'

'A whiskey sour.'

His thumb caressed the soft skin at her wrist. 'Can you play blackjack?'

'With the best of them.' The nearest she'd come to gambling was the odd flutter on the Melbourne Cup. 'Although I prefer roulette.'

'I'm going to take you out dancing and gambling and drinking.'

'And I'm going to hang off your arm and gaze up at you adoringly. And I'm going to laugh and tease you and be every kind of a temptress I can think of.' His mother would have a fit.

'And I'm going to kiss you.'

And then his mouth came down on hers in the dark of the night, hot and demanding, and it stole her breath. His kiss wasn't polite or quiet. It was dark and thrilling and she threw all sense of caution to the wind, winding her arms about his neck and kissing him back.

He pulled her in closer, trapping her between lean, powerful thighs, and deepened the kiss. She didn't resist. His hands curved about her hips and explored them completely, boldly and oh-so-impolitely. She moved against him restlessly as the thrill became a dark throb in her blood. Thrusting her hands into his hair, she held him still to thoroughly explore a mouth that set her on fire, inciting him to further bold explorations of her body with hands that seemed to know exactly what she craved.

Aidan's kiss made her feel impulsive and young.

It made her feel beautiful.

It made her feel like a woman.

She wanted him, fiercely and deeply, as if his lovemaking would be an antidote to some secret hidden pain she carried inside her.

She broke off to gulp air into starved lungs. His lips found her throat—no butterfly whispers here, just hot, wet grazes and suckles that built the inferno growing inside her. His hands were beneath her dress. They were beneath her panties, cupping her bare buttocks, kneading and pleasing and building that inferno. Her hands went to the waistband of his shorts—

*Wait.*

No, no, she didn't want to wait. She wanted to lose herself in sheer sensation. She wanted to forget her troubles and soar away in mindless and delirious pleasure. Oh, please let her…

*Ask the question.*

She froze. Aidan's clever, heat-inducing, pleasure-seeking fingers started to move and she knew that in a moment she would be lost. Totally and completely.

With a groan of pure frustration, she slapped her hands over the top of his, the fabric of her dress between them.

He stared up at her. 'Oh, God, Quinn. Please don't pull back now.'

'I have to ask a question.'

'Ask away.' His breathing was as ragged and uneven as hers.

'Not of you, of me.'

She pulled his hands out from beneath her dress. She stumbled back over to the blanket and lowered herself to it, drawing up her knees and wrapping her arms around them. Aidan didn't move. She could still taste him on her tongue. She needed a drink of water, but she didn't want to wash the taste of him away.

'What's the question, Quinn?'

The question scared the beejeebies out of her. 'Would I be prepared to fall pregnant to you?'

Although the fire was now completely out, she saw the way he rocked back at her words. She didn't blame him.

'You see, twice now I've fallen pregnant without meaning to. When precautions had been taken. So I've had to make this my default position.' It played havoc with her sex life.

Her non-existent sex life.

He came to sit on the blanket too. But not too close. 'Wow.'

'You should ask it of yourself too—would you be prepared to make love with me if it would result in me getting pregnant?'

She couldn't read his eyes. She suddenly laughed. 'Boy, wouldn't that throw a spanner in your campaign?'

He didn't laugh.

'But I don't think we want to scare your mother that much.'

'Quinn…'

When he didn't go on she pulled in a breath. 'I like babies and I like you, Aidan, but I'm not prepared to get pregnant to you.' She would never again give a man the chance to accuse her of ruining his life.

He moved in closer. 'We wouldn't have to…you know. We could improvise, set boundaries and rules.'

She edged back. 'No, we couldn't. That kind of passion—' she gestured over towards the boulder '—is dangerous. Boundaries get crossed and rules get broken. And in the heat of the moment neither one of us would care.'

And she'd woken up before to the cold, hard light of day.

'Maybe I'd risk it if I'd been on the Pill for three months and had a diaphragm and spermicide cream with me and you used a condom, but…'

'I don't even have a condom!' He sat back with a curse. She didn't blame him.

'Aidan, if you want me to play the role of wild woman in Adelaide then you have to promise me that won't happen again.'

Even in the darkness she could see the way his eyes narrowed. 'Why not?'

She could almost see his mind ticking over—there were condoms and diaphragms and spermicide creams and any number of things available in the city.

'Because we're from different worlds, that's why not. We—us—are not going to happen. It can't go anywhere.'

'What the hell are you talking about?'

'You're all corporate meetings and flash hotel suites. I'm P & C committees and bedtime stories.'

'Lawyers and politicians have kids.'

'Not with me, they don't.' Not when they worked eighty-hour weeks. 'What would your parents say?'

That shut him up. She twisted her hands together. 'I mean after Adelaide we won't even see each other again.'

'So we're not even friends?'

Friends? She swallowed. 'We're just ships in the night.'

'Without the benefits,' he bit out and she had to close her eyes and give her reckless self a stern talking to.

'Adelaide,' she croaked. 'Are we on the same page?'

He didn't say anything for a long moment. Finally he nodded. 'Publicly affectionate but hands off in private.'

A quick kiss dropped to the lips or pressed to the cheek was very different to—

*Don't think about it!*

'I'm glad that's settled.' But she had to force the words out from between gritted teeth.

# CHAPTER SEVEN

TWO DAYS LATER, Quinn stretched out on the five-star comfort of a queen bed and let out a low satisfied groan. She, the boys and Aidan had spent the majority of the day at the aquatic park. The boys had had a blast on the water slides. So had Aidan.

And so had she, though she didn't doubt for a single moment that she deserved a mid-afternoon rest. Somehow she'd managed to keep her hands to herself and her mind mostly on the boys rather than with fantasies filled with Aidan, which was no small feat considering he'd been parading around in his board shorts for most of the day.

Robbie abandoned his Gameboy to climb up onto the bed beside her. The door to the boys' adjoining twin room stood wide open. Rather than watch television in their own room, however, they'd chosen to settle in her room to play their Gameboys.

'It's been the funnest day,' he said, nestling in beside her.

'It has, hasn't it?'

'Is there a water park in Pokolbin?'

She shook her head and watched carefully to see if his face fell. It did a bit.

Chase climbed up onto the bed too. 'I love holidays! What are we going to do tomorrow?'

She opened her free arm so he could snuggle in against

her too. 'Well, now, if you two let me have a sleep-in, maybe we could see our way to visiting the zoo.'

Both boys started to bounce.

A knock sounded on the door. Before she could move, a voice on the other side called out, 'It's Aidan.'

'Come on in,' she called back. Reclining on her bed probably wasn't the best place to receive visitors—especially one as alluring as Aidan—but she did have the safeguard of two young boys tucked in at her sides and they'd banish anything loaded from the situation.

When he saw them, Aidan's grin hooked up one side of his mouth. 'That rest you said you were going to take...' He glanced at the bouncing, wide-awake boys. 'It looks... uh...successful.'

She forced her eyes wide. 'Oh, yes.'

They both laughed.

Chase launched himself off the bed and across to Aidan. 'Mum said we might go to the zoo tomorrow.'

Aidan lounged in the doorway, all hot, relaxed male, and it made her stomach tighten and her breath shorten.

'But only if we let her have a sleep-in first.' Robbie joined them in the doorway.

'That sounds like a fair exchange.' Aidan glanced at her and she suddenly realised she was alone, adrift on this enormous bed. He sucked his bottom lip into his mouth and his eyes darkened.

She hitched herself up higher against the headboard and made sure her dress covered her legs to below her knees. She avoided direct eye contact, but couldn't stop herself from looking in his direction. He bent down to whisper something to the boys. They glanced at her with barely contained excitement and raced off to their room.

And then Quinn found herself alone in all of this five-star luxury with Aidan, and she couldn't move a muscle.

It took all of her strength to wrestle the fantasies rising through her to the ground.

'I hope you're not going to be upset by what I've just organised.'

She had to get off this bed!

She swung her legs over the side, forced steel to watery knees and moved across the room to one of a pair of tub chairs. She motioned for Aidan to take the other but he remained lounging in the doorway and she suddenly realised he didn't trust himself to come any further into the room.

Heat scorched her cheeks. A whimper rose inside her. She cleared her throat. 'What have you organised?'

'An afternoon of pampering for you while I take the boys to the movies.'

'Oh! Oh, that sounds divine, but...'

'Please don't refuse. You put everyone else's needs before your own and...' He folded his arms. 'I wanted to thank you. I really appreciate what you're doing for me.'

'You've repaid me tenfold by helping me give the boys a holiday they'll never forget.'

'I'm enjoying it as much as they are.'

So was she.

'So...?'

There was something in his eyes, something hopeful and happy that she didn't want to wound. *Pampering*? She smoothed her dress down over her knees and lifted one shoulder, glancing at him sideways over it. 'What exactly have you organised?' What kind of *pampering* were they talking about here?

'A massage, a facial, a manicure, a pedicure and a stylist for your hair and make-up.'

Her eyes widened. She did her best not to drool.

'And someone from the hotel boutique will be up with a variety of outfits for you to choose from for tonight.'

'Oh, that's too much!'

'It's not half of what you deserve.'

'But…'

'Look, Quinn, I suspect you'd rather just stay in and watch a DVD with the boys than hit the town tonight.'

Then he thought wrong.

'So I'm trying to make this as pleasant for you as possible.'

She really should say no.

'I suspect you don't have anything appropriate in your suitcase to wear for this evening—it wasn't the kind of trip you had planned—and I don't want to put you to unnecessary expense and the bother of having to go out at short notice to buy something.'

It was true. She didn't have a single thing in her suitcase that would do. She'd been hoping to dash out to buy something. And there was still time, but…

She should've known he'd have taken all of this into account. The allure of a few hours all to herself circled around her, warm with promise. She hadn't had the kind of pampering Aidan was proposing since the afternoon of her eighteenth birthday party. 'I should refuse.'

'There are no strings.'

She smiled. She already knew that. 'I really should refuse, but I'm afraid your offer is far too tempting. It sounds heavenly, Aidan. Thank you for thinking of it.'

He grinned at her. Her heart started to thump. She moistened her lips. 'I'll just make sure the boys are ready to go to the movies.'

She started to rise, but a hand on her shoulder kept her in her seat. 'Leave the boys to me. I'll collect you for dinner at seven-thirty.'

And then he was through the adjoining door into the boys' room with the door between them firmly closed, as if he'd been afraid to linger.

She hugged herself. He was taking her hands-off

policy seriously and it touched her, made her feel safe. Even as it left her body clamouring with frustration.

Quinn swung from surveying herself in the full-length mirror to answer the knock from the adjoining door. The boys' babysitter stood on the other side—a fresh-faced eighteen-year-old with a wide smile and a winning manner.

'Robbie and Chase want to say goodnight.'

'I'll come through.' She went to step into the room but Holly didn't move. She just stared at Quinn. Quinn swallowed and ran a hand across the electric-blue knit of her dress. 'What do you think?'

'I think you look hot!' Holly straightened. 'Oh, I mean—'

'No, no.' Quinn laughed. 'That was perfect.'

Both boys' eyes widened when she walked into their room. 'You look beautiful,' Robbie breathed.

'Beautifuller than beautiful,' Chase whispered.

She kissed them both, told them to be good for Holly, double-checked that the sitter had her mobile number, and then moved back into her own room to pace. That was three votes in the pro camp so far, but Aidan's was the vote that counted.

Would he think she looked 'hot' and 'beautiful'?

She sank down to the bed and lifted a leg out to admire her strappy black sandals. A bow studded with diamantés sat high at each ankle. These were definitely wild woman shoes.

A glance at the clock told her she still had five minutes before Aidan would arrive. She checked her hair in the mirror. It had been swept up into a loose French roll. A couple of tendrils curled by her ears to brush her shoulders and neck. It was an elegant style to counter the sexiness of her dress and shoes and the glitter of dangling diamantés in her ears. She hoped Aidan would approve.

She stepped back to survey her overall image again. Oh, Lord! What if she'd gone too far and—?

A knock sounded.

She swung to stare at the closed door. Her fingers curved around her stomach to try and counter its crazy churning. She suddenly wished herself next door with the boys, watching whatever movie it was that they'd chosen.

There was another knock.

*Oh, get over yourself!*

She kicked herself forward and opened the door. Aidan stood there in black trousers and a white shirt with a black jacket casually tossed over one shoulder. Her mouth dried. He looked…

Divine. Scrumptious. Sexy.

And like a stranger.

She held her breath and waited for him to smile.

His gaze swept her from the top of her French roll to the tips of her ruby-coloured toenails, and back again. Her blood thundered in her ears.

His eyes flashed and his lips pressed into a thin, hard line. Her heart slithered to her knees. She wanted to close the door and hide behind it, but she forced her chin skyward.

'We'd best go if we don't want to be late.' Clipped and short, the words shot out of him like arrows, barbed and flinty.

'I'll just get my purse.'

She turned, blinking hard against the stinging in her eyes.

Aidan punched the elevator button and kept his eyes firmly fixed straight ahead.

Damn it! He should've arranged to meet Quinn in the foyer. It would've been a heck of a lot safer. What had he been thinking? He tried to slow the tempo of the blood in

his veins. He tried to remember to keep breathing. In out.
In out. He gritted his teeth. It wasn't hard.

The elevator doors slid open on a silent whoosh. He
motioned Quinn ahead of him, careful not to touch her.
He caught a glimpse of long tanned thigh and swallowed
a groan.

*Pull yourself together.* He'd seen more of her body at
the aquatic centre earlier in the day. He slammed a finger
to the button for the ground floor. *Hurry up!* He didn't
need a confined space at this point in time. He'd made
her a promise—a promise he wouldn't break. His hands
clenched. But all he could see from the corner of his eyes
was a vibrant tempting blue.

Her swimsuit had been a simple one-piece designed
for modesty. The dress she wore now was anything but.
It was flamboyant and provocative. And those heels! She
was wearing take-me-to-bed shoes. What he wouldn't give
to do exactly that and—

Nostrils flaring, he forced his gaze straight ahead to the
polished metal of the elevator doors. He stared at them,
willed them to open onto the ground floor asap and de-
posit them into a crowd and safety.

'I'm sorry, Aidan.' Quinn pushed the button to halt the
elevator's progress. 'But I can't do this. I can't go out if
what I'm wearing is inappropriate.'

He turned. She'd caught her bottom lip between her
teeth, but not before he'd seen its betraying wobble. He
closed his eyes and tried to collect himself, resisting the
urge to run a finger around his collar. 'Quinn, what you're
wearing is perfect for this evening and—'

'You hate it.'

He'd hurt her feelings? *Careless brute!* 'I love it!'

'No, you—'

'But I'm in danger of forgetting my promise to you so I'm
trying to get us out of the danger zone as quickly as I can.'

She blinked. Not an ounce of comprehension dawned in her eyes. He leaned in closer. 'At the moment all I want to do is haul you back to your room, toss you onto your bed like some darn caveman and to slowly and very thoroughly explore every—'

Her hand clapped over his mouth. 'I get the picture.' Her voice came out hoarse and she pressed the button to set the elevator in motion again. 'Sorry, I thought…'

She brought her hand back. 'I've never worn anything this risqué before and I thought maybe I'd taken the whole wild woman thing too far. I mean, look how short this hem is! Not to mention that this material hugs every curve, leaving next to nothing to the imagination.'

He closed his eyes again.

'And now I'm rambling. Sorry. Nerves. I have to try to get your suggestion out of my head or…'

He bit back a groan.

'Not that what you suggested would work in practice.'

He opened his eyes and raised an eyebrow.

'I mean, the minute the boys heard we were back they'd be straight into my room and I expect that would be something of a mood killer.'

He laughed then. He couldn't help it. The door whooshed open and he took her hand to stride out into the foyer. He said now what he should've said at her door. 'Sweetheart, you look absolutely ravishing. I am going to be the envy of every man that claps eyes on you tonight.'

She beamed back at him. 'We're going to have so much fun this evening.'

They would. Just as long as he remembered the promise he'd made. And kept reminding himself that he was a man of his word.

Quinn was right. Dinner was fun.

She recounted the pampering she'd received that afternoon, and her sheer enjoyment of it touched him. Life had been unkind to Quinn, but she didn't waste time feeling sorry for herself. She took full responsibility for her own happiness. Still, it felt good to have given her a treat.

'Have dessert,' he urged. 'I mean to.'

She shook her head. 'I couldn't possibly fit it in. But I'd love a coffee.'

That made him grin. 'Not used to late nights, Ms Laverty?'

Her eyes danced. 'Not ones that don't involve earaches or tummy upsets.' She glanced around. 'I have to say, Aidan, this is a really lovely restaurant.'

They sat at a window table that overlooked Adelaide's streetscape. The lights of the city twinkled beneath them with an effervescence he found infectious.

He ordered coffee for Quinn and chocolate mousse cake for himself. When the waiter had gone, Quinn turned from the view to survey him. 'So…how will the press know that you're out on the town tonight?'

'They've been tipped off.'

'Right.'

'When we leave here there'll be a photographer somewhere. He could be hidden or he could be brash and in our faces.'

'If it's the latter, how should I act? Natural or furtive?'

He considered that. 'It won't matter.' Either would garner his mother's full attention. 'And there'll be more of the same at the nightclub we're going to.' He'd arranged for a photographer to get in and take photos of him and Quinn dancing. He didn't tell her that, though. He didn't want her feeling self-conscious the entire evening.

She stared out of the window with pursed lips and he frowned. 'What's the matter?'

'I'm feeling a little uneasy…'

'You don't need to. I promise to look after you and—'

'About doing all this to sabotage your campaign.'

He was prevented from answering when the waiter arrived with dessert and coffee.

'But that's the whole point of the exercise,' he said when the waiter was gone.

'The point is to rouse your mother from her depression and make her look beyond her grief.' She reached out and touched his hand. 'Why can't you just tell your parents the truth—that you don't want to be a politician?'

How could he tell Quinn that her plan was a losing game? His parents loved him, sure, but it had never been on the same scale as they'd loved Danny. Besides, he didn't want to have that particular conversation with his mother. It wouldn't be a conversation but an argument. It would end in her tears and his guilt. Lose-lose. This way...

'Aidan?'

The lights of the city were reflected in her eyes and it made something inside him start to pound. He swallowed and tried to ignore it. 'If I tell my parents I don't want to embark on a political career they'll be mortally offended.'

She frowned.

'What they'd hear is not that I love my job as a human rights lawyer, but me criticizing their entire way of life and value system. What they'd hear is me *spurning* their way of life and all they hold dear. And most of all, Quinn, what they'd see is me refusing to bring Danny's dream to fruition.' He stared down at the chocolate cake, his appetite all used up. 'They'd see it as a betrayal.'

Her lips parted a fraction and her eyes almost seemed to throb. 'Oh, Aidan,' she whispered.

He ached to reach out and touch her.

'So instead you're going to let them devalue all you hold dear, to belittle the life you want to lead?'

'I can live with that. My losing the campaign will be a blow to them, a major disappointment, but it's always been on the cards. That's the nature of politics. But me walking away from it all, they would find that unforgivable.'

'What if you're wrong?'

A weight settled on his shoulders. What if they didn't forgive him for 'going off the rails' and *inadvertently* sabotaging his political career?

'What if you're short-changing them? It's possible that they'd understand your position, you know. They don't sound like ogres. You're not narrow-minded. Danny doesn't sound as if he was narrow-minded, which makes me think they're not either. You're not giving them a chance to support you.'

'Danny has only been gone for eight months. I might not be prepared to sacrifice myself to a career in politics, but I'm not prepared to cause them any more pain than necessary. Not at this point in time.'

They stared at each other for several long moments and he clocked the exact instant she decided to leave it be. He should've been relieved, but he wasn't. Which didn't make any sense.

She reached across with her teaspoon and snared a spoonful of his cake. 'Oh, that is really good. I mean *seriously* good.' He went to push it towards her but she shook her head. 'The last thing you need is to be seen on the dance floor with a woman who has a distended stomach.'

Her wryness made him laugh. 'Quinn, when all of this is over, I'd like to keep seeing you.' Pokolbin was only two hours north of Sydney, maybe two and a half. It wasn't that far.

She snagged another spoonful of his cake and shook her head. 'Not going to happen.'

He forced himself to have a spoonful of cake too. Forced himself to hide how much her easy rejection cut at him. 'Why not?'

'Because I refuse to be a part of your strategy to ruin

your political career. And we both know a woman like me—a single, unmarried mother with a low-paying job and few qualifications—is not the kind of woman to stand at an aspiring politician's side.'

'That's not why I want to see you!'

'Maybe not.' She ate more cake and she looked utterly in control but the spoon trembled in her hand. 'But I remind you of Danny. I remind you of better times and I wonder how much of the real me you see.'

He flinched and abandoned all pretence of eating. 'You're just grasping after any excuse. You want to deny what's happening between us.'

She set her teaspoon to her saucer. 'There's an element of truth in that.'

Her simple statement made his jaw drop.

'You're a nice man, Aidan. I like you a lot, but…' She glanced up and met his gaze. 'Honesty is important to me.'

A chill slid beneath his ribs.

'Phillip lied to me about what he really wanted because he thought that was the right thing to do. The same way that you're lying to your parents.'

Her words couldn't hurt him. His heart had numbed and frozen over. 'You're saying you don't trust me.'

'Are you saying you'd never lie to me?'

Of course he wouldn't! He could say that till he was blue in the face, though. She'd never believe it. Phillip had done a right royal job on her.

'Your actions speak louder, I'm afraid.'

His parents and his relationship with her were two different issues!

'I'm not some child that needs protecting and I refuse to ever be treated like that again.'

He sat back. He scowled at his cake. Quinn drained her coffee. 'Stop being so glum,' she chided. 'We're supposed to be having fun, remember? You promised me dancing.'

Quinn was running scared. That was what all this was about. He scrubbed a hand down his face. He had the rest of tonight, all day tomorrow and tomorrow night to work on her.

If he dared.

Aidan woke to the piercing ringtone of his mobile phone. He fumbled for it. 'Hello?' he mumbled.

'Aidan Carter Fairhall, have you seen the papers today?'

His eyes sprang open. 'Mum!' He sat bolt upright in bed. He dragged in a breath. Right. 'Hold on.'

He padded to the door of his room and opened it. As requested, copies of all the national newspapers awaited him. He scooped them up and moved back to the bed. 'I have them all here. Which one in particular were you referring to?'

'All of them!'

He flicked through to the society pages and then grinned. Perfect. 'Ah...' He hemmed and hawed, injecting what he desperately hoped were notes of equivocation and vagueness into his voice.

'What on earth did you think you were doing?'

'I was just having a bit of...fun.'

'You're practically pawing that woman in public!'

'She's a very nice woman.'

His mother snorted.

'Look, what's the big deal? I went out. I had fun.' The irritation that edged into his voice wasn't feigned.

'The big deal is that photographs like this—where you look drunk, not to mention *lewd*—will do untold damage to your political image! What on earth do you think you were doing?' she repeated as if she couldn't believe his stupidity.

He scrubbed a hand across his chin.

'Aidan?'

'Do you know how far it is across the Nullarbor, Mum?' Silence greeted him. 'And it's all just endless sand and scrub for mile upon weary mile. It gives a man time to think.'

'What do you mean?'

The wobble in his mother's voice made his gut clench. He wished he could've spared her all the pain she'd suffered in the last eight months. 'Ever since Danny...' He couldn't finish that sentence. 'For the last eight months I've thrown myself into work to try and forget, but it doesn't work like that, does it? I need a holiday. I'm *taking* a holiday.'

'You don't have time for a holiday! You can have a holiday once you've been elected to office. You listen to me, Aidan. You are going to haul your backside out of whatever seedy hotel it's currently residing in, you will say goodbye to your slutty little friend, and you will get yourself to the airport. *Now!* We have work to do if we're to minimise the damage you've already done.'

*Slutty?*

'Do you hear me?'

He thrust out his jaw. 'No.'

An indrawn breath reached him down the end of the phone. 'I beg your pardon?'

That tone had made him quail as a kid. A part of him was glad to hear it now. He hadn't heard his mother this riled in a long time. But Quinn *slutty*? 'No can do, Mum. I'm not ready to come home. I'll call you in a couple of days to let you know my plans.' And he cut the line.

They spent the day at the zoo.

Aidan took every opportunity that presented itself to touch Quinn—a hand in the small of her back at the turnstile and again in the queue for the canteen, a brushing of fingers when he handed her a drink, the touch of arms and shoulders as they sat on a bench for a rest, a hand at her elbow when they ascended some steps. The startled glitter in her eyes and the flush that developed high on her cheekbones had him biting back a groan, along with the urge to rush her off somewhere private.

He wanted her mind filled with the sight, smell and feel of him. He wanted it to plague her with the same insistence it gnawed at him. He wanted the frustration of unassuaged hunger to batter down all her defences until not a single one was left.

He didn't know how far he and Quinn could cultivate their relationship but, presented with the stark fact of parting company with her tomorrow, he knew he had to try something.

*She's a single mother. Leave her alone. This is just lust. Scratch that itch elsewhere.*

He thrust out his chin. It went deeper than mere chemistry and it deserved to be explored.

*Aren't you hurting your mother enough?*

A fist clenched in his chest. This had nothing to do with his mother!

*What would Danny tell you to do?*

Everything stilled. His mind went blank.

'Will we get to see them eat?' Robbie asked as they moved towards the big cat area.

It had just been dinner time at the seal and dolphin enclosures. The boys had been fascinated.

'Not today,' Quinn said, reading a nearby sign.

Robbie pouted. 'Why not?'

'Because lions and tigers don't get fed every day. The zoo tries to mimic how they'd feed in the wild. It keeps them healthy.'

Aidan nudged her arm. She started. He bit back a grin. 'How'd you know that?'

'You'll be sorry you asked,' she warned.

He folded his arms. 'Go on.'

She shrugged. 'I've been reading up on some of the latest research into human health and nutrition.' He raised an eyebrow and she shrugged. 'It appears that just as it's healthier for wild animals to intermittently fast, the same might be true for humans.'

His mind flicked back to those textbooks in her car.

'There are links that suggest fasting can decrease both the incidence and growth of some cancers, reduce the risk of developing diabetes, and perhaps even Alzheimer's. It appears that fasting could promote cell renewal. I mean, the research is only in its infancy, but it is fascinating.'

He listened in astonishment and then awe as she rattled off facts and figures with an ease that spoke of close scholarship. She eventually petered off with a shrug and an abashed grin that speared into his heart. 'I told you you'd be sorry.'

'It's amazing and interesting,' he countered. He thought of the way she'd just spoken, of the fire in her voice, of those darn textbooks and the lecture she'd given him that first day about his probable cortisol levels. He pulled her to a halt. 'Quinn, why are you wasting all of this passion and talent? Why aren't you at university, conducting your own research?'

She stared at him for a moment and then pointed—to Robbie and Chase.

Ah.

In the next instant he rallied. 'But there's nothing to stop you from going to university now.'

She glanced pointedly to Robbie and Chase again and then raised an eyebrow.

'You could study part-time. You'd get government assistance while you were studying and—'

'You mean I'd end up with a big fat student debt.'

'And a bright and shiny qualification.'

'Look, Aidan, I made my decision nine years ago when I found out I was pregnant. I have to work full-time to make ends meet, that's non-negotiable, and I'm also a full-time mum. Studying even part-time would mean spreading myself too thin. Robbie and Chase deserve more than my part-time distracted attention. They deserve at least one fully involved parent.'

He opened his mouth, but she held up a hand. 'Maybe I'll rethink that when the boys are in high school and a bit more self-sufficient.'

By which time he didn't doubt she'd have come up with a whole new set of excuses. Her shuttered expression, though, told him the subject was closed.

That evening they went to Adelaide's night races.

Quinn instantly fell in love with the pageantry, the colour and the sheer excitement.

'Which one do you fancy?' Aidan asked her as the horses paraded in front of them.

'Number four,' she said, selecting a giant chestnut. The jockey wore the exact same shade as Aidan's shirt.

'Come on.' He took her hand and led her to one of the betting windows and handed her an obscene amount of cash. 'Put it all on the nose.'

'All?' she breathed.

He just grinned and it made her heart hammer. Heaven's, how on earth was she going to adjust to reality again tomorrow? When Aidan would be gone. For good.

She pushed the thought away. Tonight was for fun. There'd be time enough to miss all of this, to miss him, tomorrow.

She watched the race with her heart in her mouth, gripping Aidan's arm. As the horses hit the home straight she started jumping up and down and shouting along with the rest of the crowd, cheering on her horse with all her might.

When number four crossed the finish line a nose ahead
of the rest of the field, she flung her arms around Aidan's
neck. 'We won! We won!'

He swung her around before setting her back on her feet
and grinning down at her. She eased away, the hard imprint of his body burnt on her brain. Did she really mean
to let this man go? 'I'm having the best time,' she breathed.

*You don't have any choice.*

'Me too.'

*Live for today. Tomorrow will take care of itself.* It
wasn't a view she tended to subscribe to, but she threw
herself into it wholeheartedly now.


Despite the heat that flared between them and its insidious
insistence that throbbed deep in her blood, Quinn found
herself laughing when she and Aidan entered the foyer of
their hotel later that evening. Even the knowledge lurk-
ing at the corners of her consciousness that their fun was
at an end couldn't prevent her from holding tight to these
last precious moments.

The foyer was empty except for the concierge and a
receptionist, and an elegant woman sitting stiffly in one
of the easy chairs. Aidan froze when he saw her. Quinn
frowned up at him, completely attuned to his mood. 'What
is it?'

The woman rose, her chin tilted at a haughty angle.
'Hello, Aidan.'

Aidan turned to Quinn, his smile stiff. 'Quinn, this is
my mother, Vera Fairhall.'

# CHAPTER EIGHT

AIDAN'S MOTHER!

Quinn's eyes widened and her jaw slackened. One glance at the other woman and she decided not to offer her hand. She swallowed and did her best to push her shoulders back. 'How do you do?' she said. She didn't say, 'pleased to meet you'. She doubted she'd be able to pull that lie off.

Mrs Fairhall didn't reply. Beneath her chilly gaze, Quinn's flirty red skirt seemed too short and her cream silk singlet top too skimpy. Which, of course, was true on both counts. She wore her strappy black sandals again, the ones with the bows, and the look they received basically said, 'woman of the night shoes'.

She choked back a giggle. Oh, Lord, they were in the middle of a farce!

'And who is this, Aidan?'

Tension vibrated through him and Quinn's desire to giggle promptly fled. His eyes flashed and his hands clenched. All of his easy politeness had disappeared, leaving a deep, burning anger she found hard to associate with him. She curled her hand around his arm and squeezed, tried to silently transmit that he not do or say anything he'd regret later.

Eight months might've passed but he and his mother were still both in deep mourning. People did and said things they didn't mean when operating under such stress. And Aidan mightn't be drunk, but they had been drinking.

He stared down at her for a moment and his face relaxed, and then a gleam she didn't trust lit his eyes. He slipped his arm about her waist and pulled her in close to his side. 'Mum, I'd like you to meet Quinn Laverty, the woman I mean to marry.'

The foyer spun. Quinn sagged against Aidan's side. She kept her eyes firmly fixed on the floor, knowing if she didn't they'd betray her. She closed them. What did he think he was doing? She should bring this lie to a close. It wouldn't do any of them any good, not in the long run.

'You expect me to congratulate you?'

He coiled up as if he were ready to spring. She leaned against him harder to keep him where he stood.

'Just once it'd be nice to hear you congratulate me on something that actually mattered to me.'

The words might've been drawled, but she sensed the very real pain beneath them. An innate loyalty for this man shot to the fore. 'Aidan,' she chided. 'We weren't going to tell anybody about this just yet.'

She lifted her chin and met his mother's gaze squarely. She didn't want to add to this woman's pain, but she'd do what she could to prevent her from adding to Aidan's. 'It's getting late.'

The dismissal was unmistakable and Vera Fairhall's eyes widened, and then they just as quickly narrowed. 'I will leave the two of you to say your goodnights. Aidan, I expect you in my room——' she gave her room number '——in ten minutes.'

'I really think you ought to leave that till the morning,' Quinn ventured.

The other woman spun to her. 'Don't you dare presume to tell me how to deal with my son!' And then she turned on her eminently respectable court shoe heels and stalked away.

Once she'd disappeared from view, Quinn pulled out of Aidan's grip, lifted both hands and let them drop. 'What on earth did you tell her we were engaged for?'

'I didn't say we were engaged. I said you were the woman I mean to marry.'

'You knew it's what she'd think!'

He scowled. 'She said you were slutty.'

Quinn went back over the conversation. 'No, she didn't.'

'Not just then.' He slashed a hand through the air. 'This morning, when I spoke to her on the phone. She called you my slutty friend.'

Quinn planted her hands on her hips. 'What's wrong with that? It was the look we were aiming for, remember? I'm *supposed* to be the wildly inappropriate woman.'

He stabbed a finger at her. 'She had no right to say it. It seriously cheesed me off.'

That was more than obvious.

'And just now she looked as if you were something unpleasant she'd stepped in.'

'It doesn't matter what she thinks of me.'

'Yes it does!'

Her heart started to pound. She pressed a hand against it. She was *not* going to travel this road with Aidan. 'You're going to have to tell her we're not engaged.'

He thrust out his chin and glowered at her. 'Or you will?'

Not on her life! 'I'll leave that particular joy to you.'

He didn't say anything. Tension crawled in all the spaces and silences between them. 'I'm sorry if this hasn't turned out the way you wanted,' she whispered. She tried to find a smile. 'But you've certainly galvanised your mother to action.' She wanted to reach out and touch him, but the fire burning between them was too fierce and she was afraid of getting burned. 'I just didn't know that it would create so much upheaval in you too.'

He dragged a hand down his face. 'Quinn…?'

She pulled herself up and glanced at her watch. She was *not* inviting him back to her room. 'Please don't lose your temper with her tonight. Try to get out of there as quickly as you can and sleep on it. See how you feel in the morning.'

'Will I see you in the morning?'

'Of course you will.' To say goodbye. She turned and made for the nearest elevator. Aidan didn't follow her and she didn't look back.

Quinn hadn't been in her room fifteen minutes when the phone rang. She grimaced and picked it up. 'Hello?'

'I suspect my mother is on her way to your room.'

Oh, great. Just great. 'You gave her my room number?'

'No, but I know how she operates. She'll have rung down to Reception to get it. Do you want me to come by to intervene?'

Aidan and all of his sexy male temptation in her room? No way! 'I'll deal with it.'

'Are you going to tell her we're not engaged?'

She let out a sigh and she didn't care if he heard it. 'No, but you're going to have to.'

A knock sounded on her door.

'Goodnight, Aidan.'

'A moment of your time, if I may?' Mrs Fairhall said when Quinn opened the door.

She'd have swept into Quinn's room if Quinn hadn't blocked the way. 'On one condition—that you keep your voice down. My boys are sleeping next door and I don't want them disturbed.'

The other woman's eyes flashed, but she nodded and Quinn let her pass.

'You have children?'

'Two boys—eight and six.'

Vera's gaze went to Quinn's left hand.

'And, yes, I'm unmarried. I've also been working in a low-level admin position and I have no tertiary qualifications worth speaking of.'

'That's none of my business.'

'But it's what you came down here to find out.'

She suddenly realised she stood in front of Aidan's mother in an oversized powder-blue T-shirt nightie with the words 'Super Sleep Champion' plastered on the front in big glittery letters. She pulled on the complimentary towelling robe provided for guests and tried not to feel at a disadvantage.

'That's not the reason I came down here, Ms Laverty.'

Quinn gestured to a chair. 'Would you like to sit?'

'I won't be here long enough to bother.'

Quinn sat. She did so in the hope it would help ease the acid burn in her stomach. 'You're here to offer me money to leave Aidan alone.'

'I see you've played this little game before.'

Just the once.

Vera whipped out a chequebook. 'How much will it take?'

And Quinn said now what she'd said back then. 'I don't want your money. I won't accept your money.'

'But—'

'Spare me the arguments. I already know the things I could do with the ludicrous amount of money you'd be prepared to offer me and, yes, I know the advantages my boys could gain from it, but I have too much self-respect. It's more important for me to be able to look my sons in the eye.'

Vera opened her mouth again, but Quinn kept talking right over the top of her. 'I have too much respect for

Aidan too. Do you have any idea how furious he'd be if he found out about this?'

Vera fell into the other chair as if she couldn't help it.

'I don't care about the insult offered to me. After all, what are we to each other? But the insult offered to Aidan...' Her hands clenched about the arms of her chair. 'How can you show him such little respect?'

'You will ruin him!' The older woman's face twisted. 'You will ruin everything good that he stands for.'

'How can you give him so little credit?' She sat back, her stomach churning harder and faster. The people from Aidan's world, though, would agree with Vera, would believe what she said with every conceited, supercilious bone in their bodies. They'd believe that a woman like her would blight Aidan's life.

Aidan was from that world, just as Phillip had been, and eventually he'd believe it too. She pulled in a breath. She and Aidan were *not* going to travel down the same path she and Phillip had. She'd make sure of it.

Not that Vera Fairhall knew that. She thought she was fighting for her son's reputation. The only son she had left.

Quinn reached across and squeezed Vera's hand. 'I know of your recent troubles and I'm very sorry for your loss. More sorry than I can say.'

'You know nothing!' Vera pulled her hand away, but she looked as if she might cry.

'You're right. I've never suffered a loss like that. The very thought of it makes me feel ill.'

Vera turned back.

'Aidan has talked to me about it a little. I know he and his father have been very worried about you and that they've been searching for ways to try and help you in your grief.'

'This is none of your business!'

'But in amongst all of this awfulness, who's been look-ing out for Aidan?'

'Don't you dare!'

Why not? Somebody had to. She leaned towards Vera. 'He's lost a brother he loved more than he's ever loved himself.'

'And you're taking advantage of his grief!'

Vera's pain was almost tangible. Quinn's eyes burned. 'No,' she said as gently as she could. 'I'm not the one who's taking advantage of him.'

Air hissed out from between Vera's teeth.

'If you continue trying to turn him into Danny, Mrs Fairhall, you'll have not only lost one son—you'll have lost the both of them.'

Vera rose and left Quinn's room without another word.

'That went well,' she whispered to the ceiling. And then she flung herself face down on her bed and burst into tears.

Quinn mightn't have slept much, but nevertheless she was up before either Robbie or Chase the next morning. The knock on her door, when it came, didn't surprise her.

Vera or Aidan?

She opened it.

Aidan.

She stood back to let him in and then went to the win-dow and pushed the curtains even wider, flooding every inch of the room with as much sunlight as she could. It didn't erase the seductive appeal of the queen-sized bed, but it helped. A bit.

'The boys?'

'Still asleep.'

'Right. Okay.' He adjusted his stance. 'There's been a change of plan.'

Her stomach started to pitch and her heart grew heavy. 'Oh?'

'I'm going to accompany you as far as Sydney now.'

She gripped her hands together and shook her head. 'No.'

He frowned. He started to open his mouth.

'You're not invited,' she said before he could speak. 'This was always where we were going to part ways and we're sticking to that original plan.'

He turned grey then and she ached for him. It took all of her strength to remain where she was rather than racing across and flinging her arms around him.

He strode across and thrust a finger beneath her nose. 'We are more than ships in the night, regardless of what you think.' His voice was low and it shook, but there was no mistaking his sincerity.

Maybe. Maybe not. But one thing was certain. 'I will not be used as some kind of distraction or delaying tactic. You need to sort your life out, Aidan. Not tomorrow or next week or after you've lost the campaign, but now. And if you think putting it off is helping anyone then think again.'

He glared. She glared back, but she couldn't maintain it. 'I want to tell you something.' She sat in one of the tub chairs, though fell might've been a more accurate description.

He folded himself into the other. 'Go on.' His voice was so chilly it raised gooseflesh on her arms.

She met his gaze. 'Children don't owe their parents diddly-squat.'

His head rocked back. 'Steady on!'

'If parents inspire respect and love, that's great, but it doesn't mean children owe their parents a damn thing. It's the parents who owe their children.' She leaned towards him to try and drive her point home. 'It's the parents—or parent—who made the decision to bring a child into the world. It's therefore the parents' responsibility to keep that child safe and healthy. It's therefore the parents' responsibility to give that child as good a life as they can.'

'And the good schools and the extracurricular sporting activities and music lessons and the overseas trips, they all count for nothing?'

'Be grateful for them, by all means, but it doesn't mean you owe your mother and father for having provided them for you. And it definitely doesn't mean you have to lead the life they'd like to lock you into. Parents, if they've actually been successful at parenting, should've instilled in their children the strength to choose their own paths.'

'You're calling me weak?'

'I am not! But I think your grief and your worry for your mother has clouded your judgement.'

He leaned towards her and her throat tightened. 'You know what I think? I think this reasoning of yours is flawed, coloured by your experience with your own family.'

She tried not to flinch.

'Do you really think complete self-abnegation and self-sacrifice is a healthy example to give your kids? Do you want them to grow up thinking that finding a job they don't like but that will pay the bills is the best they can hope for out of life?'

Her jaw dropped.

'I don't know what you're scared of, Quinn, by refusing to go to university. Maybe you're afraid that you'll turn into your parents.'

She shot to her feet, shaking. 'That will *never* happen.'

He leapt up too. 'Or maybe it's the fact that some of what they said nine years ago was the truth.'

'They said we'd ruin our lives. I don't consider my life ruined.' Regardless of what Phillip thought to the contrary. 'But it's been no bed of roses.'

Her chin shot up. 'Do you hear me complaining?'

He stared at her for a long moment and then swore softly. 'I'm sorry. I shouldn't have said any of that.'

She rubbed her nose. 'I'm not going to apologise for what I said. I meant every word of it. And I think it needed to be said.'

Aidan tried to tamp down on the fear that rolled through him. This couldn't be goodbye. It *couldn't!*

He shoved his shoulders back. Quinn was running scared and who could blame her? For pity's sake, she was a single mother with more than one life to consider. *And* she'd met his mother.

The world they'd been living in for the last…eight… nine days? It had been a strange, contained and intense time—time out of time was what she'd called it—but that didn't make it any less real.

Everything had changed.

It occurred to him, with a wisdom he'd totally lacked these last few months, that a little time apart could be good for both of them. He needed to think. Hard.

But he wasn't letting her leave without extracting a promise that he could see her again. 'Can I come see you and the boys once you're settled?'

He could see the refusal forming on her lips when Chase burst into the room. He flung his arms around his mother's middle and beamed at Aidan. 'We had fun with Holly last night. Can we stay another day? I love Adelaide!'

Quinn chuckled, a rich warm sound he knew he'd miss. 'I'm sure you do, but today we hit the road again, buster.'

Chase pouted, but his heart wasn't really in it. And then his face changed completely from fun and mischief to something sombre and glum. 'Are you really not coming with us, Aidan?'

Aidan swore that every muscle Quinn possessed tightened until she practically hummed with tension. Chase had just handed him the perfect tool to worm his way back into their car for the rest of the journey. A glance at Quinn told him it wouldn't win him any Brownie points, though.

He crouched down in front of Chase. 'I'm afraid I have to get back to work, but I've had the best fun hanging out with you guys.'

Chase's bottom lip wobbled. Aidan whipped a business card from his wallet. 'See that number there?' He pointed. 'How about you ring it this evening to tell me where you are and what you did for the day?'

Chase's eyes widened and he was all smiles again. 'Okay!'

Quinn smiled her thanks. A guarded thanks, admittedly, but at the moment he'd take any kind of smile from her that he could get.

He rose to find Robbie surveying them from the doorway—*scowling* from the doorway. 'Hey, buddy.' How long had he been standing there, watching and listening?

Robbie didn't answer. Aidan had learned that Robbie, unlike his brother, wasn't precisely a morning person, but he sensed this was more than a case of the just-out-of-bed grumps.

Robbie glared at his mother.

Aidan pushed his shoulders back. He wasn't having Robbie blaming Quinn for this situation. 'I'm really sorry to abandon ship on you guys, but I have to be back in Sydney today.'

Robbie blinked and he looked so suddenly vulnerable an ache started up in Aidan's chest. 'I know, mate, I'm really going to miss you guys too.'

When Robbie started to cry, he couldn't help himself. He strode across, picked the young boy up and moved across to Quinn's bed. A glance at Quinn and her too-shiny eyes told him she was close to tears too. Chase pressed his face into her side.

'Boys aren't supposed to cry, are they?' Robbie eventually hiccupped, his storm over.

'Of course they are.' Aidan shifted, except... He glanced at Quinn. She wouldn't like it if he told the boys otherwise.

He glanced at each of the boys again. Darn it all! 'Chase, come up here too and I'll let you both in on a little secret.'

Chase raced over and climbed up beside him. Quinn folded her arms. Her eyes narrowed.

'It's always okay to cry with your mum. She's probably the absolute best person in the world to cry with. And I bet your Aunt Mara will be a good person to cry with too.'

'She is,' Robbie confided. 'And so are you.'

It was the strangest compliment he'd ever received, but a stupid smile spread across his face and his chest puffed out.

Chase nudged him. 'What's the secret?'

He sobered. 'It's not fair,' he warned, 'but life will be much easier if you don't cry in front of your friends at school. It's okay for girls, but not so much for boys.'

Chase looked across to Robbie. 'Is that true?'

Robbie bit his lip. 'I think it is, even though everyone says it's not.'

'Aidan!'

Quinn stood with her hands on her hips and her eyes flashing.

He lifted a shoulder. 'Look, I know it's not fair, but it's true. And I want the boys to have an easy time of it at school.'

Her lovely lips parted and a wave of desire washed over him. He gritted his teeth and searched for a way to soothe ruffled maternal feathers. 'Boys, I think if someone should cry, though, that's okay and that he shouldn't be teased for it.'

Robbie stared up at him.

'So if that ever does happen—' Aidan met Robbie's gaze square on '—I don't think you should join in the teasing. What's more, I think you should stick up for him.'

Robbie scratched his nose. 'That could be hard sometimes,' he finally ventured.

'I know.' Aidan pulled in a breath. 'Doing the right thing often is.'

And so, he was discovering, was parenting. It sure as heck wasn't for the faint-hearted. It wasn't all days at the beach and trips to the zoo. Which reminded him...

He met Quinn's gaze. He hadn't used the opening Chase had given him earlier as leverage, but... Her eyes narrowed, as if sensing he was up to something. Man, she wouldn't like this.

But he wasn't letting her go without a fight.

'Robbie and Chase, remember how I said we should all go to Taronga Park Zoo in Sydney?'

They both nodded vigorously.

'How about we do exactly that this Saturday?' It was Monday today. It'd give Quinn plenty of time to get to Pokolbin—she'd probably be there by Thursday.

Both boys leapt off the bed to jump and cheer. Quinn gaped at them, and at him. 'But...but we just spent a day at a zoo.'

He rose with a grin. 'Boys can never have too much of a zoo, Quinn.'

She pointed a finger at him, her brows darkening. 'You—'

He caught her finger and brought it to his lips. The pulse at the base of her throat throbbed and a deep ravaging hunger shook him. He had to get out of here. 'That evening is my parents' anniversary party. Please say you'll accompany me.'

Her jaw dropped. She hauled it back in place and nibbled at her lip. 'I...'

'We'll hire a couple of motel rooms in the city, just like we have here, and maybe we could do something on the Sunday before you have to head back to Pokolbin.'

'Say yes, Mum,' Robbie breathed.

She tried to tug her hand free, but Aidan refused to release it until he had her answer. She shifted her weight from one foot to the other. 'You were very good with the boys just then.'

He could be very good for her too, if she'd let him.

As if she'd read that thought in his face, her cheeks flamed. Finally she nodded. 'The zoo sounds like fun.'

'The party will be too,' he assured her. Maybe by then he'd have worked out which was the wiser course—to leave Quinn alone or to pursue her with everything he had.

'What do you mean, you don't want a political career after all? You were the one who decided to step into Daniel's shoes!'

This was not going to be an easy conversation, but Quinn had been right—trying to live Danny's life was never going to work. Not for anyone. Not in the long run.

'I will not allow you to let him down like this!' Every perfectly coiffed hair on his mother's head rippled in outrage.

'But it's okay with you if I let myself down?'

She stiffened. She stared and his heart ached and ached for her. He loved his mother. He loved both of his parents. He'd loved Danny too.

*And Quinn?*

He swallowed. Quinn understood him, she'd fought for him, she was strong and full of laughter and she'd made the sun shine in his miserable life again. He wasn't sure what any of that meant.

Maybe they were only ships in the night, but everything inside him rebelled at that thought.

'Aidan!'

His mother's words snapped him to. He pulled in a breath. First he had to fight for his life—for the life he wanted to lead. He wouldn't deserve Quinn otherwise. 'Dad asked me to take Danny's place.'

She sat, slowly, as if her bones hurt. 'Why?'

Her voice came out hoarse and he had to close his eyes for a moment. 'He thought it would give you a reason to... to keep going.'

Her eyes filled and his chest cramped. 'And I agreed to do it because I love you both and I wanted to do whatever I could to make you feel better and to fill the void Danny had left behind. But I'm not Danny. I'm never going to be Danny. And nothing is ever going to fill that void.'

'So on the strength of that you're going to let Danny's legacy die?'

His head came up. 'Danny's legacy wasn't his political career.' He stared at her for a long moment and then said, 'Do you know how long it's been since I went surfing?'

She waved an impatient hand. 'Grow up, Aidan. We all put away childish things.'

'Danny didn't.'

'Of course he did! He—'

'He attended every single home game the Swans had last year,' he said, naming one of the premier football teams in the country. 'He had a box.' Aidan found himself grinning. 'He told you and Dad it was for networking and hobnobbing, but it was really because he loved his footy.'

His mother gaped at him. He lowered himself down to the seat beside her. 'Danny's legacy wasn't his career, Mum. It was his love of life and how he managed to instil that into everyone he came into contact with. It was his support of my surfing, Dad's golf and your book club. Danny wouldn't want you sitting inside four walls constantly grieving. He'd want you out and about, doing the things you love and sharing that love with others, just as he did.'

She leapt up and wheeled away. 'You think it's easy to move on? You think a person—a mother—can do it just like that?' She snapped her fingers.

'I know it's not easy.' He rested his forehead against his palm and drew in a breath that made him shudder. If he continued to pursue Quinn it would cause his mother yet more grief. Could he really do that to her at the present time? 'I realise I'm not your firstborn, and I know I'm not your favourite son, but—'

She spun around. 'Your father and I didn't have favourites!'

Aidan lifted his chin. 'Danny was everything you wanted in a son. He was your golden boy. Mum, I don't mean to sound harsh, I loved Danny, but his life is not worth more than mine.'

She sat as if in a dream. She reached out as if to touch him, but drew back at the last moment. 'I didn't realise that's how you felt. Why have you never told me this before?'

He shrugged.

Her eyes flashed. Her hair quivered. 'You stupid boy! You should've said something!'

He blinked.

'That rotten reserve of yours, Aidan! Danny was always effusive and affectionate. It was very easy to show him affection in return and to be demonstrative with him. It was always much harder to break through your reserve.'

His jaw dropped.

'I can see why you might think we favoured Danny, but, son, that just wasn't the case.'

It wasn't? He'd spent all this time thinking he was the second son in every sense and yet…

'Come along, Aidan, it's time for us to catch a plane and head into this brave new world of ours.'

He caught hold of her hand. 'I've had a thought about our brave new world. Mum, you're as passionate about politics as Dad and Danny ever were. Why don't you stand for office?'

'Me? But that's nonsense!'

'Why? You're only fifty-three, and an energetic fifty-three at that. You know the ropes. You know how to play the game. You'd be an absolute asset to the party.'

Her jaw dropped but he could see her mind ticking over as his idea took hold.

'I'll go and pack.' Aidan rose, and he left with a lighter heart than he could've thought possible.

# CHAPTER NINE

THE MOMENT THE knock sounded on Quinn's motel room door the following Saturday evening, a tempest burst to life in her stomach. The knock wasn't loud—a firm unhurried rat-tat—but it was clear and distinct. It *wasn't* enough to send a stampede of a thousand thrashing wings thumping through her.

At least, it shouldn't have been.

She pressed a hand to her stomach, moistened her lips and eased the door open, fighting the urge to fling it wide to feast her eyes on the man who stood on its other side. She'd already feasted her eyes on him earlier in the day when she'd found him waiting for her and the boys at the entrance to Taronga Park Zoo.

He'd feasted his eyes on her then too—just as hungrily, just as intensely, and with an intent that had made her stomach tighten.

The boys hadn't considered hiding their excitement. They'd hurled themselves at him, talking ten to the dozen. She'd envied them their lack of restraint. She'd have loved to have hugged him, but she hadn't. She'd merely nodded. He'd given her a quick peck on the cheek and his scent had filled her with so much longing it was all she'd been able to do to not run away.

Robbie and Chase had had the most brilliant day.

She hadn't. And she hadn't been able to tell if Aidan

had or not either. She'd tried to take pleasure in the boys' joy, in the gorgeous views of Sydney Harbour and in the antics of the meerkats, but her awareness of Aidan drove everything else out of her. That awareness had grown as the day progressed—a deep prickling burn that wore away at her. Conversation didn't ease it. At least, not the kind of polite surface chit-chat they'd maintained.

She gritted her teeth. They'd maintain it this evening too if it killed her. And then they'd never see each other again and she'd be free to get on with her life. Whatever sense of obligation had prompted Aidan would be allayed.

The thought made her want to throw up.

It also made her want to heave a sigh of relief.

He frowned. 'Are you feeling all right?'

She snapped a smile to her face. 'Of course.'

He stared at her. She stared back. Okay, polite chit-chat *but* with a little drop of honesty thrown in. 'Are you sure you'd still like me to accompany you this evening?'

'Why would you ask me that?'

His voice came out deceptively soft. It raised goose-flesh on her arms. She tried to rub it away. 'Aidan, this is a party to honour your parents. I imagine your mother, and probably your father too, will be far from thrilled that I'm attending as your date.'

'You leave my parents to me.'

Gladly, but would they return the favour? Or would she be trotted off to some quiet alcove and offered some other sweetie to disappear into the night and never return?

'I won't be offended if you've changed your mind.'

The aggressive tilt to his chin made her mouth water. 'I will be if you've changed yours.'

She bit back a sigh. 'Fine, okay. So be it.' She collected her wrap and purse. 'I guess we'd best set off. We don't want to be late.'

'Are you determined to treat this entire evening like an unpleasant chore?'

That pulled her up short. 'Of course not!' But it was true. She expected this evening to be an ordeal. Which was hardly fair to Aidan. 'I'm just concerned that...' She'd ruin everything for him.

'Well, don't be.' He took her wrap—a shot silk stole that matched her dress—and settled it around her shoulders. 'By the way, you look lovely.'

His breath disturbed the hair by her ear and sent a shiver arrowing down to pulse at a spot below her belly button. 'Thank you.' Her voice wobbled, betraying her.

His grip on her shoulders tightened and he pulled her back against him to show her how much she affected him too. Her breath caught. She closed her eyes, but rather than help her regain her balance it only highlighted the hardness pressing against her.

'If this were any other night I would do my best to seduce you here and now.'

She wasn't sure she'd have the strength to resist him if he did. With a superhuman effort she moved out of his grasp. 'But it isn't any other night. Besides, you look very debonair in your dinner jacket and black tie and it would be a shame to wrinkle you.' She could just imagine his mother's face!

She turned. 'I left the vamp behind tonight to dress as a lady. It's how I expect to be treated.'

He stared back at her, his eyes darker than she'd ever seen them. The very air throbbed. 'Have I ever treated you as anything else?'

'No.' He hadn't.

'C'mon, let's go.'

He took her elbow. She had to grit her teeth and lecture herself long and hard to keep her inner vamp under wraps.

* * *

The party was held in the ballroom of one of the city's grand hotels. It had glorious views of the Harbour and the Opera House. Lights twinkled on the Harbour and fairy lights winked on the two hundred guests—the elite of Sydney society—who mingled in all of their glamorous finery, and Quinn wished herself back into the isolation of the Nullarbor Plain and a night sky filled with an entirely different kind of light show.

She'd known Aidan would have hosting duties this evening. She'd known he would have to leave her for long periods of time. She hadn't minded. He'd introduced her to nice people. She'd made pleasant conversation. And it had given her a chance to observe him without his knowing.

'I understand you and my son had quite the adventure.'

Quinn swung from surveying the Harbour to find Aidan's father holding out a glass of champagne to her. She took it—without a single shake or quiver and all while maintaining a smile. Well done her! 'Happy anniversary, Mr Fairhall.' She touched her glass lightly to his. They both sipped. 'An adventure?' she finally said. 'Yes, I guess it was.'

Mr Fairhall opened his mouth, but his wife chose that moment to glide up between them. 'You look lovely this evening, Quinn. That dress is quite charming.'

She and her aunt had spent an entire day searching for this dress. She'd told Mara everything, of course. Mara had chuckled and decreed that Quinn needed a dress fit for a lady—a dress fit for Audrey Hepburn. And they'd found it. Pink silk shot through with the merest shimmer of black. Cocktail length with a scalloped hem, embroidered in black and with matching embroidery on the bodice. It was pretty, demure and very, *very* chic.

Quinn, however, caught the underlying meaning to Vera Fairhall's words. 'Thank you, Mrs Fairhall. The dress cost a bomb, but it was worth every penny.' She named the designer and had the satisfaction of seeing Vera's eyes widen. 'But we both know clothes don't make the woman.'

'That is very true, my dear.' She raised an eyebrow. 'I hear you've had quite the day of it.'

Had Aidan told her about their trip to the zoo? Or did she have spies? And, either way, did it matter? 'Yes, indeed.'

'I certainly understand if you're feeling tired and would like to sneak away early to go and check on your children. I mean we can't spare Aidan, of course, but we'd be more than happy to cover a taxi for you.'

'I'm sure you would,' Quinn said drily. 'Your reputation for hospitality precedes you.'

Tom Fairhall chuckled. Vera drew back. 'I'm only trying to be polite, Quinn. I'd understand if you felt slightly out of place here this evening.'

'Vera,' Tom chided softly.

'Not in the least,' Quinn sent back with all the fake sincerity she could muster. 'I see you even invited my parents. I do hope you didn't do that on my account.'

She gestured across the room. Vera swung to stare and her jaw dropped. 'You're *that* Laverty girl?'

Quinn raised an eyebrow, but her stomach sank. 'You don't need to concern yourself with me, Mrs Fairhall. I won't be troubling you for a taxi. I have a strong constitution and I don't tire easily.'

Vera stalked off. Tom patted Quinn's shoulder. 'Don't mind my wife, my dear. She's always been far too protective of Aidan. It's just become worse since...'

She glanced up uncertainly. 'I understand that. I...' She bit her lip. 'I did say to Aidan it might be best if I didn't come this evening.'

'My son, however, can be very persuasive.'

She smiled at that. 'Still, I don't want to ruin your or

your wife's enjoyment of the evening and if you think it's best I leave, I will.'

He stared down at her. He had eyes disarmingly like his son's. 'That's very generous of you, Quinn, but no. While Vera can't see it yet, we owe you a huge debt of gratitude. I'd unknowingly pushed Aidan into a course of action that was wrong for him and I didn't know how to reverse it. You helped him do that instead.'

So Aidan had stood up for himself? He'd turned his back on a political career? Her heart lifted. 'I'm not sure I can take too much credit.'

'I'm sure you're being far too modest.'

She recognised the guilt behind the dark amber of his eyes. 'I don't think you should feel guilty about pointing Aidan towards politics. Grief is a process. I think it helped Aidan more than hindered him.'

He smiled then. 'Thank you, my dear.'

Her parents glanced in her direction, pushed their shoulders back and she read the resolution in their faces. 'Now, off with you,' she shooed, not wanting him to witness whatever was about to transpire. 'You've neglected your guests for long enough.'

With a chuckle he strolled off.

She'd noticed her parents the moment they'd walked into the party—her father in an impeccable suit and her mother in sensible shoes. She wasn't sure how long it had taken them to recognise her. She suspected a percentage of the room was abuzz with news of Aidan's unsuitable girlfriend. Her name would've been passed from group to group and her parents would've heard it.

Not that she was Aidan's girlfriend.

*You'd like to be.*

It'd never work.

'If you have any sense of shame whatsoever,' her father said without preamble, 'you will leave this party at once.'

She and shame, at least her father's version of it, had never been close acquaintances. She pasted a big fake smile to her face. 'Hello, Daddy, lovely to see you too! You and Mummy look well. I'm sure you'll be delighted to hear that your grandchildren are healthy and happy.'

'Don't embarrass us in front of all these people, Quinn,' her mother snapped.

Quinn stared at them and shook her head. She hadn't seen them in nine years. It seemed strange to feel so removed from two people who had once been so important to her. But it was a relief too. She couldn't believe that once upon a time she'd wanted to be just like them.

'So you have your sights set on the Fairhall boy now, taking advantage of a family's grief, determined to ruin yet another man?'

She lifted her chin. 'The two of you lost any right to have a say in my life when you disowned me nine years ago. You are horrible people who lead sterile lives and I really don't want anything to do with either one of you.'

She'd have told them to go away, but Aidan chose that moment to return to her side. He glanced from her to her parents and back again. 'Quinn?'

'Aidan, these are my parents, Ryan and Wendy Laverty.'

She didn't say 'I'd like you to meet my parents', because that would've been a lie.

She recognised the shock deep in his eyes. Perhaps she should've been a bit more forthcoming about her background on that long drive from Perth, but it had all seemed so separate from her. 'My father is a vice chancellor at a nearby university and my mother is a leading researcher at another.' She gestured to Aidan. 'I expect you both recognise Aidan Fairhall.'

They all shook hands, but nobody smiled. It didn't surprise her when her father was the first to break the silence.

'Young man, I hope you'll take my advice and steer clear of this woman.'

Beside her, Aidan stiffened.

'I assure you that she is nothing but trouble and will only bring you grief.'

'I'm afraid, sir, that I have to disagree with you. Quinn is a remarkable woman with more integrity and true kindness than anyone I've ever met.'

Man, he was good. Smooth, unflappable and unfailingly pleasant.

'And if you say one more disagreeable thing about her I will have to ask you to leave.'

He managed to maintain his smile the entire time. She wanted to applaud.

He turned to Quinn, effectively dismissing her parents. 'Your drink is warm. Let's go get you a fresh one.'

And, with that, he took her elbow and whisked her off to the bar. She slid onto a stool as Aidan ordered their drinks, and when he handed her a mineral water she started to laugh. 'That was masterfully handled.'

'Jeez.' He settled on the stool beside her. 'And I thought my mother was a nightmare.'

Quinn grinned. 'She is.'

He choked on his drink.

She nudged his shoulder. 'I want more for you than a woman who has been around the blocks a few times.'

He winced. 'You heard that?'

'Uh-huh.' As she'd no doubt been meant to. It had been said much earlier in the evening. There'd been some mention of all the baggage Quinn carried too. She'd taken that to refer to Robbie and Chase. When Aidan had turned back to her she'd pretended to be absorbed in studying the table decorations to save him from embarrassment.

But he'd just witnessed her embarrassment.

Was an embarrassment shared an embarrassment

halved? She grimaced and sipped her drink. She suspected it might in fact be an embarrassment doubled.

'I'm sorry, Quinn. My mother—'

'Aidan, we put on one heck of a show in Adelaide. Your mother has every right to her reservations. She only has your best interests at heart.'

'Your parents don't, though.' He reached out to squeeze her hand. 'I didn't know they'd be here this evening.'

She squeezed it back before releasing it on the pretext of lifting her drink. The less she and Aidan touched the better. 'Neither did I. I'm sorry if they came as a shock to you. I probably should've been more candid about my background, but...' She glanced up at him. 'It all feels so remote from who I am now.'

Something burned in the backs of his eyes. 'We can leave if you want to.'

'Absolutely not.'

'I'm not buying into this casual nonchalance for a moment, sweetheart.'

Tears burned the backs of her eyes. She forced her chin up. 'But I do have my pride. I have absolutely no intention of giving either your mother or my parents that kind of satisfaction.'

He swore so softly she hardly heard it.

She sent him a smile. 'Besides, I promised your father I'd be one of the last to leave.'

He smiled then too. 'Wanna dance?'

She slid off her stool. 'I thought you'd never ask.'

Aidan walked Quinn to her hotel room. Neither one of them spoke. He didn't touch fingers to her elbow on the pretext of guiding her. He didn't take her hand. He didn't touch the small of her back. He kept his hands firmly—and deeply—in his pockets, did what he could to control the rapid pounding of his heart and reminded himself to keep breathing.

One foot after the other

One breath after the other.

He could do this. His hands clenched. *He could do this.*

They reached her door. They both stared at it for two beats rather than at each other. Finally Quinn seemed to give herself a mental kick and fumbled in her purse for the plastic key card.

He took it from her, inserted it into its slot and pushed the door open a crack. Quinn stared up at him, her eyes wide and uncertain, her lips a tempting promise in the dimly lit corridor.

*You can do this!*

He didn't step any closer. He would lose all pretence of control if he did that, if all of her sweetness pressed up warm and inviting against him.

Still, he couldn't resist dipping his head to kiss her.

Her lips met his, hesitant perhaps, but undeniably awake to the consequences that could ensue.

She kissed him back as if inviting those consequences. More than anything, he wanted to back her into her room and kiss her until they were both mindless with need. He ached to peel her clothes from her body and explore every inch of her to find what would make her gasp, what would make her moan, what would make her call out his name. He wanted to make love with her, frantic and fast. He wanted to make love with her painstakingly slow. He wanted to lose himself in the mindless pleasure they could find with each other.

But he couldn't let that happen.

He wanted more than one night with this woman. That had come to him swift and sure as he'd watched her make polite conversation with perfect strangers tonight. Quinn mightn't have wanted to attend the party, but not a soul would've guessed it. Meeting her parents had sealed the deal. Despite the pain it would cause his mother, he wanted to keep Quinn in his life.

Although she didn't know it, she held his heart in her hands. One misstep from him and she would drop it cold. And instinct warned him his heart wouldn't bounce. It would take a long time to get over her and he didn't want to have to try.

He deepened the kiss, wanting her aching so hard for him that she couldn't turn and just walk away. She tasted of champagne and coffee. She fizzed in his blood until he felt as if he were riding the biggest, most perfect wave of his life. Bracing one hand against the wall, he sucked her bottom lip into his mouth, nibbled it, laved it with his tongue. Her hands flattened against his chest and started to inch up towards his shoulders. Her tongue tangled with his and she made a mewling noise that angled straight down to his groin.

He broke free. 'Thank you for coming to the party with me this evening.' He didn't try to hide the hoarseness of his voice.

'Aidan?' Her hands slid against his chest and she made no move to hide the glitter in her eyes or the need in her face.

He backed up a step. Her hands fell to her sides. Her eyes dimmed. Disappointment flared in their depths… and relief. The relief kept him strong. Until she wanted him as unreservedly and unashamedly as he wanted her, he wouldn't let things go any further.

*He could do this!*

'I'll collect you and the boys at ten in the morning.'

'But…' She opened the door wider in silent invitation.

He shook his head. 'Goodnight, Quinn.'

He turned and walked away. He shoved his hands into his pockets and clenched them. He gritted his teeth and placed one foot in front of the other, pulled in one breath after the other.

* * *

They spent the following day on the Harbour. Aidan had booked a lunch cruise—family friendly—and he couldn't have ordered more perfect weather. The sun shone, but not too fiercely. A fresh breeze played through their hair, caressing their skin in a way that made it hard for him to think of anything but Quinn naked and his fingers trailing across her flesh. And hers trailing across his.

A burst of laughter from the children on the deck below snapped him back to himself. The colour on Quinn's cheekbones had grown high and he knew she'd read the direction his thoughts had taken. And if the pulse pounding at the base of her throat was any indication, she might have in fact added her own embellishments to the fantasy. His groin started to throb in time to the beat of her pulse.

'Why didn't you stay last night?' The words shot out of her as if some resistance had been breached. They sat alone at a table overlooking the foredeck, but she kept her voice low.

He leaned towards her and he didn't try to temper his intensity. 'Because I want you to want me with the same fire I want you.'

Her lips parted. She swallowed and her tongue snaked out to moisten them. 'Do you doubt it?'

He forced himself back in his seat. 'Are you telling me you didn't feel a thread of relief when I walked away last night?'

She glanced away. It was all the answer he needed.

'Aidan, neither one of us needs this kind of complication in our lives at the moment.'

He took a sip of his soda, but his eyes never left hers. 'Here's a newsflash for you, Quinn, but I don't consider you a complication.'

Her arched eyebrows told him what she thought about that. It might've made him smile a week ago.

'I like your father.'

He let her change the subject. 'I do too.' She laughed, as he'd hoped she would. He wanted to banish those lines of strain around her mouth forever. 'He likes you too.'

She glanced at him and quickly glanced away again. She tucked her hair behind her ears. 'He said you're making the break from politics.'

Thanks to her, he'd found the courage to be honest—to himself and to his family. 'Yes.'

'How's that working out for you all?'

'Very well so far. I'm taking some time off to sort out where I want to go from here, while my mother is still going into the office to sort out everyone else. My father watches us both indulgently from the sidelines and tries to fit in as many games of golf as he can.'

She grinned—one of those loving life grins that could transport him to a better place. 'That's excellent news.'

He reached out and ran a finger across the back of her hand. 'Can we talk about your parents for a moment?'

Her hand clenched and then she moved it out of his reach. 'If you want.' Her words came out reluctantly and his heart burned for her. 'But if you're thinking there's a chance for any kind of reconciliation, I'd counsel you to think again.'

He ached to hug her. 'Unfortunately, sweetheart, I agree with you.'

She blinked. Though whether at his words or the endearment, he had no way of knowing.

'Until they realise they're the ones who should be asking your forgiveness rather than the other way around, they're lost causes as far as I'm concerned.'

Her eyes filled and something snagged deep in his chest. This woman deserved so much more. She deserved to be loved and cherished.

And occasionally challenged.

'That's not going to happen. They have very rigid views about life and how it should be lived and anyone living outside of that box is given a wide berth. It's as if they're afraid it will pollute their ambition.' She drew a smiley face in the condensation of her glass. 'Their status at their universities and within their research communities is what matters to them. It's how they measure their success and happiness. They love their jobs and their institutions.' She scrubbed out the smiley face. 'What they haven't realised yet is that jobs and institutions can't love you back.'

Her parents lived in a rigid, narrow-minded world. The same world he'd been in danger of locking himself into.

'What was it like growing up with them?'

'Oh, I had all the privileges any girl could want.'

'It's not what I asked, Quinn.'

She glanced down at her hands. 'Lonely,' she finally said. 'It was lonely. My parents worked long, hard hours and when they were home their favourite thing to do in the evenings was work some more.'

He swallowed back the acid that burned his throat. When he'd been growing up his father had had to put in the hard yards, but it hadn't stopped either of his parents from finding time for him and Daniel. And he couldn't forget that for all of his childhood he'd had Danny as a playmate and companion too.

'So when Phillip and I started dating I fell hard. So did he.' She shrugged. 'For a while.'

He understood that completely, but...

'C'mon, out with it.'

He grimaced. It was lucky he had a poker face in the courtroom because it was obvious he didn't have one around Quinn. He drummed his fingers against the table. 'Look, I understand your resentment towards your parents.'

'Resentment?' She shifted. 'Oh, Aidan, so much of that

is just water under the bridge. All I want to do now is protect my kids from that kind of influence.'

'By turning your back on a whole way of life?'

She frowned.

'It's why you've shunned university, isn't it?'

Her eyes flashed. 'That was *their* dream, not mine. I'm living my dream.'

But she wasn't, was she? The childhood sweetheart was no longer at her side, helping her to negotiate parenthood's tricky waters or sharing love and laughter and all of those other things that made life worth living.

He wanted all those things for her. He wanted to share all of those things with her.

'And, quite frankly, I don't know why you have to keep rabbiting on about it.'

'Because, in a way, you're in danger of becoming just as narrow-minded as your parents.'

She gaped at him. 'I can't believe you just said that.'

Nor he. He had to be crazy. This was no way to woo a woman. But in his heart he knew he was right. Until Quinn fought to lead the life she wanted—the life she deserved—she'd never be truly free to love him. And he wanted her to love him. He wanted that with everything good he had inside him.

'Shunning university and a chance for a better life; is that a way of punishing your parents? Or do you believe that if you reject everything your parents value that you're giving validity to your current life?'

In a twisted way he could see how that might make sense.

'Oh, for heaven's sake!' she snapped. 'I'm not eighteen any more. I know that not everyone who has a degree is as inflexible or as detached as my parents...or as selfish as Phillip.'

She did? Then why wouldn't she even consider exploring her passion for science further?

She leaned towards him. 'You really want to know why I haven't considered furthering my education? It's because I don't want my children growing up lonely like I did.'

He saw then, in a light all too clear and blinding, the full effect her lonely childhood had had upon her. 'Oh, sweetheart.'

'Don't you *Oh, sweetheart*, me.' She batted his hand away. 'You don't understand how many hours I put into my schoolwork. It was something intelligent I could discuss with my parents.' She gave a harsh laugh. 'Oh, they trained me well. Those were the only times when I had their full attention and approval. And nobody could accuse me of being a slow learner. It got that I studied almost obsessively just so I could get a pat on the back from one or other of them.'

She'd learned to throw herself into her studies in the same way her parents had thrown themselves into their careers.

'My boys deserve to have a mother who is fully focused on them, not poring over some dusty old tomes in the library during their soccer games and forgetting parent and teacher evenings.'

He finally caught hold of the hand that had been making agitated circles in the air. 'Quinn, honey, you already have more life experience than either of your parents. You haven't been constrained by the narrowness of their world for nine years. You just told me you're not eighteen any more. And you're not. Nor are you going to turn into your parents. Ever. Regardless of whatever else you decide to do with your life.'

She stilled. Beneath his fingertips, her pulse pounded like wild surf.

'Quinn, these days your life is full and rich. It's better

than the kind of life you'd be leading if you'd followed your parents' path, yes?'

'Of course.'

'You no longer need to find something that will plug up the loneliness, do you?'

She shook her head.

'Then why don't you believe that you can reinvent your old dreams into the life you're living now? Why don't you trust yourself to make it work?'

She stared at him as if in a daze, as if what he was proposing had never occurred to her before.

'For some reason, your parents couldn't manage to be good scientists and good parents. Phillip hasn't been able to manage that leap either. But you're better than all of them. If you want to, you *can* make it work.'

Her chin came up. He wondered if she realised how tightly she gripped his hand. 'What makes you so sure?'

'Your love for your sons.'

She bit her lip.

He squeezed her hand and then he released it. 'You showed me I had to fight to live the life I was meant to be leading. You showed me I had the right to that life. Exactly the same goes for you.'

# CHAPTER TEN

Quinn glanced up from the kitchen table when she heard a car pull in behind the house. Aunt Mara's sturdy farmhouse was set well back from the lane, hidden in among the olive groves like a house in a fairy tale. The driveway was marked 'Private' so it was rare for tourists to accidentally wander down this way, though it did happen.

Mara had left for the shop over an hour ago. Quinn had manned the shop yesterday so today she and the boys were having a traditional lazy Sunday morning. She marked her spot in the university prospectus and moved to peer out of the door, ready to offer directions to whoever might be lost.

A man unfolded himself from the car. She blinked. What on earth…? Aidan!

Her heart hammered up into her throat, making her head whirl. She clung to the doorframe, unable to drag her gaze from the long clean lines of an athletic male body that filled her with a vigour and energy completely at odds with lazy Sundays.

After last weekend she hadn't thought she would see him again. She'd spent a ludicrous amount of time during this last week silently detailing all the reasons why that was a good thing. Absurdly, all she wanted to do now was jump up and down and clap her hands. Which was exactly what Robbie and Chase did when they caught sight of him from where they played in the side yard.

They bolted up to him and he hugged them both as if it were the most natural thing in the world. He grinned as if he were truly delighted to see them. And then he glanced to where she stood and he grinned as if he were truly delighted to see her too and her stomach twisted and turned like a purring cat weaving around its beloved owner's legs. Before she was even aware of it, she was across the veranda and down the back steps. 'Aidan, what a surprise.'

He bent to kiss her cheek. 'Not an unwelcome one, I hope.'

His scent and the touch of his lips woke her up more effectively than a strong shot of espresso. 'Of course not.'

'We can show Aidan everything!' Robbie said.

Aidan took them all in with one comprehensive glance…and that oh-so-beguiling smile of his. 'So you're all still enjoying your new home?'

He had a way of asking a question that made it seem as if he really cared about the answer. Both boys nodded vigorously.

'You can meet Auntie Mara and see the shop!' Chase said.

Chase had fallen under the spell of both, to Quinn's delight.

'And we'll take you down to the dam. We've got ducks!' Robbie added. 'And then we'll show you all the olive trees and—'

'Boys,' she hollered over the top of them when they both started to shout out their plans, 'let Aidan catch his breath first. You must've left at the crack of dawn to get here by ten.'

One shoulder lifted. A lean, broad shoulder that made her mouth water. 'I'm an early riser.'

She shook herself. 'Coffee?'

'Love one.'

It wasn't until they were seated with their coffees

that the urge to run hit Quinn. She couldn't explain it. It might've been the way those clear amber eyes surveyed her. It might've been the way they widened when they registered the university prospectus sitting on the table. It might've been the way his presence seemed to fill the kitchen. Whatever it was, it had her wanting to back up and run for the hills. Of course her inner vamp called her an idiot and dared her to sit on his lap instead. The idea left her squirming in her seat.

'Are you here for the whole day?' Robbie demanded.

'If that's okay with your mother.'

Three sets of eyes swung to her. 'I…' She swallowed. Why was he here?

He sent her a winning smile. 'I've heard so much about the place that curiosity got the better of me. I had to see it with my own eyes.'

'We can show you our new school too,' Robbie said.

'And where my friend Andrew lives,' Chase said.

'And the olive presses!'

'And—'

'Boys!' She clapped her hands. 'You're going to give Aidan half an hour to catch his breath after his long drive, while I make him something to eat.'

'Aw, but—'

'No buts.' She shooed them outside. 'You can make up an itinerary for the day.'

Robbie's face lit up and he grabbed Chase's arm. 'Will we start with the dam or the shop?'

She turned back. 'Eggs on toast?'

'I couldn't possibly put you out like that.'

'It's not putting me out at all.' It'd give her something to do, other than sit at the table and stare at him. 'Scrambled okay?'

'Perfect.'

She busied herself with breaking eggs into a bowl.

'It's not that far, you know?'

She glanced across at him. 'What isn't?'

'The drive from Sydney. It's two hours of mostly good road.'

'Oh.' She didn't know what else to say and the silence started to grow. She tried to focus on not burning anything—the eggs, the toast or herself. Eventually she slid a plate of scrambled egg and toast in front of him and hoped it'd ease the itch that had settled squarely between her shoulder blades.

The smile he sent her and his, 'This looks great,' only made her itch worse.

And the silence continued to grow.

'You were right,' she suddenly blurted out, slapping a hand down on the prospectus.

'I wasn't going to ask. I figured I'd hassled you enough. But I've been sitting here dying of curiosity.'

He grinned. She absolutely, positively couldn't help it. She had to grin back. He paused mid-bite to stare and those amber eyes of his darkened. Her heart stopped. Heat scorched her cheeks. She dragged the prospectus towards her and tried to focus beyond the buzz in her brain.

'Food technology is incredibly interesting,' she babbled. 'And can you believe it? Here I am, living on an *olive farm* and the processing of the olives is far more complicated than I ever thought it could be. Not only that, but there's the potential for us to expand our operations from providing just table olives. We could make our own olive oil too. And, I mean...' She knew she was jabbering, but couldn't help it. 'Obviously, that's down the track a bit, but...' She shrugged and forced herself to stop.

'It sounds fascinating.'

She glanced up to see if he was making fun of her, but sincerity radiated from him. 'You sound as if you've hit the ground running, Quinn, as if you've found your groove.'

'That's exactly what it feels like.'

'I'm happy for you. Really happy.'

She believed him.

He set his knife and fork down and patted his stomach. 'That hit the spot. Thank you.'

She collected up his plate and cutlery. 'I should be the one thanking you. If you hadn't kept hassling me about the possibility of going to uni I'd have continued to dismiss it. You made me shine a light on my own irrationality.' She grimaced, shrugged and tried to scratch the spot that itched. 'I felt that I'd lost my parents and Phillip to higher education. I mean that's utter rubbish, of course. I lost them to their own ambitions and prejudices. And you were right—in pursuing further study I won't become like them. I'll never be like them.'

'I'm glad you can see that now.'

She wouldn't have if it hadn't been for him. The sense of obligation weighed heavily on her, though, and she didn't know why. She rinsed his plate. 'I can't believe how many different study options there are. I have the choice of full-time, part-time, distance and all sorts of mixed mode delivery methods.' It made it very easy for people like her to fit study in around a busy timetable.

But enough about her. 'How are things in Sydney?'

'Excellent! I'm doing some freelance work for my old law firm.'

His grin told her how much he was enjoying it.

'And the big news is that my mother is running Derek Oxford's campaign.'

She did her best to pick her jaw up off the floor. 'Derek… your old second in command?'

'The very one.'

She sat. 'Wow! We've created a monster.'

'She's brilliant at it.'

'I don't doubt it for a moment.' She found herself laughing. 'I don't envy the opposition parties at all.'

'Mum, is it time yet?' Robbie and Chase stared from the doorway.

Aidan smiled, his eyes alive with fun. 'Are you up for a day of showing me around your new life, Quinn?'

A thrill shook through her. She leapt up. 'Just give me a few minutes to get ready.'

Quinn raced off to her bedroom with its tiny en-suite bathroom. It wasn't until she'd pulled on one of her prettiest blouses, though, that it suddenly hit her—she'd just put on a full face of make-up and pulled on her best jeans. A slow churning in her stomach had her dropping to the side of her bed. *What on earth do you think you're doing?*

She and Aidan, they weren't going anywhere. Things between them weren't going to progress beyond friendship. *They already have.*

Then she had to put a stop to it before it was too late and someone got hurt.

She was not going to dress up for Aidan. She was not going to try and look pretty for him. She was not going to flirt with him. He might not consider her a complication yet, but he would eventually and she wasn't *ever* going to let that opportunity arise.

Slowly she stowed her pretty blouse back into the wardrobe and then went to scrub her face clean. She slipped on a long-sleeved button-down shirt that covered her from neck to mid-thigh. It was respectable, boring and asexual.

She glanced in the mirror and grimaced. Perfect.

Even though Quinn did her very best to maintain her guard, she had a day filled with laughter and fun. Aidan even taught them all a new fun novelty song.

'You've chosen a spectacularly beautiful place to live,' he said.

'I can't believe how beautiful it is here,' she admitted. Pokolbin was Hunter Valley wine country. Vineyards and grapevines spilled across gently rolling hills that spread out lazily in every direction. The vistas that greeted her whenever she topped a rise could still make her catch her breath. 'I never realised I was such a rural girl at heart.'

'Aidan, I have a problem,' Robbie suddenly said, his face serious and his eyes puckered.

They'd stopped for cake and coffee—milkshakes for the boys—and his young face looked so serious she straightened on her seat. He hadn't mentioned anything to her!

'What's up, buddy?'

Aidan took her son's words completely in his stride. She rolled her shoulders and forced herself to sit back in her chair.

'I don't like olives,' he whispered. 'And Chase doesn't either.'

She had to bite her lip to hide a smile, her heart filling with love for her serious elder son.

'We don't like olives, but Aunt Mara and...' he shot her a glance '...Mum love them. And I know that they're the reason we live out here and that we have money for food and other stuff. And we love living out here, but... they taste awful!'

'I see,' Aidan said, just as serious as her son.

Robbie crumbled off a piece of his cake. 'It makes me feel bad that I don't like them.'

She opened her mouth, but a swift glance from Aidan had her shutting it again.

'It's not that you don't like olives, guys. It's just that you don't like the taste of them. And, frankly, mostly it's adults who like to eat olives anyway so I don't think you should feel bad.' He leaned in closer. 'You know what you could say?'

Both boys stared at him. He had their complete attention and her eyes suddenly burned. They hungered for a male influence in their lives. Problem was, it was the one thing she couldn't give them.

'You can say that you love olives, but you just don't like to eat them. And by not eating any that leaves the farm all the more to sell.'

Robbie's face lit up. 'And that means more money for the farm!'

'Precisely.'

With both boys happy again, Aidan winked at her over the rim of his mug and she realised she had to put a stop to all of this as soon as she could. When she'd been worried, earlier, about someone getting hurt. She'd been thinking about him. She'd been thinking about herself. Not her boys. With each visit he won a little more of their trust and was given another piece of their hearts.

Her mouth dried. What had she been thinking? She couldn't risk their happiness like that.

She glanced down into her mug. She hadn't been thinking. That was the problem. She'd been too busy enjoying the ride, enjoying feeling like a desirable woman again, which just went to show what a fool she was.

'Are you okay?'

She glanced up to find those amber eyes focused on her. They narrowed to slits at whatever they saw in her face. He glanced at his watch and then slapped a hand to the table. 'Eat up, guys. It's almost time we were back at the shop like we promised your aunt.'

Mara had conscripted the boys into helping for the last hour this afternoon. It had been her way of tactfully ensuring that Quinn and Aidan had some time alone. Luckily, the boys loved helping in the shop. At the time Quinn had gritted her teeth at these machinations, but now she was grateful for them.

The sooner she brought a halt to all of this, the better.

Her heart slumped. So did her shoulders. There was nothing she could do about her heart, but she forced her shoulders back, forced a smile to her face. 'My cake was delicious. How was yours?'

It occurred to her then that it'd be a long time before she could face a piece of cake again with any equanimity.

'You want to tell me what's wrong?'

Quinn and Aidan strolled among the olive trees, back towards the house after having walked the boys to the on-site shop. The Olive Branch was a small but charming sandstone building stocked with olives picked from Mara's olive groves along with sourdough bread sourced from a local bakery, cheese from a local cheese maker and an assortment of recipe books.

Tourists found the place irresistible. To be perfectly frank, so did she and the boys. She and Aidan had stayed to watch the boys serve several customers and the way their chests had puffed out at Aidan's praise had made her heart burn.

'Quinn?'

Oh, how to do this gently?

She turned and swallowed. 'Aidan, I really like you. You're a lovely man.'

He closed his eyes and swore. Her heart clenched up harder and smaller than an olive stone.

'Give us some time, Quinn, please, before launching us into this kind of conversation.'

He opened his eyes and they flamed at her.

'Why?' she croaked. 'What would be the point?'

'The point?' He straightened. He shifted his stance, as if trying to hold back a torrent of angry words. Beyond him, the sun had started to lower behind the ridge of the ranges, turning the day smoky even as the edges of everything somehow retained their clarity. She glanced around at all the golden greenness and blue afternoon beauty and wondered how despair could eat away at her so completely.

This morning she'd been happy!

*This morning you were still hiding your head in the sand.*

He leaned towards her, his jaw set. 'The point is we have the chance to develop something not just good but spectacular if you give us a chance.'

Her heart pounded and her every muscle twitched. If she'd been a bird she'd have taken flight. Even thinking about what he proposed hurt. Hoping for what could never be hurt.

*You ruined my life!* She would never give Aidan the chance to hurl those words at her.

'You're wrong.' She might be crumbling inside but her voice emerged strong and sure. 'You have to stop coming around. The boys are coming to love you too dearly. They're starting to depend on you too heavily. This has to stop before someone gets hurt.'

His gaze held hers, fierce and strong. 'It's too late for that, Quinn. I'm already in too deep.'

A tremble shook her. She swayed. Whatever golden was left of the day leached out of it. 'Oh, Aidan.'

He stood straight and proud like a warrior and it occurred to her that he must cut a commanding figure in a courtroom. She might have just dealt his hopes a deathblow, but he was neither cowed nor vanquished.

His chin lifted. 'I can't believe you won't even consider the possibility of us.'

Scorn, closely held in check, rippled beneath his words. She flinched.

'Why?' he demanded. 'Why won't you even consider it?'

She flung an arm out. 'Let me count the ways!'

He widened his stance and folded his arms. 'Then let's have them.'

The amber of his eyes glowed and the longer she looked at him the more her mouth started to water. She clenched her hands to stop from doing anything stupid like reach for him.

'You don't want to make this easy, do you?'

'Not on your life.' And then it seemed as if he almost might smile. 'I have no intention of making it easy for you to walk away from me.'

She had to bend at the waist and draw in a breath, draw in her courage. She straightened. 'I know you don't think the distance between here and Sydney is prohibitive, but I do. I'm not into long distance relationships.'

'But if I set up a practice in either Newcastle or Maitland that problem won't exist. Did you know,' he said pleasantly as if they were talking about nothing more innocuous than the weather, 'that Maitland is one of the fastest growing regional centres in the state at the moment?'

He would relocate. For her?

*No!*

'Your mother doesn't like me and she's been through enough.'

'Once she gets to know you properly, my mother will love you.'

Her eyes suddenly narrowed. 'Is that why you hassled me so much about going to university? Because in my current "uneducated" state—at least in your and my family's estimation—I wouldn't be good enough for you all otherwise?'

'I'm not even going to dignify that with an answer.' He glared. 'I can see how this stupid inferiority complex of yours has been created by your parents and Phillip.'

'Stupid?' Her mouth worked but no other words emerged.

He stabbed a finger at her. 'I have never wanted anything for you but your happiness. A happiness you're pig-headedly determined to avoid.'

'Pig-headed?' She ground her teeth together. She told herself he had a right to his anger. She was dashing his hopes, hurting him. She tried to settle a mantle of rationality about her. 'We haven't known each other long enough to fall in love.'

He was quiet for a long moment. His eyes never left her face and it was all she could do not to fidget. 'I believe that's true of you,' he finally said, 'but it's not true for me.'

Her stomach gave a sickening lurch.

'It's why I've tried to take things slow.'

She flashed back to her hotel room last Saturday night.

'I fell in love with you the moment you ordered me to take a deep breath and relish the day.'

'Because I reminded you of Danny.' He was in love with a mirage!

'Because you reminded me that the world was good, that life could be good again and that it should be lived.'

The mirage vanished. He loved her? He truly loved her? She tried to gather her scattered thoughts, tried to seize hold of her common sense. 'Do you have an answer for everything?'

'Of course I do. I'm a lawyer.'

A laugh shot out of her, just like that. *This is no time for laughing!* She snapped her mouth shut.

Aidan's face gentled. The afternoon had started to cool, although they weren't far enough into autumn to need sweaters yet. A flock of sulphur-crested cockatoos wheeled around an ancient gum tree further up the hill, their raucous cries filling the air and masking the soft chirrup of a flock of rainbow lorikeets that swooped through the olive grove, heading for the bottlebrush trees on the opposite hill.

She tried to not let it all filter into her soul and relax her—or relax her guard.

'Quinn, what are you really afraid of?'

She moistened her lips. 'That you will eventually accuse me of ruining your life.'

'You'll only ruin it if you walk away.'

His eyes urged her to believe him. Her heart wavered, but she shook her head. They were just words and while she didn't doubt that Aidan meant them in the present moment she had no faith in their longevity.

She prayed for strength. 'You and your family, Aidan, you come from the same world as my parents, the same world as Phillip and his parents. Phillip's parents told him, and me, that I would ruin his life. Before he left, Phillip told me that was true—that I had wrecked his life. Your family believes the exact same thing. And eventually you will too.' She gripped her hands tightly in front of her. 'I'm sorry but I'm not prepared to go through all that again.'

He stared at her. And then his face changed, darkening until thunder practically rolled off his brow and lightning flashed from his eyes. A torrent of angry words shot out of him, most of them not repeatable.

'Of all the idiotic, cock-brained ideas!'

She blinked. Her shoulders started to hunch as he continued with a list of adjectives to describe her way of thinking. Her wrong-headed way of thinking, according to him. Aidan had never yelled at her before. Not really. And it was strange to discover that she hated it. Really, deep down in her gut hated it. She'd finally snapped his control. And she hated that too. Because...

She loved him.

She'd have laughed at the irony, only she didn't have the heart for it. She might love him, but that didn't change a damn thing. She already knew that love wasn't always enough.

He wheeled away from her, only to wheel back again. 'So, in essence, this all comes down to courage and the fact you have none?'

She stiffened at that. She might've lost her heart, but she still had her pride. 'I beg your pardon?' The way her voice shook, though, destroyed the effect of the iciness she'd tried to inject.

'You demanded courage from me when I was dealing with my mother.'

'That was completely different!'

'How?' he shot back. 'I wasn't leading the life I should've been leading. Just as you're not leading the life you should be leading.'

'Yes I am!' But, while they held vehemence, her words lacked conviction.

'You want to know your problem, Quinn?'

She folded her arms. 'What, I only have the one?' She knew she was being immature but she couldn't help it.

'You don't believe you're worth fighting for.'

Her mouth dried.

His eyes were hard, but strangely gentle too. 'I can slay all the other dragons for you. I can offer you all the assurances in the world. But this particular dragon is one you have to slay for yourself.'

He was going to walk away now, just as she'd wanted him to. And everything inside her wanted to sob.

His face twisted. 'Damn it, do you really think I'm like your parents? Do you really think I'm like Phillip?'

Her head rocked back. Of course not! But…

But what?

The ground lurched beneath her feet. She tried to steady herself against the branch of an olive tree, but it was thin and threatened to snap. She reeled over to a weathered fence post and leaned against it, careful not to catch herself on the barbed wire. She'd have to ask Mara why they had barbed wire on the property—an idle thought that filtered into her head and out again almost immediately.

She glanced across at Aidan. 'No.' The word croaked out of her. 'I don't think you're like Phillip.'

The hard light in his eyes died, replaced with an uncertainty that tore at her. 'And?'

She moistened her lips. That fact changed everything. If Aidan wasn't like the others—and she knew with everything inside her that he wasn't—then...

'Quinn?'

'It means something about my reasoning is wrong.' She slid down to the ground. 'I'm...I'm trying to work out just what that is.'

He lowered himself to the ground. Reaching out, he took her hand. 'I'm not rushing you, I swear I'm not, but... do you think there's even the slightest chance that you could ever love me?'

Her throat ached. 'Oh, I love you, Aidan, there's no doubt about that.' She held up a hand to keep him where he was when he made as if to gather her up in his arms. Tears burned behind her eyes but she refused to let them fall. 'The thing is, you see, I know that sometimes love isn't enough.'

He stared at her and she swore she saw the life drain out of his face inch by inch. The lump in her throat nearly choked her.

'So that's it, is it?' The words dropped out of him, flat and colourless.

Was it? Slowly she shook her head. 'You're not like Phillip. You're not like my parents. I...I need to think that through more thoroughly.' She had to work out what it meant for them—if it meant anything for them.

He continued to stare at her, but she couldn't tell what he was thinking.

'You said you wouldn't rush me!'

He dragged a hand down his face.

She chafed her arms against the rising tide of fear that threatened to swallow her. 'If you give me an ultimatum—make a decision now or else—I...I would have to tell you goodbye.' It almost killed her to say it, but she forced the words out all the same.

He shook his head as if it were a weight he could barely lift. 'I'm not going to give you an ultimatum, Quinn.'

But his face had gone grey and lines fanned out from his mouth and she had to close her eyes. 'Forgive me for dragging this out, Aidan,' she croaked. 'But I have to be sure.'

She set her back against the post and pushed upright. 'Not just for my sake, but for Robbie and Chase's too. And for yours.'

With that she turned and headed for the house.

'Quinn!'

It was a cry of raw pain. Tears scalded her eyes. 'I'll call you. I promise.' She didn't turn around. She didn't break stride. She kept her eyes fixed forward.

Quinn spent the next week missing Aidan so much her mind refused to answer a single question she needed it to. And those questions went around and around in an endless litany, denying her even a moment of peace. What if Vera never warmed to her or the boys? What if Aidan's friends refused to accept her, convinced she wasn't good enough for him? Would she be able to cope with seeing her parents at other society 'dos'? What if Aidan regretted setting up a practice locally? What if he found himself pining for his firm in Sydney? He'd blame her. What would she do if he broke her heart? It'd send her into the kind of spin she shied from even thinking about.

*What if...? What if...? What if...?*

She woke in the middle of the night, cheeks wet, and aching for him with everything she had. She stood on the brink of something amazing and exhilarating that could end in disaster. And she couldn't work out if it was worth it or not.

The following Saturday night she and Mara played Monopoly with the boys. Robbie turned to her. 'Mum, do you think I'll ever find a girl I'll want to marry and who'll want to marry me too?'

She handed Chase the dice for his turn. 'I'm sure you will, honey.'

'But Alison at school says I have to marry her!'

Mara chuckled. Quinn sucked her lip into her mouth and bit on it until she could school her features. 'I promise you don't have to marry anyone that you don't want to.'

He gazed at her gloomily. 'But she's nice. I like her. So why don't I want to marry her when she wants to marry me?'

Ah... 'That's the way it goes sometimes, honey. We can be friends with lots and lots of people and we can like them lots and lots, but it doesn't mean we want to marry them. You can't force someone to want to marry you. It doesn't work that way.'

He stared back and finally nodded. 'Okay.'

He seemed happy to take her word for it.

'Is Aidan going to visit us tomorrow?'

She didn't like the way the conversation moved from marriage to Aidan as if...as if it were some logical leap. She fought back a frown. 'I don't think so.'

'Doesn't he like us any more?'

'Sure he does,' Chase chimed in. 'He likes Mum and us best of all. He was sad in Perth. But he wasn't sad when he was with us.'

It took all her strength to choke back a sob. 'Bedtime,' she croaked.

She fell into her chair after putting the boys to bed. Mara pushed a mug of tea across to her. She tried to dredge up a smile. 'Some days they're exhausting.'

Mara merely raised an eyebrow.

Quinn burst into tears.

'Sorry,' she mumbled when she finally had control of them.

Mara sipped her tea. 'Would it be of any interest to you to know that Aidan is staying at the Ross's bed and breakfast at the end of the lane?'

Quinn shot to her feet. He was? Really? She half turned towards the door and then halted. She sat again and chafed her arms.

'Are you afraid of being happy, Quinn?'

She curled her hands around her mug. 'I'm afraid of making another mistake.' And then all those questions that had been plaguing her came pouring out—about his mother and his friends and his job and her parents and what ifs galore.

Mara sat back and surveyed her. 'Does what your parents think have any bearing on your decision to see Aidan again or not?'

'No, of course not.'

Mara didn't say anything, but she lifted that darn eyebrow again. 'Aidan is a grown man. And an intelligent one. He knows his own mind.'

She hunched over her mug. 'You're saying I should extend the same trust to him that I do to myself.'

Mara remained silent. Quinn stared into her tea. Suddenly, just like that, everything stilled. Her head snapped up. She'd been hiding behind all of those issues when... when it all came down to a simple question of trust.

Did she trust Aidan?

She shot to her feet. 'The B&B at the end of the lane?'

'That's right.'

Quinn grabbed a wrap from the hook by the door and set off down their lane at a run. She didn't even stop to catch her breath when she reached the B&B, but burst up to the front door and knocked.

She stared blankly at the man who answered. Oh! She kicked herself. Of course Aidan wouldn't answer the door. 'Hello, Mr Ross, it's Quinn Laverty from the olive farm. I understand that Aidan Fairhall is staying here and I wondered if I could have a word with him.'

'Sorry, love, but he's not here.'

He'd left? Her shoulders sagged. She backed up a step. 'I'm sorry to have bothered you.' The words almost choked her. 'Goodnight, Mr Ross.'

She turned away. The door closed behind her, shutting her out in the dark. Tears stung her eyes. She tossed her pashmina around her shoulders and held on tight. Of course Aidan had left. What hope had she given him?

'Quinn?'

She halted mid-sniffle. With a heart that barely dared to hope, she turned. 'Aidan? But...but Mr Ross said...'

He'd said that Aidan *wasn't there*. He hadn't said Aidan had decamped back to Sydney.

'I went out for a walk.'

She couldn't drag her gaze from him.

He shifted his weight. 'You wanted to see me?'

A smile built through her. He was here and it had to mean something. It had to mean he hadn't given up on her. Oh, how she loved him! 'Shall I be a hundred per cent honest?'

He folded his arms. 'It's the only way.'

She pulled in a breath, pulled her wrap about her more securely. 'I've spent all week wanting to see you, Aidan.'

'All you had to do was pick up the phone.'

She took a step closer, breathed him in. 'I've not just wanted it, but craved it with everything I am. It freaked me out.'

'I see.'

He stared at her. In the moonlight his face looked beautiful but grim and her heart caught. 'Yes, you probably do. You've seen everything much clearer than I have.'

Something quickened in his face. Suddenly she recognised what it was—hope. 'Oh! I'm not trying to drag this out and make it harder for you, Aidan! I love you. I want to be with you. I want there to be an *us*. If that's what you still—'

She didn't get any further. She found herself in Aidan's arms, caught up in a vortex of desire, relief, frustration and remembered pain as his mouth came down on hers and they kissed like wild things rather than the polite civilised people they pretended to be to the world. When they eventually broke apart they were both breathing heavily. Quinn rested her forehead against his jaw. 'Wow.'

He cupped her face and drew away to stare down at her. 'You mean it?'

'Yes.'

He smiled then and it held so much joy it swept all of the old pain away. 'I love you, Quinn.'

'I love you, Aidan.'

'I love your boys too. I'm going to be the best father I can be to them.'

Father?

He grinned at the way her eyes widened. 'When I ask you to marry me you are going to say yes, aren't you?'

She didn't even hesitate. 'Yes.'

'Excellent. Now that we have the important points out

of the way, you want to tell me how you *finally* came to the right conclusion—that we *could* work and that we *should* be together?'

She smiled up at him. 'I only realised it all a moment or two before I came hurtling up the lane to find you. All of those reasons I'd been giving you for why we couldn't be together, I realised they were just issues I'd been hiding behind. The question I should've been asking myself was—Do I trust you? When I finally asked the right question, it all fell into place.'

She sobered. 'I do trust you, Aidan. I asked myself what you'd do if you were unhappy in a relationship.' She shook her head. 'You wouldn't just walk away. You wouldn't seethe or fester in silence either. You'd work at making things better.' Communication was important to him. 'You don't have a shallow heart. You have a heart that is deep and true and will weather storms.'

His eyes darkened. 'I'll weather any storm with you, Quinn. But do you believe that you have a heart that is deep and true too?'

That was the risk Aidan took, she suddenly saw.

Her heart pounded. Ice touched her nape, but she refused to let the fear overcome her. She thought back over her life and how she'd dealt with her parents...with Phillip...and with her two gorgeous boys. Gradually a weight started to lift and the chill receded. 'Yes,' she breathed, beaming her love straight at him. 'Yes, I do.'

His hands went around her waist, drawing her closer. 'My lovely girl,' he whispered against her lips.

She cupped his face in her hands. 'I'm sorry it took me so long to realise the truth. Tell me you forgive me. I love you, Aidan. I love you with my whole heart.'

'Sweetheart—' he grinned down at her '—there's nothing to forgive. I needed you to be as sure about us as I was.'

She sobered. 'And are you?'

'I love you. I want to build a life with you. I have never been surer of anything in my life.'

His lips descended to hers and if she'd had any lingering doubts they'd have melted away. She flung her arms around his neck and kissed him back with all the love in her overflowing heart.

\* \* \* \* \*

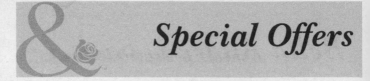

# *Special Offers*

Every month we put together collections and longer reads written by your favourite authors.

Here are some of next month's highlights— and don't miss our fabulous discount online!

**On sale 21st March**     **On sale 4th April**     **On sale 4th April**

# *Bella Andre is back...*

The US sensation Bella Andre is back with two brand-new
titles featuring the one and only Sullivan family.
Don't miss out on the latest from this
incredible author.

Now available from:

## www.millsandboon.co.uk

 *Book Club*

# *Join the Mills & Boon Book Club*

Subscribe to **Cherish**™ today for 3, 6 or 12 months and you could **save over £40!**

We'll also treat you to these fabulous extras:

-  **FREE L'Occitane gift set worth £10**

-  **FREE home delivery**

-  **Rewards scheme, exclusive offers…and much more!**

*Subscribe now and save over £40*
**www.millsandboon.co.uk/subscribeme**

Discover more romance at

# www.millsandboon.co.uk

- ❤ WIN great prizes in our exclusive competitions
- ❤ BUY new titles before they hit the shops
- ❤ BROWSE new books and REVIEW your favourites
- ❤ SAVE on new books with the Mills & Boon® Bookclub™
- ❤ DISCOVER new authors

PLUS, to chat about your favourite reads, get the latest news and find special offers:

- 🅕 Find us on facebook.com/millsandboon
- 🐦 Follow us on twitter.com/millsandboonuk
- ❤ Sign up to our newsletter at millsandboon.co.uk